About the author

Tina Greig is an author and English teacher living in France. Tina has a passion for writing epic fantasy novels which chaperon the reader throughout the worlds of the unknown and their perceived knowledge.

Her books focus on strong female antagonists, therefore introducing her readers to a new kind of badassery.

Being Purgatory incorporates Tina's personality inside her own unique writing style, bringing humour alongside passion, magic, and romance within the pages of her books.

DOMAINS SERIES: BEING PURGATORY

Tina D. Greig

DOMAINS SERIES: BEING PURGATORY

Vanguard Press

VANGUARD PAPERBACK

© Copyright 2022
Tina D. Greig

A CIP catalogue record for this title is
available from the British Library.

ISBN 978 1 78465 934 9

*Vanguard Press is an imprint of
Pegasus Elliot Mackenzie Publishers Ltd.*
www.pegasuspublishers.com

First Published in 2022

**Vanguard Press
Sheraton House Castle Park
Cambridge England**

Printed & Bound in Great Britain

Dedication

For Lee and Adam,
my boys.

Chapter 1

The world, as it is today, has disjointed ideologies of how to behave in this vast melting pot of living things. The multitudes of human entities spanning it are individual and unique, yet disastrously flawed.

People live, love, marry, work, reproduce, slave, spend, laugh, cry, care, and finally die. Not necessarily in that order but all humans are born and all humans die. FACT.

People believe in gods from all religions: they believe salvation is only possible with complete and sometimes unrealistic infatuation and over-exaggerated faith.

People in power abuse it, using the position and trust they have been given to initiate their own wishes, leaving common sense and humility devoid of attention.

I watch people. I watch the young ones play, the adults struggle and the old ones die. I sit on a higher plane and watch the destruction of the world, a wasted world filled with wonders and miracles, yet I remain disappointed.

Why fight your fellow man? Or poison water supplies? Why cut down habitation that belongs to people or animals? And this is the question that burns through me: why kill for religion or a difference in beliefs? WHY? No one has yet answered my questions, to tell me why peace does not reign within a people so vastly intelligent.

I watch and I am constantly watching as the people are gradually extinguishing themselves.

For years I have watched, waiting for death and disease to snuff out the fragile human body so I may harvest the soul before it dissipates. When I harvest, I do not care who you are, if you are rich or poor, male or female, child or adult. I do not care for your religion or beliefs, nor do I care if you wanted to die or not. All I require is your soul.

I harvest and collect souls, good or bad. I retrieve them before the harvesters from the other domains arrive and I keep them safe.

I am a soul catcher. I am fed by the energy of the souls I harvest so I may maintain the form I currently use. I have been described throughout the centuries as many creatures, vampire, werewolf, monster, beast, demon or dragon. Alas, I am none of those beings, yet I encompass them all, for I contain the power to be whoever I need to be in order to harvest and feed from the souls of humans.

As the world turns, ageing as it does, I have found that people have evolved rapidly but not as a mature race; more a cruel and demanding collective.

With access to technology and medicine, I would have expected humans to develop into a far more intelligent race. They have the ability to live longer and enjoy the life they have been given; yet for some unfathomable reason, the people deny themselves.

Before the disruption of the afterlife, when people died, they were sent for judgement. Then, they either descended to Satan or ascended to the god they believed in.

I do not care which god a person believes in: there are so many sitting on a multiplex of higher planes awaiting their believers. Still, as I watch I can observe that the people see only their own beliefs as important and are intolerant of those who do not share such beliefs.

The equilibrium has shifted within the afterlife and because of this, we now fight for the souls of the human deceased. The three of us co-exist for the need of the people but as people become more indulgent, we must fight to capture the complex souls.

When a person is nearing the end of their lifespan, their soul displays itself to the afterlife. The soul allows us to see the person, who they are and how they lived. When they are ready to release their soul, we fight: a bloodthirsty fight between heaven with its angels, hell with its demons, and me.

I am Purgatory, ruler of the domain that sits nestled between heaven and hell. Once I was the judge of souls and now I am their harvester. When we fight, we are fighting for the souls of the people. Heaven for the good and hell for the bad. And me? I fight for as many as I can.

The people have developed into an untrustworthy society where violence is at a catastrophic level. If all souls were to remain judged by me, hell would become a soulless domain and diminish the number of angels. Therefore, heaven dramatically intervened, pardoning souls at the latter stage of death to ensure a good soul leaves the deceased body.

Hell counter-intervened by ensuring hateful and evil souls remained untouched by forgiveness in order to secure their downward passage.

Me? I became weak: souls were devoured by angels or demons before they reached my domain for judgment. This, in turn, was the causation of the equilibrium shift as my domain began to collapse.

For people to survive and thrive in the world, three aspects must remain: heaven, hell, and me – Purgatory. Without any domain, the earth loses its afterlife, cascading the people into a situation of everlasting life or complete extinction.

Therefore, I am forced to harvest souls for myself to feed my domain and maintain my life. As a person dies, we fight: we fight for our domain but I fight to maintain the tri-status to protect the dissolvement of the people and ensure my own demise is avoided.

Today, I am watching. Many souls will be claimed before the start of a new day. I can sense demons tirelessly pacing, projecting their influence on respective souls. Frequent vibes from angels flutter close by, waiting for the opportunity to allow repentance for sins or comfort in death.

In contrast, I sit and wait. I do not need the large numbers of souls that heaven and hell require, but the fight is the same for one or one hundred souls.

I like to win children. Although the life of a child is short, it means they do not have good or bad influences. Children are not born good or bad: they are born pure and unfortunately easy to influence. It is the influence of the adult that lays the path a child will walk, but they do not fully understand the problems the people have developed, such as religion, racism, sexism etc. Children do not judge until taught how to do so.

That is why I like them within my domain. Their souls are content and energetic, so they feed the domain beyond the capability of the adult.

I am Purgatory: consequently, I cannot keep souls indefinitely. Eventually, they will be claimed by heaven or hell but delaying the process for as long as possible guarantees my domain will thrive.

At this moment, I am watching a soul. The body is dying quickly and the soul is panicking. With heaven and hell thirsty for this particular soul, I am about to do something I do not predominantly like to do with so much presence from the other domains: I am going to harvest this soul. I do not enjoy walking in the human domain but if I can reach the soul first, I can catch it for my own.

This soul, however, intrigues me. Why is this one so sought after? From my vantage point between ascension and descension, I can see heaven's most noble angels and hell's leading demons preparing to walk amongst the living to intercept this soul.

For millennia, angels and demons have battled individually to bring about my downfall, but I will not succumb. The fighting is vicious, callous and causes a multitude of unnecessary casualties for each domain.

I have the power to heal myself and – in circumstances I deem appropriate – others, too. Rarely demons or angels, but people; those caught in our battles. Or I do it to deny any domain of a particular soul.

Heaven and hell are aware of my powers yet neither knows how I can be killed. I do not know, either, but some injuries can take longer than others to heal when certain weapons are used to inflict them. However, due to the interest in this fastidious soul, the risk is warranted.

The hospital is quiet as I enter. I nod briefly to a bored security guard sitting behind a small desk of CCTV monitors. He reciprocates, then returns his gaze to the flickering, monochrome screens.

Making my way to the elevators, I consult a large board denoting the five floors of the building and the departments to be found on them.

Scrolling my eyes over each department, I rule out the definite places I know the soul will not be held: Maternity – no! Children's – no! Pathology – no! Haematology and other 'ologies – no!

Still standing and deliberating, I wondered whether to use my powers to find the soul. I decided against this idea, considering it too risky, as the other non-humans frequenting the hospital at this time would sense me.

Pressing for the elevator, I decided that I would ride it to every floor. I should be able to sense the impending death before I see it and can intervene before the soul is influenced otherwise.

"Excuse me, dear. Can you press for me, please?" A tiny old lady had slowly entered the elevator after me.

"Sure," I answered, looking down at her mop of immaculate grey-rollered hair. "Which floor?"

"Fourth, please." Her pained voice failed to hide the aching deep within her eyes.

Pressing the number four button until it illuminated, I observed the ancient lady process a number of emotions before settling on exhaustion, although I do not believe it was by choice but sheer lack of energy.

"Are you okay?" I asked, realizing that she was the first human I had spoken to whose soul I wasn't trying to harvest.

Her eyes met mine once more and she allowed a small smile to briefly visit her features.

"My husband is sick, so sick. I come every day to see him but he has no recollection of who I am," she offered.

"Is he dying?" I questioned, not for the benefits of harvesting but I wanted to know.

Tears threatened behind the little grey-haired women's eyes. Patting her face before the tears could escape, she nodded slowly.

"He is. He has cancer but it is his dementia that keeps him from me."

I gave her my most sympathetic smile and gently touched her forearm to offer some comfort. Juddering to a stop, the elevator landed on the fourth floor.

"May I walk with you?" I asked.

"Of course, my dear," she replied, casually grabbing my forearm as we exited the metal box.

After a short walk, we came to a halt outside a small room. There was an absence of medical equipment: the room held only a hospital bed, facing out towards the door, containing the outlined figure of a pale, fragile, grey-haired man.

The antique lady smiled as she saw him, wiping the hankie over her face once more.

"My Harry," she said softly. "Such a good kind man. I never wanted for anything. We have been married for over sixty-five years," she proudly informed me.

"Sixty-five years: such a long time," I responded, kindly.

"The best sixty-five years of my life. But he does not remember me," she uttered, solemnly.

"But you still keep coming?" I asked, intrigued by such human behaviour.

"Of course, dear. I hope that he may remember me just once so I can say goodbye." Her voice hitched as she spoke.

"Please - go to your husband. Do not let me keep you." I patted her hand whilst guiding her through the open door to her husband, searching as I did so. I found the soul of the diminutive, greying man; he would indeed be dying soon. I could sense the purity of his soul and decided I would allow heaven to collect him. I had another soul waiting.

Watching his wife straighten his bedding and kiss his forehead, I felt my own heart deflate with sorrow for them both. Before I realized what I was doing, I sent a small amount of healing power to this man: not too much, as his time was so near. I wanted him to have just enough strength to spend his last minutes in this domain with the woman he had loved and cared for throughout sixty-five years.

I knew my power has reached his soul as he flickered his eyes and turned to look into the face of his wife.

"Helen... My Helen." He spoke softly, gently lifting his hand to her face.

Tears were given permission to cascade down the timeworn face of his beautiful wife.

"Yes, Harry it's me – your Helen." She leant forwards and speckled his cheek with kisses.

I watched as the couple rekindled their love for one another until I saw a ripple appear at the back of the room. A hole from another domain opened up and through it stepped an angel. He paused, searching the room with concern, before continuing towards Harry.

"Oh shit!" I mumbled as I darted out of sight and away from the room. The angel would have sensed the small amount of power I had given to Harry, hence his reluctance.

I maintained a vigil over the couple to ensure the angel was no longer suspicious and would fulfil his role. Within ten minutes, I felt the angel leave with a good soul. I released the breath I had been holding and questioned if I was going soft. I must have been to take such a risk.

Today was my first involvement in the emotions that humans

experience: I have never interacted with people who were not for harvest. I saw unconditional love and I was surprised at the effect it had on my own ancient soul.

Taking a deep breath, I composed myself for whatever lay ahead. The fourth floor was quiet now; no lingering essences of angels or demons and no other souls ready for harvest. Deciding to visit the fifth floor, I found the stairwell and ascended to the next level.

The atmospheric change in the stairwell was immense. The build-up of essences was phenomenal. Pushing open the door, I was violently hit by a cacophony of scents and essences.

Both angels and demons wandered through the corridors, cloaking themselves – or in disguise – to make them acceptable to the human eye.

Human souls were in abundance: I could feel so many good and bad souls awaiting their harvest.

I had stored my own powers to remain undetected. Only if an angel or demon tried to locate my soul would they possibly recognize me. Keeping a distance from my foes, I hastily made my way down the corridor.

After walking through the peaceful hospital ward, I reached the nurses' station.

"Excuse me," I said, leaning over a tall desk in order to spot the blonde nurse, writing notes, behind it. "So sorry to disturb you: which ward is this?"

Looking up from her work, she smiled briefly. "This is the hospice wing. Are you looking for someone?"

Of course - the hospice wing: that explains the abundance of angels and demons present. However, it did not explain why I hadn't realised that this was where both domains waited to gain the majority of the souls. It also did not justify why I needed to fight to gain the few souls I harvested.

Making a mental note of the availability of 'ready-to-harvest' souls, I thanked the overworked nurse and continued down the corridor, watching the activity as I went.

Eventually, I sensed what I had been searching for. As I rounded a corner at the far end of the wing, I found half a dozen angels in close proximity to the same number of demons, sitting, standing and waiting.

Waiting angels and demons lined the walls of the sterile, white room and took every available seat, politely ignoring each other.

Ensuring that my essence was completely cloaked, I filled my lungs with a deep, cleansing breath and advanced towards the waiting harvesters.

The slight ripple that became noticeable as I passed the waiters was shrugged off without question. Obviously, whoever they were waiting for was far too important for them to contemplate any problems at present.

Refilling my lungs once more, I stepped silently through a slight crack in the door of the bleached hospital room. Inaudibly, I crept around the outskirts of the room. Heaven occupied the left and hell the right: these were not your everyday harvester angels and demons, but high-ranking beings.

"Holy crap!" I muttered under my breath. This does not happen often: someone of great significance to both heaven and hell was about to pass. Obviously this was bound to shift the equilibrium one way or the other: a reckoning was about to transpire. Yet I could not understand the calmness between the two enemy domains and that frightened me.

Continuing to make my way through the unaware hordes of good and bad, I stopped when I reached the far end of the room and felt the crack as my jaw hit the polished linoleum floor.

Two beds stood slightly apart from each other, each containing a dying body with a trapped soul. Beside the beds of each of these bodies sat one angel and one demon, each muttering words to their selected figures.

I searched my mind for some recollection of the angel and demon, yet came up with nothing but blanks. I couldn't have gone for years not knowing of the union of good and evil that had produced offspring, could I?

Glancing toward the head of the bed, I searched for the nameplate. CONNOR BARD was written on one; RYAN BARD on the second. Again, blanks fired fruitlessly within my synapses, triggering extreme frustration.

One male angel, one female demon, two children... Nope – still nothing!

Stagnantly sulking, I placed myself on a windowsill at the top of the room, looking down on the scene before me. I took time to study each and every person until finally I turned my attention to the young men; one blond, one dark haired; muscular, fit and tanned and extremely good looking.

Huh! Still nothing. I focused on the demon: I knew all the demons. Living so long and needing to fight them regularly resulted in a love/hate relationship. I loved to fight them and they hating losing.

Female demon? She was dark-haired with a hidden beauty; tall, muscular but not recognizable.

Frustration was grinding down on me, mocking my memory bank and causing me to question my own sanity. I do not usually forget but this was ridiculous. Something important enough to warrant the presence of high numbers of good and evil should not have seeped out of my membranes.

I stole a sideways glance toward the blond-haired angel. His face remained embedded in his cupped hands, his breathing fast and irregular. I continued to stare, tracing the outline of his head, hands, body, wings. WINGS!

Bright red, feathered wings, punishment for comfort and love found in the arms of a demon.

Chapter 2

DEVON!! Recognition flashed its bright, attention-seeking light directly into my face.

"Oh shit!" The words formed in my mouth and I managed to shut it before they could escape.

The curse, of course! Devon had fallen in love with Elenor, twenty-five years ago. She was a demon who found authority difficult to respect; therefore, she constantly disobeyed her master and would leave hell without permission.

It was during one of these times that Devon had spotted her walking through Central Park, stomping on flowerbeds and cursing at hell from his hiding place above.

Devon had admired her audacity and watched her from the safety of Heaven for many hours. From that night on, he watched for her every night, waiting patiently until she would return to her favourite corner of the park, laden with bad attitude and mischief.

One summer evening, Elenor appeared in the human domain, battered and bleeding. She walked softly, stepping over the multi-coloured carpet of flowers, wincing frequently when pressure was placed on her left hip.

Devon continued to observe her, as he had done for so many nights, but tonight his heart felt heavy. She was a strong demon: he could tell by the way she carried herself, yet tonight she was broken.

Taking the risk himself, Devon left heaven for the human domain and came close enough to Elenor to see her injuries, yet far enough away that she would remain unaware of his presence.

She tentatively sat down by the side of an ancient, fallen oak tree and nestled herself into it, hiding from view. Gradually, she tended her wounds, one by one, wincing with every movement.

Devon continued to observe, edging closer. He watched a small, beaded line of glistening tears as they ran effortlessly over her cheeks as she tended to a laceration on her outer thigh.

Even from where he was hiding, Devon could see its depth. It took seconds for him to engage his mind and decide to make himself known to her.

Leaping down from the tree branch, Devon landed only feet away from Elenor, startling her and causing her to jump. Horror crossed her features and she immediately grabbed her weapons and elongated her wings. Her wings emerged painfully from her back, ripped and bleeding; one stood correctly at her back, though damaged, and the other hung lifeless by her side. Had it not been Devon who was standing before her, she would have been dead before her good wing unfurled.

She stood, blue bruises forming on her skin. She was battered and bruised, yet she was combat-ready in an instant.

"I mean you no harm," Devon called to her, without moving.

Dropping her guard for a moment and tilting her head, Elenor listened to the angel. Once he had finished his words, she regained her position and waited for his next move.

"My name is Devon and I can help you. Your leg wound is extremely deep. I can heal you," Devon told her from the position he had backed into and where he would remain until she gave him permission to approach.

Elenor stood firm, looking at the angel as she questioned herself about why he would offer her his help.

"Angels do not help demons," she stated, carefully adjusting the weight on her painful leg.

Devon smiled briefly at her.

"I am not like most angels: I do not fight unless I have reason and you do not give me a reason." He paused, allowing her time to process his words before continuing. "Please put down your weapon and allow me to help you. I am unarmed."

Dropping her battle-ready stance and re-sheathing her weapons, Elenor allowed herself to fall back onto the tree and slide awkwardly down on it until she sat heavily, back on the ground.

Devon rushed to her side and bent down to her bleeding thigh.

"May I?" he asked, his hands poised over the wound, ready to start healing.

With her gaze downcast, Elenor nodded gravely, giving her consent.

Devon worked quickly. Elenor's haemorrhaging laceration threatened to increase the blood loss as the surrounding skin withered with fragility. Devon held his palms above the wound, allowing his healing magic to pull the lower skin flap over the wound, sealing the subcutaneous layers of skin together. Once homeostasis had been achieved, Devon turned his attention to the numerous superficial wounds that covered Elenor's body.

He could feel her strength returning as he healed her. Her blood was reviving itself with each cycle it made through her heart, as it pumped less precipitously the more she relaxed.

Devon purposely kept the conversation brief and as impersonal as possible, still sensing Elenor's anxiety and caution. When finished, Devon sat a few feet away from the tree and the recovering demon.

"You should feel your strength returning shortly," he told her, taking time to rest to replenish his own energy. Healing Elenor had drained him more than he had anticipated.

Elenor watched the angel as he closed his eyes, encouraging his strength to build.

"Thank you, Devon," Elenor spoke, softly.

"My pleasure," he answered, without opening his eyes but allowing a smile to tug at his lips.

The odd couple sat in each other's company, silently uncomfortable.

Fifteen minutes passed before Devon opened his eyes and turned to face the demon.

"Forgive me, but I do not know your name," he stated.

"My name is Elenor," she replied holding out her right hand to Devon.

Taking her hand in his, Devon brought the top of her hand to his lips and pressed a brief, light kiss on the top of it.

"A pleasure to meet you, Elenor," he said, allowing her to retract her hand. "What happened? Who were you fighting?" he enquired.

Keeping her eyes fixed on the ground, Elenor took a forced breath before answering.

"I was being punished," she confessed, still avoiding meeting Devon's eyes.

"By whom? And what did you do to deserve such a punishment?" Devon fired questions at the broken demon, looking for an answer to explain such a beating.

"Was it something to do with you hiding in the human domain?"

Elenor was shocked by his words. How had he known that she came to escape hell?

"Something like that," she mumbled. "How did you know that I frequently come here?" she asked.

Embarrassment tinted Devon's cheeks to a dusty pink.

"I have watched you these last few nights," he confessed.

"Oh," Elenor responded. "Why?"

"I enjoy the way you take your frustrations out on the poor defenceless flowerbeds." He smiled as her embarrassment made itself known in the flushing of her cheeks.

Elenor thought momentarily before questioning Devon once more.

"Is it you who fixes the flowerbeds?" she asked.

"I fix them when you leave so that the humans may enjoy them during the day and you can enjoy them at night," he confessed.

"Oh." Eleanor's brow furrowed. "Thank you."

"My pleasure," Devon replied, dipping his head slightly towards the demon.

Elenor started to move, stiffly, into an upright position and turned to face Devon.

"I need to stretch my legs. Would you like to walk with me?" she asked, keeping her eyes diverted to her feet.

"Are we walking around or through the flower bed?" Devon teased her, whilst standing up.

"Around, if you wish," Elenor giggled, retracting her newly healed obsidian-black wings back into her shoulders.

Devon and Elenor spent the next three hours walking carefully around the fragrant flowerbeds that were scattered throughout the park, until a red and orange glow in the horizon signalled the morning. The sunrise threatened to expose both demon and angel to the eyes of the human domain.

"Thank you, Devon, for everything." Elenor halted beside him, causing him to stop also.

"The pleasure was mine and I do believe that I heard a number of flowers breathe a sigh of relief," he jested.

Smacking him briefly on his upper arm, Elenor appreciated the joke with him. "I did enjoy your company but I must get back to hell. I have probably been missed already."

Stealing her hand, Devon brought it to his lips and placed a light kiss on top of it.

"Be careful Elenor. I look forward to our next meeting."

"As do I," she smiled, taking back possession of her hand. Turning to walk away, Elenor deliberately detoured across a flowerbed full of red blooms. Rotating towards Devon, she feigned horror. "Someone stood on those," she stated, before throwing him a smile and disappearing.

Speed on a few years later, where one angel and one demon fall in love and then you encompass a major problem. It is forbidden in both domains for angels or demons to be anything other than enemies. The relationship between Devon and Elenor caused a massive shift in the equilibrium of all three domains.

Consequently, Devon was banished from heaven, his healing powers were reduced and his wings were tainted blood red as punishment. He was cast out of heaven to live in the human realm without heaven's support.

Eleanor received a harsher punishment for her treachery. She endured hours of cruel torture. She was burned with ice and her wings shredded until they hung, lifeless, from her body. They were also turned red to indicate a punished demon.

Eventually she escaped, finding Devon in the park where they had first met. He had waited for her every night. In the daylight hours he worked as a human, eventually finding a home for them both.

Integrating into the human domain was a difficult task for a fallen angel and his fugitive demon. The only experiences each had had with humans were death and the harvesting of souls. Becoming part of a living human society was a wholly different matter.

Unlike demons or angels, humans express emotion in the most complex of ways – laughing, crying, anger, and love – all of these thoughtlessly displayed in public for all to see.

Elenor found it extremely difficult to adapt to life as a human female: she was a product of hell and having to gain sustenance for Devon and herself meant she had to embrace the toughest challenge of her life – the supermarket.

This task was completed by the human race in the most complicated, unnecessary manner and it drove Elenor crazy. Promising to harvest the soul of an old lady with a wayward walking frame did not help her cause when meeting the friendly security man after the old lady reported her for abuse.

As time passed, Devon and Elenor became part of their community, marrying after a year in the human domain and welcoming twin boys two years later.

The boys, Ryan and Connor, grew into handsome children: one with blond hair and his father's features and the other with dark, unruly hair, similar to his mother.

On their 15th birthday, the boys fell sick. Over the next five years, doctors fought to keep the boys alive through intensive drug regimens and surgery but failed. Before the twins were admitted to the palliative care ward, Elenor received a message from Lucifer, brought to her via one of the hounds of hell she had trained over twenty years ago.

The day the twins were born, they were cursed by Lucifer never to reach their 21st birthdays. Instead, they would become victims of human disease and die as a human deserved, too.

Upon their deaths, Ryan and Connor would have their souls harvested, one would be chosen for heaven and the other, hell. Elenor had pleaded with Satan to spare them and to take her back to hell in their place. Lucifer had refused, of course, as this was her punishment for her betrayal of him.

Relentlessly, she begged that if they must die because of such a curse, then they should be harvested together and delivered to the same domain. Again, Lucifer refused her request and ceased any further communication on the subject.

Devon, for his part, had asked heaven to intervene, to abolish the curse or to keep the twins together in death. However, heaven recognised Devon only as a fallen angel: he had been issued his red wings when he abandoned heaven for a demonic reject. Therefore, intervention on his behalf was denied.

Resigning themselves to losing their sons, Devon focused on supplying them with the information they would need to survive within either domain to which they were harvested.

Elenor and Devon included the names of demons or angels who might help them and those to avoid.

Now, the punishment for the fallen angel and fugitive demon had come to finalization on this day, the eve of the twins' 21st birthday. Both domains were represented, ready to harvest a twin either to heaven or hell and both parents relentlessly pleaded for mercy for the boys.

It was a sad sight to witness. I was pissed that I had not been officially made aware of the fate of the twins. However, I knew that my domain choice was not an option if this was to be a punishment harvesting.

Remaining cloaked, sitting perched upon the window sill of the suffocatingly full hospital room, I watched the spectacle that was the dying process. I made up my mind.

Chapter 3

The boys did not have long left in this domain; both cursed to die together. In unison, their breathing started to become shallow, slowing in rate and depth.

Slipping off of the window sill, I made my way back through the torrent of demons and angels to stand in between the two sterile-smelling beds containing two very unlucky men.

Keeping cloaked, I reached down and placed my hands on the top of Connor's and Ryan's heads. I could feel their souls becoming detached from their soon-to-be-redundant bodies.

Motionless, I readied myself. Shit was going to kick off very shortly and, as usual, I was going to be smack in the middle of it.

Waiting silently, I listened to Devon and Elenor flicker between begging for the twins to remain together and telling their children how much they loved them and how sorry they were.

Knowing that I had to act quickly once the twins died, I reached inside the heads of each young man and grazed their souls with my fingertips. I was not going to allow the souls to leave the bodies before harvesting, I knew that as the soul detached from the body, it would cause the heart to beat its last beat; it would be at this point I would harvest them myself.

Moments later, the twins began to Cheyne-Stokes as their bodies began the final stages of shutting down. Each shallow respiratory effect brought the heart to a slower beat: the relaxation of the limbs and pallor of their skin tone made the surrounding angels and demons become restless.

They were waiting for their chosen twin: however, the expected twin remained unclear. It would not be until the souls of the boys were ejected from their extinct bodies that either demon or angel could claim them.

I smiled: the twins were to be mine. I was going to keep them both with me, just to piss off heaven and hell that little bit more than I already did.

The moment a soul is released, it needs to be claimed by either angel or demon – or me. Very rarely are all three of us present. Usually, if a person has been good, it is the angels and I who fight. If the person has been bad, I fight the demons.

I watched as Elenor came between the two beds, leaning first to Ryan as she kissed him lightly on his forehead, just missing my cloaked hand: a centimetre higher and she would have known someone was there and compromised me.

She turned and kissed the forehead of her second son before making room for Devon to say goodbye.

Meeting at the end of the beds, a grieving angel and demon each held a hand of their sons and watched as each young man took his last, slow, shallow breath.

Elenor drove herself into Devon's chest as he embraced his wife, together allowing their tears to cascade from their reddened eyes.

Around them, demons and angels swarmed about the beds of the deceased twins, awaiting the detachment of their souls. The room fell silent, listening for that last faint heartbeat ... and there it was. Both men at the same time: one faint heart bump, then click. Two immediately released souls.

"Devon! Elenor!" I cried, exposing myself to the room. All eyes turned in my direction, shock and horror painted on the faces of demons and angels alike.

I smiled, absorbing the disbelief advancing towards me.

"Devon, Elenor…" I spoke once more. "I have harvested your boys. The twins will come with me now, together."

Elenor fell to her knees, hitting the floor with an almighty crack, closely followed by Devon.

"Purgatory…" Devon addressed me from his kneeling position. "Thank you."

I nodded back, in acknowledgement of his word, and taking each soul by the hand I turned to leave.

A cacophony of angry voices raised themselves behind me as disbelief shattered the mutually agreed truce between harvesting angels and demons. Fights broke out and blame was disseminated. Turning just once to look behind me, I observed the carnage and smiled.

The newly expelled souls of the twins waved goodbye briefly to their parents and as Devon and Elenor blew them multiple kisses, I began the journey back to my domain.

Our transparenting souls slowly dissipated until we became removed from the hospital room, leaving the human realm behind us.

Chapter 4

Bringing a new soul into my domain gave a boost of much needed energy but bringing two, twenty-year-old hybrid twins made the energy meter elevate upwards so hard and fast, it almost lifted the roof.

I have humble dwellings. I do not have some of the finer aspects other domains require: I have only what my people and I need.

Hell seems to be ostentatious in its surroundings; fire pits, brim stones, flames, hell hounds, and the odd rotting-flesh mountains of punished souls. In contrast, heaven is all fluffy white clouds, halos, wings, harps, and hymns.

All domains need the energy a soul produces or they will deteriorate and eventually cease to function. Hell acquires its energy through working the souls extremely hard, unmerciful in its consistent triad of arduous and gruelling tasks within the bowels of the earth.

Primarily, hell is punishment for bad souls in the afterlife: therefore, the continuation of that soul will experience punishment-defining labour and chores until it has redeemed itself fully. Only then will the tasks change, but hell will always be difficult and hard.

On the flip side, nestled neatly above the clouds, heaven obtains its energy in their own way. Heaven is where the good people go to encompass the afterlife. The souls of heaven work within the domain but unlike hell, heaven's work includes fluffing clouds, polishing halos and brushing wings... Well, that's what I believe they do.

Purgatory, my domain, is neither punishment nor reward. Souls are not yet judged as good or bad; therefore, all aspects of work are participated in by all, including me.

We need to live, so together we provide for the domain as a whole. We farm, we cook, we eat, we work, we produce energy, therefore we live. I, however, am privileged. If I meet a difficult soul, I can judge them and expel them into the open arms of a hairy-arsed demon. Or if a soul is so pure that it is almost sickening, I judge them onto the nearest cloud to float up to an expectant angel. Win-win, I believe.

However, I have stirred up both heaven and hell by harvesting the twins and I am not looking forward to the consequences; though I genuinely believe that I have done the right thing.

It is believed that I exist to receive the souls of humans who have died in grace but are required to atone for their sins. This is not so. I am not a babysitting service for naughty souls who need to apologize. However, I do judge souls as either good or bad: eventually, each one has to make their permanent afterlife journey. I ensure they go to the right place, so if you were to ask me what happens in purgatory, I would tell you that purgatory has evolved to protect souls, to ensure they are never misjudged by their harvester.

This is what I did with respect to the hybrid twins, Connor and Ryan. The boys were victims of Lucifer's cruel punishment of their parents, because they turned their backs on their respective domains to live together in the human domain.

Ensuring that the twins died was an evil, unjust action at the hands of Lucifer, but to dictate that the boys be harvested into different domains was despicable. It was a punishment diverted from their parents to the twins themselves, due to the nature of their existence as the product of an unconditional love between good and bad.

This is why I made my decision, standing by the twins' beds. They were not being judged fairly in accordance with the harvesting and judgement laws by which we are governed. Instead, judgement was from one sick megalomaniac.

Purgatory was the only harvesting option the boys should have been given: hence, that is what I did. But now the hard work begins. I was under no illusion that my bad-ass stunt was going to severely tarnish any acquaintance I had with heaven and I was as sure as hell itself that I had totally wrecked the tentative relationship I had with Lucifer.

Reaching my domain with Ryan and Connor, I called my small council of long-staying souls together to explain my predicament and prepare them for the inevitable backlash which would probably come soon.

I left Ryan and Connor with Michelle, an older lady who played mother to the new arrivals. She escorts them around the domain and gives them an orientation tour.

The emergency council meeting was, as I imagined, conducted deep within the confines of my castle. Five of us sat around a large cherry-wood, circular table, held rigidly against it by high-backed, semi-comfortable chairs.

I gazed at my council members, one by one, awaiting the bollocking I was about to receive.

Raymond, one of the first souls I harvested as a young immature domain ruler, was also the head of the council, my mentor and father figure. He was also the person I feared most when I messed up because of his honesty in telling me exactly how much I had buggered up.

I invited Mai onto the council a millennium ago: she is our voice of reason and advocate for all.

There is Porter, my partner in crime and sounding board: a young man who died at the hand of a madman with a gun. He was killed protecting four children by shielding them with his body. He remains part of my council as he keeps me grounded and is absolutely hilarious.

Finally, we have Henry. In life, he was a professor and has extensive knowledge of the multitude of religions humans believe in. He advises me with regard to correct religious protocol for the individual person and their religion, ensuring that they are judged in accordance to their beliefs.

As the meeting began, I immediately felt I should justify my actions before any discussions issued. So I spoke and waited for comments. Porter thought I was a bad-ass, with which I concurred; Henry agreed with my decisions believing, as I did, that the boys were being unfairly punished and harvested.

Mai agreed, also, that I had little choice and had to protect the boys from misjudgement, whereas Raymond thought that I had been a dick!

Apparently, I have opened up purgatory to an ass-whooping of extensive magnitude by both heaven and hell.

I argued my case and reminded Raymond of my need to put the souls first and that Lucifer was an ass-hat for doing what he had done.

In conclusion, we had decided to up the security around the gates of purgatory and prepare the domain in case fighting occurred.

Chapter 5

I caught up with Ryan and Connor about an hour after the meeting had finished. Michelle had been brilliant as always: the twins were fully orientated, fed, clothed, and allocated their lodgings.

I chose to meet the twins in a more relaxed environment within the castle. I was waiting in the lounge when Michelle escorted them in. The young men sat on the bright green sofa opposite me, their eyes conveying mixed emotions. As I looked at them, it was obvious that they were in shock. Such a shame for them to be caught up in such a wicked predicament. I wanted to know how much the twins knew of their parents' past and the curse Lucifer had placed upon them.

It was evident that Ryan and Connor had, in fact, been well educated by their parents on every aspect of heaven and hell. They did not, however, understand who I was.

So I told them.

"I am Purgatory. You can call me Tory. I am the domain between heaven and hell where the souls I harvest are protected from misjudgement by angels or demons." As I spoke, I retained an essence of anger, knowing that I had been totally absent from their education.

"So why were we not told about you? I don't understand why our parents didn't tell us that you were an option," Ryan said, running his hand through his mop of blond hair.

"That's because I wasn't an option, Ryan. I knew nothing about your intended deaths," I responded.

Connor fidgeted in his chair. "How did you know about us? I mean, how did you know we were going to die today?"

"I didn't. I was watching souls as I always do, but today something was different. I felt a shift: it was unlike anything I had felt before so I decided to leave purgatory and investigate on earth. Something had heaven and hell on edge and I wanted to know what it was," I answered.

"And it was us," Ryan stated.

"And it was you," I verified.

The twins became quiet for a moment before Ryan spoke, once again.

"Why did you harvest us if we were to go to heaven and hell?"

"We are grateful," Connor continued, "that you took us together, but will our parents suffer for your actions?"

"I was not aware of your deaths, as I have already said. Therefore, I couldn't have pre-empted the harvesting. Both heaven and hell kept you a secret from me. It was only a story I had heard about a fallen angel, his fugitive demon and their twin children that re-ignited the memory," I explained.

"If heaven and hell hadn't acted with such weirdness today, I would have never have found you. Your parents did not know that I would intervene to harvest you: therefore, they have complete deniability. They will not come to any harm. I do, however, believe that they are relieved that you have been harvested together. If anything, I have brought a shit-ton of trouble upon myself by denying Lucifer a twin."

The three of us sat in silence for a few moments. I watched a number of emotions flood across the twins' faces.

"Tory, thank you for what you did," Ryan began. "We know our parents are grateful that we are together."

"It was my pleasure. You were both wrongly judged because of an issue Lucifer had with your parents," I said, smiling at the two young men sitting before me.

Connor then stood and addressed me, causing Ryan to stand, also.

"We wish to pledge ourselves to you. We acknowledge the risk you have taken for us: therefore, we offer our services for the protection of yourself and your domain," Connor announced, before Ryan continued.

"We can fight. We have been trained well by our parents and we also have a small amount of demon and angel magic."

I was gob-smacked. Never had any of the souls I had previously harvested pledged themselves to me in such a manner. They didn't have to: I have been fighting against heaven and hell for thousands of years but I did kinda like the idea of some badass hybrid backup.

"Ryan, Connor – you must realise that if you fight with me against heaven or hell, you will never be able to leave this domain. You will not be welcome in either domain, ever. Heaven and hell will become your enemies." I sat on the edge of my overly floral, double-stuffed armchair, looking at them and awaiting their answer.

Ryan was the first to speak.

"Heaven and hell became our enemies when they issued our parents with red wings and banishment from their domains."

Connor agreed, nodding rapidly as his brother spoke. "Not only that..." He turned to address me, leaving Ryan to continue nodding. "Lucifer punished us for our parents' love, harvesting us to two separate domains, and heaven agreed to it. We have an enemy of heaven and hell, Tory. And now we will protect and serve only you." The twins stood together in solidarity, pending my response.

I smiled at them both and stood up before them.

"It would be my honour to have you both fight with me. We shall train together and armour shall be made for you both. What weapons are you familiar with?"

"The sword," Ryan answered.

"The bow and arrow," Connor responded.

"Perfect!" I replied.

Both men bowed before me and I bowed back. Something in the back of my mind told me this was right, that purgatory and the hybrid twins were to become a force to be reckoned with.

"Training starts tomorrow," I called back as I left the room to find Porter to give him the order for armour and weapons for my new guards.

Chapter 6

Within two weeks, Ryan, Connor, and I were armoured up and the twins had their weapons made to their specification. I had commissioned new sai weaponry for myself to commemorate our new union.

Today, once training had been completed, the twins were going to accompany me to their first harvesting. Ever since that day – two weeks ago – that I harvested Ryan and Connor, I had met with overly aggressive demons and manipulative angels, all trying to deny me a harvest.

The harvest today, however, was for Ryan and Connor to observe. They needed to understand which souls should be harvested and which to leave alone.

"So – anyone who is really evil we leave to the demons?" Connor questioned.

"Yes," I answered.

"And everyone too good, leave for the angels?" Ryan asked.

"Yes," I answered again.

Ryan frowned. "Why?"

Re-sheathing my sai, I turned to the twins. "It is not fair to bring an uber-good or bad soul to purgatory, just to move them onto another domain. If we can tell where they should go from the beginning, then we should let them go," I explained.

Again, Ryan cocked his head to me, in question. "But Tory, don't we need the energy their harvesting will bring?"

"Sometimes I can expel more energy fighting for a soul that rightly belongs in another domain. Therefore, I leave it and continue onto the next. In the human domain, approximately one hundred and fifty-five thousand men, women, and children die each day, all needing to have their souls harvested. However, there are thousands of angels and demons across the globe to do the bidding of their master, but there is only one of me to bid for purgatory. So you see, I do not fight for the ones who belong elsewhere," I explained, as clearly as I could, hoping to

34

avoid further questioning.

"Oh – okay. That sounds sensible," Ryan said, turning away from me and nodding to Connor.

"Yeah! It does. Cool," Connor added. "We need to shower before we go."

"Please do," I responded, motioning for them to carry on and prepare for what I imagined to be an eventful harvesting.

Henry and Mae visited me briefly, in the armoury, as I finished preparing myself, wanting to double-check that the twins were ready to accompany me. Mai worried that although Ryan and Connor were there, primarily, to observe, the excitement may cause them to act.

I did admit that I was also worried about this but I reassured them both that if I could fight angels and demons, I could easily handle twin hybrids.

Approaching the outer aspects of the inner castle, I could see the twins checking the weapons and discussing tactics. Their pent-up energy bubbled uncontrollably from their insides, igniting their adrenaline-fueled conversation.

It was quite refreshing to have such young blood and minds working with me. I did feel safer having them with me, especially as they were so significant in the domains of the afterlife. Their presence would be taunting Lucifer and heaven but this did not worry me: we were ready as a team and prepared to fight for our domain.

Leaving the castle, I took the twins through our first steps. Firstly, we needed to find the souls to harvest: therefore, we needed to visit the '*iuxta portis mortis*' (Italian for 'the portal of near-death') to find harvestable souls for purgatory.

The twins and I watched the portal for about fifteen minutes. I was able to show Ryan and Connor a prime example of a woman who needed to go straight to heaven. She was sickly sweet, kind to all people and never had a nasty word to say to anyone. She would have done my head in with her over-the-top-niceness.

We were able to watch her being harvested by an angel and this was a good first experience of how the process could be easy and straightforward.

The *iuxta portis mortis* shows all the souls that are nearing release from their human corpse. In contrast, when the twins were dying, the portal could not see them due to a blindness imposed by Lucifer. The portal shows a brief insight to the person's life, thus pre-judgement can begin before moving in for the harvest.

The twins and I watched as the life of a small child developed before us. All domains want children: this is because their innocence feeds the domains a higher concentrate of energy.

I like to harvest children, keeping them for about five years before sending them onto their god. I have never sent a child to hell: nor will I ever. They are too innocent for the crypt environment that hell produces.

"I will need to fight for this child," I informed the boys. "Hell always tries to harvest because of the innocence; heaven wants them because they are good; and I harvest because children are a pleasure to have in the domain. Come. Watch and learn." I motioned to the twins to follow as I stepped through the *iuxta portis mortis*.

I was nearly into the human domain when I was sideswiped by one of Lucifer's leather-backed scaled demons. A metallic-tasting liquid trickled backward into my mouth, after my lip had split.

My first response was to turn towards the ugly-arsed demon and backhand him as hard as I possibly could, allowing myself to fully exit the portal and take a few steps forward.

The midnight mass of stench-filled demon picked himself back up from the hard concrete and began to rush at me. I was prepared this time. Sai in hand, I awaited his attack.

Just as he reached a few feet in front of me, the pair of combat-ready twins erupted from the portal, armour glistening, weapons drawn and intent on their faces.

"Tory?" Connor questioned, turning toward me, as Ryan remained eagle-eyed, facing the stunned demon.

"Just a scratch," I reported, making my way to stand between the hybrids.

"Demon!" I bellowed. "So impolite to attack a person midway through a portal." He, it or whatever it was stood motionless, breathing deeply and rapidly. I allowed him the time to order his thoughts, as he was obviously having a difficult time thinking.

Finally, the demon spoke. "YOU!" he shouted. It was not worth the time waiting for him to speak.

"Yes, demon – me. What?" I replied, goading him.

"Are… Purgatory!" he stated, stumbling over the four-syllable word.

"I am," I verified.

Turning to address the twins, the dumbass demon spoke again.

"You!" He pointed to Ryan, who nodded with a grin.

"And you!" The demon now pointed to Connor. "TWINS!"

Oh, what a shit conversation! The twins were being less than helpful, laughing between themselves at the stupidity of this particular demon. Taking a cleansing breath, I threw the twins a 'shut-up' look, which worked immediately. Ryan and Connor now flanked me closer, one at each side, weapons drawn, waiting for my next command.

"I am indeed Purgatory, and these gentlemen are Ryan and Connor. I do not wish to harm you but I am here primarily to harvest, not to make my blades drip with sticky, sleek, black demon blood. I will forgive your unprecedented attack on me if you go from this place immediately, demon."

Demons are unpredictable, therefore we maintained our stance.

The demon's skin became darker in colour as his body inflated in size.

"Get ready," I said to the twins. "He is preparing to fight."

"Cool!" yelled Ryan, from my left.

I turned on him, quickly. "Ryan – demons are dangerous. This is not a joke."

Connor then interjected on his brother's behalf.

"Tory, we are half-demon: we were trained to fight by a demon so we know how to kill this one. Angels, too. Dad taught us how to fight and kill angels, as well."

"I apologize: I forgot," I confessed. "Please – be my guest and show me what you can do."

I side-stepped past Connor, allowing him to buddy up with Ryan.

High-fiving each other like a pair of ten-year-old children, the twins prepared for battle. Connor had notched his first arrow and Ryan was swishing his sword, from side to side, in front of him.

Now doubled in size, the bulky, scale-skinned demon headed

straight for the waiting twins. I stood, gob-smacked, as I watched the demon get an extreme arse-whooping. The twins were more than capable of protecting themselves during a fight. Devon and Elenor had taught them well.

Arrows of gold flew rapidly through the air from Connor's bow, each one hitting the demon where the young man had intended. At the same time, Ryan's sword pierced the scales of the beast as if it was a hot knife slicing butter.

Every piece of weaponry in the demon's arsenal was thrown at the twins and, apart from the odd, minor scratch, they remained unscathed.

The fight was nearing its natural end: the black, bloodied demon lay face-up on the ground, arrows sticking out from his soft underbelly, like a giant hedgehog, while large, gaping, sword-administered lacerations speckled throughout his body in the areas most likely to cause most damage.

Ryan held his sword up over the beast's heart, while Connor notched his next arrow and aimed it at his forehead.

"Hold still, demon," Ryan ordered, breathing heavily, post-fight. Connor remained focused, looking up to find my position as I walked towards them.

"Tory – do you want us to finish him? Your call!" he yelled.

I smiled. "You have one choice, boy. Send him back to Lucifer as an introduction to the way harvesting demons will be treated from now on by Purgatory and her domain."

I knew their decision before I had finished my sentence.

The demon struggled slightly, hissing at the twins. "Kill me, cowards!" he spat. Blood ran alongside saliva through sharp, broken, yellow teeth and cascaded over his chin.

Connor unhitched his bow, while Ryan brought his sword back to his side. The brothers stepped away from the injured demon.

""I believe," said Ryan, turning to his brother, "that this demon does not wish to return to Lucifer, fearing punishment."

Connor grinned. "He is the coward." They both laughed, directing it at the demon who tentatively stood upright, snarling at them.

I took my opportunity to speak with the wounded, beaten demon.

"Leave and tell your master that the twins are thriving together in purgatory. Oh – and tell him I said 'hi'."

Taking a step forward, the demon employed as much effort as his weakened body would allow to throw a punch at me. I took a step back and blocked him, pushing him back onto the ground.

"Nice try, demon. Go now," I ordered.

Without moving from the ground, where he had face- planted, the demon slowly began to evaporate through the concrete as if he were melted snow, dripping through a storm drain, until he was gone, leaving behind a speckle of black residue.

Turning from the scene, I congratulated the twins on their fighting skills.

"Your parents taught you well."

Continuing to wipe demon blood from the blade of his sword, Ryan answered.

"Our parents knew that, one day, we would have to fight either demon or angel."

"Or both!" Connor interjected. "We knew that we were going to die young. We also knew one of us would be harvested to hell and the other to heaven, but we did not know which one."

"So we were prepared for both, but I prefer this option," Ryan continued, pointing at all three of us as we re-sheathed our weapons and readjusted split clothing.

I nodded in agreement. Hell and heaven were pissed to have lost the twins: therefore, any interaction with either domain was going to be difficult, as the demon had just proved.

"We need to go. The child is nearing release and we do not know who we will encounter on the way." As I walked away, Ryan and Connor fell in line, either side of me. This felt good and I questioned myself why I had spent thousands of years fighting and harvesting on my own.

We found the child at home, in her bed, with her parents seated each side of her. The pain of death for any human weighs heavily on my heart, especially a child. This little girl was so close to death; her eyes were closed, her breathing shallow and her tiny heart beating slowly.

I kept the twins at a distance. They not only needed to observe but also to learn to respect the situation that was unfolding. Death for the child would be a welcome release: she would be freed from a young life that was lived in hospitals with innumerable medicines and interventions.

However, she would not want to leave her parents: they were all she knew. This is where angels are particularly successful: children believe angels are good, have soft, fluffy wings and will take them to heaven, which they will do, once they have completed the battle for that privilege.

Children also know demons are bad, so they will veer away from them on release. My problem is that no-one talks to a child about purgatory: they do not understand who I am and that is why I need to fight to ensure that I am the only one waiting when the soul disembarks from the lifeless body.

The child flicked her eyes open for a brief moment to meet the eyes of her mother. She smiled as if to say goodbye and closed her eyes once more.

I made my way to the top of her bed and rested my hand on the pillow close to her. Before she was released, I looked back up at the twins. They stood, side by side, with their heads bowed in respect for the dying child. I reminded myself, then, not to underestimate these two hybrid twins: they carried the traits of both parents and right at this moment, their angelic empathy was at the forefront.

The child stopped breathing. I listened for her last heartbeat, indicating the release of her soul. Within moments I heard it: one last bump of her heart and I took her hand as her soul lifted away from her failed body.

"Don't be frightened," I immediately told her. "My name is Tory and I am here to help you."

She nodded and rewarded me with a small grin.

"Has the pain gone?" I asked, maintaining the grip on her hand.

"Yes, it has. Have I died now?" she asked, her innocent eyes searching mine for an answer.

I nodded slowly. "Yes, my darling: you have died, but do not be frightened. I am here to take you to a better place where you will no longer be ill," I told her. "You can say goodbye to your parents before we go."

Keeping hold of one hand, I indicated for her to use her other hand to touch her parents as she said goodbye. Touching the shoulders of her mother and father, they gave a brief acknowledgment to the place where her hand had settled.

"What's your name, sweetheart?" I asked, drawing her attention away from the over-enthusiastic touch she was giving to her parents as she enjoyed their reactions to each of her touches.

"Beth," she answered.

"Come on then, Beth. We must go now," I explained.

"Are you an angel?" Beth asked.

"No, honey. I'm not," I replied.

"But you're not a demon!" she declared. "So what are you?"

"I am Purgatory. I am the domain between heaven and hell. People come to stay with me before going to another domain," I explained.

"Oh, will I go to hell after?" she asked, sombrely.

"No child ever goes to hell," I verified.

She smiled brightly back at me. "Oh, good."

After our conversation, we left her bedroom together.

Meeting up again with Ryan and Connor, I introduced them to Beth. She found them astounding, as this was her first encounter with twins. Ryan and Connor talked with her during the journey back to the portal, explaining why they were so similar in some ways, yet so different in others.

Whilst they spoke, I mulled over the harvesting around in my brain box. Apart from the demon we had fought and sent back to hell, we had not encountered another being from either domain. Immediately, my senses were alerted to the high possibility that something was not quite right.

I stopped and called the trio over to me.

"Ryan, Connor – this was too easy. Harvesting is not this quick or uncomplicated, especially when a child is involved. Stay focused. I don't believe this is over."

They nodded in unison, immediately changing their demeanour to being on guard. Beth shuddered and grabbed Connor's hand, pulling herself closer into his body.

"Protect her, Connor. Whatever happens, you must get her through the portal safely," I said, as our walking pace turned into a gentle run. Connor nodded back and lifted Beth into his arms, close into his chest.

Smiling down at his new ward, he comforted her with his words.

"Come on, little Nugget. I've got you and I will keep you safe."

I think I actually saw her fall in love with him, there and then. She also seemed to like her new nickname.

Rounding the corner that would take us to the portal, my fears became reality as demons and angels stood before us.

"Oh, shit! Word must have gotten out about you two. Maybe we should have killed that Demon?" I commented to Ryan, standing on my right side.

Coming to a standstill, the three of us were greatly outnumbered – approximately a 5-1 ratio – plus, we had a vulnerable, newly harvested child with us. I had experienced worse odds before.

"Ladies and gentlemen: if you would please remove yourselves from my portal, I would be grateful," I stated nicely, not wanting to start a fight in front of Beth.

Taking a step forward from the group of good and bad, the badly beaten, hobbling demon glared at our small group.

"See – I told you all. The twins fight with the whore purgatory," he hissed, flicking his gaze between us and the group standing behind him. "I told you they came. Now do you believe me?" The demon back-stepped to align himself with his fellow demons.

"Do demons and angels fight together now?" I asked the collective that barred our exit.

One higher angel stood out from the group to speak.

"We do not fight with the demons. We were interested to learn of your co-harvesters, the demon-angel twins. Why do they do your harvesting, purgatory?" he asked, not challenging but seemly confused about our alliance.

Ryan spoke up before I had chance to reply.

"We fight with purgatory because we desire to. She harvested my brother and me in order to keep us together after death. Therefore, it is our honour to do so."

Connor, still holding onto Beth, stated his opinion. "From now on, we will always travel with purgatory to every domain, to each harvesting." Turning, he fist-pumped his brother with his free hand.

A second angel joined his colleague.

"So you are declaring war on the demons and angels, young

hybrids?" He directed his question at the twins.

"No, war is not our aim," Ryan replied. "But we will fight when necessary. Now, please may we pass? This child needs to be taken to our domain and she should not bear witness to fighting between us."

"You will meet us again, young hybrids. It is only because of the presence of the young human that is just of age, Tory, that we will engage with you no further today." With this statement from the first angel, the majority of the group obstructing the portal rose up into the sky on white feathered wings and disappeared.

"WOW!" Beth voiced, loudly. "That was so cool. Do you have wings, too, Connor?" she asked her protector.

Connor sighed, loudly. "I do, but I keep them hidden. So does Ryan."

"You do?" she questioned, with surprise. "Cool!" Beth said again. "Can I see them?"

"Not right now, Beth," Connor told her. "We need to get you through the portal safely."

Distracted by the conversation, I had forgotten that it was only the angels that had left. A sea of onyx-coloured bodies stood in formation, snarling and goading one another.

"Shit! Ryan – are you ready? Connor – get Beth through the portal when a window opens up." I gave my orders to the twins, which they acknowledged with a head nod.

Stepping forward from our small group, I addressed the writhing mass of stinky-arsed demons.

"You have one opportunity to leave before I descend you, demons. Go back to your master and live until we meet again. Next time, I will not give you the option to go: you will just descend!" I shouted at them, using my authoritative voice and trying to look mean.

The demon we had fought previously smiled: he was still extremely wounded and blood continued to seep from him, causing bubbles of black, rancid clots to form at the base of his injuries.

"We have been ordered to fight you, purgatory, and we shall fight until you give up that harvested child. That one will also come with us," he said, pointing at Connor.

"That will not be happening," I said, drawing my sai from their

43

holsters on my thighs.

Ryan followed suit, unsheathing his sword, as Connor pulled an arrow from his quiver. Maintaining Beth's safety meant he had to keep one hand around her, freeing the other to fight.

We were ready for whatever the demons could throw at us. Ryan and I shielded Connor and Beth behind us and waited. I was not going to make the first move and place Beth in danger.

Moving as one gelatinous mass, the mob of demons began to close the gap between us.

"Now!" the first demon addressed me. "Now purgatory: you shall feel what it is like to bleed as I slice you with my claws. I will make you beg me to stop, whore…"

The demon was interrupted by the movement of a golden arrow. It sped past Ryan and me, hitting the demon in the middle of his forehead, descending him immediately. Silence fell over us all as we watched the demon fall to the ground. He was rigid. Falling like a slab of stone, he hit the floor with a crack. His head split underneath his weight and exploded the majority of his cranial matter over the demons behind him.

I spun around to face Connor. "What the fuck, Connor? I didn't want to start the fight!"

Connor held no remorse, he effortlessly pulled another arrow from his back and kept Beth facing over his back, away from the commotion.

"He was rude – twice. You are not a whore," he said.

"Thank you, Connor."

"No problem," he shrugged, flashing his bad-boy grin at me.

Ryan called back to Connor, over his shoulder. "Great shot, bro. Did you see his head explode? Nice work," he congratulated him.

Connor tapped his brother on the back, arrow still in his hand and replied, "Oh yeah, it was sweet."

I rolled my eyes at them both and turned back to the demon brain puddle. The remaining demons were pissed right off. Stepping over their dead, liquifying colleague, they began to come at us, en masse.

Demons are dirty fighters, biting and clawing at their victims, with no mercy, for a quick death. They will rarely surrender, usually fighting to the descension, or if they live and do not fulfil their orders, they must face the wrath of their master. If given the option, I would rather die.

Lucifer is a satanic bastard.

Rushing headlong into the fight, Ryan and I tried to make a path through the fighting demons to allow Connor to get to the portal with Beth.

We made good progress, considering the number of demons coming at us. Connor was shielding Beth with his own body as he ran, instructing her to keep her head down and not look up until he told her to.

Connor threw his arrows at the demons, who managed to get past Ryan and me. I was still in awe at the quality of the twins' training and found myself smiling at certain kill-shots or evasive manoeuvres.

Eventually, we battled through to reach the portal, creating a space between Ryan and me allowed Connor the access he needed to go through the portal with Beth.

"I will come back!" he shouted, passing me at speed with his precious cargo.

"No – we are nearly finished here!" I shouted after him, not one-hundred per cent sure he had heard me.

Ryan and I stood in front of the portal, side by side. Six large, jet-black scaly demonic figures surrounded us. Glancing at Ryan, I could see that he had been injured: teeth and claw marks punctured his arms and torso.

Demon saliva is poisonous: it contains some sort of venom similar to that of the blue-ringed octopus. This neurotoxin is designed to paralyze the opponent, rendering them unable to defend themselves. Thus, the demon moves in for the kill.

We continued to fight together until, eventually, the last demon slid from the end of Ryan's sword, flopping lifelessly on top of the already established pile of necrotic bodies.

Placing my back against the side of the portal, I took a few cleansing breaths before sliding myself onto the ground. Ryan joined me, to get his breath back.

"Are you okay?" he asked.

"Yep. You?" I countered.

"I am so pumped, right now," he replied. "That was an awesome fight."

"I guess it was… And the venom is not affecting you?" I asked, concerned, although I already knew the answer.

"Nope. If anything, it feeds the demon part of me and encourages me to fight," he said. "Which isn't always a good thing."

"If you can control it, you will be fine, Ryan. Both you and Connor fight very well. I can see the angel in your attitude and control. I think you two are the perfect fighting team," I said, offering him a smile.

"Thank you, Tory," he replied, smiling back.

"My pleasure. Shall we go and find your brother? We also need to introduce Beth to Michelle," I said, bringing myself to an upright position and re-sheathing the sai. Ryan followed suit and together we stepped back through the portal.

Chapter 7

Meeting up with Connor and Beth on the other side of the portal, Ryan and I relaxed and allowed our bodies to drop their guard. We walked the short distance to the edge of our compound and we were met by Michelle, Porter, and Henry.

Henry stepped forward with bottles of water and handed them to us.

"A success, I see," he stated, as he reached us, sidestepping to allow Michelle to reach us.

Connor gently placed Beth on the ground, close to him, and bent down to talk to her at her eye level.

"Little nugget, this is Michelle. She will take care of you. Go with her and she will show you everything that you need to know and introduce you to the other children." Beth nodded at him, as he stood and ruffled her hair. "See you later, Nugget."

Beth flashed a smile at him before she became enveloped into Michelle's arms. Connor waved as they left, promising to check in with Beth that evening.

Standing next to Connor, I lightly elbowed him in his side.

"She likes you," I teased.

He nodded. "Yep! Kids love me," he boasted.

Gathering together, our small group sat on a nearby cluster of rocks to drink our water and rest.

"Apart from harvesting Beth, what else happened?" Porter asked. "You and Ryan obviously fought something."

"Demons," Ryan stated, whilst chugging the remaining water from his bottle and crushing the plastic within his hand.

"I introduced the twins today. Both angels and demons met us as we returned. The angels threatened us but left because of the child accompanying us, but you know what arseholes demons can be. They instigated a fight and we killed and descended them," I informed Porter and Henry.

Porter smiled. Henry frowned. "Eventful day, then?" Porter smirked.

Henry, however, voiced his concerns. "Have we entered into a war because of this? With heaven and hell?" he asked.

I answered Henry. "We have always been fighting heaven and hell, Henry, but I have always had to do it alone. As I harvested the twins together, I knew the other domains would be pissed but it was the right thing to do. Unfortunately, the angels and demons see it as war because the twins fight with me and I am no longer fighting them alone."

Henry nodded. "I, too, believe it was the right thing to do, harvesting the twins together. But I worry," he added.

I smiled at him before answering. "As a council member, it is your job to worry and advise me. That is why I chose you."

"I guess it is," he agreed. "Come – let's get you back to the compound to freshen up." Henry held out his hand for me to take.

The twins and I decided to clean up and tend to our wounds first, then we would meet up to de-brief over dinner. We peeled off to our designated lodgings at the compound, agreeing to meet in an hour in the small meeting room behind the banqueting hall.

After sitting on my own in the meeting room for half an hour, I decided to go and find Ryan and Connor, taking with me a plate of cold meats and a loaf of freshly baked bread.

When I reached their lodgings, the short walk from the castle had taken less than five minutes. The door was ajar. I knocked, then entered, calling them as I walked through the hallway.

Draped over the seating areas, the twins were fast asleep, wearing nothing but their underwear. They had obviously showered and tended to their wounds, as small adhesive dressings peppered Ryan's torso and Connor had a few spotted along the arm with which he had protected Beth.

Around them, medical paraphernalia was scattered over every surface available. Depositing the food I had brought with me in the kitchen, I sat in an empty corner chair, debating whether or not to wake the twins or leave them to sleep.

The decision was made for me when Ryan farted and scratched his balls to adjust himself.

I stood, clearing my throat loudly which, in turn, startled them both awake. Sheer horror crossed Ryan's features, causing him to bolt off of the sofa and dash into the hallway, toward the bedrooms. Conor stood, said "Hi", pulled his boxer shorts out of his butt and excused himself to get dressed.

While waiting for the twins to make themselves decent, I set about relieving the over-burdened coffee table of empty wrappers, dirty plates, cups, magazines, and an arrow. Once wiped down and ready to receive the food I had brought with me, the table looked a lot bigger.

"Hi, Tory," Ryan said, sheepishly, wandering back into the lounge and standing as far away from me as he could. "I apologize," he blushed.

"What for?" I jested. "For being late, falling asleep or being found in your pants?" I stifled a giggle.

"All three." He breathed out with his head hung and his cheeks resembling raspberries.

I giggled again. "Ryan – it's fine. Honest. Here – I brought some food. I thought you may be hungry."

Making his way back to the sofa and avoiding too much eye contact, Ryan sat himself back on the sofa and made himself comfortable.

"Will we de-brief here?" Ryan asked, leaning forward to take a plate and beginning fill it.

I took the chair next to him. "We may as well, since we are all here," I answered, just as Connor bustled through the door.

"I am starving – cheers, Tory," he blurted, loading a plate and depositing himself, unceremoniously, next to his brother on the sofa.

Taking a moment, I watched the brothers' mannerisms. It was evident which one had received the majority of the angelic and demonic genes. Ryan reminded me of a angel: he was quiet, non-threatening, protective, yet a badass fighter with the benefit of complete tolerance of demon venom.

Yet Connor displayed demonic traits: carefree, unaware of his surroundings with regard to inappropriateness, he fought with arrows and fought well, but he flashed his angel side during his protection of Beth.

These hybrids held within them a concoction of good and bad, which ultimately made them extreme fighting machines. Each tolerant of demon venom and the light forces used by the angels, both men had been taught to fight as angel and demon: therefore, there was a distinct possibility they could be indestructible.

I encouraged the hybrids to speak about the experience today, whilst we ate. Both Ryan and Connor apparently enjoyed 'kicking ass'. However, their concern focused on the harvested soul; why a child should be witness to such fighting.

"Usually, we fight before the soul is released. The domain that wins the fight then goes forth to harvest the soul and take them back to their own domain. Fighting should not occur once harvesting has been achieved."

Connor looked up from his plate, masticating rapidly before he could speak.

"So," he said, spitting the remittance of his mouthful down himself. "Today was different because we were with you?"

"Yes," I verified. "I knew there was something different happening when we fought only one demon. Sometimes, I have had to fight demons and angels for hours, just to earn the right to harvest," I explained.

"That's why so many angels and demons waited for us at the portal, to verify our allegiance with you?" Connor questioned.

"Exactly. I am sure that the next time we harvest, we will need to fight more before the release of the soul," I said, continuing to let the boys know what they were letting themselves in for.

This time, it was Ryan who had questions.

"Tory – may I ask, did you always fight on your own? No others have ever helped you?" he asked, with concern.

I smiled at his question before answering. "Nobody was able to fight alongside me during these times. Remember all of the souls resident in this domain are human: they have neither the knowledge nor the skills to fight an angel or demon. Their souls remain human until they leave, either up or down. It is then that they become either angel or demon."

"We can fight with you because we are hybrids: we are not human," Ryan stated.

"Yes," I answered.

"Cool," mumbled Connor, wiping some sort of condiment from his chin. "Who decides when people have to leave?"

"I do. The afterlife started with me, thousands of years ago, when humans started to die." I took a deep breath and checked that the twins wanted the story from the start. Both nodded enthusiastically, so I continued.

"Before I became purgatory, I was a lost soul. I was never human and I don't know how I came to be: I just existed. I watched the human domain for years as I wandered by myself. The humans began as a small race dependent on each for survival, co-operating, living and working in peace. Gradually, they found other humans and their communities expanded. The perfect circle of life made by the first humans continued peacefully for a time until spirals began to form. More people created more spirals; more spirals equalled more difficulties, and more difficulties instigated conflict. These times of conflict brought death; and the consequence of death was the release of souls that wandered over the Earth – lost!"

"These souls remained relentlessly within the human domain, influencing the human for either good or bad. This was when I decided that I had to step in and thus created purgatory. I harvested the souls from earth and brought them here. Raymond was my first harvested soul and he can tell you how hard it was in the beginning."

I paused to take a much needed breath and refreshed my drying mouth with lukewarm water.

The twins finished their food and deposited their plates on the coffee table. Both were now perched on the edges of their chairs, listening intently.

"Go on," Ryan encouraged. Taking a deep breath, I continued.

"Harvesting the souls meant that I had to be responsible for them. Although detached from their bodies, the souls still require substance, hydration, shelter, clothing, and validation. Therefore I created this domain to allow the souls to thrive within it.

"I developed homes within the rugged white cliffs that were here a millennium ago, creating accommodation for either individual use or as a commune arrangement. An example is Michelle: she is the guardian for all the child souls, keeping them together in one specific place that accommodates their needs."

Resting my voice briefly and sipping from an oversized glass, I encouraged discussion and questions from the twins. I could see their inquisitive minds buzzing with the words and appreciated their patience.

Ryan was the first to question me after I had finished the remains of liquid collected at the bottom of my glass.

"So you made purgatory? And you are called Purgatory? Why name the place after you so completely? Does it not get confusing?" he questioned, pulling a frown and contorting his forehead.

I laughed quietly at his question. I had been asked that so many times.

"Back then, I was extremely egotistical: hence the megalomaniac name of a whole domain after myself. This delusion of grandeur wore off the older I became: therefore, all the souls call me Tory," I explained, a little embarrassed by my confession.

"Who created heaven and hell?" Connor piped up, chewing something else he had found that was edible.

"I did," I confessed.

"You did?" Connor stumbled on whatever he was eating.

"Yep," I responded.

"Why?" Ryan asked, this time.

This time, I sat back in my chosen chair and bringing my legs to a bend underneath me, I refreshed my lungs with an oxygen-rich breath and continued my story.

"Humans are an extremely complex race: either dead or alive, they have personality, determination, and the ability to be influenced. I would watch the souls interacting and living with each other. Humans display a wide variety of behaviours which govern their abilities to communicate or interact with others.

"Harvested souls feed this domain. It is their energy that flows alongside the natural energy created within it, thus keeping it alive. However, different personalities create different energy, either positive or negative. Unfortunately for humans, their souls do not change because they are dead: the amount of good or bad in the human domain is also prevalent in the afterlife.

"Purgatory was becoming the afterlife version of the human domain and that was not my intention when I harvested the souls. The amount was increasing and the domain was becoming more and more like a badly managed refugee camp than a peaceful afterlife.

"So I viewed my options and I felt that those who were good should be rewarded and the bad should be punished. Heaven and Hell were then created. Creating my Purgatorial Council first, we chose who needed to ascend and those who should descend, but these new infant domains needed leaders to develop them and guide its occupants.

"Lucifer, the soul chosen for hell, was a vindictive, evil human being. He performed a multitude of sins as a human and once harvested, he became aggressive and uncooperative: the ultimate asshole. So when he was asked if he would consider leaving purgatory to lead hell and its occupants, he agreed.

"Similarly, the man chosen to rule Heaven was Lucifer's polar opposite: he was good, kind, considerate, and as a harvested soul and as a human, he was faultless. Therefore, I began the arduous task of ascending and descending souls: each soul was assessed and delivered to heaven or hell.

"Journey on a few thousand years and Lucifer created demons to do his bidding in order to ensure that the bad souls descended directly into his care. These demons morphed and developed into the black-blooded, midnight, scaly beasts we see now. Satan sent the demons to harvest souls from the human domain. However, they did not discriminate between good or bad: they harvested all souls.

"I have fought many demons over time. I was the only one to harvest for purgatory, yet Lucifer had hundreds of demons. In response to the influx of demons, heaven created the angels: the purest souls were given pure white wings and weapons strong enough to fight demons. Angels fought only for the good souls; hence fighting for souls became the usual practice when harvesting.

"Gradually, the divide between good and bad became more evident, as the angels took the good and the demons the bad, but both sides started to become gluttonous and began influencing humans before their deaths to secure the souls as they stepped into the afterlife. This was not my intention when the domains were fabricated.

"So I stepped in and observed the humans and their influences. It was clear that if people wanted to ascend when they died, the angelic influence was achieved more easily because of the promises of fluffy clouds and harps. Again, demons began fighting with angels as demonic harvesting reduced. Are you still with me?" I asked the twins, taking the opportunity to rest my voice box for a moment.

Connor stood and picked up my empty glass. "Drink?"

"Yes, please," I replied, touching the outside of my lips with my sandpaper-textured tongue.

Ryan was thinking. I could see the possibilities of a question resting upon his lips, then I watched as he chewed it back, changing his mind. He did this two or three times before I interrupted his thought process.

"Ryan," I jousted him out of his head. "Do you have a question?"

"I do," he answered quietly. "But I don't wish to offend you, Tory."

"I don't get easily offended. Please – what is your question?" I encouraged.

He took a deep breath before speaking, to allow the newly inhaled oxygen to enhance his confidence.

"It would seem that by creating heaven and hell, you have inadvertently caused the problems with harvesting. I mean, when human souls occupied the human domain, fighting did not happen. I'm sorry." Finishing his statement, he hung his head.

"Don't be sorry, Ryan. It is a valid statement. You must appreciate that this discrepancy has happened over thousands of years and we have all had our input into the outcomes of harvesting. If I hadn't created Purgatory for listless souls; if heaven and hell were not created; if Lucifer hadn't created a haven for demons and if heaven hadn't counteracted with angels; if harvesting was completed on the basis of good ascending and bad descending; and finally, if I was still able to harvest without a constant battle with angels and demons, fighting would not happen."

I paused, taking the condensation-loaded glass offered by Connor and relieved my dry throat.

"It was not my intention to create a problem and for that I am sorry. But evolution of all species seems to end with problems. Humans believe in a number of gods now, yet still only one devil: therefore, each believed god resides in a different section in heaven and the soul is delivered to their god. However, when in human form, these beliefs can cause unrest between the numerous belief factions."

"Yeah, we saw a lot of that," Connor said, from his chair situated in the corner of the room. "Religion, the humans call it! You cannot grow up in the human domain and avoid it. Our parents told us about various religions and the aspects involved with them: for example, each region has its one book of worship, its own places to worship and its own unique rituals and rules." He finished his sentence and immediately filled his mouth with more food.

"But some of them fight," Ryan stated. "Killing each other because they believe in different gods. Why do they do that?"

This conversation was turning out to be quite a mammoth sharing discussion! Internally I sighed: we could potentially be here for hours. I began to explain, once more.

"Surely, you could tell me more as you were brought up in the human domain," I volunteered, encouraging them to share their experiences and knowledge with me.

"We didn't interact a lot with humans," Ryan explained. "We went to a small, private school during the day, and learnt to fight in the evening. Mum is a refugee demon and although banished from hell, demons would seek us out to torment her. This meant we moved around frequently."

"What did you do for leisure?" I continued my quest for knowledge.

"Hiking up big-ass mountains or camping in the outback of anywhere that had a lack of human population," Connor explained, still eating.

"Oh, I thought you would have become more integrated," I confessed.

"We didn't want to, really. Mum and dad made friends soon after they were married but demons influenced their friends and used them as human weapons..." Ryan stood as he explained, slow-pacing the length of the lounge and running his fingers across the top of the sofa as he did so.

"...against our parents," Connor continued. "They had to fight their friends because of the demons, so it was decided that if we remained isolated, then people we knew would not become collateral damage in Lucifer's vicious games."

I nodded in agreement regarding how sensible Devon and Elenor had been.

"Can I ask another question?" Ryan temporarily stopped pacing to talk.

"Of course," I nodded, wondering what was agitating his brain.

"Why do you harvest? I mean, if the good ascend and the bad descend, who do you choose and why? Do you bring the bad into your domain? Because I think that would be asking for trouble," he added, with a furrowed brow.

"I do not harvest the very bad, Ryan, but I do harvest those who may receive the wrong judgement. I bring humans here and ensure that they receive fair judgement. They stay here for as long as necessary before ascending or descending.

"Humans are complex creatures. They have been given so much, yet they misinterpret necessity and act as they see fit. They have bodies that are amazing: they grow, develop, create new life, become diseased and healed, they learn and retain information in a brain so packed with thoughts and information that it makes me wonder why they do not explode with overloading.

"However, the way that they choose to live their lives in their domain is traumatic to observe. Good humans do well within society yet become ridiculed, whereas the failures of the bad humans become radically charged with others of the same beliefs and actions, so I ensure that the good go up and the bad go down. I try not to harvest those who have a definite route because of their behaviour. I fight for the majority of the humans so they get the correct judgement they deserve and to help maintain the energy required for this domain."

"Then why children?" Ryan interrupted.

"Children are pure energy and revitalize me excessively. They stay with me for a few years then ascend to heaven or stay if they choose. Plus, they are hilarious," I replied, feeling a little smirk wriggle across my face.

The twins sat in silence, chewing over the enormous amount of information I had orally imparted. They had verified the information I had concerning religion and had touched on some aspects of it but, as it is with humans, religion was a complex factor in their lives.

I stood and collected empty plates from the table, then made my way into the kitchen with the hybrid twins close behind me. Running the water to fill the sink, I questioned the twins as the bubbles began to form.

"What do you think, so far, of this domain? Do you think that you will be happy here?"

"It's cool. So friendly. And no demons is a bonus. We never knew when one of those little bastards would show up in the human domain," Connor answered, playing tug-of-war with the tea towel.

Ryan, who triumphantly secured the tea towel, twisted it and proceeded to flick it across the back of Connor's legs, which inevitably led to numerous unrepeatable words flowing from Connor's potty mouth.

"I am looking forward to exploring more. We haven't seen much of the domain," Ryan stated, taking a newly washed plate and beginning to dry it.

"There are maps and other domain information in the library. Raymond believed that we should explore the domain and document it, so he and Henry did just that. I am sure that they would be happy to show you." I was glad the twins were taking an interest in the domain, especially as their stay would be indefinite.

Silence fell over us, stagnating the air. I could hear light murmuring from the twins, so I waited for the impending question.

Ryan took the lead. "So, are there others like us here?" he asked.

"Hybrids? No. You are the only offspring to ever come from a demon and an angel. Usually, when the two kinds come together it is to kick each other's arses, not to procreate," I explained.

Ryan looked sheepishly at his brother before attempting his second question. "What about others our age – like twenty-ish and not just boys?" He flushed a beetroot-red, as did his brother, both fidgeting and shoulder-pushing each other.

I stifled a giggle, before answering. "Yes, there are people your own age here. Boys and girls. You will meet them shortly." I teased them slightly as I spoke.

As a collective, we decided that enough information had been shared. Ryan declared he was tired, while Connor was apparently getting hungry.

Making plans to meet the following day, I reported that I would create an agenda concerning what we needed to work on when harvesting. The twins agreed, although with sleep and food taking priority in their brains, I think that they would have agreed to anything.

I left the hybrids and began the long walk to my own lodgings.

Chapter 8

My own home was situated on the outskirts of the lodging area that the souls inhabited. I enjoyed the solitude I received up here. Very few people came this way unless specially invited or hopelessly lost. Before creating this domain for the harvested human souls, I was always alone; deep in the abyss which was my mind and my sanctuary.

I do enjoy the company of the souls but they are noisy creatures and sometimes solitude is all I need to thrive.

Reaching my home, I ascended the thirteen steps to the front door. Each step held flowerbeds each side, scored from a multitude of countries as I harvested. As I am an absolutely terrible gardener, Mia tends to the flowers. I swear it is her kind and nurturing way that encourages them to grow. She creates meticulous beds with feeding, watering and pruning schedules, whereas I tend to the garden by 'winging it'. Throwing a handful of seeds where I want them and hoping that they will grow is apparently not a successful way to create a flower-based masterpiece.

Entering my own private domain, I located the gadget I needed and pressed the button to tint the windows, giving me complete privacy. The amazing thing about humans is that they have skills: some are cooks, electricians, plumbers, nurses. The list is endless but they bring those skills into the domain with them. I have Porter to thank for tinted glass and a banging stereo system.

Pressing my back against the door to ensure that it closed properly, I turned and bolted it, allowing myself the security to relax. Making my way through the house, I disposed of my keys in a silver shiny bowl strategically placed on the worktop for such a purpose. Reaching the far end of the house, I arrived at my bedroom. It was the biggest room in the house, situated on the edge of the cliff that my house was built on.

I loved my bed: therefore, my bed was massive, occupying the majority of the back wall of the bedroom, facing out to the cliff face. A wall of glass separated me from the outside. Frequently, I would sit on my bed and watch the domain in comfort.

Porter had worked his magic here, also. Each huge window was tinted but also pivoted to allow access from the inside out, where I could enjoy the panoramic view afforded by such a geographical position.

Right now, in this moment, I needed to change. I was uncomfortable. Firstly, my shoes were discarded as I kicked them off against one of the bedroom walls. Sitting on the edge of my bed, I lightly massaged my feet. Standing, I unbuttoned my trousers from my waist, and allowed them to fall effortlessly to my ankles, where I pulled them over my outstretched feet.

Lifting my sweater over my head, I dumped it at the bottom of my feet, alongside my trousers, and in my bra and pants, I stood in the large empty space that created a void between my bed and the glass wall.

I inhaled deeply, allowing oxygen to pass through me, warming up and filling my lung capacity to the top. Exhaling the no-longer-required carbon dioxide made my body feel cleansed. I repeated this exercise a few times until each cell and tissue within my body felt revitalized and saturated with oxygenation.

Finally, as I stood half naked, looking out over purgatory, I encouraged my wings to break free from their hiding place, deep down under my flesh, unseen by all, always hidden. My wings were enormous: trailing down the length of my back, they began at the base of my neck and ran to the base of my spine. Their wing span was also pretty impressive: each at least two feet wide but what they had in size was contradicted by the little weight they held.

Fluttering them slightly to generate air between the feathers, I watched as stray fluffy under-feathers floated effortlessly to the ground. My wings are iridescent in colour, resembling that of Mother of Pearl: they are strong, protective and pretty bad-ass, although I very rarely reveal them. Maintaining the subtle flutter, I took a few steps out onto the balcony, allowing the evening air to penetrate through my wings, revitalizing them. This was another reason for my seclusion: it is difficult to see this high up from the main community areas. Therefore, occasional wing flapping would not be seen.

I permitted myself an extra few minutes, wallowing in the pleasant sensation the wind was giving me. Here, I allowed myself to temporarily forget my worries and concerns, and enjoyed being alone.

Rotating to re-enter my bedroom, I caught my reflection in one of the glass panels. Standing rigid and holding my own purple-eyed gaze, I felt a throbbing in my gums, warning me of the need for my fangs to descend. The pain is brief but fucking hell, does it hurt.

Supporting myself with the head of the bed and its supporting wall, I encouraged the fangs to move, awaiting the accompanying pain. 1... 2... 3... Aah, and there they were! Sharp, white, deadly, long fangs protruding over my bottom lip. They caused bleeding each time they descended, as they pierced my upper gums and grazed my lower lips. I breathed out, rapidly relieved that they were down.

I stood, looking pitiful, fanged and winged, still not knowing what I am. For centuries, the question has eluded me and still does. I do not know why or how I was created; I also do not know who created me, although I do have theories that I manage to regularly disprove.

I just started existing in this domain as an individual with no information regarding my purpose, so I watched humans and fed from the energy of their wandering, dead souls. Taking another quick glance into the glass well, I recalled the names I had been given over the centuries; vampire, werewolf, monster, beast, demon and dragon. Examining my body, I could understand the names: my fangs, wings and claws that protrude from my fingernails.

I do not drink blood or chew on the bones of corpses. I am no demon and have never breathed fire: therefore, the dragon analogy is incorrect.

Recalling the sorrow I had experienced wandering this domain on my own, I re-evaluated my feelings and realized that before interacting with the humans, I was only existing. Now, opening the domain to harvested souls, I was living and enjoying it.

The sacrifice of keeping my real body hidden was worth the pain and discomfort. I smiled at my reflection: I enjoyed the human company as I was glad I had made the decision to harvest them.

Although I wasn't one-hundred per cent happy with my true body, claws and fangs made fantastic weapons. I could bite through the jugular of a demon with my deadly fangs and tear flesh to the bone with my claws. They had always come in handy if I became disarmed, although I rarely use them. I hate picking demon scales from underneath my claws or peeling excess skin from the pointed end of a fang.

Sighing loudly, I retracted my wings, pulling them deep within me to remain hidden for a while longer. I wanted a shower and wet wings take ages to dry.

Wrapping a towel around my hair and changing into clothes that accommodated my wings, I made my way into my lounge area and sat comfortably on the floor, releasing my wings to ensure complete comfort was achieved. Turning to lie on my stomach, I began to make a list of everything I wanted to go over with the twins.

1. To teach them which souls to harvest. I want to show them how to recognize the good, who should ascend immediately, and the bad, who should descend as promptly as possible.

2. How to harvest a soul. They need to learn how and where to remove the soul to allow quick harvesting and the right to claim.

3. Right to claim rules. Rules that were introduced years ago to avoid soul snatching, tearing or disintegration.

4. Angel identification. Rank, powers weapons and defeating.

5. Demon identification, as above.

6. Demon toxicity. Poisons/toxin from bites, claws and weapons.

7. Hand over procedure to Mia.

8. Domain introduction.

9. Use of portal (should be number four).

10. Medical wing, if necessary.

11. Questions.

Re-reading, I felt it was a comprehensive list which could be elaborated upon. I had asked the twins to write some questions also, although I think the majority of what they really wanted to know had been discussed that afternoon.

I was looking forward to seeing them train with their weapon of choice and eager to find out if they had worked on any of the human forms of fighting. I had seen some of the disciplines when I had been watching but I wanted to learn more.

The domain had come up to date with communication technology because of Porter's engineering prowess and general ability to fiddle with all things electric, which both benefitted and hindered me at the same time. I liked the idea of being able to communicate with others, when necessary, from one side of the domain to the other, yet I also hated it.

People could contact me at any time, wherever I was, except for the human domain and the repeated beeping from my communication screen alerted me that someone was communicating now. Begrudgingly, I forced my wings to retract and my fangs to return into my upper gums. This is such an inconvenience!

Rolling my eyes skyward, I located my remote button thing and opened the connection at my end. I jumped as the audio blasted into my lounge and the visual screen was taken up by the faces of the twins, squashed right up close to it.

"You need to back up a bit," I said, decreasing the volume and plonking myself on the chair behind me.

"This is so cool!" Connor yelled, whilst poking at the screen. "Can you hear us?"

"I hear you just fine. The communication system was set up by Porter." I told them to lower the volume a little more to compensate for the excited-voice volume they were currently displaying.

"We can find Porter tomorrow and see what else he can do. I wonder if he can get TV?" Connor continued.

"Cool! We need movies and the music channels."

I interrupted Ryan rapidly.

"Ryan, Connor…"

They both turned to look at me with dopey-looking grins.

"Hi, did you want to talk to me?"

"Yes!" Connor spoke. "I saw Beth just now. She seems to be settling well. She has been introduced to a girl about her age who was harvested two weeks ago. The lodgings for the kids are brilliant. Did Porter set up the electronics stuff there, too?"

"Porter puts electronic stuff everywhere," I confirmed. "One thing I have learnt is that where humans go, technology follows. Especially here."

Ryan doubled back into his thoughts, then unleashed his burning question.

"Do you have a mobile phone?"

"No," I answered.

"Oh, why?" he countered.

"Mobile signal is shit," I smiled.

"Honest?" Connor shouted at the screen.

"Honest." I was actually being truthful. "Cross one little domain and – puff – no bars!"

"That sucks!" Ryan declared, obviously deflated, whilst Connor sulked next to him. Briefly, Connor perked up and shoved his brother's elbow. "We should talk with Porter. See what he can come up with."

"Sure. We can help him design something to communicate with when we are harvesting – you know, just in case," Ryan added.

Turing to face each other, their conversation focused on the need for a mobile device. Connor continued, "People our age could have one, too, so we can contact each other – you know, to talk and stuff."

I watched their conversation develop. They were so similar it was if I were watching someone talking to themselves. This amused me for the next five minutes until I realized that the boys had also decided to ask Porter about getting PlayStation and X-box technology.

"Ryan – Connor!" I interrupted. "Do you still need to talk to me or can I go?"

"Oh, Tory, hi! Sorry. Yes, we don't need you anymore." Ryan spluttered his words out as he realized I was still sitting there like a prize dickhead.

"I will see you both tomorrow morning in the fitness compound at nine o'clock," I informed them.

Connor threw me his radiant smile. "Any chance we could make it ten to ten-thirty?" he asked, retaining his cheeky grin.

I caved. "Ten o'clock, no later. I do not want to have to come and get you again."

"Done," he responded. "Bye, Tory."

"Have a good evening," Ryan added.

"Have a good evening, too, and please get some sleep. We have a busy day tomorrow." I waved, turning the conversation screen to emergency contacts only as I re-settled myself.

Over its young lifespan, the human domain has developed rapidly; almost to the point of leaving itself behind. As humans matured, they had to fight for food, shelter, survival, and life. This, they accomplished by developing tools, communication, diversity of foods, utilisation of rivers and seas, beginning families and working together.

Humans now farmed, moved food across countries, travelled by sea, land and eventually, air. As technology became more widely available, aspects of human life became more tolerable and sometimes easier.

However technology began as a rich man's luxury. Those able to afford it used it to better their lives, but left others behind.

Technology divides countries: available in some yet not in others; affordable in some, not in others. I have watched humans die surrounded by all types of technology. I am still undecided whether I think technology is beneficial or problematic, but the one thing I do know is that humans die and there is no technology that can stop it – yet!

Sleep was seducing me into bed and, as I was feeling exceptionally slutty at the prospect of the romance a good night's sleep would offer, I followed my seducer and walked into my bedroom. Releasing my wings, I slid under my sheets and made myself ready: bringing my wings around my body, I created the cocoon that protects and keeps me warm. It took moments for my body to relax and my breathing to regulate, inviting sleep to take me into the celestial realm for the night.

Chapter 9

Ten o'clock at the fitness compound. I was there in body, mind, and spirit. However, the two hybrids who stood before me seemed to have forgotten their minds and spirits and by the look of them, they had only just brought their bodies.

"Did you get any sleep last night?" I asked, watching the brothers yawn in unison.

"'Bit," Connor answered.

"Some," Ryan admitted.

"Why so little?" I questioned.

"We were designing a mobile device," Ryan started.

"Yeah, like an iPhone but not. It's more inter-domain friendly. Old school. Looks great on paper but we need to talk with Porter – where is he?" Connor had obviously woken up now, as his enthusiasm for the device overtook any enthusiasm for training.

"I do not know where he will be but we need to train. We need to work together when we fight." I tried to take the conversation on another tangent to encourage some sort of exercise. "I know that we have trained for two weeks together already but yesterday, when fighting the demons, you were both able to kill the demons more quickly and easily than I have ever done. I believe it is because of the training your parents had given you, especially your mother. Did she teach you a specific way to kill demons?"

Ryan paused before answering. Each time I mentioned their parents, the boys reflected before engaging in conversation. "Mum taught us how to effectively fight demons from a young age. She knew we would need the skill and ability to protect ourselves and each other."

"Dad taught us about angels as they also fight hard and well. Yesterday was the first fight against demons we had experienced without our parents," Connor said. It was obvious that the brothers were missing their mother and father.

Allowing the hybrids a few minutes with their thoughts, I tied my shoelaces. Right in this moment, I could see in them what I saw in every harvested soul: vulnerability. It was not long before the twins decided it was time to teach me how to fight properly.

"Tory! No! What the fuck! No wonder you don't kill quickly. What are you aiming for?" Reprimanded by Connor for my poor demon-killing skills, I stood like a dumbfounded child waiting for the answer to smack me in the head so I could respond.

Swinging my sai by my side, I answered Connor's question. "I was aiming at his heart."

Ryan smiled and came to stand next to me, while Connor tutted loudly and indicated for his brother to explain.

"Demons don't have hearts as a human would have," he started.

"Oh! Do they not?" I questioned.

"No, they don't. They have a type of power node that is controlled by Lucifer and is located behind their conscious mind. When a soul descends, Satan, Lucifer or whatever people call him, changes them into demons. He does this by removing their conscious mind and replacing it with his own control node-thing. The idea is to make the demons completely unaware of danger, or the thoughts and feelings of themselves or others.

"They serve only him and they are one-hundred per cent loyal because he keeps them alive, dictating what they do and when they do it. They become ruthless killers, but they do not like to be descended to face their master as failures.

So, in order to descend them completely because they are already dead as humans, you have to aim for the brain and run it through." Ryan pointed to the area I needed to aim for. How naive could I have been to not know this?

"So they don't have a heart?" I asked, again mesmerized by this new information.

In my peripheries, I could see Connor rolling his eyes again. He came towards Ryan and me.

"Think of their hearts as stopped," he began. "It sits in the chest of the demon, unused and of no use. So, over time, it petrifies and becomes nothing more than a black stone in their black bodies."

As if a light clicked in my brain, I understood. Go for the head, not the heart, because there is no heart. When I thought about it, I realized how obvious it was.

I didn't want to but I knew I had to ask. "So what about angels? I presume that they still have their hearts?"

"Tory, how do you not know any of this?" Connor asked, making me feel even more of a dickhead than I already did.

Unfortunately for him, he was pissing me off and I bit back at him. Stomping to stand close to him, I held my sai a few inches from his face.

"As I have told you, Connor, I have been on my own for centuries. I did not have a teacher or a support network as you have had. I created heaven and hell, but played no part in the creation of the beings that inhabit them. Neither domain believes I have worth or sits down to explain their own anatomy and physiology. I learn each time I fight but as you also know, demons solidify so an autopsy is out of the question, isn't it? As for angels, they just fight and if killed, just get recalled to heaven, but I have not known how to ascend them easily before, Connor. I have had to fight until I am almost ripped apart by demons or stabbed with the weapons of light used by the angels.

"I fight to keep myself alive and relevant. If I did not fight, I cannot harvest and if purgatory does not receive new energy-rich souls, it will begin to die and so will the people I protect within it. Now! Do angels have hearts?" I was panting at this point; my sai remained aimed at Connor and he had the sense to stand still and shut up while I ranted.

Very quietly, Connor spoke. "Yes, Tory, they do. Angels have hearts and I am so very sorry."

Slowly, I lowered my sai and re-sheathed it. Taking a few steps back from Connor, I too apologized.

"Angels," Connor began, "Carry their light force in their un-beating hearts. I believe that when created, their God wanted to maintain their hearts as a reward for the goodness. Therefore, he filled it with their light force that powers their weapons and keeps them flying."

"So I can aim for their hearts?" I checked, with a question.

"Yes, and if directed in the right location within the heart, you will be able to absorb their light force to re-energize," he added.

"I did not know that." I stood, stunned: all these years I could have used angels to my advantage. Fighting angels is something I do not like doing, as they ascend because they were good, but if they fight me I will always fight back.

Connor took a small step closer to me, closing the gap that seemed so large and awkward. "I am sorry, Tory. I tend to open my mouth before my brain kicks in." His eyes were cast downward, staring at his feet.

Grabbing him tightly by his shoulders, I pulled him in close to me and gave him a hug. It took him a few moments to realise it was a hug I was giving, then he held me back.

"It's forgotten." I told him, releasing him. "I am grateful to have you both with me: there is so much that we can teach each other. As I said before, this was not the way I had intended the domains to function. Giving over the power of heaven and hell has meant that I have 'shot myself in the foot' and allowed them to behave as they wished. I realize now what a mistake that was but I cannot change it." Rather deflated, I walked away from the twins. I needed a little time by myself.

In the background, I could hear the faint buzzing of the twins arguing with each other and Ryan telling Connor, at a loud, unintended volume, that he was a prick. Poor Connor had just received a gobful from me and now Ryan was dishing it out.

I gave myself a good ten minutes sulking time, sitting on my arse. As I sat there, wallowing, I watched as Ryan and Connor went from arguing to sparring with each other. They were the perfect fighting mechanism: fluid in motion, knowledgeable of each other's abilities and they worked together as if they were one warrior.

I decided that I should actually grow up and join them if we were to fight together. I needed to become more familiar with their mindset in battle. Taking myself over to where they fought, we immediately began working on demon kills and formations. As we were bringing the session to a close, I felt a shift in the domain alerting me to the ripples in the *iuxta portas mortis*.

"Do you feel that?" I asked the twins. "Stand still and feel the atmosphere around you – do you feel the ripples?"

"I don't think so," Connor frowned.

"I think I feel something, but I couldn't tell you what it is," Ryan offered. "Is it the portal?"

"It is. We need to ready ourselves for a harvest. Change into your armour and meet me by the portal as soon as you can," I told them, as we peeled off from each other.

The portal indicates that death is imminent for someone but it does not give a time span, unfortunately. We need to watch through the portal to identify the soul for harvesting. Only when we have found it, should we step through. The last thing we want is to fight for harvesting rights then realise that we are in the wrong place.

I arrived at the portal at the same time as the twins. Looking through it, I tried to locate the soul that the *iuxta portas mortis* was indicating. Eventually I found her: a women in a difficult labour somewhere nearby.

Preparing ourselves for an onslaught, Ryan, Connor, and I stepped through the portal right into a mass of writhing demons waiting for us.

"Purgatory!" one screamed and threw a clawed hand my way. I moved: he missed. I was pissed off now so, turning my sai in my hand, I thrust myself forward and planted my blades through his dirty, stinking brain cavity. I watched as he putrefied around my blade and slid from the weapon, before solidifying.

"Cool shot, Tory!" Ryan yelled from beside me. "The bastard never saw it coming."

Obviously angered by the solidification of their comrade, demons began charging us from every direction. We fought hard. Although demons do not have the capacity to know that they should protect their heads, I was finding that they were becoming protective over that particular area, which, in turn, made it harder to stab them.

Eventually, the hybrids and I stood in a mass of globular demon carcasses. They solidified into a pitch black, odorous quantity of sticky glue with the consistency of tree sap. I had gained more wounds than the twins put together, which did really make me wonder how I hadn't died years ago from battling demons and angels.

Connor had a nasty, uneven laceration ripping over his shoulder, just outside of his armour. I reached for an adhesive dressing that I carried beneath my breastplate for emergency first aid.

"Where did you get that from?" Connor asked, confused.

"I always carry these with me. Great human invention," I informed him, then told him to be still while I stuck it to him, covering the laceration.

"Cheers," he mumbled, eyeing the scraps and scratches on me. "Are you hurt?"

"Not really. Only scratches and they will heal," I answered. "Come – we need to leave and find the soul before it is released. We may have won harvesting rights by totally pummelling some demon ass but I am sure we'll meet a few angels before we meet the soul."

I was aware that the soul was dying slowly but something else was niggling at me: something was not quite right. After walking for approximately ten minutes, the twins and I turned a corner straight into a herd of angels. Before us stood a sea of white clothing and fluffy wings, spread out across the road. Internally, I giggled as the scene looked like a recent explosion in a talcum-powder factory.

"Bloody hell – that's a lot of fluffiness in those wings," Connor said, stifling a laugh.

"They look like a flock of lost sheep," Ryan remarked.

I watched as the twins' comments were winding up the angels: it made me smile.

Ryan turned to me with concern laced across his features. This twin was always concerned and displaying his inner angel. "Are there always this many?" he asked.

"Usually. Sometimes more; sometimes less," I answered.

"And you would fight on your own? Against all of these demons and angels to harvest the human soul?" he questioned.

I nodded back at him.

"Bloody hell, Tory – that's insane!" Connor piped up.

"It has to be done. Like I said, it is my fault that it has turned out this way but I can no longer do nothing about it. We have to fight for the sake of the soul and I believe this one should come with us. Something isn't quite right," I explained to the twins.

"Ok then," Connor said, notching an arrow he had retrieved from his quiver. "Let's send these angels back to where they came from."

"Fuck, yeah!" yelled Ryan, sword drawn and pointing at his first victim.

Remembering the information Ryan and Connor had given me, I aimed directly for the heart of each angel as I fought. As I pierced their hearts, I waited as their light-force fled from their body, travelled up through the sai and was absorbed into my hand holding the blade.

The energy flowing within the light force was immense. I immediately felt a jolt of energy, like I had never felt before. I carried on through the crowd of angels, piercing and absorbing repeatedly. The energy was like a drug: I couldn't get enough and I was tripping on the excess energy I carried within me.

Eventually, each angel had been collected by heaven, leaving only little scorch marks where an angel had previously stood. The odd, pure white feather puffed around in the breeze, which amused our trio further.

The complete right to harvest was ours and we made our way to the hospital room, where the human was dying. Our weapons were no longer needed and were therefore re-sheathed, out of sight.

Stepping into the room, we saw a young woman. She was definitely the soul we were looking for. I signalled for the twins to watch me harvest so eventually, they would be able to do so.

I walked around the front of the bed. There were no belongings for this woman and the only person in the room was a nurse in a chair beside her, writing notes.

Placing my hand over hers, I felt her soul fluttering beneath her skin. I listened to her faint, slow heartbeat – bump bump bump bump – then her soul released. I immediately pulled on her hand and brought her soul from her body.

"My baby…" she whispered. "My baby!" She turned to me with horror-filled eyes. "Where is my baby?"

"Oh shit, Ryan!" I called him, whilst maintaining my grip on the women, frantically scanning the bed for a baby.

"She has a baby. Find it – quick – before its soul is released and lost," I ordered him.

Searching through the bedding, Ryan found the baby nestled deep down inside the woman's lifeless stomach.

"Hold its hand, Ryan, and feel for a flutter. Do you feel it?" My voice was raised with panic. "Ryan!"

"I can't feel anything. Connor, come help me," he called to his brother.

Connor rushed to the other side of the body, narrowly avoiding hitting the nurse off of her chair as he did so. Taking the baby's other hand, Connor helped Ryan search for the tiny soul. The baby's mother was near hysteria as she stood beside me, pulling to move closer to the bed, screaming at the twins and me.

"Ryan – Connor… Anything?" I asked. Maybe we were too late and the soul was lost. I have never lost a soul and I was not willing to lose one now; especially a baby.

The room became silent and as Connor and Ryan frantically searched the tiny body for its soul, we started to hear the last beats of a tiny heart.

Bump bump bump… bump… bump…

"I've got her!" Ryan yelled, as I heard the soul release.

"Do not let go and pull the soul from the body, Ryan. Do it now!" I shouted at him.

I watched as Ryan pulled the soul from the lifeless body of the child's mother and brought the baby into his arms.

"Do not let go of her," I whispered to him. "Please."

The baby's mother was rigid with fear as we had not been able to explain who we were before the onset of panic to harvest her daughter.

"My name is Tory," I told her. "I am here to take you and your baby to the afterlife together. Right now it is difficult to understand, but you must allow Ryan to take your daughter and we will go to my domain together. Once we're there we can give her back to you." I smiled at her and she smiled back, still in a state of shock and maintaining her gaze on her infant.

Looking back, as we guided the woman away from her dead body, I heard the nurse talking to a colleague. The woman had gone into labor following a car crash: both she and the baby were unable to be saved and they died together.

"This world is evil," I thought, stepping out of the room. "What a waste of two lives."

Journeying back to the portal, I explained in more depth who we were and where we were going; also the reason why Ryan had to keep holding the baby until we reached purgatory.

Ryan walked next to the woman, ensuring that she could see her child at all times. The woman's name was Rachel and her baby, Amelia. Rachel was 25-years old. She had been disowned by her family for becoming pregnant out of wedlock.

Our journey back was uneventful. Connor primarily acted as our protection: his arrow was notched ready for action. I spotted a few individual demons hiding in the shadows, but none of them advanced towards us.

Just as we reached the portal, one angel stepped before us, his hand held out to us, proving his lack of weaponry.

"The baby, Tory…" he said, in a quiet tone. "She should come with me. She is pure and babies do not get harvested by you."

Ryan held a defensive arm around the tiny soul as Connor stood in front of him, protecting them both with his poised arrow.

Calming Rachel down as panic raced through her, I replied to the angel.

"Not this time. This child died within her mother: she must stay with her mother now," I stated, feeling Rachel relax slightly beside me.

"Do the harvesting rights not state that a baby should only be taken by an angel to ascend?" he asked.

"It does," I began. "But I did not know that the baby was present. Neither did you. You will be aware that I had to harvest the baby at that time or she would have been lost. I would not allow her to become lost to her mother. Now, however, she will stay with her mother. The rules need to adjust to the situation, angel. This baby will not be going with you."

Anger welled beneath his features and I knew the angel was in no position to fight.

"Are you willing to anger my master with this defiance?" he asked, through semi-clenched lips.

I smiled at him. "Oh yes!" I smiled curtly. "Now, please excuse us. I need to introduce Rachel and her daughter to their new home."

The angel side-stepped away from the portal. Connor kept his arrow trained on him, as Ryan, Amelia, Rachel, and I passes through.

"Beware, young hybrid," the angel spoke to Connor. "Purgatory has changed the stakes for us all by harvesting you: she may have just fucked up the afterlife."

Connor smiled back. "I doubt that!" he retorted, as he disappeared through the portal.

Chapter 10

Immediately as we stepped through the portal into purgatory, I released Rachel's hand and Ryan placed her daughter into her arms. Our usual welcome home team was waiting for us. Henry stepped forward to speak, yet no words had the chance to leave his lips before Michelle bumped him out of the way.

"You brought a baby? Tory, babies do not come here: they must ascend immediately!" she hollered at me.

I stood my ground and hushed her. "Babies need to come here if they die seconds after their mothers. What was I supposed to do, Michelle? The baby would have been lost if we didn't harvest but she is with her mother: they need to stay together."

"Of course. I apologize. I know that you would have allowed her to ascend but were there no angels present?" she asked, her tone more inquisitive than questioning.

I answered her. "We fought the angels and demons for Rachel. We did not know there was a baby until I had harvested her and she screamed for her child. I do not know why the baby was hidden from us. My only conclusion is that the baby died within her mother as a result of the car crash. It's a bit fucked up."

"Tory!" Michelle reprimanded.

"Sorry," I apologized. Michelle hated bad language and unfortunately I am a complete potty-mouth and curse words fall from my lips so easily. "Come, I will introduce you. Rachel has given little information, so maybe you can help her?" I asked.

Michelle led Rachel and her baby away after a brief and totally uninformative introduction. I was confident in Michelle's ability to retrieve information from our new souls. Her concern was lack of supplies for a baby. Ryan volunteered to slip back into the human domain to collect what was needed once Michelle had a brief verbal list of the required equipment.

"Give yourselves at least an hour to rest," Henry advised. "You have fought hard today. Rest in case you run into trouble again."

Ryan nodded in acknowledgment to Henry and went to join his brother, who was already cornering Porter to discuss the mobile device.

Turning to Henry, I accepted the bottle of water he always brought when greeting me after a harvesting. Gulping the majority of the icy-cold fluid, I found delight in the pleasant feeling it gave as it rehydrated my battle-torn body and dehydrated internal organs.

"Something isn't right, Henry. I don't know what it is but I can feel the equilibrium shifting and I do not like it. I also do not understand why the angels did not know about the baby until after she was harvested and, of course, why I did not feel her dying, either?" I squeezed the remaining liquid out of the bottle and drank it down, wiping the droplets of escaping water as they rolled over my lips.

"Come – let's walk," Henry motioned towards the compound. "You must rest but we can talk as we go."

I agreed and turned toward the huddle of men talking enthusiastically about technology. Catching Ryan's eye, I told him to check in with me before he left for the human domain.

He smiled and nodded at me before his attention was once again regained by an over-excited Connor.

"What are your thoughts, Henry?" I asked, as we began the short journey to the compound.

"I think that you will not like what I am about to say," he answered, obviously knowing me too well.

I gave him a knowing nod. "Go on, be honest," I encouraged.

Henry took a long breath in through his teeth, his demeanour indicating that I really wasn't going to like his opinion.

"I believe that there has been an extreme shift affecting heaven, hell, the human domain, and ourselves. This shift is displacing the domains and I believe it is because you brought Ryan and Connor into purgatory." He paused, awaiting my reply.

"I agree." I said back to a shocked Henry. He wasn't used to me agreeing with him. "However, these boys were being used by Lucifer as a punishment for their parents' choices, which is not acceptable, and it is unfair to split the twins up after death just to be a spiteful ass." I paused myself as something popped into my head that I hadn't previously considered. I stopped walking, bringing Henry to a halt beside me.

"Something still doesn't add up, Henry. Devon and Elenor are angel and demon in essence. They are both already dead," I stated, watching Henry as he fathomed where I was going with this particular tangent of thought. "Therefore," I continued, "They should not have been able to procreate. The dead do not reproduce! How did Elenor become pregnant in the first place?"

Thinking further, I began walking once more, indicating for Henry to walk, too.

"What are you thinking, Tory?" Henry gingerly enquired.

"I think that these events were planned by someone for a specific outcome, but when I harvested the twins, I fucked it up," I stated.

"Tory!" Henry resented my language, echoing Michelle.

"I am sorry, but the twins are half-angel and half-demon, aren't they?" I posed the question out loud, watching Henry nod in agreement. Pausing, I allowed my thought process to develop further before I spoke again.

"Henry, those boys are hybrids: half-angel, half-demon hybrids. Born to angel and demon parents; angel and demon parents who were already dead and banished to the human domain. Henry, hybrids born to a dead angel and a dead demon are born dead. How did the boys grow to twenty years of age and 'die' before their twenty-first birthday in the first place – to dead parents?" My hands were still constricted into the quotation-marks hand gesture as I continued. "I harvested dead souls that should have never been able to die in such a human way, because, well – they were always dead! This is totally fuc– I mean, messed up," I commented, resting my case at this point.

It was obvious that Henry had cottoned onto my chain of thought, rendering us both mute.

Henry broke the silence. "I do not understand. You think that someone staged their existence? So, if according to the plan, one twin should have ascended and the other descended, what would the result of the plan have been?"

"I don't know," I admitted. "But I will find out. It seems that our hybrid boys were created for something other than punishing their parents."

Reaching the compound, I left Henry to consult his numerous books for any insight, while I decided to check in on the new harvestee and her baby.

Ryan met me in the gardens outside the compound for the children. Michelle had given Rachel a room within this compound so that Amelia could interact with other children. However, never having had such a new baby in purgatory, Michelle and I did not know what to expect. We believed that she would grow up into an adult as all the children do, eventually, but this was way too new for us.

"How's the baby?" Ryan immediately asked, as we stood together in the garden under one of the big oak trees.

"Amelia is fine. Completely unaffected by her ordeal. Rachel, however, is obviously finding this situation hard to digest and understand, but Michelle is working with her. You did well today, Ryan, to harvest the baby under those circumstances," I told him, patting his upper arm. I was impressed with the compassion held within both men as they assisted the harvest.

Ryan cast his eyes downwards as embarrassment rippled through his features.

"It's no big deal," he answered, shyly.

"It is a big deal, Ryan. It's enormous. It's a big deal to me, to Rachel, and especially Amelia. If you hadn't have caught her soul, she would be lost and would have remained wandering through the gaps between the domains for eternity. Those lost spaces are no place for a child, especially a baby. You did well," I told him.

"Thank you," he replied, maintaining the rosy-red blush to his cheeks.

I smiled. "Do you want me to come with you to the human domain?" I asked.

Allowing the original colour to return to his previously blushed features, he declined my offer, stating that because he was not leaving to harvest, he should not run into any trouble.

I agreed but warned him that I didn't trust demons or angels to play fair. He continued to reassure me that he had knowledge of grocery shopping in the human domain and that he was, indeed, the best person for the job. He also declined the offer of Connor accompanying him as he wanted to remain as discreet as possible.

Leaving me in the compound, Ryan went off to find the equipment needed for one tiny little baby girl.

Chapter 11

Standing before the portal, Ryan composed himself. Taking large lung-enriching breaths, he prepared to step through. He found himself in familiar surroundings and immediately regretted his decision to go on the errand for Michelle. It was night: the sky was as black as onyx with a slight speckling of silver stars revealing themselves to the human domain.

Finding his bearings, Ryan realized that he was home; the last place he and Connor had lived before their deaths. Memories flooded his head with images of his past. Not wanting to incapacitate himself with the inner feelings that accompanied these memories, he made his way to a large baby warehouse he knew of, ten minutes-walk away from the portal. Reaching the warehouse, he entered via an old, dilapidated back door, which was so damaged that Ryan wondered how it ever kept the wind out, let alone burglars.

Recalling the list he had committed to his memory, Ryan set about finding all that he needed. With bottles, teats, bedding, nappies and much, much more all bundled into three large bags, bursting at their seams, Ryan left the store after pacing down an aisle full of toys and collecting as many as he could.

Outside of the warehouse, Ryan closed the door and stood briefly with his back against it. He had never stolen anything in his life and his conscience was disapproving of his actions, yet he countered it with the rationale of needing the goods for the defenceless child he had harvested earlier that day.

Making his way back to the portal, Ryan acknowledged his previous home.

"Nothing changes when people die," he thought to himself. "No matter who it is, we all die and the world continues revolving. Life continues without stopping to mourn death."

In his subdued mood, Ryan listlessly continued walking. He had not taken Henry's advice to rest, instead opting to converse with Porter and Connor about the mobile devices. Cussing himself, he came to the edge of the street. Looking across the road, he saw the portal shimmer into view, visible only to the dead. Ryan began to walk slowly towards Purgatory's domain.

Something stopped him in the middle of the road. He felt a presence of another but he was unable to determine if they were dead or alive; human, demon, angel or Tory. Rotating where he stood, Ryan cast out all of his senses to find the intruder. Each direction returned a distinct lack of information, causing Ryan to believe that he was being overly paranoid.

Cautiously he continued, keeping his senses sharp and his eyes focused on his intended destination. Reaching the outer rim of the portal, Ryan felt eyes fall upon him, watching him. Again, he stood still, listening and watching whilst slowly turning on the spot. He saw nothing. Dropping two of the bags on the elephant-grey, cracked pavement, he reached for his sword, disturbed by the unease he was feeling.

Throwing one of the large bags through the portal, Ryan turned to locate the others. As he did so, he came face to face with an angel.

"You never looked up, hybrid," the angel goaded Ryan, then hit him with a bolt of light force, knocking him sideways from the portal.

Ryan hit the cold concrete with an almighty thud. His head cracked heavily down and immediately caused the skin on his forehead to rip, allowing a torrent of viscous, scarlet blood to be released.

A cascade of laughter echoed around Ryan as he lay dazed, trying to find the momentum for his body to obey him and move. Lifting his head, Ryan noted that five other angels had joined his attacker.

"Not so brave without that woman or your hybrid twin!" an angel shouted at him.

Ryan began to stand, mentally checking his body for injuries as he moved: nothing was broken except the skin on his head. Ryan tasted the metallic sticky blood as it continued to run down the side of his face and accumulated at the corner of his mouth. Using the back of his hand, he wiped the blood away from his mouth and stood firmly on his feet.

Ryan's sword was thrown a few feet away from him when an angel struck him, as he stood. Chastising himself for not realizing he was being stalked by angels and losing his weapon when the bastard angel hit him, Ryan regained his composure and drew a deep breath. He noted that he was too far away from his sword to reach it before the angels descended on him. They would have gotten to him before he regained his weapon.

Inconspicuously, Ryan reached around the base of his waistband. His fingers searched until they felt the cold hilt of his dagger: it was not going to be as effective as his sword but it was sharp and he used it well.

Releasing the dagger in his waistband, he maintained his rigid posture and faced his attackers.

Six higher angels surrounded him, their light force weapons directed at him and their wings unfurled behind them.

Many thoughts travelled through Ryan's mind at this time. He had a few precious moments to defend himself before the angels attacked him again. Pulling the dagger from his waistband, he deflected the first light-force hit.

"Oh shit! Here we go," Ryan mumbled to himself, immediately defending his body as the angels began their cruel attack.

The six angels mercilessly threw light force at Ryan, one after the other or multiple shots at once, hitting him each time they attacked. Ryan was gradually closing the gap between himself and his sword. With each slight reprieve in shots he moved, eventually getting close enough to it as a bolt of light force hit him from the side. It threw him the remainder of the way to his sword, pain coursing through his weakened body.

"You harvested a baby, hybrid. Fucking idiot! Babies come with us!" yelled one angel, throwing a ball of light force at the hand reaching for the sword.

A second angel spoke: the voice was closer to Ryan. Turning his head, Ryan saw the angel they he had met earlier that day before entering the portal with Amelia, directly after the harvesting.

"What right do you have to harvest, you pathetic hybrid?" the angel spat from between his teeth.

Ryan's fingertips rested on the hilt of his sword. He inwardly smiled before answering the angel.

"I have as much right as you angels: I am part-angel, as you well know."

"No!" screamed the angel. "You are half fallen-angel and half refugee-demon! You are nothing!" The accompanying angels jeered their colleague onwards, as he continued his verbal tirade.

"You and your hybrid brother have insulted heaven by harvesting the child. You shall suffer for your actions!" As the angel finished speaking, he hurled a small cascade of his light force at the hybrid standing before him.

Mustering as much strength as he could, Ryan forced his arm to hyper-extend: this gave him the extra few inches he needed to take the hand of the angel firmly in his own. Without pausing, Ryan spun himself from in front of the angel to behind him. Taking the angel's arm with him whilst dropping to one knee, Ryan spun the angel, forcing him into a face-to-face position. With the strength he had left, Ryan plunged his sword into the angel standing before him.

The angel stared at Ryan, then at the sword protruding from his chest and laughed. "You missed, pathetic hybrid."

"No, I didn't," Ryan replied, pushing up on his feet to stand upright. As he did so, his sword moved with him, careering up through the angel's body, ripping it open and exposing its inner cavity.

"Goodbye," Ryan added, as the angel brought his eyes back to meet the eyes of the hybrid in disbelief. Ryan continued his sword's upward journey through the angel's heart, splitting the light force outward from the angel's body.

Ryan stood firmly as the light force left the angel and travelled the length of his sword to accumulate in its hilt.

The clouds above him parted, allowing heaven to claim the failed angel with haste. Ryan watched as he ascended once more to his god, to be reinstated once his life force had been re-implanted.

"Prick," Ryan whispered, rotating on his heels to meet the remaining five pissed-off angels.

The light force he gained from the recently ascended angel gave Ryan the burst of energy he needed to continue fighting. He was bleeding heavily from the majority of his body as the relentless angels bombarded hm with their weapons of sharp, flesh-penetrating light.

Ryan was losing this battle rapidly: for every positive attack he managed, three came back at him until, eventually, he found himself thrown so hard against a lamp-post that he took it down with him as he landed awkwardly back on the hardened concrete.

He was incapacitated by the amount of light force he was receiving: being part-angel meant that he was able to withstand light force to a certain level, but he was receiving so much in such a small amount of time that his own immunity was becoming overrun by it.

"Finish him!" demanded the angel that had taken leadership of this band of unjustifiable heavenly beings. "Take him to the edge of death and call the demons to claim him into hell, where he belongs." The angels readied themselves once more for the attack on Ryan.

He was defenceless: his body was broken and bleeding, he was dizzy from the numerous times his head had cracked on the pavement and his weapons had been kicked away from him.

Out of the corner of his eye, Ryan could see demons crowding, watching the attack and waiting for the angels to finish their battle and to hand Ryan over to them.

Protecting his head as much as he could, Ryan fought to distract the light force from his body with his insignificant dagger.

White, cloudy spots began to frost themselves over Ryan's eyes as he gradually began to lose consciousness. He fought to restrain the impending mass of darkness that gradually enveloped his brain, hanging onto it and protecting it until he lay motionless, unconscious and bleeding.

"This hybrid is yours," the angel turned and smirked to the approaching collective of demons.

"Like hell he is…" A voice from behind them spoke.

Chapter 12

Almost an hour had passed since Ryan left for the human domain. He had assured me that he knew where he needed to go and what he needed to get: therefore he would be half-an-hour at the most.

I became restless with worry in the compound, so I made my way to the portal. I sat as close to it as I could, without making it look as if I was waiting for Ryan to come back.

From my vantage point, I could see the majority of the domain. I was proud to see how it stood today: homes carved out of rocks, built for the humans; recreational areas and peace throughout. Considering I started with a barren landscape of rocks, dirt and nothing much else, I was pleased with the achievements the humans and I had made.

As I sat reminiscing, ripples in the portal caught my eye: only little ripples, but I continued to watch as they grew in size and frequency. I stood, waiting for Ryan to step through at any moment, but it surprised me when the first thing through the portal was a fluffy stuffed lion, followed quickly by a large bag of baby equipment.

Hitting the floor heavily in front of the portal, the bag split under the strain of the items inside. An explosion of bottles, toys, tins and plastic, multi-coloured cutlery burst over the grass before me. I watched as equipment bounced and rolled over the pathway, but there was still no sign of Ryan.

I decided to get off my arse to pick up the baby goods from the ground. The redundant bag lay lifeless, flattened and split as a result of the excessive cargo.

It took me ten minutes to recover the disseminated items this new baby would need. Each new object I retrieved was obviously required for something, but I could not fathom why such a tiny person needed so much stuff.

Piling everything on top of a small cluster of flat rocks, I began to become concerned for Ryan. Changing into my armour and gathering my weapons, I decided to step through the portal and locate the wayward hybrid.

Stepping through, I was met with such carnage. Shocked, I stood momentarily and viewed the surroundings. Ryan lay lifelessly on the ground, his body bleeding from every aspect, as a result of light force weapons. Five angels stood with their backs toward him, facing an ensemble of waiting demons.

"The hybrid is yours!" one of the angels said to the demon pack, as he smirked like a five-year old.

"Like hell he is!" I said, from behind them.

Orbiting to face me, the five angels stared at me.

"What the fuck have you done, Nathanael? Why have you attacked? There was no harvest to fight for?" I asked angrily, waiting for my answer.

I took a small step towards him. "I know all of your names: I have lived for centuries. I know each of you and every one of them," I said, pointing out towards the demons. "Now – answer my question. Why did you attack Ryan?"

I looked behind me, reassuring myself that Ryan was still breathing. I watched for a brief moment as his chest rose and fell softly.

"Answer me!" I yelled, spinning back around to the angels.

"He killed Daniel, absorbed his light force and ascended him," Nathanael answered, curtly.

"Why?" I asked, knowing full well what had happened. Scanning the surroundings by the portal, two further seam-bursting bags of baby necessities lay scattered on the pavement.

"You ambushed him!" I stated. "You attacked Ryan when he was alone and he wasn't harvesting, didn't you?" I could feel the heat at my back as my wings threatened to expose themselves from the amount of anger I had coursing through my body.

Gamaliel stood forward of the angel group to address me.

"He should not have harvested the baby. Babies come to heaven with no exceptions."

"The baby died within seconds of her mother," I retorted. "We did not know she was there and neither did you or you would have been present when the soul was released. The baby is now with her mother and that is where she will stay. Did Ryan have the opportunity to explain this before you attacked? You are angels – what the fuck has happened to you? And now you work with demons?"

I was working hard to restrain my wings, aware that the demons were crawling forward and closer to us, as I continued my accusations of the angels.

"We do not work with demons." Gamaliel stated.

"But they are here with you and did you not just offer Ryan to them?" I countered.

"The demons are present to take a hybrid twin to hell, where he should have been when harvested, until you interfered," Nathanael interrupted. "You stole the hybrids and have angered our master. You and your hybrids must be accountable for your misguided actions," he continued.

Stepping up, I closed the gap between myself and the outspoken angel.

"I – little angel man – am the ruler of purgatory. I am neither angel, demon nor dead human. You do not have any right to speak to me as you do. You are nothing but an object of heaven to do its bidding; you are of no value and you have pissed me right off. Go tell your master that the child will be fulfilling her afterlife with her mother in purgatory until the time of ascension is correct," I ordered, my voice low and loud, echoing across the human domain.

Abraxos decided it was now his turn to pipe up and add more coal to my already-roaring, inner-angered fire.

"My dear lady," he started, and my mind begged him not to speak any further for fear I may retrieve his voice box from the back of his condescending throat. "I believe you are mistaken. Angels do not and will not take command from any resident that inhabits purgatory. You have angered both heaven and hell with your harvesting antics. As you can see, we have punished this low life and you should receive punishment also," he sneered, as did the accompanying angels. Behind them, the demons acknowledged Abraxos's words and shouted encouragement and comradeship to the angels.

I wasn't concerned about fighting the band of angels and demons surrounding me. I have fought them many times; not always winning but giving them a good fight. Taking my eyes briefly from the gathering angels, I checked on Ryan. He was starting to regain consciousness: he needed to heal before he could assist me in a fight and by the look of him, he had taken enough hits from the angels' light force to be almost barbecued by the heat.

"We warned you, Purgatory. We warned you that you were to be punished for harvesting souls that do not rightly belong to you," Cassie spoke in a deep, threatening voice.

I could see his intentions crossing his features and I felt the warmth of his light force penetrating within his body, alerting me of his intent to attack.

Rotating my body away from the group of malevolent angels, I leap backwards to protect Ryan with my body. As I moved, I felt the heat from the light force aimed at us, fired by not one but all the bastard angels.

Hovering my body over Ryan, I whispered for him to stay down and then I proceeded to do something I had never done before when fighting. I took a deep, apprehensive breath and gave my wings the freedom they demanded.

Exploding from my spine like forty-thousand sharpened battle-ready daggers, I brought the iridescent wings around Ryan and me, coating us in a protective pearlized shell which was not only strong but beautiful.

Tucking my body closer into Ryan and enveloping us further into my wings, I felt an increase in the light force attacks. One after the other, they came pounding on my wings, looking for a way to get through to us. With each hit, my wings absorbed the light force, allowing them to increase in strength as the angels began to decrease in energy.

Below my body, Ryan began to stir.

"Stay down," I whispered into his ear.

"Tory!" he exclaimed, surprised to find me squashed over his body. "What are you doing?"

"Planting pumpkin seeds," I muttered, sarcastically. "What do you think I am doing?"

"I think you are either doing that wrong or we are still in the human realm," he replied, trying to get up from underneath me.

"Stay down!" I whispered, abruptly. "You were knocked

unconscious: you must have taken so many light-force hits. When only a bag of baby stuff came through the portal without you, I decided to investigate. This was happening," I said, raising my wing slightly for him to view the group of dickhead angels and their writhing demon counterparts.

"I was ambushed," he said.

"I know. The angels invited the demons to take you when you became unconscious and apparently it is all my fault." The pummelling of light force on my wings was beginning to piss me off: it was constant bang, bang, bang against my mother-of-pearl hardened wings. They were never going to break them.

"But, why are you on top of me?" he asked, wriggling slightly underneath me.

"For fuck's sake, Ryan, stay still. We are under attack," I answered.

"Then why are we not fighting and why are we not getting hit?" he asked.

"My wings are protecting us and they are getting a lot of light force at the moment. If they absorb much more I am sure I will turn angel," I said, smirking down at the squashed hybrid.

Immediately, Ryan maneuvered underneath me whilst I tutted loudly and ensured my wings remained shielding us. Now Ryan was on his back, and I was spread-eagled over his stomach.

"What is the point of this?" I quizzed.

"You have wings: I want to see them." Looking past me, Ryan's eyes scanned behind me and traced the length of each wing. "They are beautiful, Tory," he breathed, bringing his gaze to meet mine.

I blushed immediately, like a pubescent schoolgirl. "Thank you," I replied quickly, diverting my eyes and squirming uncomfortably in my skin.

I winced as a large ball of light force hit me, sliding past a small hole in the barrier between my wings and the concrete below Ryan and me.

"How many are out there?" Ryan asked, concern lacing his eyes as I breathed past the pain the latest hit had caused.

"Four, I think. Although it feels like a lot more," I told him.

"I ascended Daniel. What a prick," he said, proudly.

I smiled at him. "We need to get out of this. Are you ready to fight?"

"Always ready," he said, winking at me.

Rolling my eyes, I adjusted my position on top of him, while he smiled like an idiot. "Enjoying yourself?" I jested.

"Oh, yes!" he replied, which made me giggle.

The seriousness of our situation was reiterated as I received a blast of light force directly to my spine. I screamed as the pain filtered past my wings and in between the small slice of exposed vertebrae skin. Ryan held onto me, supporting my temporarily crippled body. My breathing was irregular, as the pain continued to reverberate the length of my spine.

"Tory, breathe. Slow down and breathe through it." Ryan talked me through the pain as slowly it began to dissipate. "We won't have long before they fire again. Are you ready?" he asked, watching my eyes for an answer.

"Yes," I nodded. "Let's go!"

Ryan allowed me to pull myself from his body with my wings still unfurled before he reached for his sword.

"Ready?" he asked.

"Ready," I told him. "NOW!"

The world slowed down as Ryan and I exploded together from underneath my wings. With our weapons drawn, we came out fighting. The angels had doubled in number and without reprieve they attacked together. Constant weapons of light force rained down on Ryan and me, lighting up the space around us.

The demons hung back on the borders of our fight: I couldn't deduce if they were encouraging the angels or waiting for permission to join in.

I kept an eye on Ryan: he was fighting hard and with each light-force bolt that he deflected with his sword, light shone and lit up his wounded body. I do not know how he was managing to stand up, let alone fight, yet each time he caught me watching him he gave me a cocky smile and winked.

We were both fighting extremely hard. We were receiving a constant onslaught from the angels and as we ascended one back to heaven, two more would arrive.

I watched as Ryan took an attack that skirted past his sword and hit him fully in the chest. He fell to the ground, dazed, but not unconscious.

Running to help him up, I was side-swiped by a cowardly demon hiding in the shadows.

"Bastard!" I yelled at the insipid beast, running him through and severing his head from his shoulders.

My upper right arm was throbbing. Turning, I briefly assessed the damage the demon had inflicted. Thick, crimson-red blood had detonated from three large lacerations.

"You okay?" Ryan called, withdrawing his sword from an angel close to him and ascending his arse back to heaven.

"Stings like a bitch! I'm good – it's starting to clot already," I espoused, wiping the blood from my dripping elbow with the back of my free hand. No sooner had I taken up my sai, another demon careered at me from the shadowed-filled alley way.

"Shit, Ryan – I have another one!" I yelled, engaging the demon. As soon as I dispatched the mass of non-necessity, another came. Allowing myself the opportunity to see where these demon bastards were coming from, I side-stepped the attacking demon and looked into the alley way.

An endless line of green venom-filled demon eyes glared back at me.

"Ryan!" I called. "There are shit-loads of the demon ass-hats hiding here. What the hell is going on?" I questioned, battling my demons, literally.

Ryan replied with the advice to "Kick their arses!" as he was engaged in a battle with two new angels. He was already weakened by the previous unprovoked attack and I could see him beginning to tire.

Fighting hard, Ryan and I came back-to-back with each other: we were now fighting angels and demons simultaneously. An ascended angel would be replaced by a demon, who, once descended, was either replaced by an angel or another demon. It was constant and I did not know how much longer we could continue fighting: exhaustion threatened to become our downfall.

The next demon lined itself up as I began mulling over strategies in my head. We needed to get through this together. Looking up and over to the portal, I could see that it was completely over-run with demons and angels, guarding it to deny us passage.

"Tory, I can't..." I heard Ryan speaking through the confusion. Turning, I saw that he was winded badly and having trouble catching his breath.

Descending the demons directly in front of me, I turned and placed myself in front of Ryan. Elongating my wings from behind me, I wrapped them backwards to where Ryan was, now on one knee and bent over, struggling for breath.

Cocooning him, with my wings, from further attacks, I gave him the protection and time he needed to catch his breath and fight the excess of light force he had received, coursing through his body.

Abruptly, the attacked ceased, but surrounded by angels and demons I remained with my guard up and my attitude fuelled with fire. A new angel appeared at the forefront of the angel/demon collective and began to address me.

"Purgatory – I am Puriel, angel of punishment. Have you had enough? Are you ready to give up the baby Amelia and one of the hybrid twins? You shall survive if you co-operate," the angel said, smirking at me like a kid with a stolen lollipop.

Rotating my sai in my hands, I stared directly at him and shook my head.

"Go fuck yourself, Puriel, angel of punishment, who is yet to actually punish anyone since you have only just got here. This ambush attack is not punishment," I continued. "It's a weak-minded attempt to bully and threaten me into giving up a baby who is with her mother; also to separate the twins who were used in a poorly executed game to punish their parents. Ryan and I have fought for hours, yet the angels and demons have failed to defeat us. How many of your angels have we ascended during that time? Oh, and the demons – are they here just to provide extra attack weapons? It's sad really, do you not think?"

Puriel smirked at me and began pacing slowly up and down in front of me. The more he paced, the closer he came to where I stood shielding Ryan.

"This moment, now, Purgatory, is your last moment on any domain. The angels and demons are united; united to bring you to your knees and wipe you from existence."

I took the opportunity to correct him in his assumption.

"Puriel, I have lived for centuries. Angels and demons have fought me for all of those centuries, yet I still stand before you as proof of their failure to kill me. What therefore, do you think has changed in this merry-go-round of a game to alter the odds against me?" I asked, placing my hands on my hips and allowing my attitude to ooze through my features.

"I believe that this will change the odds." Puriel motioned for the seven angels behind him to move forward to stand with him. One by one, they pulled a small silver dagger from their waistbands, all identical and all pointed straight at me.

In unison, the angels began reciting a verse in a language I had never heard before.

I watched as the light force from each angel sparked its way into the hilt of each dagger, filling the weapon until it shone, illuminated by the angels' power.

Continuing to speak in verse, the light force erupted from the daggers in a thin stream of power. As each stream was set free, it sought out and amalgamated with the light force from its sister dagger.

Eight angels; eight daggers; eight streams of light conjoining forces. I watched in horror as a monumentally thick-girthed, power-ridden stream cascaded towards me.

Ryan was still down. I could hear him breathing heavily, but he wasn't up yet or solid on his feet. I continued to shield him with my backwards-facing wings, knowing that if I didn't, he would be attacked by the waiting demons, who would claim and descend with him.

Light force within this almighty stream of bright illuminance was coming towards me at a pace so rapid that I had to move fast to embed my feet firmly on the ground beneath me and bring my sai up close to my chest, to deflect and absorb the oncoming attack.

Bracing myself, the stream hit my crossed sai, pushing me back and briefly knocking me off balance. Regaining it immediately, to avoid Ryan, still crouched behind me, I readjusted my position.

Light force relentlessly pummelled my sai; frequently, shards of the stream would ricochet off of the sai and hit me wherever it could. Pain coursed through every aspect of my body, ripping my skin to allow the claret haemoglobin-filled body juice to surge from it.

Using my wings as protection for Ryan, I was disabled by the inability to move or fight back. If I engaged in fighting, I would receive the full force of the dagger weapon and if I protected myself with my wings, Ryan would become demon bait. I had no option and I was becoming tired. Deep down, I was pondering over the idea that the angels might just have a weapon to end my existence and I wasn't sure if I was relieved or petrified.

I had lived for centuries and hoped that, one day, ceasing to exist would bring a close to the endless fighting for and harvesting of souls. Yet, finding Ryan and Connor had given me new hope. I was no longer alone when I fought and I liked that.

Right now, in this moment, I chose to fight, to exist a little longer. Fuck the angels and fuck the demons, too!

Chapter 13

Henry's lungs burnt wildly. The O2 he was receiving moved rapidly through him, temporarily suffocating him until relived by another snatch of breath. He needed to find Connor and quickly: he had a gut feeling and he knew he must act upon it.

He ran to Connor and Ryan's lodgings, at the far end of the compound, and he was not there. Sprinting as fast as his legs would allow, he made his way to Porter's home. He had seen them deep in conversation earlier, after the harvesting.

Running faster than he believed he had ever run before in his life or afterlife, Henry sprinted the rest of the distance to reach Porter's lodgings.

Drumming rapidly on the wooden door, Henry fought to inhale air into his overworked, air-deprived lungs. He crouched over, wondering how his heart was maintaining its excessive rhythm behind his sternum, when it felt as if it would burst through his chest at any moment.

Porter opened the door and took in Henry's appearance.

"I need Connor!" Henry managed, in between inhalations.

"Come in," Porter told him, taking him by the arm for support. "He's in the lounge: what's the problem?" Concern rippled over Porter's features.

The commotion of escorting Henry through the front door brought Connor from the lounge, to investigate.

"What's happened?" he asked, rushing to be of assistance.

"I think there is a problem," Henry voiced, quietly. "I – Ryan..." Henry tried to stutter his words out and regain his breath, simultaneously.

"Wait! Catch your breath," Porter advised, leading Henry to a chair.

Once seated, Henry began to regulate his breathing enough to sip from a glass Porter had gotten for him.

"Connor," Henry started, eager to tell him his worries. "Ryan isn't back yet from the human domain. I tried to find Tory but I think that she must have gone after him. A torn bag of baby equipment is piled in a heap by the side of the portal. I think something has happened." Henry drained the remaining water in his glass and set it down on a small wooden coffee table beside him.

Connor absorbed the information he had received.

"You are right, Henry. If Ryan hasn't returned by now, I believe he must have run into trouble, although I can usually feel if he is hurt or has a problem. But I don't feel anything..." Connor remained deep in thought, back-tracking over the last few hours for any hint that Ryan was in difficulty. They had a twin connection, which is usually indicated if one twins is hurt or needs the other.

"Maybe because he is in a different domain, you might have missed it or not felt it at all," Porter offered, still wearing concern on his face.

Connor stood. "I am going to the portal to find out what's happening," he stated, before leaving Porter's house.

Porter and Henry followed him at a slower pace, deciding to remain at the portal to see if they could help.

Arriving at the portal after a brief stop to gather his bow and arrows, Connor cut a muscular figure as he stood before the domain gateway. He agreed with Henry that if Ryan had managed to get one bag through the portal and not himself, then he must have run into trouble.

Reassuring the Council members that he would be back with Ryan, and probably Tory, Connor stepped into the portal.

As soon as he entered the worm-hole portal, Connor felt a ball starting to form in the very depths of his stomach: this ball of unease rapidly enlarged the further he went into the portal and the closer he came to his twin.

Notching an arrow and ready for battle, Connor stepped out of the portal and found the carnage awaiting him.

Chapter 14

The power from the angels' new weapon bore down on me hard: my sai had absorbed as much of the light force as it could and now streams of light were deflecting off of my weapon and hitting me.

My skin ripped with every hit, spilling my already-depleted blood and weakening me further. Behind me, Ryan was now on his feet but unsteady. I knew I needed to shield him a little longer, fully aware that if I retracted my wings too soon, the demons would attack both of us from behind and I would not be able to protect him, and myself, from full-frontal and rear attacks.

I knew that harvesting the hybrids would cause problems but I hadn't expected this level of violence. I thought that maybe we would come across heavy fighting when harvesting and lose a few souls but I was stunned by the ambush attack and its severity.

In my periphery, I could see a number of demons surrounding beside me. Flicking my head briefly to my other side, I was greeted by more encroaching slimy black demons.

"Oh shit!" I mumbled. The unfamiliar feeling of panic began to course through my body. The angels continued their attack at the front of me and I knew the demons were trying to get to Ryan, to descend with him.

Anger overtook my thoughts, allowing me the strength to move my light force-burned sai. Using the absorbed power, I used one sai to protect me and with the other, I began to shoot the light force back at the angels.

Hitting the angels with their own power caused a brief drop of the dagger they held, thus temporarily breaking the heavy stream aimed at me.

However, each angel I hit rectified themselves immediately and brought their dagger back up to reinstate the primary stream. This wasn't a very productive counter attack but it gave me a slight reprieve from the stream and it made the angels bleed, so I continued.

I managed to hit a few demons during the reprieve from the angels that descended those few, but pissed off the remaining slimy bastards. I could feel my wings being attacked as they hid Ryan. Teeth and claws cascaded over my persistent wings as each demon attacked like the rabid wild animals they were. The pain was becoming intense, bringing me to the point of passing out.

From the side of me, I felt a demon bear down on a cluster of my feathers and violently thrash his head from side to side, as if a crocodile in a death roll. Quickly, he pulled his head back and ripped a hole in my vulnerable wing.

I screamed, as red-hot, lava-like demon toxins flooded into my wings through the broken feathers.

I felt Ryan's hand between my shoulder blades, offering support and begging me to release him.

"Not yet, Ryan – please," I stuttered though my gritted teeth. "They will descend with you," I managed to say, before a shard of light force hit me in the thigh, tearing my skin and allowing more blood to escape.

I was suffering enormous blood loss from the lacerations covering the majority of my body. My head spun as I became overcome with exhaustion and struggled to fight.

As I stood, unstable on my feet, I saw a demon hurrying towards me from my right; its teeth ready, its claws extended. I had no hope of fighting him. Protecting myself from him would expose myself further to the angels.

Inhaling deeply, I filled my lungs with a much-needed flood of enriched oxygen, flicking my gaze from angel to demon. I watched as the manky-arsed demon sped towards me and then I saw a glint of something shiny fly directly past me, hitting the demon through the head.

The black beast dropped like a stone, his head severed from his body, rolling away as it hit the floor. The demon disappeared into descension.

Rotating rapidly to my left, I was greeted by a fully armoured Connor. His bow was notched with three arrows aimed at the angels. Swiftly releasing the arrows at their targets, Connor briefly met my eyes, winked, and continued to notch three more arrows.

The angels targeted in Connor's first assault ascended as soon as each was pierced through the heart.

"Wow!" I said, out loud, relieved by the cessation in light force hitting me. The daggers aimed at me still continued light force but it was weakened by the detachment from its sisters.

I watched as three more angels rapidly ascended and as another arrow hit the seventh angel, leaving a wide-eyed, open-mouthed Puriel staring at me.

"Goodbye, Puriel, angel of punishment," I smiled at the gob-smacked angel as the arrow with his name on it hit him directly in his head, breaking apart his torso and ascending his fleeing soul.

Glancing over my shoulder, the insidious mass of repulsive demons was receding back to hell, voluntarily. As the last demon disappeared, I relaxed my body. Too exhausted to retract my wings, I allowed them to fall behind me, releasing Ryan.

Dropping hard to my knees, my hands resting on my thighs and my head bowed, I closed my eyes and struggled, against my depleted energy, to locate my equilibrium. My sai lay beside me, dropping from my hands as I fell. They burned bright white, overflowing with the excess light force that had pillaged them.

Within seconds, Ryan and Connor knelt down, flanking me on each side.

"Nice wings," Connor stated, smirking as he poked one. "Strong, beautiful, and lethal."

"Thank you," I whispered, my head remaining downcast. I could feel Ryan and Connor feeling my wings and pulling on them slightly to display their iridescence.

"Are you all right, Ryan? Are you healing?" I asked, turning towards him and analysing him from head to toe. He had numerous wounds, each healing well; his body gradually bringing the torn skin together and pushing out the demon venom at the same time.

"Tory, I am fine. And thank you for coming here and saving my life. I didn't realise you had wings but they are spectacular. Why do you hide them?" he asked, flicking his gaze from me to my wings as he spoke.

Bringing my body off of my knees, I plonked myself back down on my bum, which actually seemed to be the only part of me that didn't hurt.

"I hide them so I look normal to the souls I harvest. I do not want to scare anyone. Why do you hide yours?" I questioned back.

"Because they are fucking ugly!" he replied, solemnly.

"Yep, they sure are," Connor interjected. "Plus, we had to hide them in the human domain as we grew up."

"Of course," I nodded. I inhaled sharply as I moved to stretch my legs; a violently made claw mark, courtesy of some demon arse-face, ripped itself open again, allowing an amalgamation of blood and demon toxin to haemorrhage down my thigh.

Ripping the sleeve material from his sweater, Connor wrapped it around my thigh, pulling it tightly over the wound.

"Tory, we need to get you back." His voice was laced with concern. "You need to get medical treatment so you can heal."

"Not yet," I answered. "I cannot retract my wings yet. How did you know to come?" I added.

"Henry was worried. He saw the bag of baby stuff outside the portal but could not find you or Ryan. So I decided to investigate and here we are," Connor explained.

"I think that we need to let Henry know that we're okay. Connor – take Ryan back through the portal and ask Henry to escort him to the medical wing. Then can you come back and help me, please," I asked, conscious that Henry was probably pulling his hair out and may only have a little left now.

"Will you be all right on your own?" Ryan asked, getting to his feet.

"I shall be fine," I answered. "I will just sit here and wait until I can retract my wings. Please, Ryan – go and get yourself some medical treatment. You took a lot of demon venom today."

Nodding his understanding, Ryan walked the few short steps to meet up with his brother. Shaking each other's hand, then going in for the slap-on-the-back man-hug, the twins looked relieved to be in each other's company once again.

Picking up the remaining scattered baby items, Connor helped Ryan to enter the portal.

"I will be back for you as soon as I have him in the medical compound," Connor yelled, before disappearing through the rippling entrance of the portal.

Now alone and in the confines of my own company, I allowed the pain I was feeling to escape. Tears torrented down my face. The physical pain was excruciating.

Every part of my body screamed for reprieve from the demon toxin flowing through it and the light force lacerations were beginning to self-heal. Using the last remaining piece of energy I had, I encircled myself within my wings, temporarily hiding away, cocooning myself in my own comfort zone, where I felt safe.

Tears, blood, toxins, and sweat released from my body, creating a pool of red-tinted sludge where I sat. Closing my eyes, I shut the world out. I was alone.

Chapter 15

"Purgatory – um – I'm sorry to disturb you. Are you all right? Do you need help?"

The voice was tender and she spoke her words into my annihilated wings hiding me from the outside. I remained silent, not wanting to interact with any other being at the moment.

"Purgatory…" the voice came again. "I am sorry but... Oh, my name is Elenor."

Elenor? Who the hell was Elenor? Maintaining my shield, I searched my mind for who this person could be. She obviously knew who I was but– and then it came to me: the refugee demon and mother of Connor and Ryan.

Realizing who she was and knowing that she was not a threat to me, I gradually opened my wings.

Once exposed, I was greeted by the mother of the hybrids. She knelt down in front of me, empathy riddled her eyes and sympathy quickly replaced it as she scanned the wounds on my body.

"Hi," I whispered through my dry mouth.

"Hello, Purgatory," Elenor responded.

I met her gaze with my own and offered her the best smile I could muster.

"Please – call me Tory," I asked.

She smiled back. "As you wish."

Behind her stood Devon, the fallen angel. He, too, was smiling and I kinda felt like a little child who had fallen off her bike outside their house, as they looked at me with friendly smiles, indicating that they were no threat.

"Hi," I coughed out, licking my lips rapidly but failing to inject any moisture into them.

"Hello, Tory," he said, stepping forward. "Here."

With his outstretched hand, he offered a bottle of water. I took it with a grateful nod, unscrewed the lid and drank quickly.

The ice-cold water burned my dehydrated mouth as it rehydrated. The cold burning ran the length of my oesophagus until I felt it cascade into my empty stomach.

"Thank you…" I finally managed, once I had drained the dribble of water that clung to the bottom of the plastic bottle. "What are you doing here?" I asked, baffled by their presence.

Elenor briefly glanced at her fallen-angel husband, then returned her attention to me. "We felt Ryan's presence in this domain. We began to make our way here when we felt that he was in trouble, but when we arrived the fight was over. We just caught sight of our boys disappearing into your portal."

Devon was now kneeling before me, one hand on his wife's arm and the other outstretched out to me.

"Please…" he said, indicating for me to take his hand, which I did as I felt I should. Encasing my hand in his, he looked deep into my eyes as if he were searching for something.

"Tory, you are a good person. We never had the opportunity to thank you for harvesting our boys together. We appreciate the position you had to put yourself in for their benefit and we are aware of the unrest in both heaven and hell."

I smiled at them both. "It was a pleasure to harvest your children: they are both good, kind men and badass fighters. I do not believe that they should have been made to suffer in order to punish you and that is why I took them.

"However, I was not aware of their impending deaths. They were cloaked so well that the only indication I had that something big was happening was watching the huge demon and angel presence situated in the one area. Hence the reason I snuck in. They help me harvest now. They fight well. You have taught them well."

Elenor blushed, while Devon puffed his chest, obviously filled with pride for their sons.

"As Devon said," Elenor continued. "Thank you. We are so happy that their afterlife will be a good one and that they are together."

Devon's attention was diverted, looking behind me then back to my body, and then behind again. "Are you having trouble retracting your wings because of your injuries?" he asked, concerned, as his eyes examined my wings and lacerations.

I nodded rapidly. "Yes, it hurts so much to attempt retraction with my body trying to heal the rest of me, but I can't go back to the domain with them. No one, apart from the twins, knows I have them," I explained.

Devon rose and walked around behind me. "May I?" He pointed at the wings.

"Of course," I answered. Any help would be welcomed so I could get home and sort out my ragged- looking, battle-weary body.

"He still has healing powers." Elenor leaned forward to whisper. "He can help you." She tapped the top of my hand gently and the fondness for her husband shone within her green eyes.

"Oh, I thought his powers would have been taken when he had to fall," I stated.

"So did we, but we think that heaven was in such a rush to have him fall that they overlooked it," Elenor explained.

"That is so cool," I said. "Although it was ineffective against preventing the twins' deaths, I guess."

"True. Lucifer ensured that the boys would die and that no other magic could heal them or prevent their deaths," she said, with her eyes downcast.

"Tory, this may hurt a little bit. Hopefully, not too much," Devon called from behind me.

I nodded in acknowledgement as Elenor moved closer to me and took both my hands in hers. Heat began to radiate from within the core of my body as Devon placed his hands between my wings at my shoulder blades.

"Breathe deeply, in and out," Elenor offered, maintaining the grip on my hand.

"Ready?" Devon questioned.

"Ready," I called back.

The pain was intense, the burning sensation which began in the core of my body was now reaching out and igniting my spine, my veins, my heart. Ripping sensations coursed within me, flooding every aspect with heat. I stifled a scream as I felt the heat reach my tender wing- bases, then, with one almighty steering, fire-encrusted spasm, my wings slowly began to retract.

"Forced retraction with your body crippled by so many injuries is usually painful, Tory. You did well and you can return to purgatory to recover," Devon said, as he circled back to help Elenor as I stood on shaky legs.

Neither Elenor or Devon let go of me, letting me gain my balance before removing their hands.

I thanked Devon and Elenor for their kindness, realizing where the twins gained their compassion.

"Did you want to see Ryan and Connor?" I asked, as we walked slowly towards the portal.

"We would love to see our boys. We'll wait with you until Connor returns to you, and maybe see Ryan the next time he enters the human domain. We shall keep Connor only for a short while," Elenor said, the colour in her green eyes reigniting as she spoke of her sons.

Thoughts buzzed inside my brain, rolling around and hitting the inner membrane, then bouncing back again as I thought harder. Stopping abruptly, I turned to the fallen angel and his refugee demon.

"You are not human!" I stated.

"We are not," Devon responded, unsure where my question was leading.

"You are a fallen angel and Elenor, you are a refugee demon," I continued.

"That is correct," Devon verified, glancing with a quizzical brow to his wife.

"Uh!" I verbalized, as the idea rumbled continuously, bruising my brain as it did so.

"What ties you to the human domain?" I asked. I could see the couple weighing up my sanity as I fired questions at them.

"We have been banished from our original domains and cannot return. If we wish to be together, we have to stay in the human domain." Devon explained.

"Our boys are the only reason we did not fight to live elsewhere together. No, Tory – nothing ties us to this domain. It will always be our continued, everlasting punishment. We must live in this hollow, human domain without our children." Elenor sobbed heavily, comforted momentarily by Devon's arm sneaking around her and pulling her close.

"You are not human: you are demon and angel. You do not belong in the human domain to live your constant punishment. Come with me: live where you belong," I grinned widely at them.

"In purgatory?" Elenor questioned.

"Yep!" I nodded.

"Will that not anger heaven and hell further, if we come with you?" Devon asked, with a concerned voice.

"Heaven and hell will never cease to try to punish me for taking Ryan and Connor, but if you join us, our strength can only grow. I do not harvest just for the influence, power or energy a soul brings to the domain: I do it to ensure fair trials and an alternative afterlife before ascending or descending, or sometimes staying. Therefore, I would ask you to assist me in harvesting the souls so you may break free of your punishment. You can live your lives in purgatory with your children for as long as you wish. It is your choice," I informed them.

Elenor and Devon stood dumbfounded, silently looking at each other.

"You do not need to tell me now whether you wish to come," I interjected. "Take your time. This is a big decision which will ultimately cause more unrest within the other domains and problems for the two of you." I understood their hesitation.

"We accept," Elenor blurted. "Oh, thank you, Tory!" She was sobbing, smiling and cuddling into Devon. Devon calmed his over-excited wife before taking a deep breath and addressing me in an extremely serious tone.

"Tory – what you have done and what you are willing to do for my family is not only honourable, but kind and selfless. It would be a pleasure for my wife and me to join you in your realm to live and to make our new home. As of this moment, we pledge to fight with you, to assist you with harvesting souls and protecting the realm," he bowed.

"Don't do that!" I said. "There is no need. Happy to have you on board." I had no time to breathe before I was enveloped within Elenor's arms, holding me tight and thanking me, over and over again.

I hugged her back, avoiding over-stretching my still-healing wounds and winced inwardly with every misjudged movement Elenor made in her epic hug marathon.

Eventually, Devon peeled his wife from me.

"Do you need to collect anything from this domain before you come over?" I asked. "Although we have everything you should need already, we'll find you a new home immediately."

"We need nothing more," Elenor stated.

Devon agreed. "The two things we really need are already in your domain," he said.

"Our domain!" I reminded him. "Come – let's go before anyone else decides to fight us today."

I stumbled briefly on the short walk to the awaiting portal. Devon and Elenor took one arm each, in support, as we stepped through the portal and into their new life.

Chapter 16

"Tory, I was on my way to you. Are you okay? Did–" Connor shut his mouth with such force I thought he may have actually broken all of his teeth.

"Connor," I said, bringing his attention to me. "I believe these are yours," I smiled.

He nodded, muted by the surprise, and then he cried. Big tears of immense joy rolled down his face and he sank to the floor. I steadied myself on the edge of the portal and indicated to Devon and Elenor to go to their son.

The majority of my council stood around the portal. Connor and Ryan had obviously informed them of what had happened and, as usual, they faithfully waited for my return.

Porter had now taken Devon's place as he brought his arm around me and supported me to stand. Henry looked dismayed at the unfolding events, while the rest of us looked upon the family before us.

A refugee demon, a fallen angel and their hybrid son, encircled in an embrace, comforting and supporting one another.

"Good job," Porter whispered. "But we need to get you to the medical compound: you are oozing everywhere."

I nodded in agreement. If anything, some pain relief would be welcomed right now. Porter and I started to walk, yet two steps in and the laceration on my thigh continued to rip apart. Devon had explained, when assisting with the retraction of my wings, that although he had maintained some of his healing powers, it was not effective enough to retract my wings and heal the lacerations in one healing period.

Briefly stopping as the pain coursed through me and the blood cascaded over my leg, I felt another pair of arms encircle me.

"Here, let me help," Connor said softly into my ear. Taking me out of Porter's grip, he lifted me into his arms and began walking.

"You brought my parents over!" he stated.

"I did," I responded.

"Why?" he asked.

"Because they spend their lives grieving for you and Ryan. They hide to avoid further punishment from either heaven or hell. Do you not want them to be here?" I asked, confused by his questions.

Connor smiled a bright, cheeky smile. "Yes, Tory – I want them here. They will be a good commodity to have when we harvest. You have done more for my family and me than we could have ever imagined. I am so grateful to you."

"It is a pleasure to have them here. I'm sure Ryan will also be happy to see them," I said, not needing his gratitude but accepting it.

We walked silently for a few meters, allowing my thoughts to violate my brain again.

"What are you thinking about? You frown when you think," Connor said, dislodging my thought process.

Pausing briefly, I answered him. I slung my arm around his shoulder and neck to support myself a little.

"I think that I may have caused more problems for them, Connor. I mean, when they were hiding they were as safe as they could have been, but now? They will fight again and become noticed by heaven and hell for supporting me. I do not wish them any further angst: they deserve to be together somewhere safe, with their family. I just hope that I did the right thing by bringing them here for their own sakes." I offered Connor a small smile as I struggled to hide my unease.

"They would not have come if they wanted a quiet existence in the shadows of the human domain. Remember, Mum is a demon. She comes across as a pleasant lady but get on her wrong side and she will kick your arse through your nostrils quicker than a cat on a ceiling fan," he assured me.

I giggled, immediately regretting it as pain shot through my body like a newly released ball in a pinball machine.

Connor's smile dropped with concern.

"Why are you not healing?" he asked.

"I don't know," I offered. "Usually, my tolerance to demon toxin is high and my metabolism chews it up and spits it out before the fight is finished."

"Huh," Connor replied, glancing away from me. I could see he was thinking: his concentration level had increased rapidly and his shoulders hunched slightly.

"Your father helped me retract my wings," I said, dragging Connor away from his thoughts.

"He is a kind man," he replied. "He is fair, just, and wise, but he is also an excellent fighter. Mum and dad together are the ultimate fighting team."

"I believe they are," I agreed. "Am I too heavy?" I asked, slightly embarrassed that I was still being carried.

"Yep!" Connor smirked. "But it's okay. I am strong enough to make it," he jested, carrying me with no obvious signs of fatigue.

I stifled a giggle to avoid inviting the pain back into my body. "You are an arse," I stated.

Connor threw his head back and laughed hard; a deep belly-laugh that reverberated within his body before reaching his lips. I allowed my head to gently fall against his chest, cautious to avoid his armour. I smiled as I felt the remnants of his laugh echo away inside his chest and tried as much as I could to make myself heavier.

I was placed unceremoniously on an awaiting medical trolley, once Connor and I had reached the medical compound. Cracking some joke about needing an osteopath for his back, Connor was followed out of the room by two giggling nurses, who were highly impressed by his wit and humour.

Vowing to return as soon as he could, Connor left to escort his parents to Ryan's hospital room on the floor above me. I waited in silence for the doctor to arrive. As I sat, I mulled over the fight. I needed to research the daggers: eight potent daggers that, when separated, looked like extremely ornate letter openers, yet together they were one hell of a bad-ass weapon.

This was obviously a new weapon designed to kill me but, although it did a lot of damage, I do not think it would be able to cause my death. It could fuck me up worse than today, maybe, but not death. Shielding Ryan impeded my ability to move and attack, but I still don't think light-force daggers are the weapons to end my existence.

A rather tall medic walked into my room, after knocking loudly. He was harvested after dying in Iraq, seven years ago. His name was Jason and he set up the medical compound shortly after he arrived.

"Tory – what have you been doing?" Jason asked, eyeing up the state of my grey, bloodied body.

I shrugged and allowed my eyes to roll gently in their sockets.

Jason had been taken into my confidence shortly after he had arrived. Setting up the medical unit was mainly for my benefit, as souls no longer suffer disease or illness. The hospital was well equipped to supply demon toxin antidote and treat light-force lacerations.

"You usually heal quicker than this, Tory," he went on to say. "What happened?"

"I was protecting Ryan," I started to explain.

"Ah, the hybrid, cool guy and his brother," Jason interrupted.

"Yes, they are," I concurred. "This long wound on my thigh will not heal. I have tried to squeeze the remaining toxin from it but it just bleeds and the pain is excruciating," I explained feeling my badassery falling away as I whined.

"Then that's where we will start," Jason smiled and started to busy himself, collecting sterile equipment, gloves, instruments, and drawing up syringes with a multitude of liquids.

"I will give you a local for your thigh, so that I can have a good look, and I will administer a systemic analgesic for the pain." He came towards me, wheeling his silver trolley of torture as he spoke. "I may need to open the wound to see if there is a foreign object contributing to your inability to heal."

"Okay. Sounds gross but let's get it over with," I said, watching him glove up and come at me with an impregnated swab dripping with frigid, pink fluid.

"I need your arm," he said, puddling the pink stuff on the floor by his feet.

Exposing my arm to him, Jason began the first of many assaults on my body. Within minutes I was cannulated, drugged, prepped, and ready to go. Jason had performed the "Can you feel this?" test on the open laceration and was just about to start digging around in it when Connor burst through the door.

"Hi, Jas," he said casually, allowing the door to swing itself shut behind him.

"Hi, Connor," Jason replied from behind his face mask.

Walking over to stand behind Jason, Connor observed the medical paraphernalia prepared for use.

"You going in?" Connor asked, pointing to my thigh.

"Just about to. It's numb and Tory has had morphine, so she is set," Jason replied.

"Can I stay?" Connor asked.

"If Tory is happy?" Jason said, nodding at me for consent before allowing him to access the inner aspect of my thigh.

My head was light and whizzing rapidly: human drugs affect me so well. Briefly, I took in my situation lying here on a table: Jason about to wiggle around in my leg; Connor wanting to stay; and me tripping my nut off.

"If he wants..." I slurred, my face painted with a wider, gormless grin. "You had better not throw up though," I continued, poking my finger in his general direction.

Connor smiled back. "I won't. Are you tripping?" he asked.

"Nope, I am pleasantly drugged," I managed to mumble, before dribbling down my chin.

"This is so cool," Connor verified again. "Get on with it, then." He turned to Jason and hand-gestured a digging motion.

Jason nodded and began. I could hear the sound of the instruments being lifted from the shiny metal trolley and placed back down again. Connor continued to give me a step-by-step account of how gross the whole process was and I revelled in my new-found love of morphine as he did so.

I heard Jason sigh and push whatever he was holding deeper into my thigh.

"Fucking hell, Jason!" Pain exploded through my aching body with rapid speed. Every nerve sparked and crackled into life and, in unison, they all shouted at my brain.

Withdrawing the instrument, Jason apologized as Connor raced from behind him and stood beside me, taking my hand, which I gratefully accepted.

"Has the pain settled now?" Jason tentatively asked.

"Doh! Yes, it has now that your arm is no longer embedded inside my leg," I snapped. "I'm sorry," I immediately countered.

"It's okay," Jason said. "I need to give you more pain relie–"

"YEAH, DO THAT!" I interrupted loudly.

Both Connor and Jason burst into laughter before Jason could compose himself to continue.

"Let me start again. More pain relief is needed so that I can get to whatever is on your leg. It's solid, so it should come out in one piece," Jason explained.

I soberly nodded. I didn't relish the thought of him digging further into my leg but I also wanted what was in it to come out.

With my mind numbed by the secondary dose of morphine and syringe-loads of local anaesthesia injected into my wound, I was ready to have the invader removed from my body.

Connor stayed with me, still retaining his support grip on my hand, while Jason changed his gloves ready for his explore-and-retrieve mission.

Watching in awe, Connor and I observed as Jason drove in and out of my leg with different instruments on each pass.

Retractors were holding the wound open further, giving me a front-row seat to the inner workings of my thigh.

"Found it!" Jason yelled, from virtually inside my leg. "Can you feel this?"

"Nope!" I answered, still revelling in the morphine top-up.

Reaching back behind him, without taking his hand out of my leg, Jason fumbled for something on the little silver trolley. After a few moments of picking instruments up, feeling them and replacing them, Jason took hold of a pair of forceps and proceeded to place them inside my leg.

I could feel a minimal amount of tugging and pushing until, eventually, a shooting pain reverberated throughout my leg. As I cried out in pain, Connor took the top half of my body and turned it into his chest, bringing his arm around me tightly.

I screamed a number of times as Jason pulled and tugged on whatever was wedged inside there.

"It's nearly out, Tory, I promise," Jason mumbled through his gritted teeth. "One big, final pull, okay? Brace yourself," he stressed.

I inhaled deeply and held the breath within me. Clamping my arms around Connor, I began my inner countdown to pain: 5, 4, 3, 2...

"Aagh!" I cried, as I felt the object dislodge from my body.

Jason began pulling the thing out of my leg.

"Bloody hell!" he exclaimed. "I can see your body healing itself as I'm coming out. Everything is just knitting together." He continued to withdraw slowly from my leg.

I wriggled out of Connor's grasp to see what was found, just as Jason ripped the object out from the skin of my leg. As he did, the laceration became taut as it fought the clamps that held it.

Jason, Connor, and I watched as the clamps came off and the skin healed itself, leaving only a small red line as evidence that a wound was ever there.

"That is so cool," Jason stated.

I smiled. "I know, right?"

Deciding to clear up the excessive amount of blood and demon venom, which had created a sludgy mess of clots and fluid on the floor below the bed, the three of us discussed the possibilities of the object stuck within me as we cleaned.

Fifteen minutes past and we were all seated around the sparkly clean instrument trolley, waiting for Jason to reveal the item from underneath a surgical sheet. Once the sheet was lifted, we were greeted with an ugly, black, barbed, claw-like arrowhead thing, dripping with demon venom.

"So this is why you were not healing," Connor said, reaching to poke at it.

Swatting his hand away, I pointed at the sharp, unforgiving tip. "It keeps producing venom, look! It is constantly coming out."

Jason picked up the claw with a pair of forceps and we watched as venom pumped from it.

"Demon weapon?" Connor asked. "The angels invented some daggers and the demons must have these claws. They must be working together, Tory."

"They must, I agree. The demon claws prevent healing and constantly pump the venom inside the body while the angels shoot a powerful, constant stream of light force. Sneaky bastards." I was angry now. Such an unfair game to play against three beings from purgatory while heaven and hell have armies.

"We need a plan," Connor said.

"We need an army," I responded.

Chapter 17

Ryan and I were fully recovered by the next morning, Jason had insisted that we stay in the medical unit under observation overnight, which we agreed to as we were coming down from the morphine high we were both on.

Jason had dismantled the claw while I rested and before officially being discharged in the morning, he came to see me.

"Tory, this claw is organic on the inside. It has a reproducing venom sac held in a black, hard casing, designed – as you said – to prevent healing from within. And the barb keeps it in place. Therefore, it goes in deep and cannot be removed easily while fighting. I believe it was situated on the claw of the demon that caused the laceration," he explained.

A gentle knock rapped on the door. "Come in," I yelled, too loudly, as Jason shuddered next to me.

I was pleasantly surprised when Elenor poked her head around the open door. "Am I interrupting?" she asked, before stepping into the room.

"Of course not. Please come in. Elenor – this is Jason, our medic. Jason – meet Elenor, Ryan and Connor's mother," I said, introducing both parties.

"Wow, you are fully demon, are you not?" Jason blurted out.

"Jason!" I reprimanded.

Elenor giggled softly. "It's okay, Tory. And yes, Jason, I am a full demon. Pleased to meet you." Stepping forward, she offered Jason her hand, which he took and shook enthusiastically.

Jason eventually let go of Elenor's hand and offered her his chair. She nodded in thanks and sat herself down.

"Tory, Connor told me what happened to your leg and that a new demon weapon has been fashioned. I wonder if I may be of any assistance to you?" she asked.

"We have some questions, especially about the venom," I replied. "Jason?"

Jason stepped forward and explained to Elenor the information he had already discovered when dissecting the arrowhead.

Elenor nodded her head and began to explain.

"The venom sac is based on the venom-producing ability of the black widow spider in the human realm: this is how all demon venom is produced. When we are transfigured from human soul to demon, we are given these venom sacs. Sitting within our hearts, the venom – instead of blood – pumps through our veins and we can force it into our claws or teeth when we attack," she clarified.

"So this claw head could potentially affect someone for an elongated time?" I asked.

"Yes, it will. The venom will kill a human but demons, obviously, and angels are immune. You are, too, Tory. However, you are not immune to hypovolemic shock. If you cannot heal, you will continue to lose blood, weakening you further. You may not die from the venom but you die because of a lack of blood as a causation of the venom." Elenor confirmed my fears.

"So demons are working with angels?" I asked.

"I am afraid it would seem so, Tory. I am sorry," she replied.

"Then this means we need a new plan," I said, determined that the human souls would not suffer due to the anticipated all-out war between heaven, hell, and me.

I called a council meeting for that evening, inviting not only council members but also the growing number of human souls that were familiar with my non-human status.

I had time for a brief wing inspection when I dashed home to shower and change my clothes. I unfurled my wings, allowing the space they need to overstretch. Standing in front of the mirror, I allowed myself to suffer the moment of agony as my fangs descended. Unfortunately, the morphine residue floating around my system had been metabolized in seconds, when the claw head was removed and my body began healing itself.

Roaming my eyes over my wings, I was surprised by the amount of feathers I was missing. The big, strengthened feathers that had been shot or pulled out were now replaced by tiny little fluffy chicken feathers. They would not take long to reach full size, but I felt a little pathetic and weakened by them.

After my shower, I heard the doorbell sound.

"Tory – it's Connor," he bellowed from behind the closed wooden door. "Can I come in?"

I made my way to the hallway to unlock the door. Conscious that I was still in a towel, I adjusted it to ensure that nothing was peeking out. Connor already knew I had wings, so I didn't bother retracting them, instead opting to fold them behind me.

"Hi, come in," I said, peering at him over the side of the door, hiding behind it so he could enter.

Connor entered slowly, staring as he did so. Once in the hallway, he turned, still staring, as I shut the door behind him and placed my back against it.

"You have fangs!" Connor stated, looking from my mouth to my eyes in rapid succession.

"Oh, shit!" I exclaimed, slamming both my hands across my mouth to hide them.

"Do you drink blood?" Connor asked, still gawping at my mouth.

"No, I do not," I mumbled from behind my hands.

"So you are not a vampire or anything weird like that?" Connor continued.

"No, Connor. I am not a vampire. I don't know why I have them: I just do," I mumbled louder from beneath my hands.

"Oh, okay then," Connor said, walking over to me and gently taking hold of both of my wrists. "Can I see?" he asked.

Initially, I shook my head violently.

"Please?" he asked again.

Loosening my strength in my arms, I allowed Connor to take my hands away from my mouth, slowly, and as he looked at me, I gave him an awkward smile. Maintaining a light grip on my wrists, Connor gently held my arms at my side.

"They are beautiful. Why do you hide them?" he quizzed.

"So people don't think that I am a vampire or anything weird," I responded, feeding back his own words to him.

"Of course," he smiled. "So you have beautiful wings and beautiful fangs. Is there anything else that you're hiding?"

I shook my head. "Nope – just my claws, but you know that I have those, wings and fangs," I responded, with an embarrassed shrug.

Connor lost his words and wandered into his own mind for a brief moment. Bringing his hands up the length of my naked arms, he held my upper arms within his hands. His eyes met mine and he breathed an elongated breath.

"You seem to be neither demon nor angel, so may I ask what you are?" he said calmly, gauging my response.

Freeing myself from his grasp, I pulled the towel tighter around my body and shook my head.

"I do not know what I am, Connor. I have never shown anyone my true form. Only you and Ryan know about my wings but you are the sole owner of the fang information. I am embarrassed by the way I look and do not wish to frighten the human souls whilst harvesting."

Confessing, I allowed my feelings to roll off of my tongue as I said the words. Tears pierced my eyes, acknowledging that I had shown Connor my core – who I really was – and he hadn't yet rejected me.

Stepping closer into me, Connor took me into his arms and held me against his chest. No words were needed as I allowed myself to embrace him back, signalling my brain to let me cry, to let me take comfort in the only person who was able to see me for who I am.

"Please, don't cry, Tory," Connor whispered into my hair. "You are beautiful. I think that you are the most beautiful woman across the four domains." Tenderly breaking our embrace, he wiped the tears from my stained cheeks with his thumb and tucked a stray tendril of hair back behind my ear.

I smiled at him and when he dipped his head to kiss me, I reveled in the feelings that exploded from within my body; feelings that I had never felt before or ever knew I could feel. Connor pulled me against his body and I gladly melted into him. He deepened our kiss, taking me along with him until I could taste a metallic taint on my tongue.

"Shit, oh shit!" I yelled to myself, as I realized what it was. Pulling myself away from Connor, I looked at his mouth. "Oh Connor, I am so sorry. So, so sorry…" I apologized.

He smiled, wiping the droplets of blood that had accumulated on his lip where my fangs had pierced it.

"It's just a scratch. It's fine," he said. "I can feel it healing already."

I watched as his hybrid healing ability began its magic and started to knit his bleeding lip together.

"No!" I said, pushing him away.

"Tory, I'm sorry. I should not have kissed you," Connor blurted, taking his hands from me, also.

"No, Connor – it's fine. I just want to get rid of these first," I said, pointing at my fangs.

"Oh, okay. But do you have to lose the fangs? I am finding them extremely sexy," Connor said, giving me a smouldering look that nearly made me drop my towel.

"I do. I have never kissed anyone before and I was enjoying it until I hurt you," I admitted.

"Never kissed anyone?" he asked.

"Not in the way you just kissed me. Hello and goodbye kisses but never – you know – intimately," I continued to confess.

Connor took both my hands and gently began rubbing his thumb over them.

"Why not?" he asked, mesmerizing me with the softness of his touch and the unintentional thumb-rubbing.

"There has never been anyone that I had wanted to be intimate with. I have shown you all of me, Connor. Only you. I trust you with my secrets." I kept my eyes focused on Connor, watching as he absorbed the information I had given him and hoping he realized how vulnerable I was feeling right now.

He smiled and lowered his voice, creating a sensual deep, dark rumble within it as he spoke.

"Every women should be kissed. But you, Tory – you should be kissed by a man who sees who you are. You are the bravest, most badass woman I have ever met. You are beautiful, Tory. Every inch of you radiates a beauty so divine that I want to kiss you as often as I can. Your secrets are safe and you never need to hide your true self from me. Your uniqueness, encompassed with your passion for the human souls, makes you the most perfect woman I have ever laid my eyes on. However, I have a secret, too," he said, keeping his eyes firmly fixed on mine.

"Your wings," I whispered, still overwhelmed by his words.

"My wings," he verified.

"Can I see them?" I enquired.

Connor briefly dropped his gaze and furrowed his brow.

"I cannot deny you this as you have shared all of you with me and I want to share all of me with you," he said, dropping my hands lightly and taking a few steps back from me. "Ready?" he asked.

"Ready," I countered, keeping my eyes fixed on his.

Standing before me, Connor pulled his t-shirt over his head and discarded it on the floor, to his left. Taking a deep breath, he began to release his wings. Blood-red metallic feathers began to erupt from his shoulders and travel down his spine as they were released.

Connor obviously felt the same pain I experience when allowing my wings their freedom. He stood rigid, his eyes downcast with the most fantastic wings protruding from his back.

Closing the gap between us, I wanted to see his wings up close.

"May I?" I asked for his approval and after receiving a nod indicating granted permission, I walked slowly behind him. I stood back to gain the full view of his gigantic set of wings.

Reaching out, I ran my fingers over the red, soft feathers that tickled where they touched. Using both my hands, I traced the perimeter of his wings as he maintained his rigid stance.

"These are beautiful, Connor. The colour is perfect," I said, bringing the palm of one of my hands up the skin of his spine nestled between his wings.

"The colour represents shame and banishment. They are the same colour that both my parents were given as punishment," he replied, taking a few steps forward before turning to face me. "Tory – I also hide my wings because I do not want others to see. Angel and demons will know who I am immediately. They will recognize the colour and the embarrassment that brings," he finished.

"I think that they are cute," I informed him.

"They are not cute," Connor countered.

"Have you ever seen your wings from the back, fully opened?" I asked.

"No, I haven't," he shook his head.

"Well, then – you must believe me when I say they are cute!"

"I believe that we both have some issues about ourselves. I will beg to differ with you about my wings and you may regarding your fangs," Connor said, taking my hands and placing a small kiss on each.

"Beautifully flawed is how I would describe us," I said, leaning forward and capturing his lips with my own. Slowly bringing my body closer to him, Connor deepened our kiss.

In the distance, I heard the chiming of my bedroom clock reminding me of the time.

"Connor," I whispered against his lips. "We need to go to the meeting."

Breaking the kiss but keeping his face close to mine, Connor muttered his annoyance. "I know, but you cannot turn up like that. I don't mind but the others might," he giggled, giving me a final peck on my forehead before allowing me my own body back.

"That's true. I'll go and change." I made my way reluctantly into the bedroom, leaving Connor in the hallway concentrating on retracting his wings.

Twenty minutes later, I had dried my damp hair, changed and retracted both wings and fangs successfully. Connor and I left the house after finding it impossible not to kiss each other just one more time before leaving.

Chapter 18

The room Connor and I walked into was stuffed with human souls alongside Elenor, Devon, and Ryan. The original council members were sitting at the oval wooden table in their regular positions, while bodies occupied any space where a chair or pair of standing legs would fit.

I took my chair at the head of the table as Connor made his way to the back of the room to perch on a window sill, next to his brother. Once he'd settled himself, he threw me a wink accompanied by a smile, designed to melt me.

It did. I needed to take a few moments to regain my equilibrium before I could concentrate on the task ahead.

Raymond was obviously worried about the events and the expected reason for this meeting. He was an old soul and he did not like feeling as if he were being kept in the dark. Not only had I brought a fallen angel and a fugitive demon into purgatory without his knowledge, I had also invited them, alongside others, to the emergency meeting.

I could feel his eyes glaring at me over his notepad as I settled myself, ready to begin.

"Raymond, it's fine. They are fine," I whispered out of the side of my mouth to him. In response, I received an extremely heavy huff. Good old Raymond never said a bad word but huffed like the wind when dissatisfied.

Porter was deep in conversation with Ryan and Connor. All three sat on the window sill like school boys plotting something they shouldn't.

Michelle and Mia were discussing the latest harvests, especially how a baby should not be harvested to purgatory. However, they did agree that the infant should stay with her mother and that it was nice to see a baby again.

Henry was talking with Devon and Elenor. He was always the welcoming committee and information distributor. They were discussing the accommodation given to Elenor and Devon and they were apparently really happy with it.

The other souls I had invited included Jason. His knowledge and recent discovery of the demon claws made him a valuable commodity within the council.

Four other hospital workers accompanied him, all of whom had treated me after battles and were fully aware of my abilities, wings, and fangs. They comprised two nurses – Chris and Jackson; one orderly – Luke; and a surgeon named Andrew. They were all extremely intelligent and valuable souls who decided to stay in purgatory rather than ascend.

Another group of men who I harvested over ten years ago stood in repose in the corner of the room. Five badass but soft-as-shit bikers who died together in a huge accident. Angels, demons, and I all attended to harvest. No fighting occurred that day: there were so many deaths, we didn't need to.

Those men had also decided to stay, providing an exuberant vibe within the domain, and assisted in descending the souls unwilling yet worthy of an afterlife in hell.

"The Rose Daggers" biker club included Gator, the 55-year-old leader, who ran his men like a well-oiled motorbike. His second was his son, Wolfman, an extremely hairy man with a perfect plaited ponytail hidden under his bandana. Raven was the whitest man I had ever seen; his skin so pale and almost insipid, yet his hair and eyes were as black as... Well – a raven.

Bones apparently used to be an orthopaedic surgeon – hence the name – and finally, the youngest member of their gang was Poet. He was a brand new probate and had just been awarded his colours.

All of the Rose Daggers wore their colours and tattoos with pride, continuing to use their legal names or street names in the afterlife and continuing with their brotherhood bond. Apparently, they had had a few run-ins with the law but no murders or violence: hence why I harvested them and not the demons. These men were genuine and an asset to purgatory and to my cause.

Taking stock of all the souls around me, I smiled at their continued dedication.

"Good evening," I started breaking the conversations and initiating silence as the entire room came to a halt to listen. "Thank you," I continued. "Ladies and gentleman, this meeting has been called due to new information and weaponry being used against me when harvesting. As you are aware, Ryan and Connor accompany me when harvesting but unfortunately this has angered both heaven and hell. Yesterday, Ryan was ambushed in the human domain. Realizing that he may have had a problem, I joined him.

"Both angel and demons attacked us with two new weapons that I have never seen before. The angels have eight, light-force daggers that, when amalgamated, create a stream of pure light force. The demons have claw weapons which seem to be mounted on their own claws. These arrowheads are planted inside lacerations created by these demon claws and constantly pump demon venom into the bloodstream to prevent healing.

"It would seem that the angels and demons are working together: demons embed their arrow heads whilst the angels throw their light-force daggers at the same victim. I have brought you here today to ask for your help. I need to be able to harvest to maintain the energy that purgatory needs to survive, but I am unable to do that if an ambush disassociated with harvesting is waiting each time the twins or I cross through the portal.

"Please let me also introduce Devon and Elenor, Ryan and Connor's parents. I have asked them to join our domain to escape the constant punishments from heaven and hell. They have also agreed to accompany me to harvesting, alongside Ryan and Connor.

"However, our numbers are also small, and although we are excellent fighters, we need new members to help in being successful: hence the reason why you are all here."

I paused to survey the reactions of the souls present.

Gator was the first to address me.

"Anything you need, Tory, the Daggers will be with you," he announced, as the remaining club members agreed by patting each other on the back and nodding.

"You know that we are with you," Jason said, speaking for his colleagues, also. "However, Tory, it worries me that our human souls will not be able to adequately fight for you or to tolerate demon venom or the angels' light force," he continued.

124

I nodded in acknowledgment, recognizing his concerns. I chanced a quick glance at Raymond, who I could see was getting ready to give his counter argument.

"We will, of course, provide you all with training before we would contemplate taking you into the human domain," I addressed the room. "Also, Michael should be joining us soon, with Julian."

"Tory – may I?" Raymond said, from beside me.

Inwardly sighing, I sat and allowed the wise old misery-guts to stand and say his piece.

"I would like to just air my thoughts, Tory," Raymond began, and I knew we were in for a lecture. "It vexes me that human souls are being asked to fight against demons and angels without the skills or knowledge to do so. I fear that creating an army of your own will anger heaven and hell. I believe that Tory should continue to harvest souls the way she has always done. Having an entourage with her will make her and them more obvious to the demons and angels and therefore to their attacks."

I placed my head in my hands and bit my tongue hard. Raymond always had words to say, yet little understanding of what they meant. He had no idea what it was like to fight heaven and hell, yet because he was so old and my first harvest, I felt I should allow him his opinion, although I rarely agreed with him.

From one of the chairs situated next to Porter, Devon stood. His brow furrowed and his lips were held tightly in a thin line.

"Your ideas, Raymond, are outdated and dangerous. Tory places her life at risk with every single harvest she performs; she battles heaven and hell each time she crosses the portal, and you would deny her help from those who wish to give it?"

Devon was not happy. He gave Raymond a dressing-down as he explained exactly what I did and the numbers I had to fight individually. Unfortunately for Raymond, it was not what he wanted to hear, so he sulked as usual.

Those that wanted to verified their help, leaving Raymond to agree to disagree as he continued scribbling in his notepad and mumbling under his breath.

Devon had re-taken his seat and was talking to Elenor about how inappropriate Raymond was and how he knew nothing of the risk I take for purgatory.

I caught his eye briefly and nodded my thanks to him and he offered a bright smile in return.

A stagnant silence fell over the room, post-argument, and I knew next week's newsletter was gonna be a bad one. Raymond always managed to stick the odd moan in, when creating the domain newsletter he insisted we had to keep us all informed.

Loud thuds on the door brought the uncomfortable silence to an end with the arrival of Michael and Julian.

"All right there, Tory? Apologies for our lateness," Michael said, as he and Julian closed the door behind them and leant their backs against it.

Standing once more, I continued my speech regarding issuing everyone with armour, weapons of their choice, and where and when training would begin.

"So you can see, I will take every precaution to maintain your safety while in the human domain. Michael and Julian will be creating your armour and weapons, so please make yourselves available to them.

"Jason is also working on a vaccine to help counteract the effects of the demon venom. You are already dead: therefore, you cannot die. However, the venom is extremely painful and can render a soul incapacitated and vulnerable. That is when the demons or angels will try to descend or ascend you, so please be aware. Any questions?"

I glanced around the room at the numerous souls shaking their heads, grateful for their loyalty.

Eventually, Poet indicated he had a question.

"Who will train us?"

"Devon, Elenor, Ryan, Connor, and I will. We all have experience fighting both angels and demons. We will begin training in two days, so please find me if you have further questions," I responded. "Can I take the opportunity to thank you all for your help? I am sure that having numbers will help with our cause, but remember we do this primarily for the good of the newly harvested souls."

I smiled and sat back down, reaching for the water before me, the condensation glistening on the outside of the glass.

Gradually, the room erupted into a cacophony of conversations allowing me the time to sip from the frigid glass. Raymond had excused himself and left the room, while Mia slid into his chair to offer encouragement for my correct decision.

An hour later, I remained at the table, accompanied only by the hybrids and their parents.

"My dear," Elenor began. "This is the right thing to do. If heaven and hell are becoming united in order to fight you, you will need help. Remember these people have volunteered: they support you and we shall become a formidable force for anyone who believes they can beat purgatory."

Rounding her words off with a hug, Elenor patted me briefly on the back. This was what I had needed: verification.

As I sat listening to the family talking strategy and what to teach the human souls, I felt the same feeling I had every time a new soul was soon to be released.

"A soul will be released soon," I announced, interrupting the conversation. "I need to get to the portal so I can find out where we need to go. Shall we meet there in fifteen minutes?" I asked.

It was agreed: in fifteen minutes, the five-strong amalgamation of demon, angel, hybrids and me would be introducing ourselves as a team. Now this would definitely piss off heaven and hell even further. I couldn't wait.

"I'll come with you," Connor said, "so you can teach me what to look for," he added, smiling.

"Okay, come on." I stood and left the room with Connor falling in behind me, leaving the strategic meeting to continue without us.

Chapter 19

Connor and I arrived at the portal and sat down before it, in the velveteen heaps of grass.

"You are watching for the change in essence," I told him. "An alive person has a golden essence signalling life but when a person is dying, the essence shifts to a pale blue colour."

"Why?" he asked.

"I don't know why: it just does. When the soul is released, it turns red, so it can be found easily and harvested," I explained.

"That is so cool. But they don't stay red," he stated.

"No," I verified. "When the soul is taken to its domain to begin the afterlife, it changes back to the version of itself as a human. Look!" I said, pointing into the portal. "See all these alive souls? We just need to be vigilant and find the one we need."

Connor wriggled himself closer to me and followed the point of my finger.

"Wow, Tory – how do you find anyone like this? There are so many gold essences." He turned to face me and smiled. Leaning forward, he placed his hand up to the side of my face and gently tucked a stray strand of hair back behind my ear.

"You are beautiful," he said, bringing his hand to the back of my neck and running his fingers through my hair. Pulling me gently towards him, he captured my lips with his own. Softly, he kissed me, as if I were so delicate and he could possibly break me.

Deepening our kiss, I brought my arms around him and pulled myself closer into his body. He responded by enveloping me within his arms and gradually pushing me down onto my back.

Melting into him, I allowed myself to explore his body with my eager hands. My fingertips gently skipped over his muscular arms and guided me over his back, learning each contour of his upper body. He, in turn, had balled my hair up in his fist and it was a sexy as hell. I was becoming lost in him. Opening my eyes, I watched his face as he kissed me. He was carefree and handsome.

"Stop watching me," he mumbled against my lips.

I giggled, causing him to open one eye and smile, tickling my mouth with his own.

The releasing soul called to me once again. Pushing my hands against Connor's chest, I reluctantly broke away from him.

"The soul is calling to me, Connor. We must watch for it," I told him.

"Okay," he replied, stealing another quick kiss before sitting upright and taking me with him.

Holding his hand for fear of letting it go just yet, Connor and I peered into the portal.

"The correct name of this portal is *iuxta portas mortis*," I informed him. "It means portal of near death, in Latin. It enables us to see the souls that need us; almost like a two-way mirror and GPS at the same time." I pointed out the different aspects of the portal and their meanings.

"Okay – there, do you see?" I began frantically pointing at the top right-hand of the portal. "Do you see? The blue-tinged soul." Pulling Connor to the portal, we looked closer into the waves of souls that rolled over one another.

"That is minuscule and so faint. How did you see that through all the other souls?" Connor asked, squinting his eyes and adjusting his position to view the blue soul better.

"Thousands of years of practice," I replied. "If you continue to watch, you will see the soul gradually become darker the nearer to release it becomes. We need to go soon, especially as I am expecting demons or angels, or both, to be waiting for us."

Connor nodded in agreement and in silence we prepared our armor and weapons in anticipation of a fight.

"Tory, can I ask you a question?" Connor said, tucking his arrows neatly into his quiver and securing it on his back.

"Sure," I replied, my gaze still fixed on the ever-deepening blue soul.

"Why do you save people? I mean, humans know about demons and angels, heaven and hell, yet they know so little about you," he stated.

"I help the souls because they deserve a better afterlife than being lost in the human domain. I am also ensuring a fair trial for those who do not belong in purgatory for a long period of time. Heaven is selective in its harvesting, whereas hell doesn't give a shit about who they harvest, except children. There is an unwritten rule about children. I also do it because humans are fascinating, different ages, skin tones, hair colours, genders, jobs, abilities, statuses. "However the one aspect of the human race I do not understand is religion and beliefs. Humans live and die by their beliefs and their gods. I have watched their wars, fought in their name of religion and I still don't understand this behaviour.

"Every human was created the same, whether male or female. They were given one body and one brain, as equals, but somewhere in evolution human beings began to distance themselves from one another, becoming enemies. And the reason for this was pathetic," I continued, briefly turning to face Connor, then turning my attention back to the portal.

"What reasons?" Connor asked, also eyeing the portal.

"I am sure you must have seen some of the things when you lived in the human domain," I said.

"We were pretty sheltered, Tory, so we were protected. Please go on," Connor encouraged.

"The human race began attacking each other because of people's differences, ridiculing and creating thousands of excuses for their behavior towards each other. I have yet to find any of them valid," I told him.

Connor paused before speaking. "So why do you save them, if all humans behave this way?" he asked.

"Because I am the boss in my domain. All souls that enter are equal and remain equal until judgement is needed and they either descend or ascend. It may seem a bit hypocritical but humans need structure and authority to enable them to accept one another and I provide it," I concluded.

"What about heaven and hell?" he asked.

"They provide their own structure in their own domains. Very rarely does a soul leave either, once it has been harvested to these domains." Pausing to take a breath, I was disturbed by the sound of approaching footfall.

"Tory, Connor," Ryan greeted us. I received a nod whilst Connor received a punch to his upper arm.

"Hello, Ryan – are you ready? Devon, Elenor?" I said, as the fallen angel and his fugitive demon caught up with us.

"Are you expecting trouble?" Elenor asked.

I nodded. "I always anticipate trouble, then I can be pleasantly surprised if it doesn't appear," I smiled back.

"Judging by what happened last time, we need to be vigilant," Ryan added.

"I agree," I said. "The angels and demons are aware of you twins, but I believe they will be a bit pissed when they realise I have your parents with me, too."

Moving closer towards the portal, our little group of five spoke briefly about tactics and harvesting. I was not looking forward to more fighting, I never did like it but I was happy that I would not be alone.

"We need to go," I interrupted. "Connor – see how blue the soul is now?"

Connor stood closer to me and nodded in agreement that now was the time. Knowing the portal would take us where we needed to be, Connor and I stepped through first, closely followed by Ryan, Devon, and Elenor.

Taking a deep breath and holding it, we stepped into the human domain. I readied my weapons and threw Connor a small smile, which he returned with an accompanying wink.

Chapter 20

There was silence as our group clustered together, all hyper-aware and ready for action.

"Why is it so quiet?" Ryan asked, from behind me.

I shrugged. "Sometimes it is at first. Come – let's go." I motioned with my hand and as a unit we all moved to our intended destination, a makeshift military hospital approximately ten feet away.

We were in a war zone, hence the reason we had yet to encounter any angels or demons. War equals death, and death equals a large amount of harvesting. Therefore, our one soul target would be easy to find without bringing too much attention to ourselves.

Reaching the outer perimeter of the hospital, I was optimistic that the ongoing fighting and deaths would occupy the harvesting demons and angels. I did not know exactly where we were, but the environment was broken: crumbling building lined the streets, the intact buildings had smashed windows and graffiti slashed across them.

Fragments of burnt-out cars and waste bins frequented each street corner, accessorized by scattered shards of glass and discarded cigarette packets. In the distance, the comprehensible sounds of fighting reverberated between the annihilated buildings. Screams resounded over the auditory abuse of gunfire.

Frequent portals opened from heaven and hell. We hid and watched as angels and demons stepped into the mortal domain, ready to do their bidding and harvest souls.

Allowing them to pass, we remained cautious. I did not want to instigate a fight: it would be a fruitless waste of effort. The number of available souls for harvest were in excess: however, I was also concerned as to why I had one soul calling me when so many others needed harvesting, too.

Finally, our collective made its way to the front of the building after conquering the convoluted maze necessary to get there. Military personnel were stationed at the door and, from what I could see, throughout the whole building.

Circling the temporary hospital, Ryan found an entry point approximately eight foot up. Devon and Elenor flew up to investigate the possible entry point: no alarms or guards reported. Looking around to ensure that there were no passing demons or angels, I released my wings, creating swirling dust plumes rising up from the ground beneath me.

"I'm not carrying you two up!" I said, standing with my arms folded, staring at the reluctant twins. "Come on – get 'em out!" I back-handedly encouraged. I looked at each twin, still wingless and searching for a hole in the ground to swallow them up.

"Ryan!" I called, forcing him to meet my gaze. "Are your wings the same as Connor's?"

Ryan looked shocked at this question. "He showed you his wings?" he questioned, glancing sideways at his brother and being rewarded with a shrug from Connor.

"You both saw mine, so it's only fair," I stated, grinning back at him.

"I don't like to show my wings," Ryan responded, looking for the hole in the ground once more.

Connor fluttered his newly exposed, metallic, red wings, puffing dust from his body with them. Walking up to his brother's side, Connor lay his hand on his brother's shoulder.

"Brother, it feels good to allow your wings their freedom. We are not in the human domain any more, but where we belong. We should not be ashamed."

"They represent punishment and disgrace," Ryan mumbled under his breath.

"Ryan," I said, stealing his attention. "They represent your family. The colour only amplifies the love your parents felt for each other; to fall and become banished for one another, the bond that brought them together and the two children they brought into the world. If others see your wings, so what? They will know the trials you have suffered and overcome to be here. In the now, it is the only thing that matters. Created of heaven and hell, but you belong in purgatory." I kept Ryan's gaze throughout my speech, allowing him the time to digest my words.

Gradually, after his few minutes reprieve, Ryan began to allow his wings to gently push out from between his shoulder blades. Vivid red feathers began to cascade and stretch from his body. His wings were not metallic like Connor's, glasslike but flexible, tinted a bold red. His feather shards eventually became his wings.

"They are beautiful," I complimented.

Ryan nodded, controlling an escaping smile. "It does feel good to allow them their freedom."

Connor shoved him harder than necessary across his arm.

"Told you," he quipped.

Ryan gave him a crooked smile and punched him back on the upper arm. Rolling my eyes, I tutted loudly as the boys exchanged a few more slaps. I interrupted them when I had gotten bored of watching.

"When was the last time you flew?"

"When I was a kid," Ryan replied.

"No idea," Connor added.

"Okay, well – we need to go. It is getting closer to the soul's release," I said, preparing to fly. "I will go first." Bringing my wings into their airfoil shape, I began rotating them forward, down, then back up, allowing the air to pass over and underneath them. Connor and Ryan both began their pre-flight ritual, obviously also enjoying the air circulation.

"Come – let's go!" I called, as I began to agitate my wings, permitting me to rise and begin to fly. Undulating my wings, I flew up from the ground and revelled in the freedom they gave me.

Glancing down briefly, I saw that both Connor and Ryan were sky-bound. Cautiously, the twins were becoming reacquainted with their wings: the odd flutter to the side or judder didn't seem to faze them as they followed behind me.

Standing on the ledge in front of an ancient wooden door protected by steel bars, we five winged creatures jostled for space.

Devon had begun to pull the bars obstructing the doorway out of the wall they were embedded in. Rubble flew, debris scattered, and dust showered our group as we stood observing.

Elbowing Connor in the side, I encouraged him to assist his father with an over-exaggerated head-nod directed at Devon. Winking once, he nudged his brother into action.

Elenor and I protected ourselves from the dust with our wings, taking turns to peek at the progress the men were making.

"I am sure that we could have completed this in half the time," Elenor jested from behind her wings.

"Obviously!" I retorted, dipping my wings to throw her a grin.

In all honesty, it did not take long for one angel and his hybrid sons to remove the steel bars, but Elenor and I thoroughly enjoyed teasing them. When the last bar had been removed, Ryan stood back and kicked the rotting wooden door. A gentle shove would have been as efficient since the door crumbled before him like the losing move of a Jenga game. The men entered the war-torn hospital, leaving Elenor and me to follow behind, stifling giggles.

Once inside and re-grouped, we took the opportunity to adjust to our surroundings to evaluate our next move. I could feel the soul calling loudly, so close to release. I begged it in my mind to stay connected until we arrived. The sense of urgency I had was willing me to snap my next sentence.

"We must just go: we have no time to chat. I can feel the soul calling. We need to follow it: it will guide us."

Suddenly, I became aware of a possible downfall in bringing others with me to harvest. When I harvest alone, I follow the calling soul but now I was standing still, discussing which way to go and who would tackle the guards.

I took a deep breath: firstly I apologized to my comrades for being a complete bitch, then suggested that we follow the call of the guards and worry only about other humans if we encountered them.

Encouragingly, my suggestion received nods of agreement and following my lead, we headed down the dark corridor to the waiting soul. I tracked the soul to another four floors up and cautiously we entered the only lit area of the makeshift hospital.

Cloaked and with retracted wings, our group made our way into the ward. Before stepping through the door, behind me Elenor caught my arm.

"Tory – Devon and I will stay here and guard the entrance. Take Ryan and Connor with you," she whispered.

"OK," I agreed. "Call us if you have any problems. We should not be long as this soul is straining to remain connected," I informed them, nodding my thanks as the hybrids and I entered the ward.

Military healthcare personnel littered the over-capacitated ward. Each room we passed held at least four injured service men and women; some connected to machines, some staring into space and others consoling their colleagues.

Shivers raced the full length of my spine. Once again, the impact of the destructive nature of the human race astounded me. I felt a light touch on my upper arm and turned to meet Connor's gaze.

"You okay?" he asked, with concern lacing his eyes.

"I'm fine," I assured him. "I see this so often but it is a shock to see the extent of the injuries these humans receive and survive. It is good that some survive, but what a waste." I sighed deeply.

"I know," Connor concurred, still rubbing my arm lightly and offering me a small smile. "Come. Let's find this soul and get out of here."

I smiled back at him and continued searching for the soul.

A red light above one of the rooms indicated the position of our intended soul. Doctors and nurses were running in and out of the room carrying equipment and armfuls of blood sachets for transfusion.

"Here," I whispered, bringing us to a halt. "This is the soul we have come for. Wait here a moment," I told the twins.

"Of course," Connor replied, and as I walked into the room, Connor and Ryan started sentry duty either side of the door.

"He's crashing. We're losing him," a senior doctor was communicating with his colleagues while beginning CPR on a heavily bleeding solider. Nurses continued squeezing the life-sustaining donated blood in their elevated bags into the soldier via numerous intravenous lines and gradually the soul prepared to evacuate the body.

Taking a moment to assess the patient myself, I could see he had lost one leg up to his hip and half of his other leg. All of the dressings covering the wounds were saturated and leaking copious amounts of life-preserving blood.

Walking past the medical staff working fruitlessly to save this soldier's life, I took hold of his blood-stained hand and pushing deeper inside, I felt for his soul.

His soul was ready to leave: it had wound itself around my hand before I had chance to take it myself. I could feel the gentle slowing of his heartbeat that was being maintained only by the CPR administration from the medical staff.

"Okay. Hands off. Let's see what he is doing," the senior doctor said, encouraging all staff to withdraw their hands from the body. In silence, all personnel became transfixed by a black screen with a thin, green rhythm strip containing small and inconsistent mini mountains, crossing the width of the machine. I watched with them as the heart rhythm stopped and the mountains faded to create one straight green line, accompanied by an insistent beep, indicating the stoppage of his heart. Personnel within the room hung their heads, a few mumbled prayers, and an aged healthcare assistant cracked open the window of the room in the belief that this allowed the soul to be free.

As he released, I pulled the soldier's soul from his crumpled, battered, worn-torn body.

"Time of death: 02:42," the doctor muttered soberly, peeling the gloves from his hands and tossing them into a nearby clinical waste bin, his head downcast and his own soul evidently aching because he could not save this soldier.

A flurry of activity began around the soulless body. IV lines were removed and the cleaning and preparation of the traumatized body began.

"Hello – I'm Tory," I said, turning to face the new soul I held by the hand. "I am here to take you to your afterlife."

"Sergeant Daniel Harris," he replied, looking me over then looking past me at his own torn-up body.

"It's best not to look," I said, quietly.

Nodding passively, he turned away and we began to walk out of the ward.

"This is Ryan and Connor," I said, introducing the twins as we exited. They greeted each other with a handshake, accompanied by verbal introductions as we continued through the building.

As we walked, I explained who I was, where we were going, and what would happen to him now. Daniel remained silent, observing each fallen comrade as we passed the overcrowded, medicalized rooms.

"These are the survivors," I said, lightly. "All of these men and women you see here will not die in the war," I offered, trying to give him some comfort.

Daniel stopped walking and paused briefly. "How do you know that?" he asked.

I smiled, sympathetically. "I am purgatory. Souls call to me before they are released from the body so I may come and retrieve them to their afterlife. These souls here in these rooms are strong: there are no souls calling, therefore the bodies are able to be repaired. Your body, Daniel, was damaged severely and your soul called for me to receive you when your body failed."

"I understand," Daniel responded.

"It will get easier," Connor interjected. "My brother and I were saved by Tory, so now we assist her to save others, ensuring that no souls are left to wander the earth, lost. Ryan and I will show you the ropes once we're back in purgatory." Connor patted Daniel on the shoulder and continued explaining the whole heaven, hell, demon, and angel paradigm.

Before long, we reached Elenor and Devon, where introductions were made. Then, as a group of six, we left the makeshift hospital. I walked ahead, accompanied by Devon and Elenor, while Ryan and Connor walked with Daniel, continuing to inform him of what to expect in the afterlife.

Cautiously, we made our way back to the portal avoiding detection by the demons and angels as they continued their harvesting on the battlefield.

As the portal came into view, our group sped up to rapidly cross back into purgatory. Fighting continued around us as we travelled. Our cloaking ensured our invisibility to the human eye and we were seemingly ignored by heaven and hell's parasitic minions.

A vehicle came towards us, at speed, amongst a shower of bullets, hailing from above, originating from within one of the destroyed buildings.

Connor had called me back to Daniel as he was refusing to move. I reached Connor. Daniel was transfixed, his eye tracing the movements of the bullet-ridden vehicle.

"British," he mumbled, indistinctly. "My regiment. They shouldn't be here. Not this far from the base. I don't– For fuck's sake, they shouldn't be here!" Daniel's staccato words fell from his lip, dripping in confusion. "They are disobeying orders. They should not have come back for me," he continued.

"They are your squad?" Ryan asked, trying to calm Daniel.

"Yes: I am their squad leader. They were under orders not to return for me," Daniel explained, becoming both agitated and emotional.

We watched as the vehicle carrying Squadron 14 continued towards the hospital in an obvious bid to find their leader. Bullets cascaded upon the vehicle without reprieve, although the damage inflicted was minimal on the armour that encased it. Transfixed and unwilling to move himself, Daniel continued to watch as his comrades passed us. Abruptly, my ears were assaulted with the enormous, deafening sound of an explosion. Clamping my hands over my ears, I tried to barricade my eardrums from the ringing that currently violated them. The military vehicle had been catapulted off the road into the air by a blast from a roadside bomb. I watched horror overtake Daniel's features as the vehicle exploded: incandescent yellow flames, tinged with orange and red spikes, effortlessly engulfed the van and its contents.

Immediately, time slowed down. The deafening explosion demanded the attention of those surrounding it. Demons and angels began to migrate toward the direction of the vehicle, the direction toward us.

"Do something!" Daniel screamed at me, violently shaking my arm.

"How many are in that truck?" I questioned rapidly, conscious of the unwanted attention the exploration had created.

"It's a Mastiff 2, so two in the front with a possibility of eight in the back. It shouldn't have gone up like that. I don't understand!" Daniel's desperation was mounting as panic invaded his thought.

"Daniel, this is not just one IED," Ryan interjected. "Look!" He pointed out the IED casings scattered in the street.

"Four…" Daniel countered. "They didn't have a chance."

Watching in horror as time began to speed up to its normal momentum, the truck continued its fire-engulfed roller-coaster roll. Roll after roll, the vehicle kicked past buildings and debris as it gravitated with the excelled propulsion the IED cluster had given it.

"Tory," Elenor caught my attention as she stood close beside me.

"Look, there – what should we do?"

Bringing my gaze into the direction she was referring to, I saw a sight that I had never seen in the hundreds of years I had completed in harvesting.

"Ejected souls," I muttered. "Souls are never ejected this way." My own confusion blinded me temporarily, impairing my ability to think.

Daniel fidgeted unconsciously beside me, watching the souls of his squad being catapulted like rag-dolls from their dead bodies and from the military vehicle.

"Daniel, stay close to me," I told him, controlling his fidgeting with a firm hand on his shoulder whilst addressing my team. "We need to harvest these souls: there could be as many as ten, so be vigilant." My group of misfit demons and angels immediately acknowledged me and set off running towards the ejected souls.

"Come – let's go. Stay close and keep with me," I ordered Daniel.

Connor had already reached one soldier and was briefly explaining who we were as he travelled to find the next fallen soldier. Ryan was assisting a soul trapped by debris, whereas Elenor and Devon had just harvested a group of four souls.

Cautiously observing the distant, oncoming demons and angels, I could tell that they hadn't noticed us due to their lack of speed and arrogant saunter over to the explosion site.

"We need to speed up!" I called, reaching a female soldier with Daniel, who immediately began informing her of our current situation.

"How many in the truck?" I enquired.

"Eight," she replied, still stunned from the hurried information Daniel had just given her.

Looking around, I took a tally: Elenor - four; Ryan - one; Connor - two; and the soul I had harvested totalled eight: we had all the souls.

Gathering the group together, I began to assess the situation and decided our next move. We had now been discovered by the advancing demons and the angels had taken to the air to reach us more rapidly.

"We must go: explanations will have to wait. I have never harvested so many souls at one time, so be vigilant and keep the souls between us and protected at all times," I demanded.

The group fanning out into a pentagon, I began leading them toward the portal. Connor and Ryan were positioned behind me, while Elenor and Devon covered the rear. The nine, newly harvested souls walked between us, close together and silent.

"Ah, purgatory," a voice spoke from above me. "Your stupidity knows no bounds." Abraxos hovered over me, fluttering his dove-white wings and intentionally pluming dust up from the road, engulfing us.

"Back for another ass-whooping?" Connor called to him, notching his first arrow as he did so.

"Nice one," Ryan called to Connor, nodding his head with respect to his brother's quick wit.

Abraxos smirked and allowed his wings to set him firmly on the ground before us. "Foolish hybrids, your demise is eminent and I will personally see to it that your descension continues to be one of pain and suffering," he declared, directly to Connor.

Connor, being Connor, was not going to be taking any crap today and with a huge grin slapped across his face, he allowed his arrow the freedom it desired and released it. "Ascend, you bastard!" Connor called, as the arrow whispered softly past me and embedded itself firmly into Abraxos's heart.

Abraxos's light force dripped freely from his chest, surrounding the arrow with his light. A portal of heaven opened up to accept the defeated ascending angel and, as Abraxos was recalled to heaven, Ryan turned to Connor and high-fived him.

Turning to the hybrids, I smirked. "You know that will just piss him off more."

"Oh yes," Connor smiled and winked at me.

Unable to control my own smile, I shook my head and turned back to face the next onslaught of abuse in the form of one ugly-ass demon.

Chapter 21

Flanked by numerous fang-toothed, black-scaled demon colleagues, the collective group rapidly closed the gap between them and us.

"Ready?" I asked my group, pulling my sai from my waistband. A resounding "Yes!" echoed from behind me with an accompanying "Fuck yeah!" from Connor.

"Daniel – keep your squad between us at all times. Do not stray, do not try to help. Dispatching these demons will not take long," I said, turning my head slightly to allow him to hear me.

"Understood," he replied and immediately relayed the instruction to his squad.

Standing firm, I waited for the demon posse to come close enough to avoid yelling at them. "Let us pass, demons. We have harvested and wish to return to our domain. We have no wish to fight you as there are plenty of harvestable souls for you to take." I addressed the head demon as I did every time my path crossed theirs, yet each time they chose to fight and I would descend them. You would think that they would have learnt by now.

"Give up your harvest, Purgatory," the head demon ordered. "War means descension: therefore, we will collect."

Keeping my sai ready, I responded. "War is created by those with power, who then order soldiers to fight, human against human, until the created war is won and the creator is victorious and remains safe behind their walls. War is not descension: it is a product of misguided beliefs and power-hungry bigots. Maybe you need to concentrate on the creature of war and leave the innocents to me!" Anger bubbled away beneath my skin. I had witnessed human war for centuries and the ignition for each war was either religion or power.

"Creators do not die as frequently as the fighters: therefore we descend who we harvest in war, no exceptions." The head demon had a point: creators are hidden away, untouched from the reality of war, but these souls were mine and their afterlife was to be achieved in purgatory.

Inhaling deeply, I began my speech on the harvesting treaty and once claimed, no other demon should seek to influence the soul. The head demon smirked widely, allowing his yellow teeth and putrid-smelling breath to become visible.

"The treaty no longer stands: therefore I will take those souls from you and descend them for eternity." Pausing for my reaction, he licked his front fang with his repulsive, discoloured tongue.

"The treaty stands, demon. It cannot be dissolved. It protects all souls," I countered, becoming more frustrated.

Laughing at me, the demon then composed himself enough to respond.

"Your recruitment of the hybrids has enabled heaven and hell to unite in our fight to destroy you and your halfway-house domain of hapless souls. We have decided that you have failed in your bid to uphold the treaty: therefore it is null and void." Cackling loudly and encouraged by his entourage of scaled beasts, the head demon took a step closer toward me.

"Be dignified, Purgatory. Fuck off and allow history to erase your failed attempts to save the souls of humanity."

I stood in silence. The treaty was the building block for fair judgement and harvesting and now it was devoid of respect.

"With or without the treaty, I fight for humanity and always will, demon. Relay to your heaven and hell consolidation that I will not be stopped but become stronger. Purgatory will grow and defend the human souls at all costs." I felt Connor take a step closer behind me, showing his support with such a small but powerful gesture.

"Then prepare to fight," the head demon continued, bringing his hand up to his face to wipe away the saliva that had dribbled from his foul mouth as he spoke through his fangs. "The hybrids and their disgraced parents, who you have brought into your circle, only give us further incentive to bring about your downfall."

"As you wish," I replied, determination now replacing the adrenaline assaulting my body.

Taking his cue, Connor immediately released his arrows, allowing Ryan and me to drive forward and begin kicking some demon ass.

As previously discussed before leaving purgatory, Elenor and Devon protected the harvested souls. Being military, they were respectful and regimented, making it easier to protect them.

"Get to the portal!" I yelled to Devon, ducking to avoid a swipe from the head demon. Devon nodded and immediately began moving the troop to the portal, while battling any attempts from the demons to attack.

Standing as a trio, Ryan, Connor, and I fought the demons, descending them one by one until only one remained.

"It is your turn to descend, demon," I said, taking a step forward. He closed the gap between us quickly and continued to run as my sai hit him hard: one in the chest, the other piercing his neck severing his spinal cord and descending him immediately.

A familiar light-headedness gradually started to cloud my head. Wiping the demon inners from my sai, I started to re-sheath them but stumbled forward. As I regained my balance, I noticed crimson drips pooling on the ground by my feet.

"Bastard," I said, aloud. The demon had descended itself by lancing his body on my sai, thus being able to get close enough to me to embed a bloody claw.

Following the channel of dripping blood, I traced it to a reasonable-sized gash in my upper arm. Blood was continuing to seep radially from the wound, along with the excess demon venom.

Before I could call his name, Connor had his arms around me. "They got you again, then!" he teased, as his muscular arm encircled my waist. Ryan had also made his way to my side and was examining the laceration. "I can't see a claw," he said.

"It's there," I verified. "I can feel it pulsating. You need to get it out," I told him.

Ryan looked at the wound then back up at me and shook his head, slowly. "How?"

"You need to get your fingers in there and pull it out," I said, obviously not relishing the idea of him doing so. "I believe the angels will try to attack soon, as they think that the demons have incapacitated me. Please, Ryan…" My head was becoming increasingly heavy and I could feel Connor needing to take more of my weight.

"Sit!" Connor ordered and brought my body down to the ground, positioning me between his legs with my back against his chest. "I've got you," he whispered.

"Do it, bro. I'll hold her. We'll need her if we get attacked again," Connor told his brother, encouraging him to perform the minor surgery.

Kneeling beside me, Ryan took hold of my right arm and examined it further. "It must be deep, Tory. I can't see it at all." He gently prodded the area and withdrew his touch when I winced.

"Just shove your fingers in and see if you can feel it," I demanded, nodding my head in encouragement.

"Okay. Connor – hold her." Gently pulling the laceration open, Ryan placed his forefingers inside. Stifling a scream by holding my breath, I closed my eyes and allowed Connor to pull me closer into his body.

"I can't feel it." Ryan's frustration was evident in his panic-tinged voice.

"Go deeper," Connor told him "The last one was embedded in her bone. She can't heal with it in there and the venom will ensure she is weakened if the angels attack."

Taking a deep breath of his own, Ryan pushed his fingers deeper into my arm. I squealed as pain coursed through my body. As Ryan poked further, Connor whispered words of encouragement onto the top of my head. He calmed me and I liked the feel of his touch upon my skin. I concentrated on Connor's words, hoping to get some reprieve from the pain and wishing my consciousness to pass out but it didn't happen. My body remained hyper-aware, allowing me to feel every nerve sing as Ryan touch them.

"Got it!" Ryan called. "My finger is on it but I can't move it."

"Wiggle it out," I offered. "Or put your thumb in to grab it." A slight smile tickled the corners of my mouth as I watched Ryan's face turn white, then green, then back to white. He gulped deeply. Then, taking a long breath and giving himself a tiny pep talk, he advanced his thumb into my arm.

The pain was excruciating. Turning further into Connor's arm, I screamed into him. Tears filled my eyes and began to pour down my face as if they were torrential rainfall. Placing his mouth firmly onto the top of my head and enveloping me closer to his chest, Connor kissed me, apologizing for not protecting me.

Each move Ryan made within my skin caused the laceration to rip as he struggled to take hold of the implanted claw. I felt every internal tug, begging for Ryan to grab the bloody thing and get his fingers out of my arm so I could heal.

An almighty crack came from deep within my arm. "Oh, good god, Tory! I have the claw in my fingers but I think I just split the length of your bone." Ryan had become even more white as guilt overcame his features.

My arm was humming in pain and I was fully aware of the break. "Ryan, do you mind just bringing your hand out of my arm so I can start to heal, please," I snapped, then immediately apologized.

Pulling the claw from my arm, the skin ripped once again to allow Ryan's fingers to exit, holding the demon weapon. Regulating my breath, I calmed as the pain ebbed away. The five minutes it had taken to remove the claw had felt like a lifetime and as I pushed myself gently up on my free uninjured hand, I thanked Ryan for completing his almost thankless task.

Pocketing the claw, Ryan stood and wiped my blood from his hand. As he did so, he threw his brother a side- glance wink and turned away from us.

"So I guess he knows something happened between us," I said, turning within Connor's arms.

"I guess so," Connor smirked, leaning forward as he re-adjusted his arms around me and kissed me hard.

I absorbed his kiss: my lips opened to encourage him to enter my mouth and allow his tongue to find mine. My arm was tingling, fast somatic sensations jolted from the inside of my body and out toward the opened skin, indicating its now uninhibited ability to heal.

"How's your pain?" Connor asked, against my lips.

"Gone!" I smiled against his mouth. "Only tingling."

"Are you sure it is the healing tingling you are feeling and not the side effects from my kisses?" he asked, keeping his lips lightly on mine.

"Nope," I giggled. "I do not get tingling in my arm when you kiss me." I continued struggling to talk and kiss at the same time.

Breaking our kiss, Connor stared into my eyes. "What do you feel then?" he questioned.

"Butterflies," I admitted. "In my stomach."

"Me too," he concurred, and leant forward to claim my lips again.

Moments passed and I was lost in him. I had forgotten where I was or what I should have been doing. All that mattered right now was Connor; was us.

A loud, abrupt cough brought our attention back to the present.

"If you two love birds have finished eating each other's faces, I would appreciate some help with these oncoming angels." Ryan was trying to avoid eye contact with both Connor and me. We giggled like school kids as Connor stood and pulled me up with him.

"I knew they would be close behind," I said to the brothers. "It's further proof that heaven and hell are working together."

"How's the arm?" Ryan asked.

"Healing. It's fine, thank you. Might invest in some longer armor," I replied. "Come – stay together and let's try to get to the portal. I am expecting the daggers from the angels since there are eight of them standing there."

I was correct. Eight angels, each grasping a dagger. I rolled my eyes as we made our way closer to the portal. It was going to be become pretty boring if, after every harvest, I was to be clawed by a demon and stabbed by an angel with a glorified glow-stick.

To my right, Connor had notched his arrow and held it ready to lift and fire. Ryan's sword was drawn. Taking my sai from my waistband, I turned to Connor.

"Do you want to start this off? Hit as many as you can in quick succession. The light force in the daggers weakens as their numbers decrease," I told him.

"Sure," he answered, unleashing one of his sexy grins and a wink in my direction.

I smiled briefly as I heard Ryan let out an over-exaggerated huff behind me.

"Behave!" I mouthed back to Ryan.

"Connor, just shoot! They are expecting me to try and talk to them first, as I always try to do. I am tired of talking, just shoot the bastards," I lightly demanded, raking my fingers through my wayward fringe and replacing it back behind my ear.

"As you wish, babe. My pleasure," Connor replied, lifting his bow upward and aiming towards the horde of cutlery-wielding angels.

Before the angels could contemplate what was happening, a portal released from heaven fell to receive the first ascended angel. The dagger fell from his hand as he ascended, thus having the reaction I wanted – a reduction of the light force in the angel's hands. Immediately after the first ascension, a second portal opened and another angel buggered off to where he belonged.

"Ryan," I spun radially toward him. "We need one of those daggers to take back to Porter to investigate how it works," I said, rotating quickly back to face the six angels before me.

"Two down!" Connor called, notching his third arrow.

"Perfect – keep going," I replied.

The arrow sped past me, aimed perfectly at one of the angels. However, eventually using the space within their brains, the angels realized that we had opted for the straight 'cull' attack.

Moving to avoid the deadly arrow, the angels clustered together and brought the remaining six daggers to form one light-force stream. This time, instead of directing it at me, the angels pointed their daggers at Connor. I pre-empted this move, as I didn't think that the angels were stupid enough to allow Connor to ascend them all.

Unfurling my wings, I stepped in front of Connor with my wings towards the angel attackers and facing Connor.

"Hi, babe," he said, with an innocent smirk overtaking his face.

I shook my head, waiting for the blows from the daggers. "You're an idiot," I smiled back, as the stream hit my wings and deflected away from Connor. Calling Ryan to also stay behind my wings, I relayed my plans to the hybrids.

"Use me as a shield. Keeping firing your arrows and Connor, I would be grateful if you would hit the angel you missed with the last shot," I teased.

He shrugged and stepped forward into me. "I promise not to miss again," he said, gently placing a chaste kiss on my lips before readying his arrow.

With every step back I took to close the gap between the angels and us, Connor let fly his arrows. The light-force stream was relentless and I could feel my strength starting to waiver.

"How many more?" I questioned Ryan.

"Three," he answered. "Two daggers have been dropped. As soon as I can, I'll retrieve them," he continued.

"Okay. How close are we to them?" I turned to Connor.

"A couple more steps and you will be giving them a lap-dance," he responded.

I rolled my eyes at him with a smirk and he replied with a wink.

"On my mark, I will turn to fight. Ryan – get the daggers, and Connor – just kill things," I said, preparing my sai as I counted down from 3, 2, 1 – "NOW!"

Turning rapidly, I realized how close we had gotten and a lap-dance was not far wrong. Lunging forward, I began fighting the angel before me. The light force was weakened by the small number of daggers now that the angels were fighting individually, rather than as a collective.

I received a few hits on the bare skin on my thighs and upper hands before the angel slipped his guard and exposed his chest. My sai slid easily into his chest cavity and as the tip pierced his heart, the light force within it began to escape and allow itself to be absorbed by my weapon.

"Goodbye," I taunted. "Bid your master good day from us." As I retrieved my sai out of the bloodied chest wound, the angel ascended quickly, leaving his comrades to continuing fighting.

Connor dispatched the seventh angel as it charged me while Ryan was locked in battle with angel number eight. Three daggers were abandoned on ascension. Placing them in my waistband, I turned once more to Ryan. He was fighting hard. Connor had his arrow trained on the angel but was struggling to find a clear shot.

I gasped as Ryan's sword landed at my feet: it had been knocked out of his hand by the angel's light force. Preparing to step forward, I heard a blood-curdling scream. Dust and debris from the ground restricted my view as Connor and I tried to find Ryan.

Suddenly, a portal from heaven slipped silently down and picked up its failed angel. Relief coursed through me. Rushing forward, Connor and I found Ryan. He was on one knee, several burn wounds were scattered over his body and in his hand he held the demon claw he had retrieved from my arm.

"Turns out…" He puffed his words trying to regain his breath. "That demon venom ascends angels pretty quickly." He smirked and accepted the high five offered by Connor.

Temporarily celebrating our success of the ascension and descension of our attackers, we left the area before any further attacks came.

Devon and Elenor had now stepped back through the portal from purgatory to see if we needed help.

"The harvested souls are safely with Mia and Henry," Devon reported. "Any problems?" he enquired.

"Nothing we couldn't handle," Connor replied, nudging his brother.

"One claw removed from my arm and three daggers collected. I'm hoping Jason can shed some light on the development of these weapons," I elucidated.

"We do know now that demon venom will ascend angels with little contact. I was de-weaponed of my sword and used the claw instead. Slit the angel through the heart and it ascended in seconds," Ryan reported.

"That is good to know!" Devon retorted.

"Come," Elenor motioned to the group. "We can continue the discussion back in purgatory."

Before following her back, I took one more look around. Demons and angels were continuing their harvesting as the war raged on. A lot of men and women were unnecessarily losing their lives today and it saddened me.

"You okay?" Connor asked, taking my hand.

"Yes. I just find all of this so sad," I said, squeezing his hand gently.

Bringing up my hand to his mouth, Connor kissed the back of it, softly. "There is nothing you can do, Tory, to influence the humans. They are independently minded, I'm afraid, but at least they have you fighting for them and protecting their souls after death. I, for one, think you are awesome."

Embarrassment coursed through me and I felt my cheeks flush. "Thank you," I whispered coyly, keeping my eyes downwards. With my hand in Connor's, we left the human realm and re-entered purgatory.

Chapter 22

Arriving back, we were met by the usual team: Henry buzzed close to me waiting for a rundown of the harvesting, while Porter was immediately drawn to Connor and Ryan, eyeballing the daggers that Ryan held in his hand. Henry informed me that Mia had the newly harvested souls and was in the process of information-giving and finding them residence. Apparently, Sargent Harris was keen to talk to me but, as per my usual routine, I needed to clean myself up and rest for an hour or so.

Briefly talking with Elenor, Devon, and the twins before we departed from each other, I expressed my gratitude for their help and my relief that we were successful in our harvest. Elenor had insisted that we should all meet for dinner that evening, as she wanted to ensure we were having a good meal to compensate for the fighting we had undertaken. I readily agreed. I love it when someone else cooks. I was a horrendous cook and I did not have the patience to learn how to do it better.

"I will come and pick you up for dinner, if you like," Connor said softly, touching my arm and causing a torrent of goose bumps to erupt with excitement from his touch.

"Thank you," I agreed, already excited with the anticipation of his visit. Taking a step forward, he kissed me swiftly on the cheek.

"See you later," he smiled, as I melted and continued to walk with Henry who was commanding my attention.

"Each volunteer has been measured and work has begun on the armour; Jason is currently working on an antidote for the demon venom. He says it is very close to a venomous spider in the human domain," Henry recounted, frequently looking up from his notebook to avoid tripping over or misguiding his step.

"What about the skills assessment aspect for each person? I want to ensure that everyone has either some sort of skill we can use to our advantage or ascertain who we need to train. I think more archers would be of benefit. Connor's ability to reduce large numbers of oncoming enemies is extremely helpful when fighting hand to hand," I explained.

"I have organised a meeting in two days with all volunteers," he responded. "You will receive the debrief then."

"What would I do without you, Henry?" I asked, giving him a cheesy grin. "It is a weight off of my mind to know that you have everything under control."

"You are very welcome, Tory, and it really is my pleasure. Now, I shall take my leave so you may clean up a bit. You have dried blood, dirt, and what I believe is demon black blood covering the majority of you. It's gross!" Henry bowed, as he always did, and left me at the bottom of the hill leading to my home.

"He just didn't want to walk up the hill," I mumbled to myself as I watched him walk away.

Once through the door, I began my routine: blinds down, clothes off, wings unfurled and fangs descending. I sighed as I did each time the real me was given the opportunity to escape. Giving myself a general, visual once-over, I noted a few healing scars alongside the mud littering my skin. The deep wound on my arm was healed; however, dry blood and venom fragments clung stubbornly to my skin.

Fetching myself a glass of wine, I took it into the bathroom to sip while I showered. Standing underneath the waterfall of warm water, I gave permission for it to cleanse me and to wash the day from my skin.

Liquid mud mixed with reconstituted blood and water accumulated at my feet before circling the drain and disappearing.

Wrapping an extra-large, fluffy towel around my naked body, I sat on the downturned toilet seat and drank the majority of my wine in a couple of gulps. I had about an hour before I expected Connor to arrive: therefore, I decided to treat myself to another glass of wine and relax.

Lying on my back in the middle of my bed, I stared at the ceiling, debating whether I should close my eyes and get some sleep or use the time to get myself ready. Making up my mind to allow my body to recharge after such an intensive fight, I set my alarm for half an hour and snuggled under my duvet, closing my eyes.

I was woken by heavy banging on my front door. Still encased in my towel, I answered the door, chancing a look at the wall clock as I did so. I had slept the whole hour and Connor was bang on time. Being rapidly jolted from my sleep was not a good start to this evening, I felt more exhausted now then I had done pre-nap.

Connor stood the other side of the door, leaning against the side of the frame. He wore a white shirt with the first few buttons open, teasing me with the tiniest view of his muscular chest. His trousers of choice were tight, ripped jeans, accompanied by Dr Martins. Raw sex stood dripping on my doorstep and I was mesmerized, visually taking in every inch of the hybrid as he smirked.

"I am fine taking you to dinner in your towel, but I am sure that my parents would object," Connor said, knowing that I was drinking him in as he stood in front of me.

"I fell asleep," I admitted, eventually finding his eyes.

"I can see that. Can I come in?" he asked, looking me up and down as I stood with just enough towel to cover the bits it needed to.

I nodded but before I had the chance to move, Connor had his hand in my hair, his arm around my waist and his lips on mine. Lifting my body off from the ground and closer into him, he walked into the hallway, kicking the door shut behind him with his booted foot.

I revelled in his kiss, enjoying the closeness of our bodies and his touch as his hand gently balled up my damp, wayward hair. Keeping me in his arms, Connor maneuvered to place my back against the wall and pressed his body into mine. The passion between us rose rapidly as our kiss deepened, allowing our tongues to come together.

"Tory," Connor whispered against my lips before releasing them, so he could speak. "If I had known that you would have been here waiting to harvest me, I would have died years ago."

Devoid of words, I smiled at him and reclaimed his lips. My hands explored his muscular arms, travelling to run my fingers over his chest through his shirt. He felt exceptional to touch. Sliding my fingers underneath one of his buttons, I popped it open with ease, followed by the second, third and fourth until I had exposed his chest to my eagerly waiting eyes.

My hand glided effortlessly over his collar bone, continuing down over his pectoral muscles and abs. Bending forward, I placed light kisses into the middle of his chest and gradually worked my way over his clavicle. Connor relaxed his head, allowing it to drop back, exposing his neck. Taking the opportunity, I grazed my kisses up his neck. Appreciating his body, I took my time to breath him in.

He never took his hands away from my body. He kept me close and placing my legs around his hips, he leant further into me and moaned with pleasure. Bringing his head forward, Connor met my eyes with his and my mouth with his own.

"Are you two coming to dinner or are you just going to suck each other's faces all night?"

The voice echoed from the communication intercom Porter had installed to all the TV's. I froze and stared at Connor.

"Sorry," he whispered and placed me gently on my feet.

"I will go get ready then," I told him, adjusting the towel around me and tucking a stray hair behind my ears.

"Okay. I will go see what he wants and – Tory…" Connor paused. "You look beautiful." Winking then turning away from me, Connor began rebuttoning his shirt as he entered the lounge.

"Brother! Your timing is shit."

Revolving, I wandered back into my bedroom, retracting my wings and fangs as I did so.

Ten minutes later I was ready, killer stilettos and a dress: not my usual style but I wanted to make a good impression on Elenor and Devon. I pulled my hair up into a messy bun and applied some light make-up. Connor had given me a raving torrent of compliments alongside a vow that he couldn't promise he would be able to keep his hands off me this evening. Threatening him not to attempt anything in front of his parents, we left the house rapidly to avoid the sexual tension that was gaining momentum as we stood admiring each other's bodies.

Elenor and Devon had made a lovely home for themselves, carved from a rock not far from Ryan and Connor. A long wooden table commanded the majority of the space in the dining room. It sat heavily laden with cutlery and matching crockery, plus a beautifully ornate candelabra residing over the entire spectacle with its ambient glow.

"This is beautiful, Elenor. Thank you," I said, addressing her but continuing to eye up my surroundings.

She smiled and offered me an outstretched hand. "I like to keep my home a place of comfort and homeliness. It is something I learnt in the human realm: the home is where the family lives, therefore it should retain a family atmosphere. Come – I'll show you around."

Elenor and I paraded throughout the small house leaving Ryan and Connor talking with their father, whilst under strict instructions to watch but not touch the simmering pots on the oven.

As we visited each of the rooms, Elenor took me through her choice of décor, why the colours were chosen and where they were sourced. Devon had taken Ryan back to the human realm shortly after Elenor and he had arrived to collect the family's belongings. Elenor explained to me why she needed the numerous photo albums and old books that belonged to the twins when they were children.

Ten minutes had passed when Devon caught up with us in his study. He likes to read and ensured that the majority of his literature accompanied him to purgatory.

"Elenor!" he yelled, as he burst through the study. "The big pan is bubbling all over the oven – what shall I do?" he asked, with concern etched over his features.

"I will come," she told him, gently indicating for us all to move out of the way so she could attend to her pots. "Take Tory back with you: I will serve soon," Elenor told Devon, before giving him a smile and ushering us off quickly. I, too, offered a shrug and smile to Devon as we headed to the dining room.

"You have a beautiful home," I said, trying to make conversation with the fallen angel.

"It has nothing to do with me, my dear. Elenor designs and creates the rooms and I do what I am told. She likes our home to be comfortable and welcoming," he said, speaking in awe of his wife.

Following Devon through the door to the dining room, I was relieved to be in Connor's company again.

"Hi, babe," he said, standing from his chair and walking over to me. I smiled as he planted a tender kiss on my cheek and whispered an apology for his parents in my ear.

Sitting around the monstrous oak table, we had begun our meal and the conversation had changed tangent from food to today's harvesting.

"I agree, Tory," Devon stated. "I believe that heaven and hell are indeed working together with a focus on your demise."

I nodded, finishing my mouthful before speaking.

"Twice, I have been attacked by demons who have succeeded in embedding these new claw weapons into my body. I think the idea is that I become weakened by the demons' first attack, the angels then appear with their light-force daggers. It is obvious that the demons are to weaken me and the angels try to kill me. I don't believe this is just because I harvested Connor and Ryan: it must be something bigger," I told him.

"I don't know," Elenor began. "By harvesting my boys, you ensured that Devon and I were not continually punished. If the boys had descended and ascended, then Lucifer would have completed that aspect of our punishment. Denying him that victory, I believe, has angered him further: hence the reason why we are here in purgatory. We are, in essence, mocking heaven and hell by assisting you to defeat their messengers." Pausing to breathe, Elenor took the opportunity to take an elongated sip of her wine.

I nodded sullenly. "I am afraid that you may be right," I added.

"It doesn't matter why angels and demons fight together," Connor interrupted my thoughts. "It's the fact that they are attacking you, trying to find your weakness, and it is obvious that they wish to kill you and break apart your domain."

We were all in agreement that we needed to ensure the domain was protected and that we were now assembling a small army of our own. Purgatory would have to bring about the termination of the alliance formed by heaven and hell in order to protect ourselves and the human domain.

The evening was pleasant but intense. The conversation regarding domains and strategy later developed into technology adaption, then Connor's favourite subject – sandwiches.

I enjoyed being part of this family group. They were so at ease with each other and it was obvious that they relished the time they had together. I sat in silence, listening to the back and forth conversations. It was hard to believe that I was sitting across the table from an angel, his demon wife and their hybrid twins. I giggled, earning a sideways glance from Connor, followed by his trademark wink.

Finishing coffee and bringing the evening to a close with polite conversation, a series of loud knocks then rapped at the door. Devon stood and made his way to the front door, leaving silence to descend over the table.

Voices echoed from the hallway but they were too inaudible to hear what was being said. Footsteps followed the sound of the front door closing. Devon reappeared, closely followed by Henry. The poor man was red in the face, breathing heavily and sweating profusely.

"Tory," he breathed, leaning heavily on the back of a dining chair.

"Henry! Sit! What is the matter?" Standing, I indicated for him to rest in the chair I had just vacated, unsure whether he would pass out if he remained standing.

Reluctantly, Henry sat, taking some deep breaths as instructed by Elenor before she disappeared into the kitchen. Returning with a large glass of water, she handed it to Henry, encouraged him to drink it first, before he was able to speak. The silenced table waited eagerly for the important information Henry had for us.

"Tory – there are souls that need to be harvested as soon as possible. Mia was watching the portal when souls rapidly became evident for harvesting." Draining the remaining fluid from the condensation-wrapped glass, Henry thanked Elenor and handed it back.

"It is not unusual, Henry, for a number of souls to need harvesting. As you know, I can't harvest everyone," I gently reminded him.

He turned to face me, with concern etched into his features. "Something isn't right. I don't know what it is but this does not feel as it should. The souls are calling for you before death; they are calling for help." Finishing the sentence, Henry immediately brought his thumb up to his mouth and starting chewing on the hard skin surrounding the nail.

Okay. Now that was not how souls behave. The soul shows evidence of release but never knowingly calls for help, especially not by my name. "I shall go and assess the situation; see what's happening."

"I'm coming."

"Me, too!"

I looked up from Henry to see both Connor and Ryan rising from their chairs. Elenor and Devon were also standing and were readily agreeing to the investigation mission.

I smiled at my companions. "Thank you."

Chapter 23

Approaching the portal, I could see numerous people listening to Mia as she spoke, obviously explaining what she was seeing, as the lights flickered widely within the portal. Gator and Wolf were in amongst the crowd while the remaining Rose Daggers were huddled with Porter, discussing something intensely, and Michael and Julian were deep in conversation with Sergeant Harris.

Making eye contact with Mia, I waved her over to speak to me, without the crowd in tow.

"What's happening? Why are there so many people here?" I asked as she approached.

Stress played across Mia's features. She was worried and her demeanour gave away her inner panic. "Souls are nearing release over the majority of the human domain," she began to explain.

"That is not uncommon," I interjected.

"I know," Mia continued. "But these souls flagged up at the same time and they are all calling for you. It would seem that they all originate from the same areas as previous harvested souls."

"Do you think this is a coincidence?" Ryan asked from behind me.

I shook my head. "No, I don't, I'm afraid. This sounds as if this scenario has been constructed to draw me out or to make us take notice."

Looking past Mia, I saw a sea of worried faces searching for answers. Slowly, I began to walk towards the portal, watching as the blue lights screamed my name and doubled in number.

Connor walked with me as I continued my approach. "Plan?" he queried, briefly grazing my hand with his own as they fell silently by our sides.

I sighed. "We investigate."

Reaching Gator, I shook his outstretched hand. "Do you need us to come now?" he asked. "We are prepared, minus the armour, but we will assist if you want us there."

"Not yet, Gator. I need to get an idea of what is happening. How long until your armour is ready?" It was going to make a massive impact for me to harvest with my own ever-expanding army but I was not prepared to risk a forced descension or ascension of any of them.

"Yo, Mike!" Gator yelled, jogging me from my thoughts.

As Michael turned towards us, Gator beckoned him over. Both Michael and Julian had finished their conversation with Daniel and walked the small way to join us.

"Tory... Gator." Michael offered his hand to Gator and then to me, followed swiftly by Julian. "When do you think the armour will be ready?" Gator asked, pushing his hand deep into his trouser pocket and adjusting himself.

"I can't let anyone cross without armour. It's just too dangerous with the light force from the angels and the demons' venom," I added, trying to ignore Gator's self-groping.

Michael thought, briefly. "Two days max for these guys," he said, pointing at Gator and the Rose Daggers standing behind him. "I thought that I would be on time until you gained nine more recruits."

"Nine?" I questioned.

Michael thumbed over to Sergeant Harris, who saluted back, acknowledging him.

"Oh, I didn't know."

"He insisted. In fact, they all insisted," Michael continued. "So we will need at least until the end of the week for all the armour to be ready."

Gator voiced his disapproval of our investigation trip without the Daggers. Appeasing him gently, I asked them to stand guard at the portal and assist with any harvested souls. I had an uneasy feeling and I wasn't happy to leave the portal unguarded.

"We must go. I need to see what's happening." I turned to Connor. He nodded in agreement, calling Ryan and his parents as he did so.

Gradually, we walked through the portal, one by one, and gathered on the other side in the human domain. Silence greeted us; an eerie, deathly silence that penetrated the subconscious, encouraging anxiety to come out and play.

"I don't like this. It's too quiet," I whispered to Connor, flanking my right.

"I agree. This is unusual," he replied, bringing an arrow from the quiver and notching it, ready for action.

"Be alert!" I called to the group, as we embarked on our journey towards the souls screaming my name. The closer we came to the souls, the louder the voice became, becoming more desperate until it screamed.

My body froze momentarily as I listened to the screams. I could not decipher whether I was listening to male or female, child or adult. It was just a frightening non-stop screaming. Finally, bringing my mind back into focus, I ran. The momentum in my legs carried me faster than they had ever done before.

I could hear the others following me, so I continued relentlessly until I realized that Devon was yelling, rallying for my attention.

"Tory – STOP!"

Eventually stopping, I bent over, resting my hands on my semi-bent knees to allow air to circulate back into my gasping lungs. "Devon?" I huffed through my rapid panting.

"Tory, you have wings! Flying will get you where you need to be a lot quicker." Standing beside me, he also took the opportunity to re-oxygenate his body.

I smirked, feeling very foolish. "Of course I do. I use them so infrequently that I forget I have them."

Patting me on the back, Devon shook his head in exasperation. "So use them now or I swear this running will exhaust us and weaken our fighting skills."

Feeling stupid, I watched as Elenor bade her wings to unfurl, agitating them gently to allow air to circulate within them. Devon followed suit and the twins were already airborne.

"Come on, babe. Get those beautiful wings out!" Connor goaded from his elevated position. Flipping him the bird, my wings exploded from my back, free from their binds and aching for their freedom.

Connor's feet touched the ground in front of me. Placing his hand on my cheek, he leant in and gently kissed me. "You are the most beautiful woman I have ever laid my eyes on," he said, temporarily breaking our kiss.

I smiled as I accepted the compliment and cast my eyes down, feeling the rose-blush tint my cheeks. Connor kissed me lightly on the top of my head. "Come – let's find out what's happening so that I can take you home."

I nodded, just as another scream sounded from the opposite direction to where we were headed. "Shit! We need to split up if the souls are in different locations."

"Elenor and I will follow this new soul, Tory. Connor and Ryan will go with you," Devon spoke up, making an immediate decision.

"This is why we need a communication device," Ryan mumbled to his brother, as we took to the sky.

"You know Porter is working on it. Don't be a dick!" Connor responded, punching Ryan lightly on the arm.

I was relieved when we finally found the source of the screaming: a pale blue light radiated from a house situated in a small urban street. On the second story of the building, a window was open, inviting us to enter and investigate.

"Tory, babe – this is obviously a trap if they left the bloody window open for you," Connor said, grasping my arm to momentarily stop me bursting through the window like a fat kid in a sweet shop.

"I can't let the soul suffer any more," I responded, acknowledging that he was probably correct.

Ryan infiltrated. "Tory, take a breath. Let's not storm in, but be cautious: we will save this soul, I promise."

I nodded and stood on the edge of the window sill. Peeping through the dirt-smudged glass, I was taken aback by the scene playing out before me. A young woman was lying in her bed, her eyes were closed and beads of sweat glistered on her body.

One demon and one angel stood either side of her, mumbling words into her ears. Before she screamed, the demon would slice her with his claw, ordering her to scream for me and promising that the angel would take the pain away quickly if she did so.

As my name left her lips, the angel intervened and gave her the pain reprieve she craved, healing her with his light force.

Ryan and Connor were either side of me as we perched precariously on the inadequate window ledge. "They are torturing her," I whispered. "Killing her slowly with demon venom but keeping her soul from releasing by healing her with light force. What the fuck is going on?"

This time I heard the skin of the woman rip open as the demon dragged his rancid claw against her fragile thigh, carving a huge, harsh laceration. Fresh, cardinal-red blood ran to fill the expansive laceration, dripping rapidly over her leg and pooling beneath her.

"SCREAM!" the demon demanded. "Scream for Purgatory!" he ordered.

Leaning over her, the angel whispered to her with a menacing edge to his voice. "Scream, girl. Scream for Purgatory and I will take the pain away. SCREAM!"

"Purgatory! Purgatory!" she screamed, torrents of salt-tainted tears raced down her cheeks, endlessly chasing each other. The demon placed his thumb into the laceration he created and pushed down hard. "Purgatory!" Her blue light was fading fast, indicating her soul was readying itself for release.

Placing his hands above the haemorrhaging thigh wound, as the demon withdrew his thumb, the angel pummelled her body with his light force. Immediately, her face calmed as the pain subsided, leaving her soul to re-establish itself again.

"Pin them to the wall but do not kill them yet," I said to Connor, through gritted teeth. "Ryan, take her elsewhere: her soul is exhausted and may fail to heal, so stay close in case she needs to be harvested."

The brothers nodded their understanding and I watched as Connor readied his arrows and allowed them their release. I entered the room, closely followed by Connor and Ryan. Ryan picked the terrified woman up in her bedding and flew out of the window with her, nodding to Connor and me as we prepared to confront her tormentors.

The demon was held against the wall on one side of the room and the angel, the other.

"You are an awesome shot," I complimented Connor. He winked and voiced his own opinion on how awesome he actually was.

I had the angel as my primary target. I stood in front of him and placed my finger on the top of the arrow that protruded from his chest, through his body, holding him to the wall. The angel grimaced in pain with each slight movement of my finger on the arrow.

"This arrow sits just millimetres from your heart, angel. One slight, accidental movement and it will collide with your heart and ascend you.

Do you understand?"

The angel brought his eyes up to meet mine, his face contorted with a mixture of hate and pain. "Fuck you, bitch!" he spat, through his gritted teeth. Abruptly, his head snapped expeditiously to the right, closely followed by Connor's clenched fist.

"Mate, that is no way to speak to a lady," Connor teased the angel, retracting his fist from the angel's bloodied face.

Spitting blood from his mouth onto the floor below, the angel spoke. "I understand," he replied, dribbling blood and saliva over his chin.

"Good." I turned to address the demon, leaving the angel hanging in situ. The foul stench that accompanied the demon assaulted my senses as I drew closer.

"Demon, the arrow that holds you to the wall is millimetres from your spinal cord, as with your buddy over there. One movement closer and you will descend. Understand?" I looked at the demon, teasing the head of the arrow with my fingers.

"I understand, Purgatory, but do you?" he critically answered.

"Understand what?" I questioned, removing my fingers from the protruding arrow. "Tell me!"

Sniggering like a bully in a playground, the demon smirked. "You have angered our masters with the decisions you have been making. We will be working to bring about your demise. Purgatory will collapse, taking you with it, and we shall be present to harvest the souls you have stolen to their rightful domain." Showing his discoloured teeth, the demon laughed boorishly, while breathing heavily on me with his rancid breath.

Behind me, the impaled angel sniggered, bringing my anger to the surface. I rotated rapidly and punched the angel's protruding arrow through the rest of his body, embedding it into the wall, piercing his heart, and spilling his light force. The angel ascended slowly and painfully.

"Since you are divulging the information I need, I will not descend you just yet," I said, spinning back to face the staked demon. "Why are you torturing humans? You were forcing the souls to near-release, then bringing them back to prevent it. That is a cruel practice and for what benefit?"

"For your benefit, Purgatory," the demon slobbered a thick, black drool from his mouth as he spoke, accompanied by a contusion of pain. The arrow lodged within him was obviously causing him discomfort.

"Explain," I demanded.

"It worked: semi-releasing the soul brought you from hiding behind your portal. Angels and demons all over the earth will continue to torture souls until you are snuffed from existence. You are an insignificant aspect of the afterlife and therefore should be aborted, like the disease you are."

Smirking, the despicable creature before me finished his sentence. Connor had made his way to stand beside me, positioning himself to introduce the demon to his right fist.

"Stop!" I caught his fist, mid-swing. "Let me."

Releasing Connor's fist, I allowed my anger to accompany my own fist, as I punched the demon on the right side of his stench-filled face, fracturing his nose. Charcoal-black blood-like fluid fell from his face.

"Remind me never to get on your bad side," Connor breathed close to my ear. He chastely kissed my cheek and winked before turning his attention back to the demoralized demon.

"Who gave you these orders?" Connor asked, towering over the demon in height and allowing his own demonic side to rise up, thus enhancing the threat he posed to the demon.

"His highness, the King of Hell: Lucifer, my master, and your rightful true ruler," the demon replied.

"And the angels?" I interrupted.

"They have orders from their own master; their god," he spat through his continuously bleeding teeth.

"Are others being tortured now?" I asked, remembering the numerous blue lights of near-release souls speckling the portal before we entered the human domain.

"Temporarily, Purgatory. Because you are here, the humans will get a reprieve until our masters decide to summon you again." He continued, "You are to give the hybrids back to the domains they are destined for, to end this, purgatory. This is your ultimatum or human suffering will continue in this manner."

"Over my dead body," I replied.

"As you wish, Purgatory!" a voice called from the window.

Turning sharply, I saw Abraxos standing just inside the window, and a thrown dagger heading for me. I smiled back towards the demon.

"Goodbye," I said, watching confusion spread across his features. Then, releasing my wings, I deflected the dagger, directing it towards the stationary, fear-filled demon. The dagger wilfully greeted the demon's flesh, piercing it with ease, as the blade continued its journey into the spinal cord of the paralyzed creature.

Opening his mouth, the creature screamed as the light force contained within the dagger choked him. Rancid, blackened blood cascaded from the creature's nose and droplets of tear-stained blood fell from his eyes. Relentlessly, the blood exited any orifice it found, creating a mass wave of blood and venom. Continuing to scream, the life-force of the creature poured out until he had been completely drained.

Flicking his bloodshot, frightened eyes at me, I waved; like the bitch he thought I was.

"Imagine how your human victims felt as you tortured them, you rancid bastard. Descend into hell and tell your master that I will never back down, and remind him where he came from."

As I concluded, the inner capacity of the demon's body fell out through his mouth, gradually bringing his feet, legs, abdomen and chest through also, as he slowly decimated in front of me. His whole body turned inside out and spewed out through his screaming mouth, chased out by the light force contained within the dagger.

"Abraxos!" I called his name, as I spun to face him. "Do you realise the demon venom has a similar effect on angels?" I teased. The horror that overcame his features led me to guess that he didn't.

"I don't understand," he retorted. Panic replaced the confusion and as swiftly as he arrived, he turned to leave.

"Hi!" Ryan said, coming to stand in front of Abraxos. "Need help getting where you are going?" he asked, before plunging his sword into the surprised angel's chest. As a trio, we watched as Abraxos's body split in two sections that dribbled apart from one another.

"Abraxos, you can give your master the same message!" I yelled to him. From above us, the light arrived as his body rapidly ascended. Stepping further into the room, Ryan made his way over to Connor and me.

"Nice trick with the dagger, Tory, but come on – that was a gross descension," Connor greeted his brother with a slap on the shoulder, throwing me a grin.

"It is a bit gruesome. I'll be peeling demon guts from my shoes for weeks to come. How is the woman, Ryan?"

"She is fine. Asleep on her sofa and unaware of today's events."

I was relieved that she was not affected by her tormentors, but livid that this was the grand plan implemented by heaven and hell.

"Your parents?" I enquired.

Ryan smirked and wiped the angel inners from his blade. "Kicking demon and angel arse."

"We need to discuss what this means," I frowned. "I will not be threatened. I do not wish to have the humans suffer every time heaven and hell fancy a chat or want to get my attention."

Connor stood closer to me. Retracting my wings to allow him closer, he slid his arm around my waist.

"However, at least we know the effects the weapons the demons and angels have on each other," he suggested. "Jason will be interested to know this."

He placed a light kiss on my forehead. Turning in his arms, I captured his lips with my own. Ryan afforded us a few seconds to indulge in each other before coughing loudly from behind me. I smiled against Connor's lips as I felt him move his hand from my waist and offer his brother the middle finger.

"Let's go and find your parents to see what they've found out during their intervention. They both have knowledge of heaven and hell, respectively, so their council will be helpful to aid us in proceeding. I feel as if I am currently running in circles."

"Do you know where they are?" Connor addressed Ryan.

"Waiting at the portal. Come – let's fly."

Connor and I burst into uncontrolled laughter.

"What?" Ryan demanded.

"You sounded like a right dickhead," Connor replied, punching his brother on the shoulder as he walked past him. "Come, Tory – let's fly!" Connor jumped through the window, releasing his wings as he did so.

166

"Bollocks!" Ryan muttered and followed him, wings spread and hovering just outside, waiting for me.

Walking towards the window, I became assaulted with the heavy smell of sulphur. "Shit! Connor!" I yelled to him, as demons filled the room surrounding me. I could see Connor and Ryan outside, immediately locked in battle. Drawing my sai, I prepared to face the encompassing demons. Standing ready to fight, I saw a number of demons create a space a few feet before me. Silence fell as all demons knelt on one knee and bowed their heads.

"Purgatory," the voice said, as a figure appeared in the sphere created by the kneeling demons.

"Lucifer..."

Chapter 24

Lucifer did not intimidate me. It was I who allowed him to rule hell, once I had created it for the misfits and evil souls I believed had no place in purgatory. Facing him did not frighten me: it only angered me further.

Lucifer paced up and down within the width of the small demon circle. The apparent Lord of Darkness had an extremely tedious and repetitive slow march and it bored me watching him practice his walking technique.

Tilting my hip for comfort, I sighed loudly. "You received my message, then?"

"Loud and clear," Lucifer's pace did not change as he responded, refusing to look at me.

Folding my arms across my chest, I became well aware that this was more of a display of demon numbers than a conversation about the solidified demon that had descended less than half-an-hour ago.

Eventually, Lucifer stopped pacing and came to stand closer to me than I really appreciated. Making a huge issue of my movement, I stepped back, huffing to maintain my personal space.

"Tory–"

"It's Purgatory to you." A smirk played on my lips as a frown occluded his brow.

"You – Purg-a-tory," he spat. "Have created the problem by disobeying my orders for the punishment of my refugee demon, Elenor. By intervening and harvesting the hybrid twins, you, Purgatory, have not only angered me but have created an imbalance within the domains of heaven and hell. Devon has fallen, therefore Ryan must replace him. Elenor is banished, consequently Connor must take her place. Balancing the equilibrium is of paramount importance, not only to me but to the ruler of heaven, also."

His monolog finished, Lucifer began to pace once more.

I inhaled deeply to replenish my lungs with the little clean air available in the decaying demon-stinking room: the sulphur stench from the prevalence of demons in attendance was overwhelming.

"I cannot speak to a moving object. Would you stand still, Lucifer?" I demanded. He complied with my wishes and came to a standstill.

"It was your wish to banish Elenor, as it was heaven's wish to make Devon fall," I stated. "Consequently, it was not I who created an imbalance but the fault of those who demanded those actions. You unlawfully punished Elenor and Devon's children to elongate their punishment: it has nothing to do with the equilibrium of the domains but everything to do with your malice. Ryan and Connor did not deserve to die so young and may I remind you that I was unaware of the twins and the curse placed upon them. I stumbled upon them when their souls called for help. I made the decision to harvest them before I knew their true identity and I will continue to fight for them."

Looking past the demons and over Lucifer's shoulder, I could see Connor and Ryan had been joined by their parents, all four fighting continuously to descend the unwanted demons. Briefly, I caught Connor's eye. Worry crossed his forehead as he held my gaze for longer than he should, resulting in him gaining a swift punch from his attacker.

Lucifer stepped in front of my gaze, obscuring my view of Connor. "Your stubbornness shall be your downfall, Purgatory. When you fail in your attempts to protect the hybrids, I shall descend Connor with me, where I will allow him to experience, every day, the pain you cause my descended demons. Subsequently, Purgatory, I shall make you watch as I pull him apart from the inside out, allowing him to scream for mercy but denying him each time."

Lucifer said no more. He disappeared quickly, leaving me with a room full of revengeful demons.

Regaining my battle-ready posture, I welcomed the fight to rid myself of the anger build-up inside me. Glancing briefly at the window, I saw the hybrid family still heavily engaged in battle.

"Which one of you will be first?" I addressed the writhing mass of venom-clawed beasts and as one wretched, charcoal cloud, they lunged towards me. Protecting my back and arms from behind me, I felt no remorse or hesitation in brutally descending the demons.

Beads of sweat formed over my body, glistening upon my skin like a million inlaid diamonds. I had been fighting solidly for ten minutes and, although I was not fatigued, I had sustained a number of opportunistic demon scratches. The venom from these superficial lacerations did not affect me as I could feel my body interjecting to expel the toxin and knit the laceration together.

So far, I had avoided direct implantation of the claws. I was not so naive to think that an appearance from the angels would not happen following this demon one. Connor and Devon were now in the room with me. Stealing a fleeting glance at both men, I saw that they had sustained numerous scratches but nothing deep enough to contain a weaponized claw.

From behind me, I sensed that my wings had suffered badly from the unseen attack. Turning to the wing-scratching demons, I began descending them, quickly taking them by surprise with speed and aggression.

The demons were becoming frenzied in their attacks, desperately trying to reach me to deposit their venomous claws. Lunging forward, I pierced two oncoming demons with my sai, simultaneously. Withdrawing my blades from their rancid bodies, I was hit with a searing pain between my wings.

Immediately, I knew that I had been hit with a claw embedded close to my spine. I spun to face my attacker and found it descending slowly, with an arrow from my hybrid protruding from its neck.

Connor was making his way to me with Devon in close proximity. Shielding myself with my ripped, damaged wings, I allowed myself a short reprieve to fill my hollow lungs.

"I'm gonna go straight in and get it," Connor informed me, as he came to stand at my back, bringing his arms around the bottom of my waist.

"Okay," I mumbled.

"Steady yourself – deep breath." Connor brought his left hand to rest flat on my back and, with his right hand, he prepared to enter my body.

Filling my lungs with clean air until their capacity was reached, I held it tentatively as I felt Connor's hand inside my skin, searching for the claw. I didn't scream, I didn't need to: every nerve in my body was screaming for me. I let the retained breath out slowly; one tiny, juddering breath at a time. Focusing on anything but the pain, I could see that Ryan and Elenor had joined Devon in keeping the oncoming demons away from Connor and me.

"I've got it, Tory. It isn't completely embedded but I do need to pull back a little. Ready?" Connor rubbed my back gently with the thumb of his left hand.

"Ready," I called over my shoulder, releasing the breath I had been saving. I steadied myself. Someone took my hands from me and held them in their own.

"Squeeze tight if you need to," Elenor's concerned face came into view.

I smiled my thanks and steadied myself, using her as an anchor. Grimacing hard, I felt every layer of the wound rip open as Connor brought the claw from within me.

"Breathe, sweetheart," Connor spoke softly, taking me in his arms and bringing me into his body. Nodding to her son, Elenor turned to assist in descending the few remaining demons.

"I'm okay," I mumbled into Connor's chest, as I felt his wings encompass me in a protective cocoon.

"It's healing?"

I nodded as he kissed the top of my head and hugged me into him a little tighter.

Ryan's voice echoed around us, alerting us to a problem. Devon had been hit with a venomous claw but the effect on him was severe. He was unconscious and Elenor was cradling his head.

"I can't find the claw," Ryan's panicked voice shouted above the noise of the descending demon responsible for incapacitating his father.

"Let me!" I rushed over to Devon and skinned my knees as I crashed onto the ground next to him.

Replacing Ryan's hand, I drove mine into Devon's body and frantically searched. Moments later and my fingers grazed the end of the hard, evil claw.

"Got it!" Yelling, I pulled hard in an effort to dislodge the embedded claw. Eventually, it moved with the assistance of a rapid wiggle.

Once out, I threw the claw away from us and placed my hands heavily over the wound. Devon did not seem to be healing as quickly as

I would have liked.

"What do we do?" Ryan questioned, watching Elenor stroke the head of her husband, offering words of encouragement to him.

"I don't know. The last angel we used a claw on ascended, but I don't know what will happen to your father. He is fallen, therefore he cannot ascend."

Standing in silence, we waited for a response from Devon. Nothing. He remained unresponsive yet the silence and the shallow dip and rise of his chest indicated that he was breathing on his own.

"We need to get him back to purgatory: Jason may know what to do. By staying here, we are vulnerable if the angels return." I stood and studied the faces of the people around me.

Elenor nodded in agreement and Ryan tenderly picked his father up in his arms and took to the skies with him. Elenor, Connor, and I flanked him back to the portal.

The portal was quiet. I feared that a multitude of demons and angels would be waiting for us on our return. Breathing a sigh of relief, I touched down, retracting my wings.

Connor landed, followed by Ryan, handing his father over to Connor. Both hybrids retracted their wings and awaited their mother. Joining her sons, the trio stepped through the portal, ensuring that no harm came to Devon as they maneuvered him through the small space.

Just as I was following in Connor's footsteps, I felt as if I were being watched: the uneasy feeling of eyes scrutinizing, concentrating, and almost boring into my brain capacity. Turning rapidly, I scanned the surroundings. Nothing. I traced the buildings and walkways, yet still saw nothing unusual. Shrugging, I pirouetted back towards the portal and, in my periphery, I saw two figures quickly dive behind a tumbled-down. abandoned town house.

I stood silently, my eyes focused on the direction in which the figures had fled. I was exhausted. Deciding not to give chase, I waited for them to come to me.

I did not have to wait long before one of the figures stepped from behind the ancient building. The person holding their obviously benevolent stance seemed young and timid, standing still, aware that I could see them. My mind fought with itself whether or not to engage with the dark figure before me.

"Purgatory?" The timid, humble voice of a male reached my ears.

Beyond my fatigue and my will to walk through the portal, my curiosity pushed me to interact and walk toward the semi-cowering figure.

"Hi…"

"Purgatory?"

"Yes, I am Purgatory. How may I help you?"

The figure was a man and a demon. Although I had my sai sheathed, I casually rested my hands on the handles of each blade.

"My name is Stephen and this is my girlfriend, Florence." Pausing, he took the hand of a young girl, still hidden and out of sight behind the building. A beautiful young angel stepped out and Stephen immediately brought her into his body for protection.

"We need help. Florence and I are being reprimanded by our masters because we want to be together. We would like to pledge ourselves to you, purgatory, to live in your domain and serve with your hybrid army."

My mind flashed back to remember the story of Devon and Elenor's punishment; their banishment to the human realm and the premature deaths of their children.

"We can help you," Florence found her voice to interject. "I can help Devon with my light force. Help him to recover from the demon venom. Stephen and I know what our masters are planning for you. We have been learning the newly discovered weapons so we may be of service to you." Florence stepped forward from her boyfriend but maintained a gentle grip on his hand.

"He was my boyfriend as a human. We died together in a car crash but we were harvested into different domains. Please, Purgatory – we are begging for your help." Stephen came to stand beside his angel, consoling her as tears gently escaped from her sapphire-blue eyes.

I closed the gap between us.

"Please call me Tory. I will accept you into my domain if you are aware and prepared for the possible consequences that heaven and hell may rain upon you. The information you hold will be of great use to us in purgatory but it does not determine whether you are accepted through my portal. My domain is open to all those who require protection from heaven and hell but if it finds that your intentions are not as you state, I will not hesitate to return you back to the domains you originally came from. Do you understand?"

"We do," Florence verified, as Stephen nodded rapidly beside her.

"Come. We should go before any wandering demons or angels find us." I motioned for them to follow.

We walked the short distance from the building to the portal. I talked with Florence about how she would be able to help Devon. Apparently as a full angel, Devon can recover using the pure light force Florence holds, as a pure angel herself. Hybrid light force is not strong enough to heal a true angel.

I was unaware that the twins had light-force abilities and Stephen informed me that they most probably had some demon venom. I suspected that the twins were also unaware of their abilities.

Stephen and Florence admitted to studying Devon and Elenor, the twins and me, in order to barter for help with information. Heaven and hell had been studying us, too, trying to find a weapon to kill us all and leave the human souls of purgatory freely available for harvesting.

I was just stepping into the portal when Connor rushed into me from the other side, panic in his face as he grabbed me to stop me falling backwards.

"Are you okay?" he demanded, searching my body with his eyes.

"Connor, I'm fine," I reassured him.

"When you didn't follow, I thought there was a problem." He kissed me hard and passionately until he realized we were not alone.

"Hi," Connor mumbled over my shoulder to Stephen and Florence. "Tory...?"

"Connor – this is Stephen and Florence: new recruits." I side-stepped Connor's embrace as he shook the hands of Stephen and Florence and waited as I introduced exactly who he was.

"Another angel-demon combo. It would seem that hybrid couples are defecting and heading our way," Connor whispered close to my ear.

"We should get back to your father. Florence is pure angel: therefore, she can help him. Did you know that you have light force and venom?" I questioned.

Connor was shaking his head. "Does this mean I could have helped my father sooner?" he directed his question to Florence.

"Not really. Although you could potentially help a little, your light force would not be strong enough to give him the energy he needs. The quicker I get to him, the less time he will take to heal." Finishing her explanation, Florence looked to Connor and me.

"Okay, let's go." Connor took my hand tightly in his, whilst motioning Stephen and Florence to follow through the portal.

Inhaling deeply, Florence and Stephen remained hand-in-hand as they stepped through the portal into purgatory.

Chapter 25

Connor rushed us to Devon. He remained unconscious in the infirmary with Elenor keeping a vigil at his side. As she entered, Florence immediately ran to Devon and knelt next to him on the bed. Connor followed her in, rapidly catching his mother before she grabbed at the young angel. Understanding who Florence and her partner were, Elenor acknowledged her fellow demon while keeping her eyes focused on her husband.

Florence checked Devon's irises, gently lifting each eyelid. As she examined Devon, she explained that it is the iris of the angel that holds the connection to the light force within the body. The colour of the iris is a definitive indication as to whether an angel can be saved.

"I am here in time: his light force is extremely weak," Florence told Elenor.

"Can you help my husband?" Sorrowful tears obscured Elenor's eyes before gradually falling down her cheeks.

Offering Elenor a small smile, Florence nodded and closed her eyes. Lifting her head up to the sky, Florence began to utter unfamiliar words. She brought her hands into her chest, coming to rest adjacent to her heart. She continued to mumble until, eventually, she opened her eyes.

Florence's eyes were immaculately white in colour, representative of the light force held within all pure angels. Taking her hands from her chest, she briefly placed them together. Light force spilled through her fingers and ran effortlessly over her delicate hands that vibrated with the renewed energy she held within them. Florence inhaled deeply before plunging her palms onto Devon; one on his forehead and the other over his heart. Holding them in place, Florence encouraged the light force to dissipate from her hands and to submerge itself within Devon's body.

Moments passed in silence until Florence removed her hands from Devon's body. Transiently, Devon flickered his eyes, exposing the renewed light force currently flooding through his body, healing and regenerating from the inside out.

"He will be fine," Florence whispered softly, her exhaustion overthrowing her balance. As she collapsed, Stephen rushed to support her, holding her within his arms.

Connor released his mother from his arms, aware of her need to continue her vigil at her husband's side.

"He will awaken soon. His light force is working with mine to heal him and dissipate the demon venom," Florence advised the family.

Connor offered thanks on their behalf, as Elenor nodded to her in acknowledgment, allowing brand new tears of relief to fall. Walking over to the newly recruited hybrid couple, I also gave my thanks and told them that I would escort them somewhere to rest before we spoke again.

Leaving an already-sleeping angel with her demon protector, I was accosted by Mia and Henry when leaving the hospital room where Devon lay. After hearing a brief explanation as to why a new hybrid couple had joined purgatory, Mia confirmed that she would house Stephen and Florence close to Devon and Elenor. This was a mechanism for support for the newly acquired angel and demon and also to ensure they were observed, to validate that their refugee status was justified.

I agreed, although I believe that they spoke the truth: Florence and Stephen were lovers in their human lives, torn apart by heaven and hell. To appease both Mia and the rapidly nodding Henry, I also agreed to question the couple further regarding the information they held.

Henry and I discussed the normal post-harvesting issues. However, I hadn't actually harvested anyone myself but I had gained volunteers. After a tedious twenty-minute discussion, Connor rescued me. Devon had woken and was continuing to heal. Connor suggested escorting me home so I could rest and eat something, reminding me that we had had a fierce battle today.

Once back home, I headed to the shower leaving Connor in the kitchen, boasting a culinary specialty I would love. I showered the residual blood from my demon-assisted claw wound, allowing the rosé water to whirlpool itself down the drain and disappear. It wasn't long before Connor knocked softly on the bathroom door to inform me of the food masterpiece that awaited me.

Folding my wings into my back and maintaining the length of my fangs, I headed into the aroma-filled kitchen in my wing-adapted pyjamas. On entering, Connor smiled at my attire and motioned for me to sit, whilst presenting me with a large glass of ice-filled water.

I drank fast, refreshing my mouth and feeling the chilly liquid cascade down my throat until it rested on reaching my stomach.

"Ta-dah!" Connor announced, placing a huge bowl of mac and cheese on the table in front of me.

"Wow! Mac and cheese!" I teased.

"With bacon…" he added. "The best mac and cheese ever – with wine." He winked, placing a large, frosted glass of white wine on the table and pushed it gently towards me.

"How are you feeling?" Connor asked, bringing his own bowl of the gloriousness that was his mac and cheese. It had been hours since our meal with Devon and Elenor had been interrupted, and I hadn't realized how hungry I was.

Swallowing my mouthful, I nodded. "Fine. I can still feel my body healing where the claw embedded but I have no pain." I paused, sipping at my wine.

"Connor, I've been thinking," I started, causing Connor to place his cutlery down and listen intently. "When we fight demons or angels, they either descend or ascend. They are then reconstructed or reanimated and return to fight us once again. I think we need to avoid descending or ascending and instead, we need to somehow completely extinguish their souls. We should not allow them to regenerate or the armies of heaven and hell will be a constant threat. We shall forever be fighting and I am tired of relentless fighting."

Pausing again, Connor and I digested the information. I watched Connor process what I had said: he was acknowledging me with gentle nods as he thought.

"Do you have any ideas how to do that?" he asked before stuffing a fork full of food into his mouth.

"I believe we could use their weapons against them, somehow. The claws and daggers affect their opposite number drastically, causing ascension or descension. Maybe, if we could adapt their weapons, we could successfully rid heaven and hell of their infinite army."

Connor had devoured his meal and moved his chair around the table

178

to sit next to me.

"I agree but, babe, just remember that Lucifer has threatened the human domain because of us. If we make this new weapon, it will have to be completed quickly or we will run out of time. I am concerned that we are potentially revolving in circles: fighting, harvesting, fighting..."

"It hasn't always been this way," I told him, pushing my near-empty plate away from me to the middle of the table.

"My plan is to revert to before I created the leaders of heaven and hell, when I used to harvest individuals: judge the soul and place them where they belong. By disintegrating the armies of heaven and hell, I have the opportunity to keep the human race safe and get the heads of heaven and hell back under control. Under MY control." I looked to the hybrid sitting beside me for verification of my plan and I was rewarded with an enthusiastic nod.

"With your own army, Tory, you could achieve this. Your army is growing in numbers and ability. The recruits are all loyal to you because you harvested them and they agree with your methodology." He threw me one of his cute smiles as he finished speaking.

"That is my other concern, Connor. The army. If any of them – including you and your family – suffer at the hands of either demon or angel, you will descend or ascend for eternal punishment. How can I ask any of you to do that for me?"

This was my main issue and it grated in my consciousness that an afterlife of torment could potentially await anyone who followed me.

Scraping my chair on the floor, Connor turned me in it to face him. Taking my hands, he gently placed a kiss across my knuckles.

"Babe, we follow you because we believe in you and what you stand for. Remember, when you harvest souls you give them the opportunity to decide their own afterlife: to stay with you or to become part of their intended domain. You cannot be fairer than that.

"The masters of heaven and hell demand that their subjects become demon or angel to create their army, whereas you, Tory – you have an army of volunteers."

Leaning forward, he kissed me softly. Bringing my arms around his shoulders I pulled myself close into him enveloping him into my body.

He responded by curling one of his warm, muscular arms around my waist whilst the other stroked through my hair.

"One thing that worries me: how do I protect the others in the army from the light force of the angels or the venom of the demons? Our bodies can metabolize both of these and heal us, but a human soul cannot," I voiced, enjoying the spontaneous head massage I was receiving.

"I'll talk with Jason. Maybe we need a rapidly acting antidote for the human souls to carry, similar to that of an EpiPen for anaphylaxis treatment." Connor leaned in and claimed my lips as he spoke his last word.

Pecking him chastely on the lips, I began a new sentence, receiving an eye roll in response.

"I need to speak to Florence and Stephen; find out what they know so we can judge our next move." I stood up from the table and regrettably allowed Connor's hands to fall from my waist.

Connor stood with me.

"Yes, you need to talk to them, but not tonight. Ryan and I will accompany you tomorrow morning."

I nodded in agreement with him. I was tired, as was Florence after healing Devon. Connor and I walked to the front door, slowly elongating our time together.

"Until tomorrow. Sleep well, Purgatory." Connor caught my lips and kissed me softly. His mouth lingered on mine, neither of us wanting to let go of the other. Opening the door behind him, Connor gradually started to back out, taking me with him.

"I need to go – before I can't," he smiled, retaining his grip on my hand.

"You don't have to leave," I shyly whispered.

He smiled again. "I don't want to. But I'll call in on dad on the way home. I will be here in the morning." Taking both of my hands up to his lips, he kissed them before returning them to me.

Closing the door behind him, I stood briefly with my back against the cold wooden door. My mind spun with the inherent thoughts that vastly exploited it, brought on by the antics of today. Renewing myself with a deep breath, I pushed my weary body away from the door and made my way to bed.

Chapter 26

Connor, Ryan, and I were seated around a small melamine table situated at the back of the communal dining room. Breakfast was in full swing for those who, like me, couldn't be arsed to fumble in my own kitchen for something to eat.

Souls do not need food or fluid to the degree that they did in human lives. Here, although food creates a small amount of energy for the soul, the energy the soul formulates for the domain is huge. The human souls eat out of habit, constructing a social aspect similar to that within the human domain.

However, I needed to eat and I was starving. In front of me sat a large plate with precariously placed food groups adorning it. I was gradually grazing through the titanic amount, listening to Connor and Ryan's conversation about Devon's recovery.

Looking up from my plate, I saw Florence and Stephen making their way towards us. Connor stood to shake Stephen's hand in greeting as they approached, then immediately introduced his brother.

Florence stood timidly, just behind her demon, before greeting the twins. Having been invited to sit, the couple took their places, close to one another.

"How is Devon?" I enquired, once Florence had seated herself beside me.

She smiled. "He is fine. Awake, alert and healed," she reported nervously.

"And you are recovered?" I asked, concerned that healing Devon may have affected her more than she acknowledged.

"I am now," she said, taking a freshly poured cup of coffee from Stephen. "Healing the light force of another pure angel is exhausting: it takes the majority of my own light, so I have to allow it to regenerate before I can call upon it again." Florence blew the steam from the top of the cup before taking a small, tentative sip.

Filling my fork to capacity, I began another question.

"What did you do in heaven? I mean – it doesn't seem as if you were part of the army."

Florence allowed her amusement at my statement.

"No, Tory. I was not in the army. I was– I am a healer, although I worked primarily on those ascended during battle. I had an endless cycle of healing and regeneration. I heard about you from the angels you fought and ascended. You and your hybrids are quite the talking point in heaven."

"Oh, so they do talk about me. That's good to know," I smirked, stabbing my empty fork on the remaining morsels scattered on my plate.

"The things they say about what they'll do to you are not good, but it's how I learnt what the army plan to do and how the daggers work. I believe you are in possession of two," Florence explained, tracing the rim of her coffee cup with the tip of her index finger.

Resting my fork on the empty plate, I nodded in verification, desperately trying to swallow my remaining mouthful so I could speak. Florence waited patiently, sipping her coffee and frequently eyeing the demons and angels around her.

"We do," I huffed quickly, gulping from the glass of water beside my plate. "Our doctor, Jason, has them. He is studying them to find out their qualities and whether we are able to harness that power for our own benefit. We also have a demon claw," I added.

"Whoah, how did you get a claw?" Stephen asked, turning from talking to Connor to focus his attention on our conversation.

"Ryan pulled it out of Tory's leg," Connor interjected.

"How did it affect you? There was a lot of speculation between the demons," Stephen asked, enthusiastically.

"It stopped me healing, making me weak and vulnerable," I answered. "What did the demons think it would do?" I counter-questioned.

"Just that. They wanted to incapacitate you enough for the angels to attack you, once the venom had begun to take effect." Without realizing it, Stephen had verified the conclusion the twins and I had made.

"That's a bit low isn't it?" Ryan spoke up. "I mean, Tory – if you were still fighting on your own, you would have had no chance of removing an embedded claw, let alone be strong enough to fight angels when they arrived."

Casting my eyes downwards, I shrugged my shoulders with indifference. Connor gently took my hand from my lap and placed it in his own.

"If it wasn't for us, Ryan, heaven and hell wouldn't be so pissed. They are retaliating because Tory made the decision to harvest us." Connor rubbed his thumb softly over the top of my hand as Ryan came to realise that my problems only really began after he and Connor were harvested together into purgatory by me.

"I don't regret my decision," I rapidly stated, not wanting Connor or Ryan to feel uncomfortable.

"It was my decision and I stick by it. Heaven and hell have fought for dominance over me for hundreds of years and have failed. This stunt they are pulling now – working together in agreed disharmony – is another attempt to make purgatory obsolete in the afterlife and I, for one, will meet them head on."

Finishing my monologue, I allowed Connor to encase me in his arms and kiss me chastely on the top of my head.

"We will help any way we can," Stephen offered. "And, as I said before, we waited to find you once we had gathered as much information as we could and remain undetected. Florence and I are grateful that you accepted us, Tory, and we also understand that defecting from our realms means that we will never return." Stephen had his arms around Florence: his love for his angel radiated from his face and I knew then that I had made the correct decision.

Ryan and Connor left the table to refill the coffee pot leaving Florence, Stephen, and me to discuss how long they had been dead and how they would meet up in the human domain in order to be together. The story was similar to that of Devon and Elenor: rendered apart by death but reuniting in the domain of the living.

After I had listened to the loved-up couple talk more about how they managed to keep their meetings a secret and their decision to find me, Connor and Ryan made it back to the table with freshly brewed coffee.

I relayed to the small group the conversation Connor and I had the night before. Ryan eagerly agreed that permanent ascension or descension was necessary to assist in our battle against heaven and hell.

Briefly, I brought up the idea of demon venom/light-force antidote, although Florence couldn't understand that if venom could ascend angels, why heaven had not considered an antidote. She remained silent for a few moments, tracing her memory back to whether such a subject had ever been mentioned or approached.

I was eager to catch up with Jason to discuss his latest findings and was relieved when Mia entered the canteen. After introductions, Florence and Stephen left with Mia for a guided tour of purgatory and their new lodgings.

"What do you think?" I asked the twins, once they had left. "Can they be trusted? Their afterlife souls are still so young that I believe heaven and hell have not been able to fully influence them yet."

"I agree," Ryan added. "They seem legit and I do not think Florence would have healed dad if they weren't trying to prove themselves to us."

"So, we proceed with caution and I would also like to have their fighting skills assessed. If they join with us, it has to be during harvesting, too. I want to avoid either of them descending or ascending back to face punishment for defecting," I continued.

Ryan slurped the remains of his coffee before speaking. "I have a meeting with Porter this afternoon regarding the communications devices and then I will assess them."

I nodded in agreement. "Ensure that Florence is well enough first. It took a lot out of her to heal your father," I reminded him.

"Sure. See you two later." Ryan left the table, promising to catch up with us to show off the new devices.

Connor plonked himself on the table in front of me, capturing my legs between his. "What are you going to be up to then?" he asked, caressing my legs with his hands.

"I have an appointment with the doctor," I said, with a huff.

"Anything wrong?" Connor asked, concern sweeping across his features.

I smiled at his concern. "No, I'm fine. But he takes blood from me to test the weapons on and today is blood- letting day." I sighed deeply. I could cope with wounds from daggers, swords, or from fighting but Jason with his little 22-gauge needle was prolonged agony.

Retrieving blood from a being who healed at a rapid rate meant that my skin healed around the inserted needle. Once Jason had enough blood, he would cut the needle from my granulating skin and it hurt like a bitch.

"Can I join you?" Connor asked, maintaining the gentle rubbing over my hand.

"Of course. You can hold my hand while the blood is being taken." Taking his hand in mine, I gave it a gentle squeeze. "I will appreciate it."

Connor and I left the canteen but somewhere, in the pit of my stomach, an unfamiliar feeling of unease rolled around like a wayward marble. Dismissing it as the side effect of a gluttonous breakfast and enhanced coffee intake, I maintained my hand in Connor's to help ignore the feeling.

Chapter 27

Jason's office was filled to the brim with an enormous amount of medical paraphernalia. Not long after he agreed to become the chief medical officer, he had asked me to collect his medical equipment from the human domain.

I had accumulated a fair number of hours sitting in the same chair, watching as blood tracked down from my antecubital fossa into a clear blood bag, tilting away beside me.

Today was different. I was watching Connor play with equipment he obviously had no idea how to use. Jason hovered in the background, straightening up his office once the whirlwind that was Connor had passed.

Finally, Jason had reached his pinnacle tolerance level and pulled a second chair close up to mine.

"Connor," Jason caught his attention. "Sit, please!" he gently demanded, taking a historical medical piece of equipment out of Connor's hands and pointing to the empty chair.

The newly disciplined hybrid sat heavily in the chair, then turned to me and winked.

"Can I have some of your blood, as well?" Jason asked, lingering over Connor with a tourniquet.

"Okay. Will you test it, like Tory's?" Connor asked, giving his consent by rolling up his sleeve and holding his outstretched arm to Jason.

"I want to see if your blood is different to Tory's and how it reacts to the antidote I have created. You have both demon and angel genes, so I'm hoping to see more of a result with your hybrid DNA," Jason explained.

Moments later, Jason had stabbed Connor and we watched as we experienced the first glimpse of hybrid blood chase itself from Connor into the bag below him.

"Oh, wow!" Jason exclaimed.

"I know – right?" Connor said, grinning.

"Your blood is... Well – what colour is that?" Jason asked, mesmerized with the flowing blood.

Straining to see what the fuss was about, I too was rendered speechless for a moment.

"It's black, with silver shards in it," I said, eventually.

"Cool, isn't it? Ryan's blood is silver with black bits," Connor boasted.

"Wow! Just wow!" Jason had pulled over a chair and sat, watching the blood collect.

The bag filled rapidly and it seemed as if the night sky was draining from Connor, taking the stars with it.

Connor's mood changed rapidly, leaving a tinge of sadness to take up residence in his features. "I was supposed to descend," he said, sombrely. "I am mainly demon, whereas Ryan should have ascended: his blood is the polar opposite of mine. It's lucky that, as children, we were able to heal quickly. Imagine trying to explain our blood to doctors." His smirk returned, for which I was grateful.

"I knew demons had black blood but I have never seen the silver of the angels. And I have drawn a lot of angel blood," I said, poking at the needle still wedged in my arm.

"The silver in angel blood is associated with their light force. It is hidden, or encased, within their red blood cells to protect it. Neither Ryan nor I have red blood cells, so the silver cannot hide," Connor continued to explain.

"Remembering what Florence said about you and Ryan having your own powers, do you think that, because of the colour of your blood, you possess more venom than light force? Therefore Ryan has the opposite, more light force, less venom?" I questioned.

"It would seem that way. I need to find out how to use them both, as does Ryan," Connor responded, wincing as Jason made an extended cut from the needle-insertion point to allow the needle to be removed before Connor healed.

Jason picked up the warm bagful of Connor's onyx blood and gently agitated it.

"I will test its composition and find out the demon-to-angel ratio. I'll ask Ryan for a blood sample, too."

Jason walked away from us and over to a small table, where he began labelling Connor's blood bag while mumbling to himself.

Jumping from his chair, Connor came and stood next to my needled arm. He winked as he took my hand in his, just as Jason approached with a fresh pair of gloves and a shiny new scalpel.

Cutting the skin of the arm caused the needle to fall from the tissue, allowing healing to continue. I was healed and flexing my arm as Jason began gently agitating my blood bag, moments later.

"So, is your blood like human blood?" Connor questioned briefly, looking at me then Jason, when I shook my head.

"We have no idea what Tory's blood is composed of," Jason said, slapping a label over the front of the blood bag. "In fact, we have no idea what constitutes Tory. She is not human, demon nor angel. I have yet to find anything to explain her composition."

"That is so cool!" Connor stated. "I'm going to find Ryan and assess the new arrivals. You okay here?"

I nodded and he kissed me on the top of my head before winking and leaving.

"Bye!" Jason and I called, as the door closed behind him. Gathering up my jacket, I thanked Jason and left the surgery to watch the portal for a while.

The portal was quiet. Gently, the fluid that kept my world from that of the humans moved in waves, glistening and rippling themselves over and over again. The human domain was temporarily peaceful, allowing me to relax into the unhurried rhythm of the fluid movement.

Sitting on the grass, close by, I pulled my legs up to my body and rested my chin on them. Before purgatory became as active as it is now, I would spend hours watching for near-releasing souls; waiting for the opportunity to cross and harvest souls to replenish the energy purgatory needed, but also to bring a new personality into my world.

Losing my thoughts and whimsically chasing the ripples in the portal, I was abruptly disturbed by a dark shadow walking across the entrance on the other side.

Standing, I walked closer, as the shadow paced back again, then again, and once more, as if someone or something was looking for a way through the portal.

As I watched, the figure continued its repetitive pace: left then right, right then left.

I was becoming dizzy watching so, deciding to explore, I stepped through the portal without thinking: no armour nor weapons. Emerging through the portal, I was greeted by a demon; a young, timid demon that jumped as soon as I appeared. Immediately chastising myself for my impulsiveness, I developed into my defensive stance.

"What are you doing here?" I asked the tiny demon.

Taking a step back and further away from me, the demon cast his eyes to his feet before slowly lifting them back to me.

"My name is Jonathan," he mumbled, in an almost inaudible voice.

"Okay, Jonathan. What are you doing here?" I asked again, taking a step forward as he, once again, stepped back. As I waited for my answer, the demon continued to observe his feet and my face, deciding when to open his mouth and spit out his words.

"Jonathan, what are you doing here? Why are you pacing in front of the portal?" I was becoming impatient with his silence but also intrigued by this bizarre demon behaviour.

"Please don't hurt me, Purgatory," he whispered, keeping his head down.

Okay – really confused now. "I will not hurt you, Jonathan, unless you attack first and then I shall descend you before you even reach me," I said, unfolding my impatient arms and observing the relief that took over his face.

"My master is looking for Stephen: he is so angry. Is he here?" he eventually said, eagerly waiting my reply.

"Why would you think he is here?" I counter-questioned.

"I heard him talking to Florence. They said they wanted to come here, to you, together. So that they could be safe," he stuttered.

"How do you know this? How were you able to listen to them?" I continued, gaining as much information as I could without divulging anything to him yet.

Jonathan briefly looked around and took a small step toward me, before speaking. "I used to follow him when he left hell. He caught me one evening and wanted to know why I had followed. I told him it was so I could see the human domain but really I wanted to be his friend. He is kind and the other demons are mean."

"How old were you when you died?" I asked, guessing that he was about eighteen or nineteen.

"Fourteen. I'm tall for my age."

I was shocked: a fourteen-year-old should not have been harvested to hell unless he was particularly evil and it really didn't seem as if he was.

Jonathan wiped his face with his hands and I watched a tiny black tear make its way over his cheek. "I am being punished because I killed myself."

My heart sank. What was so bad in his life to make him do such a thing?

"Come, tell me." Perching myself on the edge of the pavement, I encouraged him to join me.

Nervously, he sat down a few feet away, which I understood. Inhaling deeply and wiping more tears from his face, he told me his story. Bullied at school for being different; bullied at home for not achieving his grades. A child so depressed with such low self-esteem, this was hard to listen to. He had hanged himself in his bedroom. Despite his young age, suicide is considered a sin in some religions, therefore it was hell that harvested him.

Demons – true demons – are not fourteen-years old. They also do not cry or twiddle their fingers in their laps. My judgements are always correct and now, as I listened to Jonathan pouring his heart out, I knew he was telling the truth. But unknowingly, he had also verified Stephen and Florence's story.

"Stephen and Florence are with me," I admitted. A smile crept over Jonathan's lips and he let out the breath he had been holding.

"Jonathan, do you want to live in purgatory, too? Is that why you are here?"

He nodded, fidgeting with excitement where he sat.

"If you come into purgatory, there is no returning to hell. I need to trust you and you shall have to gain the trust of the domain seniors. Also, if you defect from hell, there may be repercussions from your master if

190

you are caught." I paused.

"I understand. Hell frightens me and the other demons hit me because I took my life. I am sorry I did that." Jonathan's tears obscured his eyes as he spoke.

"Your afterlife should not be a continuation of your human life, just because you did something that you now regret. Regret is the acknowledgement of something you would change, given the chance. Come..."

I stood and held out my hand to the tiny, sobbing demon. Stepping back through the portal, alongside Jonathan, I placed my hand on his shoulder as he stood looking at his new domain, allowing himself to relax.

"Welcome to purgatory."

Chapter 28

Deciding that the first person I needed to speak to about the new addition to purgatory was Elenor, I made my way to the infirmary with Jonathan in tow.

Elenor had not left Devon's side since he was injured. He was now awake and healing well, but slowly. Jason had insisted on keeping him in the infirmary for forced rest for a few days.

I found the couple chatting together over tea and biscuits. I couldn't stop my giggles as I recognized the very human trait. Elenor looked up and smiled as we entered. Devon turned awkwardly and motioned us over.

"Good morning, Tory. What a lovely surprise," Devon said, as I reached his bed.

"Good morning. How are you feeling?" I asked, conscious that Jonathan was hiding himself behind me.

"Better than ever. Jason is allowing me to leave here tomorrow, although I am not so keen on this blood-letting service he is currently conducting," he responded.

"I believe that we have our son to thank for that!" Elenor stated, wiggling her finger at the small round plaster on her arm. "Jason knows we heal quickly but he insists on this tiny little thing for two hours."

I laughed loudly. This badass hybrid couple each sported little round plasters on the orders of a human soul.

"Tory," Devon brought my attention back to him. "Why is there a small demon hiding behind you?" he said, straining to look past me.

Stepping sideways, I exposed Jonathan. He began to fidget with his hands while keeping his eyes focused on his shoes.

"This is Jonathan. He was fourteen when he died," I told them.

"Suicide?" Elenor questioned.

Jonathan nodded his head, maintaining eye contact with his shoelaces.

"Ah," Devon added. "So how has it come about that you have him? You seem to bring either a true demon or angel back with you each time you leave purgatory," he smirked.

"He knows Stephen and Florence, I found him pacing outside the portal. He has defected from hell to find Stephen and to start a new afterlife," I told them. "I wanted to talk to you, Elenor. I have never experienced a demon child. We have never had a demon child in purgatory and I am reluctant to integrate him immediately with the young harvested souls," I admitted.

"Jonathan, my name is Elenor and I, too, am a true demon," she said, switching places with me to sit closer to him.

Jonathan smiled, briefly. "I know who you are. You were banished because you loved an angel, and you have children. My friend Stephen loves an angel and that is why he left," he informed her.

Elenor allowed a smile to play upon her lips. "How do you know all of that about me?"

Refreshing his lungs with a deep breath, Jonathan told us how. When the human souls are turned into demons, they receive insight to the domain that is hell. Apparently, if any demon should encounter any member of Elenor's family, they must fight to descend them for immediate punishment.

"I don't want to have to fight you; I am only fourteen. I also think you and your family are brave. I would like to live here, where I can learn to fight to help people be harvested to the places they should go when they die. I hate hell and I don't think children should ever go there," Jonathan's sadness manifested in yet more falling tears.

Immediately, Elenor gathered the sobbing mini-demon into her arms and held him tightly into her body. He cried, taking comfort from Elenor and her unspoken permission to hold her as tightly as he needed.

Devon leant forward and began gently rubbing Jonathan's back, as Elenor whispered words of reassurance to him. Briefly, Elenor met Devon's eyes. He nodded once at her.

"He will stay with us," Elenor announced. "He needs help transitioning from hell to life in purgatory. He is not a threat, Tory. I promise you."

As she spoke, Jonathan's tears stemmed. Devon passed him a tissue to wipe his eyes, as Elenor sat him back down on his own chair, without letting go of his hand.

"Thank you, both." I stood to leave, vowing to inform Stephen of Jonathan's arrival and to convince Jason that discharging a bored angel would be a benefit if he intended to ask for more blood.

I left the tiny demon answering questions from Elenor as I left to find Connor.

I found Connor and Ryan putting Stephen and Florence through their paces on a green patch of recently cut grass.

"Hi," I interrupted, watching as Stephen received a punch to his side when he turned at the sound of my voice. "Sorry," I shrugged, watching him wince.

"Never lose focus," Ryan chastised.

"How is it going, Ryan?" I asked, causing him to cease his attack on Stephen and wipe the sweat from his brow with his sleeve.

He nodded before answering, allowing him to refresh his lungs after the epic sparring match he and Stephen had just experienced.

"He's good: loses focus sometimes but an honest swordsman and quick with his claws." Ryan gave his assessment whilst showing me three claw marks across his arms from the demon's swipe.

"Florence?" I watched her spar with Connor a few feet away. "She's obviously good with a sword." I noticed that Connor sported a number of pink, healing wounds on his upper arm.

"Yes, she is good. She can also manipulate her light force to become embedded in the sword, for extra effect. I would say that they will both be assets to your cause," Ryan finalized his report with his conclusion.

"What about you and Connor? Have you had any luck finding your hidden powers?" I asked, knowing that finding them would be high on the twins' agenda.

"Not as yet," Connor shrugged, joining us. "Stephen and Florence are going to work with us to find our powers. Florence has said that she can sense both demon and angel magic within us: we just need to find it." The wrinkling on his brow indicated his frustration at the loss of the powers he was unaware he had. However, this didn't stop him placing his sweaty arms around me and kissing me fully on the lips.

Pushing him away, I complained at his sweat-soaked body and

chastised him for being so gross.

Joined by Stephen and Florence, we seated ourselves on the grass to discuss abilities. First on the agenda: Jonathan.

"I have some news," I started. "Stephen, do you know a small demon named Jonathan?"

Stephen briefly glanced to Florence, then back to me. "I do. He is a young demon, about..." He hesitated, searching for Jonathan's age.

"Fourteen," I interjected.

"Wow! That is too young for a demon," Ryan exclaimed.

Connor was puzzled and allowed the expression to play on his features before he offered a question.

"How do you know him?"

"I found him," I stated. "Outside the portal, wandering back and forth, so I went to find out what he wanted."

"You went outside the portal by yourself, with the threats that Lucifer has made?" Connor added, not amused by my confession.

I sighed at him and rolled my eyes, choosing to ignore his comment.

"What did he want?" Stephen asked, expressing concern for the young demon.

"You," I retorted. "He verified your story and sees you as his friend. He has also just defected from hell."

"He is here?" Florence asked.

"He is. I dropped him off with Elenor, twenty minutes ago."

"Mum has him?" Ryan asked, deciding to eventually join the conversation.

Connor showed his confusion with a head shake, whilst Stephen became pretty upbeat about our new member.

"Thank you, Tory. I was going to talk to you about him. He is just a child abused by the higher demons. I cannot thank you enough."

Turning to Florence, he planted a kiss on her cheek and told her that he loved her. She beamed back at him, joining him in his joy.

"I told Jonathan I would take you to see him. He will stay with Elenor and Devon: he needs guidance and a mother figure, so they have offered to care for him." I was in awe of Elenor, ready to open her heart and her home to a child, without hesitation.

It is times like these that make me wonder why souls get harvested into the selected domain of hell when they are obviously good people.

"Shall we go now?" Stephen asked, starting to rise from his seat.

Placing her hand on his arm, Florence stopped him from standing. "Honey – after you have had a shower. You stink!" she smiled.

He agreed and he and Florence turned to leave. We decided to meet outside the hybrids' house in one hour, giving everyone time to freshen up. Stephen and Florence headed toward their lodgings, while Connor, Ryan, and I left at a more leisurely pace.

I sat with Ryan on the sofa in the lounge, sipping coffee and discussing Stephen and Florence's fighting skills. Apparently, Stephen used a combination of sword and claw, taught to him during the initiation of the new venom-claw weapon hell had just introduced.

He was fast and agile, whereas Florence was calculated and methodical. He recommended that they fight as a pair due to their complementary fighting skills.

I agreed. Ryan and Connor always flanked me, therefore Elenor and Devon, Stephen, and Florence would take position behind us, bringing our immediate angel/demon quota to seven, including myself. This meant that the human aspect of the army would slot comfortably in the middle of our heptagon-shaped formation until they had gained more experience in fighting demons and angels.

Connor replaced Ryan on the sofa once he had showered the morning's fight off of his skin.

"So," Connor began, making himself comfortable on the seat next to me. "You have angered both heaven and hell, so you decide to take yourself to the wrong side of the portal and return with a tiny demon!"

I wasn't sure if he was telling me what happened or asking me. He finished with a question.

"Why did you not ask me to accompany you?"

Draining the remains of my coffee cup, I explained myself and justified my abilities to cross the portal without assistance. I could tell by Connor's deflated expression that he was hurt by my omitting to find him first.

"I worry, Tory. I know you did the harvesting on your own for years but I am here now – we all are – to help you and ensure the safety of purgatory," he said, in a just-audible whisper.

"I know. I find it hard to break my habit of impulsiveness," I admitted. Moving closer to him, I offered my sincere apologies with a kiss. He accepted my apology quickly and, without compromise, expressed himself with his lips against mine. He claimed my moans of pleasure as his own.

"Brother – once again, your timing is shit," Connor huffed, withdrawing his lips from mine and swivelling to face his brother.

Ryan smirked and the brothers began a war of words regarding perverts and randy bastards. Deciding not to offer my opinion, I reminded the hybrids that I would be escorting Stephen to be reunited with Jonathan. I asked both Ryan and Connor to join me, knowing that they were itching to be included. I reluctantly agreed that they should also assess Jonathan to see if he would be an asset to our team.

Although I was not sure whether a child should be involved in such a war of survival between heaven and hell, Ryan reminded me that he was, in fact, a demon and that he would have been trained to fight.

Agreeing to decide if he should have a role within the purgatory army, I consented to wait and see what Elenor and Devon concluded about our new addition.

A series of rapid knocks on the door reminded us that an inpatient Stephen was waiting. Gathering ourselves together, Connor took my hand in his as we left for the infirmary.

Chapter 29

Jonathan was waiting eagerly for us as our small group arrived in the infirmary. Immediately, Jonathan ran at Stephen and was swept up into his arms, encased by Florence. I glanced at Florence: she smiled broadly before returning her attention to the demons before her.

"Verdict, mum. What do you think of this Lilliputian Demon?" Ryan asked.

Elenor sighed deeply before answering, flicking her eyes to the child-demon, then back to Ryan.

"He will be all right. He has been tortured since he died; partly because he committed suicide and partly because he is young and vulnerable. Jonathan must stay in purgatory so we can protect him from an afterlife of constant pain. He has also informed me of the plans Lucifer has with heaven. It turns out that he was used as a servant during the gatherings between heaven and hell: he has remembered everything. His information is invaluable to our cause," Elenor explained.

Jonathan was still involved as the middle piece of a demon/angel sandwich. His smile took over as he explained how he came to be the newest demon in purgatory.

"Good," I said, loudly. "That's what I wanted to hear, but he is at no point to venture out of purgatory, I have an almighty deep feeling that Lucifer is not going to be happy when he realizes Jonathan has defected."

Elenor nodded her head in agreement, as did the rest of the demon and angel family.

"Tory!" Spinning at hearing my name, I saw Jason bustling through the door. "I have found the weapon. It's perfect – look," he stated, proudly.

Placing a microscope on a table to the left of the room, he began adjusting the eyepiece. From a box underneath his arm, he brought out a multitude of syringes, tubes, and other medical paraphernalia.

Once he was ready, we were instructed to gather around him as he demonstrated our possible new weapon against demons and angels.

"Here, Tory – watch!" Jason indicated for me to look into the microscope. "This is hybrid blood. Watch when I add this." Taking a pipette, Jason placed it into a small vial of thick, burgundy-coloured liquid. Drawing up the viscous fluid, he placed one drop onto the hybrid blood.

Immediately, the blood cells began to shudder and split in two. From that division, the two halves rapidly darkened until it began to shrink.

"Keep watching," Jason demanded.

"Oh, my goodness!" I continued to watch as each half of the blood cell imploded, leaving no trace of its existence on the slide.

"What's in the vial?" I asked, interested in how he had accomplished this weapon.

"It's a mix of demon venom and angel light force. Administering this weapon destroys the internal workings of the angel or demon. The blood cells implode, meaning that they can no longer descend or ascend as they can't contain the weapons of their enemy within their own bloodstream."

"They cannot, therefore, access their own domains?" I mumbled.

"Exactly!" Jason replied, proudly. "They will simply implode and be removed from existence."

Revisiting the microscope eyepiece, I watched in awe, once more, as Jason placed more of the blood onto the slide and a droplet from the weaponized vial. Re-enacting the previous death of the blood cells, the cycle of death continued until the cells were deleted from existence.

"Wonderful, Jason! Absolutely wonderful. Please show the others," I asked, leaving him to set up the microscope again.

It took twenty minutes for everyone to view the new weapon. Connor was last to look. He, too, gasped as the blood cells disappeared from the slide.

"You are a genius," Connor declared, looking up from the eyepiece. He patted the doctor on the shoulder. "How do we use this?" he asked.

Jason shrugged back at him. "I hadn't got that far." He turned to face me. "How do you wish to administer this weapon?"

After considering our options and following prolonged discussion, the group concluded that our own weapons should be able to deliver the blood-cell demolisher. Currently, our weapons were able to absorb the venom of the demon or an angel's light force, so we had to adapt them to contain the weaponized liquid in order to deploy it into the attacker on impact.

Basing our weapons on the same concept as the venom-delivering demon claw, Jason believed that this would be easy to achieve in a day or so.

A commotion of shouts echoed within the small, elongated corridors of the infirmary. Connor stood to investigate but was knocked sideways by the door being kicked open by a person on the other side.

In through the widely-swung door walked Poet, with Raven closely behind him.

"Connor, Tory! We found her by the portal," Poet breathed heavily between each word, gradually lowering a bundle, covered with his jacket, onto a nearby bed.

"It's a lady," Raven added, assisting Poet to retrieve his jacket from around her.

"Oh shit, Connor." I recognised her immediately as the woman who was being tortured by the angels and demons we had previously fought.

"Is she dead?" Connor asked, as we stood by her bedside.

"She is," Poet answered. "She has no pulse. Raven and I tried CPR for ages but she never responded."

"Is she harvested?" Devon asked, bringing Elenor with him as he made his way to her lifeless body.

Gulping down the enormous gathering of fear-induced bile, I gently lifted one of her eyelids.

"No," I whispered. "Her soul has died within her body." My muttered words trembled as they passed over my lips.

Silence enveloped the room, as sorrow for this unknown woman overcame us.

"What does this mean for her?" Poet asked, soberly.

"It means that she will not have her deserved afterlife," I answered "Her soul was purposely stopped from releasing so it could not call to me. The demon or angel – or both, if they collaborated – have taken away her right to be harvested so that she could be thrown through the portal."

Tears glassed over my eyes. How could heaven and hell be so evil and calculated to use humans as pawns in this game of power?

"How long until the weapon will be ready to be used?" I questioned Jason.

Thinking briefly, he answered. "Two days – max."

I nodded in acknowledgment. "Ryan – what about the communication device?" I asked, knowing he had been working closely with Porter.

"Completed," Ryan answered. "The human souls have been allocated their devices and have received training on their usage. It is only you guys who need yours," he informed me.

"I want all devices allocated by tonight, with training given. Tomorrow, the entire army shall meet behind the lodgings in the north field. That is Day One, where we shall ensure all communication is interacting correctly and that we can communicate with each other effectively."

Ryan nodded in agreement as I turned my attention to Jason.

"Day Two – Jason will have the weapon ready. Again, we shall meet to train with these new additions to our weaponry." The hybrid army before me muttered their understanding.

"Day Three," I began. "We shall march upon the demons of hell and the angels from heaven. We will bring them to their knees, then wipe them from existence. I shall claim back the rights to heaven and hell. I will rule once again as the only judge of the afterlife."

Adrenaline pulsed rapidly within my veins, giving me a new sense of purpose. Humans suffer enough on their mortal plain and I will not allow their afterlife to be used as weapons against them and me.

Words of encouragement resounded around the infirmary. Jason excused himself back to his lab, while Ryan went in search of Porter.

Devon, now discharged rapidly from the captive infirmary, headed back to his lodgings with Elenor and his newly acquired demon-child. Stephen and Florence accompanied them as they began to discuss Jonathan's future.

Dismissing Poet and Raven, I thanked them for their attempt at saving the young woman. The men left quietly, leaving me in the silent infirmary in the company of Connor and the dead woman.

"We need to bury her, Connor. I cannot extract her soul now she is lost, but we cannot send her back to the human realm, otherwise her soul will wander inside her body for eternity. By burying her, we will place her soul to rest."

Without words, Connor took me into his arms and held me tightly. Gently placing light kisses on my head, he asked me where the woman should be buried.

Behind my home is a patch of bright emerald-green grass. Flowers speckle across it as if rainbows sat upon the ground. We agreed that this was an ideal location to rest the soul of this unfortunate woman.

It was decided that we would bury her in the evening, allowing the cover that the darkness would provide for Connor to fly her in his arms over to the flower-encased green. Placing the woman comfortably in the bed, we left her, temporarily looking as if she was in deep slumber.

"You know this is a true act of war?" I confirmed with Connor, walking home. "Angels and demons are forbidden to kill humans."

"I know, babe. I believe that we need to fight to retain the crucial equilibrium that keeps the domains functioning for the benefit of the human afterlife, and not the rulers who command them." His words soothed my consciousness slightly. I knew, deep down inside my core, that bringing war to the angels and demons had to be done. Connor just verified that it was, indeed, the only action that could be taken.

A ball of dread wound itself once more inside my gut, pulling my fears and worries within it. Churning rapidly, the ball grew in size until I felt it would explode from within me.

"Tory, babe. This is the right thing to do. We would not be fighting with you if we did not feel the cause was worthy." Connor's words were soft and calming.

Immediately, the dreaded knot began to shrink, allowing my confidence to retain its position at the forefront of my mind. It did, however, reman; just visible and hiding itself in a guise of a tiny marble, present but not yet a threat.

I sighed deeply. Squeezing Connor's hand, I quickened our pace to bring an end to this dreadful day.

Chapter 30

The ground quickly swallowed the body of the dead women. Taking her into its bosom, the earth cradled the vulnerable, lifeless body and with every spadeful of dirt that was replaced, the garden rocked her steadily to sleep.

"She shall find peace this way," I said, perching next to the mound Connor and I had created.

"She will," Connor agreed, handing me a bottle of icicle-cold water. I drank greedily from the bottle allowing running drips to fall over my hands and cascade gently down my arm.

Hunger toyed with my body, teasing it with internal cramps and audible rumbles.

"Hungry?" Connor jested, holding out his hand for me to take.

Allowing him to pull me up, I draped myself into his arms as we made our way to the front of the house together. As we rounded the corner, Porter and Ryan stood to greet us.

"We will go to see mum and dad in an hour, with Stephen and Florence, to test these out," Ryan said, waving a handful of gadgets at us.

I smiled at his enthusiasm and greeted him with a hug.

"Thank you, Ryan. And thank you, Porter." I turned toward the second technology-laden person and hugged him, also.

"Are you hungry? We are just about to find something resembling food in Tory's kitchen," Connor piped up from behind me.

Ryan nodded. "I could eat. Porter?" he asked.

"Yep – I could eat, too," Porter verified.

Leading the group into my house, I had a regrettable feeling that I was about to lose the majority of the contents of my kitchen.

"Connor, I am going to freshen up. Help yourselves," I told him, directing him to the kitchen as I headed to the bedroom.

"Will do, babe. Don't be too long," he smirked, disappearing into the kitchen with his two partners in crime.

I sat down in the corner of the shower and allowed the cascading, raging hot water to partially drown me. Hidden tears flooded down over my cheeks, combining with the pooling of the shower water collecting around me.

The ball of dread had reappeared and was bouncing effortlessly throughout my sub-conscious, mocking my integrity and confidence as it did so.

Inhaling deeply, I composed myself enough to realize that I was making a habit of sulking in the shower. Never had the afterlife been so complicated: the weight it created on my shoulders was causing my body and mind to crumble beneath it.

Giving myself a few moments more of my self-pity party, I started to convince myself of my need to succeed and reclaim heaven and hell once again.

Emerging from the steam-filled shower cubicle, I vowed that this moment was the end of my shower-sulking grief gala. I was determined to become the being I once was.

I would never have tolerated the diabolical behaviour Lucifer and his heaven counterpart now displayed. My lenience, over hundreds of years, had allowed power to build in their insignificant power-obsessed minds.

With the enormity of the fight ahead churning within my brain, I left my bedroom with renewed purpose. I was back; back to how I used to be. Ready to fight for what I believed in.

Turning into my dining room, I could see that the boys had had a successful forage through my cupboards. The rectangular oak table that I rarely utilized was heavily laden with the majority of the contents of my fridge. Down the middle of the entire length sat open packets and plated finger foods. Pausing for a moment, I watched the interaction between the three men as they ate, talked and played with the new technology before them. Connor was the first person to come into my home and now there were three. My life was definitely changing.

Connor caught my eyes with his own as he looked up from the communication box-thing Ryan and Porter had brought with them. Smiling uncontrollably, I made my way over to the table and occupied the chair next to him.

"You look beautiful," he whispered, leaning over to me to keep his words between us. I kissed him on the lips before thanking him for his compliment.

After sourcing myself some food and a large glass of wintery-cold white wine, I began to listen to Porter's instructions on the communication device.

Twenty minutes passed, and we were all scattered in and around my house testing the device out. It worked perfectly and it had been tested for access outside of purgatory. Apparently, during its development, Ryan had spent a lot of time in the middle of the human domain at night, standing the other side of the portal as Porter remained in purgatory, fiddling with the gadget.

I stood with my back to the far wall of my bedroom, playing with my box. Ryan was outside in the garden. Connor had made his way to the far side of the house and was perched on the bath in the guest bathroom while Porter remained in the kitchen.

"They are marvellous. Porter... Ryan. Well done," I spoke into the little microphone that sat gently on my right cheek. Both men relayed acknowledgment of my praise alongside Connor's comments regarding some technical issues.

"Everyone who will accompany me into the human domain has one of these and knows how to use it?" I asked, sliding my back down the cool wall and seating myself comfortably on the floor.

"Correct," Porter verified. "I will remain in purgatory to control the primary communication board, meaning that I can keep audio on everyone and ensure all devices work properly."

"Porter – privacy settings. How do they work with a large number of active devices?" Connor asked, with the acoustic echoes of the bathroom chasing him.

"Red button," Ryan cut in, sharply. "Then say who you want to speak to. The devices are named, not numbered, to make it easier."

"Tory?" I heard through my headset.

"Connor," I answered, stifling a giggle.

"Can you hear me?"

"Yes," I giggled again.

"I'm calling you privately," Connor said.

"I know," I replied.

"So no-one can hear me."

"Okay."

"I was thinking it might be prudent if I were to stay the night to protect you," he whispered.

"Okay," I whispered back. "But what do I need protecting from?" I questioned.

"Me," he jested. "I'm coming to find you. Over and out."

The communication noise returned to include Ryan and Porter. They were deep in conversation regarding remote access and battery power. I remained sitting on the floor, waiting for Connor to arrive. My stomach bustled with a million dancing butterflies, allowing a child-like excitement to build up in anticipation of his arrival.

A few moments past before I heard rapid knocking on the bedroom door.

"Come in," I said, via my communication device and watched the door handle as it effortlessly turned, allowing Connor to enter.

"Hi," I smiled.

"Hi, I am here to protect you. Flick the switch up," he said, walking further into the room.

Fumbling with the small switch on the device, I eventually switched it up, so I could hear but not be heard.

"Done," I managed to say, before Connor dropped to his knees before me and placed his lips on mine, encasing me in his arms. Although I enjoyed the closeness and kisses from Connor, it was not a romantic moment listening to Ryan and Porter through our devices at the same time.

"Porter," I flicked the switch back on. "Are we finished for this evening?"

"I believe so, unless you have any questions."

"No questions," I verified.

"Turn the PCD to off and remove it to end the communication," he advised.

"PCD?"

"Personal Communicative Device," Ryan answered.

"Oh, turning off now," I said, removing the device and switching it off. Connor followed and kissed me again before we left the bedroom.

Reassuring Porter that we were happy with the PCD usage, we bid both Ryan and Porter goodnight. Ryan slapped his brother and winked at him before reminding us of training the next day.

I left Connor at the door, deep in conversation with Ryan and Porter, to attend to the mess that was once my dining room. Clearing the leftover food and collecting the used plates and cups, I took them into my disrupted kitchen and began the mammoth clean-up following the hybrid feeding.

Bubbles developed and popped off from my hands as I washed crockery. I heard the front door close and listened as Connor's footsteps became louder the closer he came, until they stopped behind me. Bringing his arms around my waist, he held me whilst softly peppering kisses on my neck.

"Are you nearly finished?" he asked, turning me within his arms as I nodded.

"Good," he stated and claimed my lips.

Reaching my bubble-filled hands around him, I brought his body as close to mine as I could get him.

"Come," I spoke against his lips. "We have a long day ahead of us tomorrow." I broke away from his body and continued to hold his hand. Walking out of the kitchen with Connor, I took us both back into my bedroom.

The moonlight shone in through the huge window, encompassing the majority of my external wall. Without reaching for extra, artificial light, I guided Connor around my room to stand with me at the foot of the bed.

"It's beautiful," I breathed, glancing out of the window onto the domain that is purgatory. "Even when the moon is awake, the domain is bright and alive." I continued, I was always in awe of the energy pulsing throughout the domain, the consequence of harvesting human souls.

Next to me, Connor sighed. "It is," he said, softly bringing me into his arms. "Are heaven and hell the same?" he asked.

"They were when I created them," I began. "But once I had put the chosen rulers in charge, the domains began to change and I had visited them both before all the fighting broke out."

Pulling me down with him, Connor and I landed on the edge of the bed. "What are they like now?"

"They are very much how you would imagine them to be. Heaven is extremely bright and although there are clouds, the angels do not live on them and play harps all day. In essence, heaven is good: it is quiet and very white. Hell, in contrast, is diabolical, Lucifer rules with a disciplinarian attitude. He created pits of sulphur filled with fire as punishment for the sins of harvested souls, depending on how they died or lived their lives," I explained.

Connor thought briefly before speaking. "So Jonathan would have been punished in such a way for committing suicide?"

I nodded slowly. "I am sure he was. Hell is a very dark, influential place. Lucifer and his demons are cruel."

"No wonder he followed Stephen," he mumbled and I nodded in agreement.

"I will rule the domains when this is all over," I stated. "Both Heaven and hell are necessary components of the afterlife but this was not how I envisioned them to develop. Big changes will happen, Connor, and I will not fuck it up again."

I could feel anger bubbling within my veins and then pain took over my body. Doubling up, I screamed into my hands as my fangs rapidly descended.

Connor's protective hands encased my body, lightly demanding to know the cause of my pain as he swiftly questioned me.

Allowing the pain to subside, I lifted my head and turned to face him.

"It's these bloody things," I grumbled, pointing to my newly erupted fangs. "When I become emotional, they descend and it bloody hurts."

Connor smiled and, leaning forward, he kissed me then proceeded to run his tongue along one of my fangs.

"I still think they're sexy," he said, breaking the kiss and giving me his cute grin.

I giggled like a school girl, thus encouraging Connor to claim my lips once more. Heat coursed through my body, igniting the passion that was hidden deep inside my core. Rapidly, I began to tug at Connor's clothing, encouraging it to leave his body.

I was fumbling with the stupidly small buttons of his shirt, when Connor smiled against my lips and allowed a laugh to pass through them.

"Are you laughing at me, Connor?" I smirked.

"Yep!"

I shrugged and deepened the kiss. Extending my index finger, I encouraged my claw to peep out, unnoticed by Connor. Within seconds, I had gently run my finger down the front of his shirt and ripped the material apart, as if a hot knife to butter.

Retracting my claw, it was my turn to smile against his lips. I slid my hand through the shirt and onto his chest.

Connor reacted as he felt my hand on his body. Pulling away from me, he looked down at his expertly sliced shirt.

"You do not play fair, Miss Tory," he said, faking horror.

I smirked widely, tipping my head in innocence. "And you, sir, should not laugh at girls with claws."

Connor stood and removed his ruined shirt and allowed it to fall to the floor. Taking a step forward, he towered over me, forcing me to lift my head up to maintain eye contact. Kissing me from his position of advantage, Connor gradually pushed me back onto the bed as our passion increased. My hands grazed every inch of his naked flesh. Not satisfied with just one touch, I ran my fingers over his back, his muscular arms and toned chest.

Connor began undressing me as I lay underneath him, until I wore only my bra and trousers.

His hands caressed every inch of my exposed skin. Replacing his hands with his lips, his tender mouth cut through my inner core causing a reaction of pleasure to every touch.

I felt him smile against my stomach as a million electro-filled goosebumps rose up to welcome him. I had never experienced anything in my life that even came close to the euphoria I was feeling right now. I was becoming lost in my need for Connor's touch. Fumbling, I reached for his trousers and tugged at the buttons to help relieve him of them.

"Tory, honey – let me," Connor said softly, sitting up to balance on his knees over me and, more gracefully than my haphazard try, removed his trousers.

I watched his muscles tense and relax with each movement he made.

He was beautiful: so majestic I could not take my eyes from his.

"Let's get rid of these," he smirked, tugging at my trousers.

Raising my bottom off from the bed, he pulled them down and over my feet, depositing them next to his own. He traced my body with his lips as he raised himself over me. It took every ounce of my vulnerable and wavering self-control not to explode beneath him. He continued over every contour of my weakened body until he reached my lips, where he paused.

"You are the most beautiful person I have ever met," he said, before crushing my lips under his.

Breaking away from his kiss, I tenderly began to stroke his neck with my lips. His body reacted against mine, his hands grabbed at my hair and fisted it softly into his palm. Reaching the soft skin sitting taut at his jawline, I abraded it lightly with one of my fangs; not hard enough to draw blood but enough to cause a low, guttural growl from Connor's gravel-sounding throat.

The demon within him reacted to me: a red tint encompassed the whites of his eyes and, as our eyes met, I could see his concern as I pulled slightly away from him, surprised by this unintentional lapse of control. Connor searched my eyes, his face laced with concern. I smiled at him, letting him know that I was fine with seeing the tiny glimpse into his demonic side. In fact, deep down inside my core, my veins pulsed with an adrenaline spike caused by his inner demon showing itself and it was sexy as hell.

We remained entangled, making love and exploring each other's bodies until we finally fell asleep wrapped in each other's arms.

Chapter 31

I woke early and slipped my body from under Connor's protective arm. I left him sleeping while I showered and prepared for the day of training ahead.

Throwing the doors of the kitchen open wide, I allowed a cool breeze to whip through the house, replacing the stagnant, food-soiled air from the evening before with lightly scented, easy-to-breathe, fresh oxygen.

Taking a freshly brewed pot of volcanically hot, strong coffee outside onto the decking, I poured the two cups as I heard Connor stumbling into the bathroom. The day was welcoming: the sun shone high, although it was still early, rapidly encouraging the petals of flowers to creep open and delight in the heat it provided.

Glancing across purgatory, I enjoyed its peace and tranquillity. When creating my domain, I envisaged the serenity the soul should be granted in the afterlife and henceforth, purgatory was born.

Disruption of my daydream came in the form of a hybrid's arm encircling my waist and resting his chin upon my head. Connor wished me a good morning with a gruff, morning voice and a quick kiss on the top of my head.

"Good morning. Coffee?" I asked, turning as far right as I could to meet his lips with my own.

"Please," he uttered between kisses. "Breakfast?" He enquired with just the two syllables.

"Whatever you get," I jested, passing him the warm cup.

Patting me lightly on the shoulder, Connor retreated into the kitchen and began foraging though the fridge. Moments later, he re-appeared with a plate laden with anything he could fit on it: fruit, cheese, meats. I smirked as he sat.

"Hungry?" I commented.

"Famished. Stocking up on the protein for training today," he replied, rolling up a piece of ham and shoving it into his mouth.

"Connor?" I paused as he looked up and briefly stopped chewing. "Am I doing the right thing? I mean, I know that I have said this before but the human souls: it is them that I worry about."

Connor rapidly continued chewing and nodding his head, trying to swallow.

"Yes," he finally managed. "We have them covered both with armour and weaponry. Jas has an antidote to the demon venom and the angel light stuff so, babe, it will be okay. This will be an epic fight but we will win."

"We have to!" I countered.

Breakfast continued to focus around the upcoming battle, including Connor relaying his assessments of each human.

"We can use Jonathan," he stated.

"No, we cannot! He is a child!" I countered.

"No, Tory. He is a demon. Whatever he suffered in hell still does not take away the fact that he is a demon; a trained demon. He has essential skills for fighting other demons: you do need to consider him," Connor explained.

"I don't know. I look at him and I see a frightened boy," I said, worried.

Connor smiled and took my hand. "That is your problem, babe. You need to see him as a demon when he fights and a child when he is in purgatory. We shall watch him later and you can judge for yourself," he offered.

"Okay, I will assess him, but no promises," I said, temporarily agreeing to a truce.

Arguments and counter-arguments swamped my cognitive content. My state of reason stood precariously on the edge of my doubt. I would make up my mind later about Jonathan and while I sat searching the bottom of my coffee cup for answers, my conscious was agreeing with everything Connor had said.

Connor allowed me time with my thoughts as he finished off the last of his breakfast. Eventually my unco-operative cup offered no relief for my decision and I cleared away the evidence of breakfast. Shortly after, Connor and I made our way to the training ground.

It was still early when we arrived at the vast open space used as the training ground. Porter and Ryan had set up a long row of foldable wooden tables, straining under the weight of the weaponry stacked upon it.

"You are a day early," I said, approaching the busy men.

"We worked to finalize the weapons last night," Porter replied, as Ryan stood behind him, yawning.

"Gives us two days with communications and weapons," Ryan told us, mid-yawn.

I smiled at the men before me. "Thank you. You have given us a valuable opportunity to increase our abilities together as a group."

Porter and Ryan patted each other on the shoulders. We stood together, discussing strategies and possible outcomes. Gradually, we were joined by the remaining numbers of my hybrid army.

Armoured up and standing in the formation taught by Ryan and Connor, the army – my army – awaited inspection. Connor and Ryan flanked me, escorting me up and down in front of the troop. They took turns to inform me of each member's strengths alongside their weapon of choice.

Archers and swordsmen were prevalent, with some scattered sai use. Fully armoured and weapon-ready, my army looked quite the small but adequate team.

It was decided that Elenor and Stephen would fight in their demon form whilst Florence and Devon became their true angels: I wanted the army to gain extensive experience working with the unpredictability of a demon with venom and the angels' light force.

Ryan and Connor circled the group before the fighting began. I had asked them to focus on giving support and advice to those who required it. I had included Jonathan in the army so I could observe his fighting skills. Elenor was aware that I was interested in his ability; therefore, he would be her first target.

As my communication device was activated, I began to hear a muddle of breathing from the army before me. Rapid fast-paced breaths from some soldiers were contrasted by the more relaxed, slower breathing of others.

Giving the signal to fight via the PCD, I watched as the army began to react to the angels and demons coming at them.

Swords glistened in the morning sun, while clashing with the light force emittance from the weapons of the angels. The angels fought hard against the human souls, testing their endurance, strength and skills.

Connor, Stephen, and Elenor were also encouraging the fight to develop, teaching the humans how challenging a fight against a being from the afterlife was.

The weapons used by the humans had not been activated for this intense sparring match. I did not want to risk imploding any of my own army, especially as the evidence from the hits by the blades and arrows were present in the form of pink shards of healing wounds on the accessible bare skin of the demons and angels.

On the flip side, the demons and angels were careful when hitting the human souls, although scratches were obtained as proof of the inadequate protection of the fighting human bodies.

Once either demon or angel caused a superficial scratch on the vulnerable human, the human became more aware of the need to protect themselves in those areas.

Seating myself on a section of soft grass, I began my own evaluation of our youngest member. Ryan and Elenor had reassured me of his potential abilities but I needed to see them for myself. Jonathan was quick and methodical, with an innate ability to appear invisible, hiding in obscure places and sneaking up on his opponents.

Bringing the current training to a halt, I immediately dismissed everyone for a ten-minute break before restarting.

I continued to watch Jonathan's interaction with his comrades as he made his way to the ice cooler filled with bottles of icy water. He migrated towards Stephen and Florence, who immediately checked him over. He was the only member not to have suffered from either sword or claw. Other army members congratulated him, which left his chest inflated and his smile wide.

"Thoughts?" Ryan said, as he sat on the grass next to me, sipping water from the plastic bottle.

"He fights well, individually," I concluded. "He would be able to protect himself adequately against his enemies. I'd like to see him in a team battle," I added, once again casting my eyes over the young demon.

Ryan nodded as he began to explain that he would organize a team battle after recess. Apparently, the army had already been allocated into two teams; one led by Ryan and the other by Connor. The twins had intentionally split Jonathan from Stephen and Florence to gauge his abilities away from their immediate protection.

Once the recess period was over, Connor and Ryan took their respective teams and huddled them together for a team talk before they began. Connor had Jonathan on his team and was currently strategizing his role in the formation with him.

Taking their positions on the opposite sides of the fields, the two teams of hybrids and humans faced each other and prepared for battle. Each soldier stood ready, weapons drawn and concentration flooding their faces.

Both Ryan and Connor were relaying instructions via their PCDs and a wave of nods and verbal acknowledgement rippled through the formations, ensuring the communication devices worked.

Catching Porter's gaze as he worked on the soundboard before him, I nodded to him and he nodded back, with a thumbs-up. Turning back, I watched as Connor gave the signal for the fight to begin and the clashes of swords and fleeing arrows erupted from the practice ground. I focused primarily on Jonathan and the fighting humans.

I leant back on my elbows and continued to observe a well-disciplined and structured army face each other.

I was altogether impressed with the human souls: they fought hard and enthusiastically against their hybrid counterparts. The humans were managing to injure the hybrids as much as they received hits to their own bodies.

I felt confident that the humans would be an exceptional and unexpected asset to our cause. I had never expected the humans to want to fight but again, I was pleasantly surprised at the commitment they offered and support they gave.

The fight continued at a rapid pace. I found Ryan and Jonathan deep in battle. Both opponents held swords out to each other: they were poised and reacting to each other's attempts at making contact with their weapons.

What began as sparring practice soon became a demon-against-hybrid match. Jonathan's demonic attitude started to surface as he fought

Ryan: every swipe of his sword was meant to injure. His eyes glowed with a red tinge as his demon showed itself.

"Connor," I called over the PCD. "Are you watching?"

"Yes." he replied. "I will step in, if necessary."

Getting up on my feet, I afforded myself a better position to see the fight developing.

Connor had ordered the remaining army to step back and watch the continuing fight between young demon and his hybrid brother.

Moving from my position, I walked closer to the fight and stood at the edge of the group.

"He fights well for a kid – demon or not," Daniel said from beside me.

"He does," I agreed.

Ryan, tired of Jonathan's under-hand demon jabs at him, began to rain his sword down at the boy. Blocking and manoeuvring away from Ryan, Jonathan was becoming exhausted and overwhelmed by the hybrid's insistent sword. One by one, small lacerations began to appear on Jonathan's skin. Being a demon meant that he healed almost immediately. However, as his blood ran down his body he began to slow in his attacks.

"Connor…" I mumbled, again.

"Ryan has this, Tory. He needs to show Jonathan not to be too cocky when fighting angels or other demons." Connor turned and winked at me, then returned his attention to the fight.

Rolling my eyes and tutting loudly, I turned my attention back to the fight. Ryan countered Jonathan's every advance, diverting his blade away from his body and slicing Jonathan's skin with his own blade.

I winced every time blood forced itself from the wounds Ryan's blade was inflicting. However, Jonathan persisted in his ongoing attacks. His eyes shone brightly with the fiery red glow emitted from demon eyes: his claws were extended and his aggression was increasing at a rapid rate as his frustration at Ryan escalated.

Flicking my eyes at Ryan, I saw that he was calm and focused. He watched Jonathan intently, judging his next move.

"Ryan," I said, whispering over the PCD in private.

"Yep," he replied, keeping his attention on the small demon.

"You need to finish this now," I demanded, lightly.

Briefly, he turned to me and nodded.

"As you wish," he said, inhaling deeply and returning his gaze to Jonathan.

Attacking once more, Jonathan careered through the grass field. His sword outstretched and his eyes red, he ran directly at Ryan. Diving to the side, Ryan pushed Jonathan's sword away from his body with his own. Turning to face Ryan, Jonathan spun on his heels and regained his balance, before charging him again.

This time, Ryan allowed Jonathan's sword to interact with his, the blades clashing together, scraping along each other and firing sparks from the force applied to the metal.

With one fluid movement, Ryan had interlocked with Jonathan's sword and maneuvered it from his hand. As the sword fell to the floor, Ryan kicked it out of Jonathan's reach and stepped forward. He held his sword up to Jonathan's throat with enough pressure to cause an indentation on his skin.

Jonathan froze. He remained still and, gradually, his eyes lost their red tinge and reverted to the light blue that he displayed as a human. Nodding at Ryan, he admitted his defeat. Raising his hands in the air, he diverted his gaze to his feet.

Walking over to Ryan, I was joined by Stephen and Connor.

"Good fighting skills, kid," Ryan said, removing his sword from Jonathan's throat. "But you have to control that temper or you will lose focus on your objective. Draw on your rage as a demon but think about the fight."

Closing the small distance between Jonathan and himself, Ryan gave him two pats on his shoulder. "You are a good fighter. Connor?" Ryan said, spinning around to his brother and indicating his need for a drink.

Reaching into the cooler close to him, Connor threw the first condensation-clad bottle to Ryan, who passed it to Jonathan before reaching his hand back out for the second.

The remaining members of the rally had disbursed quietly, leaving only a hybrid-demon-angel group on the field. Florence and Stephen were busy ensuring that Jonathan's wounds were healing correctly and showering him with words of encouragement.

"Are you going to let him fight?" Connor asked, closing the gap between us as we gathered beside Ryan.

"I am," I confirmed. "He fights well and his temper, although uncontrolled, should help him. But only if he wants to fight and we keep an eye on him," I finished my sentence and awaited a response.

Stepping forward, Elenor addressed the group.

"I agree, we need to ensure he is protected if he loses control when fighting, but I believe we need to be vigilant regarding all non-demon or angel fighters."

Elenor had inadvertently touched on my raw nerve of anxiety for the human souls. Devon rubbed my shoulder gently as he came to stand beside me.

"The humans have their weapons and their antidotes. They have been receiving vaccinations to build up their tolerance to the venom and light force. Are they vulnerable? Yes, they are, but they are aware of the risks and they have all volunteered. Tory, we need to go into this situation fighting. Worry about the humans, by all means, but do not let your worry overcloud your judgement."

Around me, heads nodded in agreement with Devon's words. Jonathan and his guardians had rejoined us. He was smiling brightly and had reverted to his fourteen-year-old self.

Bouncing the ball of doubt around one last time, I threw it to the back of my mind and hid it under the memories categorized as trash.

Chapter 32

The afternoon brought more training. I involved myself deeply in venom and light-force education. I was reliably informed that I was worrying too much, leaving me wondering if everyone had been under the influence of Connor and Ryan's thoughts.

I smiled inwardly as my army of badass human souls displayed a huge amount of confidence and calm.

The light slipped away from the exhausting day, leaving a plethora of resting souls scattered in a chaotic array on the trampled grass.

Florence had accompanied Elenor back to her lodgings to source supper for the ravenously hungry souls. Ryan, Devon, and Connor had also been summoned to assist and grumbling to each other, made their way back to Elenor and Devon's home.

I mused to myself silently as I watched the sun continue its tireless journey, dipping out of sight to bring warmth and light to the opposite side of the human domain.

Gradually, the iridescent glow of the moon began to expose itself to purgatory, bringing with it a million light-emitting stars, glistening for attention.

Out of the corner of my eye, I became aware of a figure coming towards me. Turning, I saw Mia racing toward me at speed. I moved to greet her.

"Mia, what's wrong?" I asked, catching onto her arm in support as she abruptly halted.

Mia allowed herself a brief moment and inhaled deeply, blowing out her words as if they were air.

"A near release soul," she puffed. "You don't have long."

Motioning her to sit where she stood, I looked around. Catching Stephen's eye as he spoke to Jonathan, I called to him.

Closing the small gap between us, Stephen picked up a bottle of water from the toolbox as he passed it, and handed it to Mia.

"Been running?" he asked.

A red-faced Mia smirked with sarcasm and began draining the bottle.

"Stephen – I have to go into the human domain and harvest a soul. Would you please accompany me?" I asked.

"Of course. Just us?" he counter-questioned.

I nodded, explaining that I wanted to be in and out of the human domain without drawing attention to myself, hence the reason I was not gearing up the army. Agreeing, Stephen called Jonathan over to sit with Mia and explain where we were when the others returned.

Moments later, Stephen and I had armoured up and were making our way to the portal: we had taken our PCDs to trial them across the portal's boundaries.

Once we had reached the portal, I gave Stephen a small pep talk. I couldn't tell him what to expect with Lucifer's threat hanging over us but I could ensure he remained vigilant and wary of his vulnerability to his previous master.

Taking the lead, I stepped through the portal with Stephen at my heels. We were immediately surrounded by flames licking at our bodies.

"Where are we?" Stephen managed, before his throat became overloaded with smoke and coughing replaced words.

"Cover your mouth and use your wings to protect your body," I demanded, placing the material from my sweatshirt sleeve over my mouth. Allowing my wings to explode from my back, I began wafting the flames away from Stephen as he began to release his own wings.

We took a moment to observe where we were. It seemed as though we were standing in a warehouse that was burning. The near-releasing soul screamed from within the flaming building, but in the distance. It begged to be released and pleaded to be harvested quickly.

Stephen and I began to run in the direction of the relentless screaming, wrapping our wings around our bodies. We cut shapes in the displaced smoke as we made our way further into the unforgiving building.

Smoke invaded my senses, making me disorientated and slow. The screaming ceased for a moment. I stood still, bringing Stephen to a halt beside me, and strained my ears to hear.

Nothing.

I turned to Stephen, but he shook his head in verification of the silence. Indicating for him to follow, we tentatively walked, continuing in the direction from where we had originally heard the voice. Abruptly, Stephen stopped, pulling on my arm as he did so.

"Listen!" he whispered.

Rumbles from the fire attacking the building and cracks from the burning wooden frame disorientated my ability to hear anything else. Eventually pushing itself through the combination of noise, a muffled scream settled on my ears.

"Where?" I questioned Stephen.

He shrugged, listening for the scream.

"This way," he pointed, slightly to the left of where we were standing.

Changing direction we gathered speed. The scream became more audible.

"Tory!" Stephen breathed over the PCD. "Demons are present here."

"I know, I can feel their essence. You good?" I questioned, continuing our pace.

"Yep! I think they are torturing the soul." Stephen said, briefly bringing his gaze over to mine.

"I know they are," I said, soberly. "They always do."

With his eyes downcast, Stephen inhaled as deeply as his lungs would allow.

"Stephen, you are not like them. Falling in love with an angel proves that," I tried to reassure him. Lifting his head slowly, he softly smiled.

"Come, let's find this soul," I continued, giving him a few gentle slaps on his shoulder.

"This way," he said, turning from me and continuing in the same direction.

The soul continued screaming, rising in speed and volume; panicked, urgent, and scared. Rounding a sharp corner of the building, we were once again stopped in our tracks.

Ahead of us stood a demon: tall, dark and dripping with evil. In his arms, he held the newly released soul. The demon had his hands over the mouth of the soul, distorting the screams that were desperate to be heard.

"You bastard!" I addressed the demon, as I took a step closer to its rancid body. "You snatched the soul before it was ready to leave." Swiping my eyes to the left of the demon, they fell upon the lifeless capsule of the body once occupied by the screaming soul. The demon stood firm with an air of arrogance allowing his lips to curl into a smug grin.

"Stephen!" The demon addressed my companion and gently nodded his head in recognition.

I felt Stephen's body become rigid beside me.

"Are you okay?" I whispered through the PCD.

Stephen nodded without speaking or removing his eyes from the demon.

"So, you now follow the whore from purgatory, Stephen, with your angel slut!" the demon mocked.

Stephen began to step forward, angered by the words spoken by hell's beast.

"STOP! Stephen!" I grabbed at his arm to prevent him moving further. He turned sharply, questioning me with his eyes.

"He is taunting you!" I warned. "If you attack, he will release the soul to wander in the human domain. We need to secure the soul first, then he is all yours."

Stephen nodded once more, acknowledging the need for patience.

Taking the lead, I stepped in front of Stephen and came face-to-face with the foul-breathed, yellow-toothed face of the demon.

"What are your intentions, demon? Do you intend to harvest the soul of this man?"

Temporarily, the soul stopped screaming; his horror-filled eyes were wide open and begging for escape.

"No, hell does not care for men like this: weak of mind and kind of heart," he said, flexing his arm around the body of the soul.

"Yet hell accepted Stephen's soul. He, too, is a good man: kind but not weak. He is strong of mind and will: strong enough to defect from hell to purgatory where he belongs," I goaded.

The demon took a step forward, bringing the terrified soul with him.

"He is a fucking traitor," the demon spat, between his teeth.

I could sense the demon within Stephen was becoming restless, growing in anger with each word that dropped from the mouth of the demon facing him.

"Steady, Stephen," I whispered through his headset.

Stephen took a step backwards, giving himself enough space to retract and control his inner demon.

"Demon, I demand that you release the soul into my care immediately." It was my anger that bubbled uncontrollably now.

"Our master is unhappy with you, Stephen. You are to return to hell and accept your punishment for your foolish behaviour." The words hissed from the demon's mouth, each one grating on Stephen's nerves.

"Lucifer is no longer my master. I shall never return to hell. Give me the soul: he is weak and no use to hell." Stephen remained calm and confident as he spoke.

Pushing the soul away from him, the demon threw the body at Stephen.

"Take him, traitor. He has a message for you."

Catching the tumbling soul, Stephen handed him immediately to me so that I could officially harvest him. Relaying the ancient rite of harvesting, I held onto him lightly as Stephen drew his sword and began his attack on the waiting demon.

Once I had harvested the frightened soul, he ceased screaming.

"You have a message?" I asked him.

He nodded rapidly.

"Jonathan..." he began. "Jonathan will be collected tomorrow evening. If he is not presented to hell at 22:00, Lucifer will begin to descend every single human, town by town, country by country, and heaven will be hell's ally." The soul closed his mouth and bowed his head.

"Lucifer," I whispered, then turned to address the soul. "I am sorry that this has happened to you. My name is Tory." The soul softened his tense muscles and momentarily relaxed.

"Ray," he said, offering me his hand.

"Welcome to your new afterlife. It's a shitty start but once we're in purgatory, it will get better," I smiled, shaking his hand.

Looking past Ray's shoulder, I watched Stephen fight the well-matched demon.

"Tory, can you hear me?" Porter's voice came through my headset.

"Go ahead," I replied.

"Connor and Ryan are on their way to you," he reported.

"Okay, thank you." Shit, Connor was going to be pissed that I had left purgatory again without him.

"Stephen, descend him quickly. We need to go," I told him.

Continuing to clash swords with his demon opponent, Stephen granted me with a verbal understanding before growling loudly and allowing his body to grow in stature. He was bringing forth his inner demon, encouraging the monster trusted to him by Lucifer to expose itself. Before my eyes, Stephen changed: his skin rippled with onyx-black scales as they appeared from underneath his armour and chased one another to the extremities of his body.

From the top of his forehead erupted two razor sharp horns and his venom-filled claws presented themselves at his fingertips.

"Demon!" I called, before the fighting resumed. "Tell Lucifer I will look forward to meeting him again tomorrow." I smirked and gave a small wave, while pulling Ray further from the fight as I took position, a few feet away.

I had seen demon-on-demon fights and they were ruthless, a no-holds barred game of maiming, with eventual death but never mercy.

Stephen was refreshed by his demonic shift and quickly engaged his opponent once again.

Both demons held swords and swiped at each other with their claws causing venom oozing lacerations. The fight was rapid and brutal. Stephen's renewal of energy kept him one step ahead of his attacker until he had thrown the sword from the hands of the demon.

Standing rigid, with Stephen's sword at his throat, the demon hissed loudly.

"Traitor!" He looked directly into Stephen's eyes and spat at him.

Stephen smirked as the liquid venom collected at the blade of his sword.

"Descend, you bastard" he snarled and stepped forward, gradually thrusting the tip of his sword into the demon's throat, laughing as the demon choked and spewed venom as the blackened blade slid further into his body, beginning his descension.

The seconds ticked swiftly by with every slide of Stephen's sword, hanging from the blade that protruded from the back of his throat, the demon lost consciousness and dangled lifelessly.

Stephen turned to me and grinned widely, holding the demon aloft before slamming its remains into the wall behind the corpse and descending him back to hell.

As Stephen wiped the black blood from his darkened blade, his demonic scales began to retrace their steps and disappear underneath his armour to be hidden, once more.

"Well done, Stephen. Come – we need to get back to purgatory," I coaxed him, eagerly, wanting to avoid any further demon interaction within the human realm.

The flames that had greeted us on our arrival had begun to die down as human firefighting crews battled the building. By the time we had reached the portal, I had introduced Ray to Stephen and explained to our new soul what to expect once we had stepped into purgatory.

Inhaling deeply and coughing out the remaining smoke assaulting my lungs, I waited for Stephen and Ray to step into the portal, before I brought up the rear and stepped through.

On the other side, I railroaded straight into Ray causing us both to tumble to the floor with the grace of an elderly pachyderm.

"What the bloody hell...? Ray – are you okay?" I asked, picking myself up from the floor before offering him my outstretched hand.

He took it gingerly, glancing behind me frequently. Once on his feet, I turned to find out what the object of his concern was behind me.

Standing row upon row, heavily armoured with their weapons sheathed but ready, my army waited behind the hybrids. Ryan, Connor, Elenor, Devon and Florence stood proud and focused.

"What are you doing?" I asked, directing my question at Connor but including the entire army.

"Waiting, in case you needed us," Ryan answered.

"We were listening in," Connor told me, flickering his eyes briefly to Ray, then Stephen. "Epic descension, Steve," he smirked.

Stephen acknowledged his praise with a nod before making his way over to his concerned angel. Florence immediately began inspecting his body for wounds that needed her assistance to heal.

Ray stayed rooted to the ground beside me, obviously shocked by the sight that greeted him as he entered into his afterlife.

"My army," I verified. "They will not harm you," I reassured him.

Reluctantly, he stepped beside me and cautiously eyed the regiment before us. Holding his hand up, he gave a wave. I smirked, relieved when I spotted Mia pushing her way through the formations to reach our newest member of purgatory. Introducing herself, Mia took Ray away to explain all he needed to know and find him somewhere to sleep.

Connor took a step forward before turning to face the army.

"Stand down. Go back to your lodgings and rest, for tomorrow we fight."

Dismissing the army and waiting for them to retreat, Connor spoke briefly to Ryan, then Stephen, before turning his attention to me. He closed the gap between us with two large strides coming to a stop in front of me.

"Connor, I–" I was interrupted as he snaked his arms around my body and pulled me close into him, capturing my lips as he did so and caressing the back of my neck with his free hand.

"Hi," he whispered against my lips.

"Hello," I muttered back, before kissing him again.

My PCD headset crackled in my ear as a rustling, exasperated voice echoed through it.

"Hey bro, you guys wanna turn your mics off? We can hear everything!"

I pulled back from Connor, rapidly grabbing at my headset and fumbling to find the off button. Unhelpful as always, Connor stood laughing, which only added to my state of fluster.

"Git," I mumbled under my breath.

He smirked again, took my headset out of my hands and switched it off.

"So you took Stephen to harvest this soul. How was he?" Connor asked, fishing for answers.

"He was good. Calm and level-headed. He is a bloody good fighter. When did you start listening in?" I enquired.

"Just after Porter told you we were coming. Ryan and I decided to gather the army and wait at the portal for you, instead of rushing in," he explained. "Hence the reason we were there when you came back through."

I giggled. "Poor Ray... He must have wondered what the hell he'd just walked into. Thank you," I added. "For waiting."

Connor smiled and nodded. Together we talked about the threat Lucifer had made to the human domain if Jonathan was not returned to him tomorrow.

"Is he aware of our army?" Connor questioned.

I shook my head slowly, before responding.

"No, it doesn't seem as if he does. We still maintain the element of surprise."

"Good," Connor began. "Tomorrow we shall end this farce and you, my queen, shall rule the afterlife."

"I am not a queen," I responded.

"You are my queen and ruler of purgatory: therefore you are a queen."

I smiled briefly, before my lips were claimed again by Connor.

"Come," he whispered. "Let's freshen up and get an early night." He smirked, ending our kiss and taking my hand. Connor and I walked up to Stephen to check that he was unharmed from his battle with a fellow demon.

Stephen reassured me that he had sustained only a few minor scratches which had healed by the time we had returned. After bidding Stephen and Florence a good evening, Connor and I headed back to my place, unable to keep our hands off of each other as we went.

Chapter 33

I hardly slept. I had watched Connor sleep peacefully for hours, smirking at his facial expressions as his dreams overtook his subconsciousness. However, my own mind raced with a thousand contradictory thoughts. Each thought collided effortlessly with its polar opposite, concluding in such valid and invalid structures that my own brain was exhausting me.

Deciding that Connor was annoying by continuing to sleep in his tranquil state, I gathered up my robe and headed outside, via the kitchen, so I could grab a large glass of juice as I passed through.

The cold pillar of the terrace supported me as I rested my back against its frigid frame. Relaxing my wings, I allowed them to drape effortlessly at my back, gently tickling my skin with every breath I took.

I began counting the floods of stars that speckled the backdrop of the onyx-black sky. Bats whisked past me causing mini tornadoes of wind, dislodging the air around me with effortless undulation.

My thoughts continued their elementary arguments deep in the membranes of my consciousness. I was relieved that it was Lucifer bringing about the war of the three domains and not me, although I had planned to overthrow the megalomaniacs running the two crucial aspects of the afterlife. This was an easier way to ensure Lucifer would be present without having to descend a shit-load of demons first, to gain his anger and interest.

I was also well aware that heaven would be joining us: since the two domains had been graciously co-operative to achieve their own goals, neither had been far from the other.

The numbers in my army were small but I was confident in their abilities. All of the army had been trained in fighting demons and angels by demons and angels; we had communication, weaponized blades and arrows alongside the antidote needed to neutralize demon venom. We were ready to claim back the afterlife.

Sucking the last droplet of juice, I gave my wings the freedom they desired and spread them wide. Fluttering softly in the escalating breeze, I enjoyed the cleansing ritual.

As I turned to make my way back to bed and hopefully some much needed sleep, my attention was diverted to the small quarry hidden deep below the cliffs that supported our homes. A small flame flickered in the distance. Curiosity pierced rapidly within me and, in seconds, I had securely wrapped my robe around my body and was airborne.

The wind whipped around my wings as they beat in unison, creating the airfoil needed to project me to my destination.

Once close enough to focus, I could make out a small, hunched figure, hidden behind demon wings which cut a shadow against the roaring wood fire.

"Jonathan?" I said, softly landing and gently agitating the earth below my feet. Startled, he lifted his head and looked directly at me, his face stained with the black tears of a demon.

"What are you doing here?" I asked, taking a step closer to the distressed child demon.

"Is this all my fault? The fighting?" he asked, wiping fresh, liquid-coal tears from his cheeks.

I shook my head and sat down next to him on his lonely rock.

"No, Jonathan. None of this is your doing." Gently, I placed my hand on his wing, encouraging him to lower it.

"The fighting has gone on for years. Tomorrow is my opportunity to permanently end it and take back what was originally mine: to create a new afterlife where everyone receives what they deserve depending on how they lived and not by heaven or hell's persuasion," I explained, encouraging his slow retraction of his wings to expose himself further.

Shrugging deeply, Jonathan fidgeted where he sat, gradually settling his wings at his back. "I can fight," he said, sombrely.

"I am aware of that," I replied.

"I can fight well. I can help tomorrow," he continued.

I smiled to reassure him before I spoke.

"I know you can help, Jonathan, but I also know that you will be a target for Lucifer, so I would ask that you decide whether to accompany us tom–"

"I will be there," Jonathan interrupted. "I want to fight for you." He turned with a dry face filled with determination.

"Then I ask that you stay within the middle of the formation and assist in protecting the human souls, also," I explained, as Jonathan rapidly nodded in acknowledgment of the role he needed to play.

"Go and get some rest, Jonathan. Tomorrow's fight will be unpredictable and aggressive. We need you at your best," I encouraged, standing upright and offering this brave little demon my hand.

Taking it firmly, he stood upright with renewed confidence.

"Thank you, Tory. For everything," he said, shaking my hand.

"No thanks needed, little demon. Come – let's fly back before Elenor realizes you are gone. Then you really will be in trouble," I giggled, giving him his hand back and tapping his shoulder lightly.

Within twenty minutes I had ensured that Jonathan had returned safely home and I was sliding into bed next to the still-sleeping hybrid. Bringing my body as close as I could to Connor, I manipulated myself to fit into the space in between his body and mine. Once positioned in a reverse spoon, I pressed a light kiss on his head before allowing sleep to cloud my mind, close my eyes and allow me access to the celestial realm of dreams.

Chapter 34

Today I had woken up in a positive mood. Sharing the morning with my demon and angel breakfast guests, we continued to discuss the implications of the impending fight, plus strategies and priorities.

We would be gathering the army on the grounds besides the portal at 8pm. This time would be dedicated to communication and weapons to determine all were working correctly. Jason would also be ensuring that the demon-venom antidote pens were administered and the instructions for use were clear.

My pinnacle army of hybrids were busy discussing formations when rapid, loud knocks abused my front door. Connor motioned for me to remain seated as he pushed his chair away from the table and stood. Making his way to the door, Connor's strides matched the impatience of the person knocking on the other side of the door.

Four of my army stood behind the wooden door, each covered in blood and panting rapidly.

"Michael – what the fuck...?" Connor asked, as I rushed to stand beside him.

"Another one," Michael puffed through blue-tinged lips.

"Another what?" Connor questioned.

"Julian!" Michael called to his apprentice. Julian stepped past Michael cradling a bloodied human body as it draped lifelessly over his arms.

"Oh my god," I mumbled.

We were now joined by the remaining hybrid cluster in the doorway, struggling to see and hear what was happening.

"Tory," Devon said in a sombre tone. "This is the human we went to when the demons and angels were tormenting the humans to gain your attention." He stepped forward and tenderly lifted the eyelid of the inanimate human.

"The soul is still connected," Devon whispered and replacing the eyelid, hung his head.

Behind me, Elenor let out a small gasp as Devon reached her and embraced her into him. I remained speechless. Lucifer's cruelty was unlimited: a barbarous act of intimidation to prove the seriousness of his threat.

"Ryan and I will bury the body next to the girl," Connor uttered, close to my ear, as he signalled his brother.

I nodded in defeat. Once again, I had failed to protect the humans from the influence of heaven and hell. Murdering a second human was continued evidence of the ongoing co-operation and support heaven and hell were giving each other.

"Stephen, Florence, Devon – I need to see what is happening in the human realm. Will you accompany me, please?" I asked, needing answers and wanting to ensure that no more humans were at immediate harm.

All three agreed and dispersed to ready themselves. Connor and Ryan left with Julian to bury the human, while Michael and the two accompanying souls left. I stood alone in my doorway and encouraged myself to breathe. Elenor had taken Jonathan back to their lodgings to prepare.

Terror, concern, worry, panic, and revenge took turns to visit my thoughts, creating a vortex of confusion and clarity. Gathering myself, I left for the portal, immediately giving my wings the freedom they desired. I flew hard and fast.

Reaching the portal first, I paced back and forth waiting for my comrades. The trio of hybrids arrived shortly after and we began making our way through the portal. The portal was not indicating any near-releasing souls so I was not expecting any demon or angel activity.

What we did find, when we crossed, was a sight so horrific that not only did I get chills deep into my core but my body froze in disbelief.

On the dusty, loose ground next to the portal entrance lay a huge pile of bodies. A multitude of dead and decaying angels and demons: each soul had been removed by either heaven or hell to wander for eternity in the voids between the domains.

Each body had been mutilated, bearing the scars from both demon and angel. Taking in the carnage before me, the left arm of a Demon caught my eye: 'TRAITOR' had been etched roughly into the skin by what seemed to be the claw of their demon attacker.

Scanning my immediate surroundings and the bodies within it, I took hold of a lifeless angel: again, 'TRAITOR' was emblazoned into the flesh, but this time by angel light force.

"They are murdering those who wish to join us," I breathed, gently closing the eyes of the slain angel.

Florence began to frantically lift the eyelids of the victims in search for anyone she was able to heal, searching for any sign of a soul. But one after another, she shook her head in defeat.

"There is nothing I can do," she wept.

Stephen comforted her as she sank to the ground, sobbing. Glancing over at the murdered corpses, I had the answers I had wanted. Heaven and hell would both be present tonight; present and ready to fight to bring about my demise.

"Come," I said, gesturing to the accompanying hybrids. "There is nothing that we can do for them now," I said, regretfully.

"We can bury their bodies," Florence murmured, wiping the remaining tears from her eyes.

I nodded in agreement. "We shall bury them in purgatory. That is obviously where they wanted to be."

Having sent Devon back through to purgatory to organize the burial, Florence, Stephen, and I began straightening the bodies, giving them the respect they deserved.

Thirty-four angels and demons were laid out before us, each brandishing the word 'TRAITOR' somewhere on their bodies. Their attackers had not considered mercy; just torture. Prolonged, agonizing, unnecessary torture.

Moments later, Devon re-appeared, bringing Jonathan, Elenor, Ryan, and Connor. One by one, we each lifted a body and carried it through the portal and into purgatory. Devon had selected a site behind the portal that was secluded. He had called the entire army to assist. Each body was buried as comfortably as one could bury a body. Florence continued to check under each closed eye to ensure she had not missed a glimpse of a potential soul to save. Reluctantly, she stepped back from the graves and allowed the earth to reclaim them, keeping the lifeless bodies warm and providing a safe resting place.

As the last body disappeared under the ground, the army stood in a circle with their heads downcast, in respect for the lost souls.

Standing proud of the army, I addressed them.

"This is what we are fighting for. Who we are fighting for," I said, indicating the thirty-four new graves, each adorned with a small cross. "The afterlife needs to be adjusted, improved and to judge the souls as they should be. These angels and demons were coming here for help, for re-judgement into a better afterlife. These thirty-four souls are now lost to us. We cannot help them but we can help the others and we will help them. Tonight, we fight for those souls who need us."

I stopped as cheering erupted from the army; each member eager and ready to fight.

"We shall assemble here at 9pm. We shall fight and we will be victorious!" I shouted over the continuous cheering.

"We are ready," I said, as Connor joined me.

"Yes, we are," he said, taking me by my waist and bringing me into his hot, muscular body.

I savoured the comfort he gave me. A sense of tranquillity enveloped my body, hiding me from the responsibilities weighing on my shoulders. My moment was short-lived. My army dispersed into groups discussing the impending fight between heaven and hell against purgatory.

I sighed, letting Connor go, and heading out to find Florence. Her distress was apparent as I came closer to her. She was fruitlessly trying to find comfort in Stephen's embrace but the actions of today's brutal murders were playing heavily on her mind.

"Do you think that you will be able to accompany us tonight, Florence? I totally understand if you do not feel as though you can," I said, softly.

"I will fight with you, Tory. Tonight and any other night, to ensure the safety of the human souls." She pulled gently away from her beau and stood firm before me. "I could not save those souls today but I will save those who are needing me from this day forward." Determination occluded her features and she allowed a minute smile to float upon her lips.

"That's my angel!" Stephen said. Snaking his arms around her tiny waist and turning her within his embrace, he kissed her lips. As their hug and kiss intensified, I took my cue to leave.

Chapter 35

Swinging on the back legs of a pine chair, I traced the second-hand as it raced across the face of a yellowing, white plastic clock that sat proudly on the wall of the meeting room.

I was early. Nerves had driven me to get to the meeting room three-quarters of an hour before everyone else. So here I sat, impatiently waiting and extremely bored with my own company.

Eventually, a trio of council members came through the squeaky-hinged door. Raymond, Mia, and Michelle entered, each greeting me as they did so. After five minutes of general chatter about the human residents of purgatory, Porter and Henry joined the group.

"You know why we are here!" I stated, standing before my trustworthy and loyal council members. A dull, audible acknowledgment of the meeting's agenda rumbled from the five souls.

"Tomorrow's outcome will either signify the beginning of a new afterlife for heaven, hell and purgatory, or..." I hesitated briefly. "Or the end of purgatory as we know it. I am confident in my army but we are dramatically outnumbered. If we fail in our mission to protect the afterlife, I need you to know what is expected of you, as my trustees."

Again, my words were acknowledged by semi-audible words and slow head-nods. All parties were massively aware of the impact the battle of the domains would have, should we fail. But failure was not an option.

Inhaling deeply, I gave my lungs the renewed oxygen that they required.

"If I do not return to purgatory, another demon, angel or hybrid must take my place. That person must be able to cross the portal and harvest souls to maintain the energy required by purgatory to survive. However, if in the event of complete failure and the non-return of any person to harvest, you must destroy the portal immediately."

"Does that mean that we shall perish?" Mia questioned, with tears evident in her emerald-green eyes.

Sympathy for her and every soul that relied on me to protect them coursed through me.

"Purgatory will not perish immediately," I replied. "The energy stored within its core is extensive but without renewed energy, it will deteriorate over millennium until eventually it will cease to exist."

"Like we will," Raymond commented, unhelpfully.

"Like we all will," I countered. "But you are free to choose, Ray. You may leave purgatory before the portal is destroyed, but your afterlife will be uncertain."

Michelle glared at him from across the waxed cherrywood table, as Mia sobbed loudly. Porter passed her a tissue and spoke softly.

"What happens if we do not destroy the portal, if you do not return?" he questioned, comforting Mia.

"If the Portal is not destroyed, it will mean that heaven and hell could flood purgatory with angels and demons. Each will fight to own it and cleanse it of its inhabitants, claiming them as their own."

Silence descended over the small crowd of souls: reassurance was futile. In conclusion, someone needed to survive this war. One of purgatory's demons or angels needed to survive to protect the souls within my domain.

My stomach lurched with unease as my mind rapidly sought solutions to the problems purgatory could face if I failed in my mission to protect it.

I had no doubt that I had made the right decision; not just for purgatory but to stop the senseless torture of innocent human souls. Having reassured my council for the final time, I dismissed them to continue their duties. Michelle and Mia left together, followed by Raymond and Henry.

"Are you ready, Porter?" I asked, as he approached me.

"Tory, we are all ready. I will keep communications open at all times until you are back here, safe."

"And if it fails?" I asked, seeking my own reassurances for the continued protection of purgatory.

Porter sighed before answering. "I will do what I have to do. Ryan has given me the key codes to the weapons for the destruction of the portal, but Tory – this mission will be successful. You have a small but elite army."

I smiled, accepting his reassurance.

"Thank you, Porter. Without your input we would not have the communications we have now." I paused briefly searching for the required words. "Porter, if I do not return to purgatory, ensure that Jonathan does not take charge. I believe, although he is demon and capable of passing though the portal, that he is too young for such a responsibility. His years were so few when he died that he does not possess the necessary experience an adult human life would have given him. You, Porter, should take the role yourself, in this instance.'

Finishing my sentence I paused, allowing Porter the time he needed to digest the information. He sat on a table close to him, obviously deep in thought and considering my wishes.

"Here…" Stretching my arm out to him, I handed him my will: a very human act I believed would help him to accept and carry out my wishes. I had written it in the early hours of the morning and included my line of succession depending on who would return, starting with the hybrids and finally ending with Porter.

"I see," he said, taking the dog-eared sheet of folded paper. "How very human of you," he smirked.

Due to the fragility of the thin, folded paper, Porter exaggerated the need for careful unfolding to prevent it from ripping down the creases. Once open, he read it slowly, mouthing each word as he did so. Nodding and shaking his head frequently, he eventually sighed heavily and began to refold the paper with the same care he took to unfold it.

"I have no doubt, Tory, that you will return. However, if it is not possible, I will ensure that your wishes are fulfilled." Porter's head remained downcast, his words soft and sincere.

"Thank you," I matched his whisper with my own.

Placing my wish-filled paper in the back pocket of his trousers, Porter stood and walked towards me, closing the gap between us.

"Make sure you come back," he said, and took me into his arms.

I returned his hugs and for a split second forgot the impending battle as I embraced my oldest and best friend for what could quite possibly be the last time. As our hug ended, I gathered my senses once more, changing the tangent of my thoughts back to this evening.

Porter and I left the meeting room together and headed towards the portal. I was ready – ready to fight and reclaim what I once had; to reclaim myself and send the current failed rulers of heaven and hell to their extinction.

A breeze of renewed confidence flooded through me. This was not going to be easy but I was determined.

Chapter 36

The army was already present as I reached the meeting point at the portal. They were regimentally lined up, with Connor, Ryan, and Jason parading past each soldier, checking their armour, weapons, and antidote.

Determination shone from the faces of each individual, all of them ready to fight for their afterlife.

I acknowledged each person as I passed, re-checking their armour, weapons, and antidote. Walking over to the tent we had erected as a make-shift headquarters, I disappeared inside to ready myself. Once dressed in my armour, I checked and re-checked my weapons.

"Ready?" Connor asked, as he entered the tent.

I nodded back at him rapidly, then stopped to compose myself. Inhaling deeply, I rushed my body with new oxygen, refilling my blood with rich, refreshed blood cells.

Allowing myself time, I walked into Connor's armoured body and embraced him. He held me tightly to him, gently speckling the top of my head with light kisses. Time stopped at that moment, allowing me to cherish the man I loved. I needed it. Right now, I did not know if I was saying goodbye, but if this was to be one of our last moments together, I wanted to own it.

Connor whispered soft words of love and reassurance. Not wanting our moment to end, I lifted my chin to meet his face and kissed him, becoming lost in his body and savouring the taste of his lips.

"I love you," I breathed against his lips. I felt him smile against my lips.

"And I love you, Tory," he whispered back.

Deepening our kiss, I brought my body as close into his as I could, wishing our armour was removed so I could run my fingertips over the contours of his chiselled body. Sliding his hand down my back, Conor groped my bottom and pummelled it with his hand.

"Do you know how gross you two are?" Ryan said, standing just inside the doorway of the tent.

"Do you realise what a pain in my arse you are, little brother?" Connor retorted, looking over my shoulder at Ryan.

"You are five minutes older than me dude!"

"Still older," Connor stated. Kissing me quickly then taking my hand, he pulled me with him as he moved to face Ryan.

"We are ready," Ryan said, talking directly to me and trying hard to ignore his brother by my side.

"As are we," Connor replied, before I had the chance to answer.

"Go," I said to the brothers. "I shall be with you shortly." Motioning toward the door, the brothers took their cue and left, while taking the opportunity to argue further as the draped curtained door of the tent wafted shut behind them.

Composing myself for the final time, I followed in the recent footfalls of my hybrid commanders.

Swiping the curtain to the left, I ducked and walked through. The sound of clapping echoed throughout purgatory. Gazing around, I was astounded by the number of people standing before me creating the thunderous applause.

The men, women and children of this domain stood with the army of humans, angels, demons and hybrids, each one brought to purgatory over the span of thousands of years to live out their afterlife.

Humility sparked within the core of my heart and radiated out to pulse within me. Gradually, as the clapping continued, the souls separated, creating a pathway leading to the portal.

I smiled and began to walk to the pinnacle of my destiny, passing Connor and Ryan first. Conor winked and Ryan beamed, following to flank me.

"What's going on?" I questioned Connor, as his steps fell in with mine.

"Mia and Michelle told the people of purgatory what was happening and they wanted to show their support," he explained, close to my ear, as the claps became deafening.

Passing soul after soul, smiling, my confidence expanded as kind words of encouragement and support fell from the lips of every person I had ever harvested.

I had tried for so long to keep the reality of the conflicts between the domains a secret, yet now, when I needed courage, the truth was spoken and the support was given without question. Reaching the middle of the path of souls, I began to approach my army

My gaze caught Mia and Michelle standing together either side of the path.

"Mia, Michelle – please come and stand before me."

I stood firm and watched as my two invaluable Council women stood before me like naughty children awaiting punishment.

"Thank you," I said and before either woman could reply, I had them in my arms and hugging them tightly. "Thank you. This is just what I needed," I whispered.

Michelle was the first to break away from our trio. Taking my hand in hers, she spoke softly. "You were there when we needed you, Tory. It is now our turn to be here for you. We will all be here waiting for you and your army. Any injured souls should return immediately so we may treat them. Porter will keep us informed of your progress," Mia added, grazing her fingers over the top of my hand. She was desperately trying to hide her anxiety but was making a really poor job of it.

Placing my hands over Mia and Michell's, I squeezed them as tight as I dared without hurting them, reassuring the women as much as I could.

"I will be back," I said, sternly. "I always come back."

Releasing them, I continued on through the path, shaking hands, patting shoulders and receiving a fist-bump from Jonathan.

"Stay safe," I whispered to him.

He looked back at me with his fourteen-year-old eyes; his young, innocent eyes.

"I will," he replied and in that moment, a flash of brilliant red streaked across his iris. It was his demon making itself known.

I smirked back at him, before turning to face the portal.

I inhaled deeply. Once we entered the portal, we wouldn't know where we would step out, and there were only three options: heaven, hell or the human domain. I was guessing that the middle ground of the human realm was going to be the battlefield of choice.

"Come," I said, turning back to the men and women of my army.

"Let's ensure the human afterlife remains as it should."

A roar of cheering ricocheted around purgatory and with a nod to the army, I stepped through the portal into the unknown.

Chapter 37

We were early. After stepping through the portal, nothing was there to greet us but the bustle of human city life in London. Our group remained cloaked from human eyes as we assembled into our chosen heptagon.

"Be ready," I communicated through the PCD. "Demons and angels will descend upon us soon. Do not engage with the humans and remain cloaked at all times."

Acknowledgement of my orders reverberated throughout the ranks. Alert, we waited. Every member of the army vigilantly scoping out the surroundings. As we stood waiting, the sun began to ebb gently away, exposing the city to the encroaching evening. Pillowy white clouds followed the footsteps of the fading sun, leaving stars to replace them in the clear, silent sky.

"Tory – I can see shadows lurking behind the buildings. Demons!" Jonathan's voice echoed through the headset before it was replaced by static.

"Demons," Stephen concurred.

"Look up," Florence stated. 'On the roof tops. There are the angels."

Adrenaline began to pump through my body, like trapped articles held within the Hadron Collider, frantically forcing the chemicals to move more and more rapidly with each palpitation of my heart.

Moving tighter into our formation heptagon, I felt Connor and Ryan flank me closer.

"Weapons up," Ryan commanded.

Sliding my sai from my waistband, I manipulated them to fit comfortably in my hands. Behind me, the sound of metal being unsheathed rattled throughout the formation. Scuffing feet adjusted themselves on the concrete, fixing them in pace and centring.

Taking the opportunity, I briefly looked behind me. I was searching for Jonathan. For some reason, Lucifer wanted him. He wanted him badly but I had yet to figure out why.

Running my eyes over my army, I focused on the short demon-child. He was close to the back sandwiched between Poet and Raven, who were flanked by Stephen and Florence. There was no way any demon or angel would get anywhere near him. I smirked as Jonathan caught my eye and gave me a thumbs up.

Returning to face into the city of London, I scanned the surroundings. Demons hid behind four enormous stone lions that sat in time-frozen slumber. Angels hung from every illuminated advertisement board and a couple stood next to Lord Nelson as he surveyed Trafalgar Square.

"Bastards," Connor stated. "What are they waiting for?"

I shook my head in response. The sun finally betrayed us and the moon ceased to provide the necessary light we needed. One by one, demons and angels crept out from their hiding places, each one holding a human. The humans were captured as they tried to leave the square as darkness fell.

"What are they doing?" Elenor spoke into the PCDs.

"A scare tactic, I expect," Ryan answered.

"Hostages?" Jason added.

"I have no idea. Be vigilant," I replied. I did not like the angel and demons using innocent humans as bait in this ridiculous game that we were currently engaged in. Heaven and hell knew my weakness for the human race and now they were using it against me.

Night continued its elevation, taking over the sky like sticky black treacle, oozing across the horizon. Street lamps flickered around us eventually sparking into luminance. The added light gave extended clarity to the scene playing out before us.

Swarms of blacked-winged demons clustered in large groups over, on and around the four lions. Among them stood the captured humans, made drowsy by the powerful sedative released into them by the claws of the demons. Not enough venom to kill but just enough to render the human helpless.

Angels had also taken human hostages up onto the rooftops of Trafalgar Square. Forced compliance was achieved by pumping light force deep into the human victims' veins.

Through the PCD, Ryan and Connor took turns to give orders and verify positions to the waiting army. I stood proud of my army and looked into the vast crowds of angels and demons. Searching each face, I wanted to find Lucifer and either end this nonsense or start this war.

My wait was temporary. Ten feet in front of where I was standing, the concrete began to crack. Rubble lifted from its secure, embedded resting place and very slowly began to move. Rising up, it tumbled over itself, creating small concrete pieces that rolled away from each other. Piece by piece the earth parted.

"Ready!" I called down the PCD.

Lucifer ascended from the smoke-filled hole the rumbling terrain had created, in his own ostentatious manner. Lucifer stood upon a coal-black chariot; blood-red rubies adorned its metallic body and hot flames licked at the blackened wheels.

Two onyx-black horses drew the chariot, their eyes as red as blood and their manes licked with the roaring yellow orange glow of the flames of hell.

"Lucifer." I acknowledged his entrance and watched as the dismantled, sliced earth began to rapidly move to meet its opposite, closing the gap Lucifer had created. Piece by piece it fused, reconstructing the hard standing for Lucifer to rest upon.

"Purgatory," he smirked. The flames of hell flickered in his eyes as he stared at me for longer than necessary. "I see that you have my young demon with you. Wise choice. Hand the traitor demon over to me now and I will spare the lives of these human souls who currently shield my demons."

Around him encroached several other demons on flame-maned horses, each holding the essences of hell's fire within their eyes.

"Why hide behind humans, Lucifer? Do we intimidate you that much for you to seek the protection of unwilling humans?" I goaded him, silently hoping he would he insulted by my remark and free the human barriers.

Lifting his right hand from his horses' reins, Lucifer extended his arm out towards me and smiled. Hyper-extending his index finger, he waved its black claw at me with a slow metronomic sway.

"Tut, tut, Purgatory. Nice try but you have failed to cause insult. We do not hide behind humans: we use them as weapons against you. Your sympathy and respect for the human population allows me to use them to draw you out, to bribe and control you. You, Purgatory, are weak." Lucifer glorified himself as his surrounding demons laughed with him at his words.

My insides churned rapidly. Boot-wearing butterflies made themselves known by slamming their bodies against my stomach with relentless force. I knew what I needed to do: I just did not want to do it.

"Tory," Connor's soothing tone settled within my ear pierce as he privately communicated with me. "Sweetheart, it's okay. You know what you have to do."

I nodded back accepting my decision with obvious support and fixed my eyes on Lucifer's.

"Jonathan will not be returning to hell,' I announced. "He is a citizen of purgatory and he has denounced you as his master." Finishing my sentence with a smile, I watched as rage engulfed the demon leader.

His face became enveloped with a crimson wave of anger, his eyes flickered like the roar of a petrol-infused fire and his claws protruded further. Lucifer did not allow words to fall from his lips: instead, he raised his right hand, tightly fisted, into the air. The dark-black demons, scattered within the shadows, stepped forward into the ambient light cast by the silver-tinged moon.

Each demon's flame-filled eyes were fixed on their master: they were waiting for the unspoken order from Lucifer. He then gave it. Opening his clawed hand, he released a vampire bat. The bat flew from its captor's grasp with flames licking at its wings.

All demon eyes kept their focus trained on the black- fanged mammal as it flapped its fiery wings, propelling it high into the evening sky. In unison, every demon holding a human plunged their black, evil-clawed hands into their victims' chests.

Screams filled Trafalgar Square; screams that pleaded for mercy, begged for death and called out for their god. One by one, the atrocious demons pulled forth the hapless soul from the core of their victim's body.

Without exception, every demon held a lifeless human body on one of their stench-coated, fisted hands and the other held the writhing, panicking, petrified soul.

I shook my head in horror, allowing my rage to surface, forcing my fangs to pierce my gums with the need to be released. The anger I held within accepted the pain my ivory fangs gave and nullified it swiftly.

Keeping my focus trained on the souls ripped from their human bodies, I assessed the situation. I had sealed their fate: their souls were condemned. As I watched the fading souls begging to be harvested, my entire rationality abruptly got up and left the confines of my conscious mind, leaving me with an intense rage that taunted my process of clear thinking by sending it into chaos.

"You cannot harvest them," Elenor's calming voice echoed through my communication device.

"I know," I muttered, in a disheartened tone.

Lucifer remained seated upon his hell mustang, and began to let out a deep, guttural laugh. To add fuel to my already alight and burning inner fire, he clapped his hands loudly and slowly, one by one, each murdered human soul faded out of sight, destined to become lost in the vast open abyss between domains; wandering for eternity without purpose.

Lucifer met my eyes with his own.

"This is just the beginning, Purgatory! Bring Jonathan forth and maybe you will spare the souls of the humans that are held by my angels."

His smirk returned as the demons flanking him sidestepped their horses to allow entry to the third player in this rancid and tedious game.

"Abraxos," I managed to verbalize, greeting the head angel with disdain. He sat arrogantly upon a white horse, completely in contrast to the steeds that Lucifer commanded. The horse had the eyes of a clear blue, cloudless sky. Its mane fell in long, white, wispy curls down its neck, while its tail resembled a host of elongated white clouds, laced together.

"Purgatory – you are stubborn and playing an extremely dangerous game," Abraxos roared from his seated position.

He didn't need to waste his breath on me: I was already aware of the damage I was bringing to the human souls.

"Abraxos – I say to you now, as I have said to your sidekick here, I will not hand over any demon or angel who chooses to find peace in purgatory. We are not here to issue threats or justification: we are here to fight for the humans and for your domains." Remaining calm and self-assured, I allowed the surrounding demons and angels to enjoy the apparent humour that met my statement.

Lucifer threw back his head and opened his cavernous mouth: his laugh was guttural and forced. I watched his eyes: those flame-filled portals were showing signs of panic. The flames within them had died down to a barely lit ember. He was worried.

Abraxos laughed hard too, briefly glancing towards the two flanking demons as his own entourage stood patiently behind him. His laughter was also forced and his enthusiasm did not reach the same level as Lucifer's.

Good, I thought to myself. They both have their doubts.

"Be ready!" I called down the PCD.

I chanced a glance at Connor: he was focused and ready. His first weaponized arrow was notched and begging for flight. Turning to my other side, Ryan's battle stance mirrored that of his brother, his sword poised and his focus rigid.

Abruptly, Abraxos turned to glare at me through his beautiful but deadly eyes. Flicking his hand up above his head, he released four light-force flares into the darkened sky.

The bright, iridescent quartet of sparks flew up over the multitude of classic statues and buildings that created the historic monuments of Trafalgar Square. The flames were orders from Abraxos, calling his angels that were still holding humans; the call to extinguish their lives and allow their souls to become lost.

I watched each angel hold their palms over the hearts of their terrified human victims. Emitting a blade-like shard of light force, the angels pierced each human they held. The shard penetrated the chest and pummelled the beating human heart with repeated light force, stopping the muscle immediately and releasing the soul.

Angels stood on monuments and buildings, gently illuminated by the retracting light force sparks emitted by Abraxos. Every angel was holding a screaming human soul, mirroring the behaviour of their demon counterparts.

My breath hitched and my subconscious battled with my reason. I needed to allow these few humans to be lost in order to save the entire domain.

Silence fell upon the square, waiting for the souls to be released into the unknown terrain between the domains.

One after the other, screeching souls were relinquished into the darkness, thus terminating their chance of harvest. Deep within me, my own soul broke into tiny shards and began lacing through my adrenaline-consumed veins. Ingesting my fear, I stroked the hilts of my sai, messaging the intricate engraving that adorned it. The inscription etched within the metal is an ancient Tamil script, engraved thousands of years ago by the first humans I had ever observed. They ignited my passion for the souls of the human race and brought me the sense of need I required to relieve my loneliness and find my calling.

"I fight for the weak,
Justice I shall ensure,
For those harvested to the afterlife,
Now and forever more."

Running my fingers again over the words that I have always honoured, I smiled inwardly. I had my weapons; I had my army; and I had waited years for the opportunity to take back what was mine and rectify my mistake.

Glancing once more at my enemies before me, I took a deep breath.

"Lucifer! Abraxos!" I called their names, disdain dripping from my descended fangs as I addressed the advocates of my created domains. "The humans you have murdered shall be buried with the honour they deserve. The souls shall be sought within the cavernous voids between our domains and they shall be harvested and given the afterlife you have denied them."

My anger had elevated into rage, yet I was aware that Connor had sidestepped closer to me. Briefly distracted by the small gesture of support, I turned toward him and met his eyes for a minute moment.

He winked.

I smiled, making the biggest mistake as pain tore into my right shoulder. I spun back to face a secondary arrow from a demon archer. Blood exploded from the fresh laceration the arrow had caused. The arrow had missed embedding into my skin, opting instead to graze my shoulder before continuing its flight into a nearby wall and falling into the street.

I couldn't feel the tang of poison that usually accompanied a demon arrow. I exhaled the breath I had been holding and replied to Connor's need for reassurance.

"He missed. No poison," I breathed back at him.

"Thank fuck for that," he said, continuing to keep his notched arrow trained on the demon archer.

"FOOL!" A loud voice broke through the tentative silence. "How could you miss?" Lucifer stood up on his horse, barking a reprimand at the archer. "Do it again! Hit her! Bring the bitch down!"

Although obviously flustered by his public bollocking, the bereft archer notched another arrow.

"Is he really going to do this?" Elenor asked, through the PCD. "Is he that stupid?"

"Oh yes," Connor countered.

Releasing his trained arrow, the archer remained with his eye focused on its intended target – me! I watched the blade of the sharpened triangle of steel rush towards me at speed.

Remaining still, I altered my eyes from the arrow to Lucifer and smiled. Lucifer stared back, his eyes quizzical and his posture nervous. Abraxos now stood adjacent to his demon comrade and followed his gaze to join mine.

Acknowledging his company, I returned my gaze to the encroaching arrow, encouraging Lucifer and Abraxos to look, too.

Curiosity had got the better of both men and their flanking officers as they watched the arrow. An unseen force hit the arrowhead, cracking the metal in two halves, as if it were made of nothing more than refrigerated butter.

Splitting in half, the arrow splintered through the middle, falling apart with the grace of tumbling sycamore seeds.

Finally the last of the arrow disappeared from the air, black and red fletchings fell effortlessly to the ground. Watching the arrow disintegrate at my feet, I felt a smile return to my lips and I lifted my gaze to the stunned demons and angels before me.

Lucifer's words evaded him: his jaw hung heavy, leaving his mouth to hang open. To his side, the demon archer was rigid: his mouth oozed black, rancid, viscous blood and his hands cupped an arrow protruding from his chest.

Connor had released his own deadly arrow at the same time as the archer. He had directed his golden-edged missile with immense precision to meet head on with the demon arrow.

Colliding at their tips, Connor's arrow shattered the metal of his opposing projectile, creating a snake-tongue effect that traced the length of the demon arrow. Metal, wood, then feather parted under the strength of Connor's missile, running through its core until the two halves dropped at my feet.

Looking down at the slaughtered arrow, I smiled hearing Lucifer's gasp. Raising my eyes, I found Lucifer and Abraxos motionless and staring at the stricken archer.

A consequence of the demon arrow's decapitation was the obstacle-free path it left for Connor's arrow. Whistling through the air, the arrow continued its journey until it pierced the archer's demon heart.

Falling to his knees, the archer maintained his grip on the protruding arrow and screamed. The weaponized venom had begun to penetrate him, gradually causing the destruction and implosion of every cell within his demonic body.

Re-orientating myself, I twisted to look at Connor. He smiled and winked as I mouthed 'Thank you' to him for saving my life, once again.

Lucifer stood, continuing to watch the elongated death of his favoured archer.

"He is not descending!" he stated, loudly. "Why the fuck is he not descending?" he questioned, as his eyes met mine.

I shrugged. I was not prepared to divulge our new weapon although I was delighted that it worked, even if it was a little gruesome.

"It works. Thank goodness." A voice from one of the harvested soldiers interrupted the screaming of the imploding demon. An entourage of cheers erupted from my army and with renewed confidence, we stood firmer.

Eventually, the only evidence that the archer ever existed was a discoloured mound of black, tarry liquid where he had once stood. He was gone; completely dead. The external circle of afterlife the demons and angels were happily experiencing was ending.

Rolling waves overtook the forces of our enemies. Demons and angels had watched and witnessed the demise of the archer and in turn, one after another, they turned to their leaders for answers.

Regaining his fragile composure, Lucifer addressed his army and the army of angels.

"Kill the fucking lot of them!" he ordered, drawing his own sword from his leather waistband.

Immediately, dozens more demons erupted from underneath the earth's crust, propelled by the angered flames from hell itself. Bursting from the heavens came reinforcements of angels. Beautifully pure white wings fluttered downwards, holding light-force weapons of dangerous intent.

Before either angel or demon had their feet firmly planted on the terrain of the human realm, they were running towards us.

Purgatory stood firmly at the back of our formation, the portal providing protection from an attack from the rear. Demons and angels surrounded our three other sides, slowly enveloping my army in a sea of black and white.

Cheers of encouragement from Lucifer and Abraxos egged the demon/angel army on, pushing them harder and faster until they were close enough for us to engage.

Chapter 38

Keeping our heptagon formation, we battled the oncoming swarm of demons and angels. My first opponent ran at me with his venom-laced claws outstretched in front of him. Ducking under his arm, I launched myself into his body, smashing my sai deeply into his rancid, skinny black fame.

Maintaining my posture underneath his weakening arms, I allowed my sai to pour the deadly toxin into him. Failing fast, the demon began to weaken and hunch himself over. Withdrawing from his body, I wiped my sai on the sleeve of his closest arm. Red, shocked eyes bore into me with surprise as I cleaned my blades; then he screamed. My opponent dropped to his knees, clutching the fresh injury my weapon had created. Two small holes were evident in the lower section of the demon's chest and as the toxin began its relentless destruction of his bodily cells, the solidified, black, blood-like fluid began to drip out of the wounds.

As the toxin increased its efficacy, it annihilated the demon body at a fast rate. The onyx blood now rapidly poured from the two sai-created holes, creating a pool of viscous fluid around his feet.

Deciding that demon innards would not look good splattered on my boots, I took a step back. Reluctantly, I met the eyes of the internally tortured demon, his red eyes were fading and bulging uncomfortably in their sockets.

With one almighty scream, the demon brought his melting hands up to his face. Hearing a sickening snap, I watched in disgust and horror as his left eye popped from its socket backwards into his head.

My breath hitched as the fascination of the sight before me approached its grizzly conclusion. A second snap, then a pop, and the right eye disappeared. Remaining on his knees, the demon began to shake violently and as I watched the continuing fluid leaking from my sai marks, one eye fell out of it and disintegrated on the ground.

In sickening anticipation, I waited for the other eye to leave the demon's body via his chest capacity. I didn't need to wait long: morbidly mesmerized, I watched the second eye slide down the demon's abdomen, then slop off of his bent legs, hitting the ground with a squishy-sounding plop before it exploded on impact.

"Gross!" I exclaimed to myself, yet I could not stop watching. The demon's head took seconds to implode into itself, collapsing from the outside in, liquidating and spilling from the chest wounds until his upper torso had completely disappeared, leaving his bottom half to rapidly disperse into a blackened puddle on the pavement.

Opportunistically looking around me, I could see a number of similar pools that were once demons. It was obvious that the weapon Jason had created was effective: none of the demons had descended; they had simply liquified and ceased to exist.

My reprieve was short. The brief distraction had allowed an angel to try her luck with a small jolt of her light force, grazing my thigh. I berated myself for my slip in concentration and readied for the fight.

I anticipated a rapid struggle as the angel was young in human years and in death. Estimating her age as appropriately nineteen, I implored her to reconsider in order to survive. However, the stubborn angel continued with her attack until, eventually, we came face to face, our weapons poised and ready.

"Reconsider," I demanded "Do not give up your afterlife. Come with us."

With an indignant snort, the girl shook her head whilst screaming a stream of obscenities that should never be heard from a lady, let alone an angel.

"Last chance!" I stated, preparing to end the fight.

"Fuck off, Purgatory!" she responded.

Those were her last words. Regretfully, I surged forward, sliding my right sai into the middle of her chest, lancing her light force. My hand steadied her falling body on my blade; light force pulsed from her body into my sai while, simultaneously, the toxin seeped from the same blade invading her body like lions ravaging meat. She had sealed her own fate. Light force began dripping from the wound my embedded sai had created, followed swiftly by it cascading through her mouth.

"I am sorry," I whispered, meeting her crystal blue eyes. Holding my gaze for one last breath, followed closely by her last heartbeat, she closed her eyes, leaving her body to shatter into millions of tiny glass shards. Each shard gently floated to the ground and melted into a tiny mound of shingle at my feet.

"Tory! Behind you!" Ryan's voice crackled over the PCD, alerting me to an oncoming attacker. Revolving swiftly, with my sai up and ready for action, I came face to face with another female angel.

She, too, had a sai as her weapon of choice. She charged at me with gritted teeth, holding her weapon high and screaming something about traitors and death.

I blocked her oncoming attack, weaving and ducking as she relentlessly stabbed at me with her blades. It was obvious that this angel had little training in the use of the weapon she was waving at me.

Her arms and chest bore small scars from my sai: the toxin was beginning to weaken her, forcing her to become clumsy and un-coordinated. Becoming bored with her constant battle cries and incompetent sai ability, I lunged forward and ran my blade through her heart.

The screaming stopped. The angel dropped her arms to her side as my weapon began delivering the toxin into her body, while absorbing her remaining light force. With her arms hanging loosely, the angel's sai fell from her dying fingers.

The clashing of each sai caused another angel to bring his attention to me, as he saw his comrade held on my blade.

This time, I did not hesitate or engage in combat. I withdrew my blade from the crystallizing female angel and plunged it deep into that of the oncoming male. Hanging on the end of my sai, like a white, fluffy kebab, the angel began to convulse as the weaponized toxin raped his body. I extracted my blade from him, his body started to become solid and gradually a large crack erupted in his chest. His body was splitting, cracking randomly as his complete death began.

Consequently, my attention was brought back to the female angel, whose whole frame was cracked like a shattered glass window hit with a stone. Her expression was blank and her eyes were falling from their sockets, piece by glass piece, hitting the terrain below her and splintering further on impact.

Her body continued to lose fragments until it eventually collapsed under its own burden and tumbled to the ground.

Turning my attention to the male angel, a large crack in his rigid glass-like body was tracing a path from his hip to his chest, spanning from left to right. The crack paused briefly before an ear-splitting screech indicated movement. The glass-on-glass noise continued as, painfully slowly, the upper portion of the angel's body slid diagonally away from his bottom half. Gaining momentum, the slipping, decapitated crystallized torso fell from its pedestal and hit the ground with a heavy thud.

Crumbs of glass sprayed around me. Hiding my face away from the initial impact, I heard rogue piece of angel glass hitting my armour. Peering from behind my armoured arm, I watched as the torso-less body began to drop to its knees.

Allowing my wings to erupt from my back, I hurriedly wrapped them around myself for more protection.

The knees caved and made contact with the pavement on Trafalgar Square. Angel glass exploded upwards with dramatic flair, sword sharp shards raining down from above me.

Taking care to ensure my body was temporarily covered by my wings, I peeped out from inside my feathers. To my horror, I could see Raven running full pelt in my direction, being chased be a nasty-looking demon.

I had seconds! Conscious that it was still raining glass, I open my wings wide enough to see Raven running as if to go past me. I knew he would run out of time to escape, becoming perforated by the remaining falling glass.

Three, two, one... Raven was adjacent to me. I took the opportunity to fully open my wings and grab him. Taking his arm as he ran past, I spun him into my body as my wings engulfed us both but exposed my back to the oncoming demon. I felt the bastard slicing at my wings trying to reach me.

"Stay still, Raven!" I demanded. "My wings will protect us."

"Yes ma'am," he responded, which made me smile.

Just as I had anticipated, the remaining glass shards rained down upon us. I could feel the slight pressure caused by the weight of the shards as they were repelled by my wings.

The attacks from the demon had ceased, leading me to believe that he had either given up or was affected by the angel glass.

Eventually, I could no longer feel the glass rain. Apprehensively, I began to unfurl my wings. Raven and I scanned our surroundings. Glass from the angel's death lay shattered at our feet. Ruffling my feathers behind me I dislodged a final remnant of angel glass, plus a few spots of my blood, from the superficial wounds the demon and glass had created.

"Are you okay?" I asked Raven, eyeing the wing debris with concern.

He nodded back. "I am. Thank you. What happened to the demon?"

I shrugged back at him and brought my wings behind me as they began to heal themselves.

"Fucking BITCH!" A deep, resonating voice echoed from behind us.

"I think he may still be alive!" I said, turning with Raven, weapons drawn to face the creature from hell. I do not know how he was still alive: the angel glass was either embedded in his blackened body or lying on the ground, covered in black demon blood, where it had sliced him.

"Fucking bitch," he repeated, maintaining eye contact for a few seconds before the weight of his injured head defeated him and he face-planted the street beneath him.

"Don't let him descend, otherwise he'll return," I turned to Raven as he readied his sword.

"My pleasure," Raven smirked, and closed the gap between him and the wounded demon.

Gathering as much strength as he could possibly muster, the demon lifted his head for the final time. "I will be back for you, human!" he spat through his rancid yellow teeth, as fresh, sooty, viscous blood dribbled from the corner of his mouth, bubbling over his chin and forming an expanding puddle beneath his heavy head.

Raven's mouth turned up into a sadistic smirk as he drew back on his sword and held it high above his head.

"I don't think so!" he roared, bringing his sword down and plunging it swiftly into the demon's neck. A crunch resonated as the demon's head separated violently from his body.

Retracting his weapon from the concrete, Raven wiped the dripping, demon body fluid from it on the back of the liquifying mass.

Turning his back on the demon, he smirked as he walked past me, thanking me again for saving his life. I smiled and watched as he regrouped with the Rose Daggers before becoming engaged once more.

For a moment, I was given a reprieve; a chance to breathe and for my body to finish healing. Turning full circle, I was able to take note of my army. All were engaged yet everyone seemed to be coping with the fight thus far.

Stephen and Florence fought, whilst Devon and Elenor were paired up, rapidly extinguishing angels and demons.

To my left, Ryan was battling heavily alongside Julia, David and Cara from his army squad. Ryan had suffered a number of small insignificant, self-healing cuts to his forearms, and the humans were showing some signs of bruising.

My last rotation brought me round to face Connor. His muscular body glistened in the moonlight, sweat beaded across his chest and abdomen and I couldn't help but lick my upper lip with desire as I appreciated his body.

Bending down quickly, he gathered his arrow from the glass angel cracking into a million shards at his feet.

"Are you okay, babe?" he asked, placing his arrow in his quiver and making his way towards me.

I nodded. "I'm fine: a few cuts but they're healing," I replied.

"Turn," he lightly demanded, pointing his index finger in the air and swirling it.

I huffed and turned, exposing my back to him.

"Spread your wings, Tory," he asked, in a low concerned voice.

Allowing myself to be temporarily obedient to Connor, I spread my wings as requested. Connor stepped closer into me until I felt his breath on my neck and his palm on my back.

"Tory, babe. This is deep," he whispered from behind me.

"I can feel it healing and I don't feel any light force or venom," I responded, trying to reassure him.

"Huh!" he sighed, pausing momentarily before speaking again. "It is healing but slowly. I think you have a shard embedded. I need to take it out of you for you to fully heal. Yo Bro!" he hollered at Ryan, as we watched him dispatch the demon he was fighting.

Checking his comrades were happy for him to leave, Ryan ran over to us.

"You alright?" he addressed us.

"Yep – you?" Connor counter-questioned.

"Yeah. What's up, Tory?" Ryan turned his attention to me.

Before I had the chance to open my mouth, Connor answered for me.

"Shard in her back. Cover us while I remove it, will you?"

"Yep, will do. Making a habit of having things embedded in your body, aren't you?" Ryan smirked, readying his sword, whilst Connor stifled a laugh and my jaw fell open.

"Ignore him. Ready?" Connor asked.

I nodded rapidly, giving consent for Connor to delve his hand into my skin once again.

"It's only small. I can feel it. Just... trying to... get my... fingers around it." Rummaging for a moment longer, Connor withdrew a star-shaped glass shard and immediately reported that I was healing at a more rapid rate.

Very softly, Connor ran his hand over my back and between my wings, before bringing his hand to the back of my neck, tenderly stroking his fingers over my collar bone.

Closing my eyes, I leaned into his touch, enjoying the brief moment with him. He brought his body closer behind mine. Breathing softly, close to my ear, he kissed me softly.

"I love you, Purgatory.'

My breath hitched, allowing my heart to burst with the happiness I felt from those three words. Twisting in his arms, I found his lips with my own and kissed him hard. Immediately, he returned my kiss and brought his arms around me further, holding me tightly into his chest.

"I love you," I whispered against his lips, as I felt them turn up into a smile. Elongating our kiss, I lost myself in him.

"Oh shit! Guys – a little help, please." Ryan's pissed-off voice broke our kiss and reclaimed our attention.

Turning in his direction, we saw swarms of demons and angels flooding toward us, like rolling waves of contaminated sea water. As a trio, we steadied our feet firmly, weapons drawn. Back-to-back, we waited for the wave to come to us.

Through the PCD, Connor checked on our comrades. Elenor reported back that between Florence, Devon, Stephen, Jonathan and herself, they were helping cover the rapidly tiring human souls.

"Do they need to go back through the portal to recover?" I interjected.

"Not yet," Elenor replied, "However, Lucas has just returned from escorting Julia back to purgatory. She sustained a pretty nasty demonic laceration. Incidentally, the antidote works exceptionally well. Neutralized the demon toxin almost immediately. She had to go back for stitches as the humans don't heal as fast as we do."

I felt a rush of relief chase though my veins. Thank goodness, the antidote worked.

"We have a large group of demons and angels advancing towards us. I think we need to re-group and fight as one," I informed them.

"Of course."

"Right away."

"Yes, boss."

Voices of acknowledgment echoed down my PCD and gradually I began to feel the presence of my army at my back. Standing proud of my army, I addressed them again.

"Our main objective is to get to Lucifer and Abraxos. Without their authority and leadership, their armies will become weak."

Again, murmurs from the army verified the understanding of our goal. Anticipation flooded through me. The enlarged demon/angel army raced at us; an unrelenting mass of black and white, the ultimate good and bad united for a brief period to fight me.

It was almost comical, as smaller battles between allies played out at the sidelines of the advancing mob.

Grounding ourselves once more, the army stood back to back and facing outwards, weapons drawn and each member battle-ready.

I focused on Lucifer and Abraxos, close enough to view the battle, yet sufficiently far away to avoid being active within it. My eyes bore into their bodies before dropping to the ground, searching for a route that would lead me to them.

"Fly, Tory!" Connor's voice stuttered through my headset.

I shook my head softly. "I would be to vulnerable," I answered. fearing that if I took to the skies, every arrow currently notched by my enemy would be following my flight path in rapid succession.

"You are vulnerable either way, Tory. You are their target by land or air, babe. You are vulnerable."

My shoulders slumped forward, allowing my confidence to lose its balance and roll off of them. I was the target! This is all because of me and it's why we all stand here waiting for an arse-kicking to come to us.

However, I was not here to be beaten or forced into handing over the human domain, alongside purgatory, to heaven or hell. I was here to claim back what was mine: the afterlife.

No sooner had I snapped myself out of my pathetic, selfish attitude, the first wave of enemy fighting hit us. Hard.

Chapter 39

Angels and demons attacked from each direction: as one was slain, another took its place immediately. Trafalgar Square resembled a battle zone. As far as I could see, demons and angels occupied every available inch of the London square and more were appearing, battle-ready and heading in our direction.

With each second that the St. Martin-in-the-Fields clock ticked, more enemy fighters emerged from the skies and the ground.

From their vantage point, the devil and his higher-angel buddy watched the fight, pausing to talk between themselves, they frequently laughed with each other.

Turning rapidly to my left as I fought a foul-smelling demon, I spotted Jonathan also battling with a demon. The more they fought, the further Jonathan moved away from our group.

I could see that he was fighting well; a little aggressive and uncontrolled, but he was kicking the demon's butt. Making light work of my current opponent, who then liquified at my feet, I stepped over his groggy residue and engaged with an elderly angel.

This was not an old and wise angel, in the context of being elderly, but a tiny, little wrinkly man. Bent over with age, he waved his light force sporadically around, hitting everything in close proximity, including his fellow angels.

I smirked. He had obviously just been harvested as his body had not started to heal itself. He had not been in the afterlife long enough for his angel powers to rid him of his aliments or straighten out his spine. Poor bugger: harvested to fight when he should be receiving peace.

It was glaringly obvious that he did not know who or why he found himself in the middle of a battlefield. Passing angels directed him to where he should be, whilst demons tormented him.

Abruptly, I was stopped by a blinding fragment of light force illuminating a motionless lion to my right.

"Shit! Jonathan!" Leaving the old man to hopefully get lost in the crowd, I ran in the direction that I had last seen the demon child. With my feet pounding the concrete, I fought my way through numerous demons before their blackened, glutinous, bodily by-products created a sticky coating under my feet.

Giving consent for my wings to ricochet from their rest, I took to the skies as a second light-force blast ignited at Jonathan's last location.

Gaining momentum, I flew hard and fast until I was stopped, mid-flight, by rapid light-force fire.

Diving down towards the origin of the blasts, I spotted a small, dark figure catapulted into the sky.

"Jonathan!" His name hung on my lips as his unconscious body continued to free-fall, earth-bound, until he collided with a massive bronze lion. His body fell awkwardly to the terrain before him, where he remained lifeless.

Raising my gaze from Jonathan, I saw Abraxos land a few feet from his body. Stoking the burning flames currently engulfing my wrath, Abraxos slowly walked towards the helpless demon. As he elevated his hands, I could see the outline of one of the dagger weapons the angels thought would kill me.

The bastard was preparing to descend Jonathan back to Lucifer. Releasing the chains from my anger, I flew hard to reach the demon child.

Abraxos had the dagger trained on the defenceless demon. The blade began to sparkle slightly as he called the light force within it.

My first foot hit the ground in front of Jonathan's head, quickly stabilized by the other. As Abraxos let loose the light force stream, I prepared my sai to intercept the weapon.

The power the force held was stronger than I remembered. Gradually, it began to push me backwards towards Jonathan. Digging my heels further into the ground, I rectified my equilibrium and stood firm.

Abraxos did not cease in his efforts to reach Jonathan. Intercepting each change of direction he made was infuriating him more and more, until he dropped the dagger to the ground, lowering his eyes in exhaustion.

I took the opportunity to check Jonathan: he was badly wounded.

His body was speckled in both demon and angel-inflicted wounds. Searching his armour, I looked for his antidote. He hadn't used it, which was probably the reason that the lacerations were not healing.

Retrieving the EpiPen-style antidote, I flicked off the lid to expose the large, sharp needle and plunged it as hard as I could into Jonathan's upper chest, not covered by armour, and into his stagnated heart.

Jonathan's body jolted in response, yet he remained still. The millisecond it took for his body to regain momentum felt like a year slowly passing by.

Eventually the antidote ran through his veins, coursing its way to his extremities and encouraging the toxins to exit via any means necessary.

He inhaled. He was alive, in the demonic sense. Relief cascaded over me as I watched his chest rise and fall with determined rhythm as his body began to heal itself.

I was reminded by a bolt of light force piercing between my wings that I had stupidly turned my back on the chief angel. Just as I was about to find my feet, Jonathan opened his drowsy eyes and looked at me. Offering him a reassuring smile, my breath hitched as a secondary bolt of light force ran the length of my spine.

"Stay down!" I ordered Jonathan from between my gritted teeth. "When you can, get back to the portal. You need to heal."

He nodded with a heavy head as unconsciousness claimed him again. Swallowing the pain ricocheting off my back, I moved to stand, leaving Jonathan at my feet. Turning towards Abraxos, I inhaled deeply, bringing my sai up to my body in a defensive stance.

"So, Tory..." Abraxos began. "You have chosen to fight. How far does your stupidity range? Seriously, I am intrigued." A grin spread across his features and it took the majority of my self-control not to attack him immediately. Deciding to use words to prolong the conversation and grant my body more time to heal, I replied.

"Abraxos, I am not here to fight, but to defend. To defend purgatory and the human domain from the despicable behaviour heaven and hell are currently displaying when harvesting. Besides, when does heaven take orders from hell?" Goading him further, I tilted my hips and smirked right back at him.

Adjusting his posture, Abraxos released his wings and began a failed attempt at intimidation.

"HEAVEN DOES NOT AND WILL NOT EVER TAKE ORDERS FROM HELL!" he bellowed.

I allowed a faint crease in my brow to show, as I feigned confusion.

"Yet you are here, today – right now – as Lucifer dictated." I could sense the anger building within the ancient angel: his wings remained outstretched while his face glowed with an intensity comparable to that of a plump, ripe aubergine.

"Bitch!" he spat through his teeth, disseminating saliva over himself.

"Touched a nerve, have I?" I retorted.

Administering a beam from the dagger held in his outstretched hand, Abraxos rained a torrent of light force at me. Blocking and diving to avoid his attack, I was momentarily distracted by a crash of rubble behind me.

Rotating to check on Jonathan, I was met with a pile of rocks just missing the hunched body of the child demon.

Jonathan had regained consciousness and scrambled to safety before the rocks had fallen. The bronze lion now stood precariously to the side: if the base received many more hits, the lion would fall and crush me.

"Go around the back, Jonathan and stay down. Hide," I managed to tell him before my distraction allowed a bolt from the dagger to hit me on the right side of my face.

The force spun me around, upsetting my balance. Falling uncontrollably, my body hit the fallen rubble as my head rebounded off of the base of the lion. Pain seared inside me, releasing blood from a multitude of lacerations and abrasions I had just received.

"STOP! HIDE!" I held my hand up to Jonathan as he struggled on his knees to reach me.

He halted.

"Please," I whispered. "Be safe."

Reluctance and contemplation played on his face before he nodded in acknowledgement and began to retract his weary body to behind the statue.

A ringing in my ear caused me to reach up and investigate. The communication device had shattered around my ear, embedding shards of plastic into the surrounding skin.

Tentatively, I pulled at the PCD until it came away from my ear. A new wave of blood pulsated from the wound from the newly evacuated earpiece.

Stemming the blood with my hand, I threw the PCD to the ground and began finding my feet.

In the few moments it took to rise to my feet, my ear and bodily lacerations had healed, leaving only tracks of dried blood as evidence.

Abraxos was laughing hard, his head swung back as he enjoyed my brief defeat. I shrugged. As Abraxos was enjoying his humour, I readied my light force-absorbed sai and aimed.

Releasing the pent-up light force, I slammed Abraxos his weapon, back into his chest, with the force of a hurricane.

Bringing his head to its correct position as his laughter abated, Abraxos was hit by his own weapon, delivered via my sai, and thrown from his feet. Falling backwards, he was unable to correct or prepare for his landing.

"HA!" I yelled. "Hurts, doesn't it?" Pretty pleased with myself, I took time to check on Jonathan. I could just make out his tiny figure veiled behind the lion's enormous front paw.

From above me, the beating of wings brought my attention back to reality. Lucifer landed a few feet away from where Abraxos remained, strung over the stones. He stared at his temporary ally.

"Purgatory." He acknowledged me after demanding that Abraxos 'get' his 'shit together'. "I see you still protect the boy. You are foolish to bring a fruitless war to the afterlands." Arrogance radiated from him as he glared at me, as though he were reprimanding a small child.

Allowing him his moment to speak, I remained quiet, assessing his surroundings. He had five demons accompanying him, flanking him at his sides and his back.

He had little armour covering his black, scalded body: the protection focused on covering his most vulnerable area – his neck. In his left hand, he held a dagger, which he unconsciously fingered as it sat uncomfortably in his palm. On his waistband hung a sword, intricate and beautiful, but contained within it was a piece of ancient dragon platinum. It is believed that dragons consume platinum to produce fire from its digested by-product.

When I appointed Lucifer to oversee hell, there was no fire or lakes of lava, but over time, Lucifer's need to create hell as a punishment forced him to look at a prolonged, inescapable, deadly penalization for being harvested to hell: heat and its accompanying fire.

Tracking down the last known reclusive dragon, Lucifer murdered the beast and cut out the platinum-filled bone that created its flames. Returning to hell, Lucifer embedded the bone into the domain's terrain, where it infected the land with its flame. Hell became hot and fire-filled, causing elite punishment for the souls of the harvested, human souls.

Once the bone had released itself into hell, a small platinum ember remained and it was this ember that had found solace and protection within Lucifer's unique sword. The ember feeds the sword its internal heat, rendering the sword deadly.

I eyed it up and down. Its beauty radiated and as the moonlight of the human domain caught its metallic hilt, it glistened with a red-hot thread interwoven within it.

"Lucifer – I do not bring war: only an end to oppression. Prepare yourself for death." Standing firm, I delivered my own speech back to the head demon.

"Interesting theory but no, Purgatory. This is definitely war," he retorted.

"Fucking bitch!" Abraxos was making his way towards Lucifer. His healing wounds were scattered across his angel body.

I stifled a giggle and watched Abraxos pushing demons out of his way.

"Nice language for an angel. Must be the company you keep, Abraxos," I quipped.

He threw me a look that could have killed me if such a thing could be done, which only made me laugh out loud.

Standing next to Lucifer, Abraxos leaned in and began whispering to him, like a schoolchild in a playground. Lucifer nodded with concern and frequently flicked his eyes in my direction.

Behind me, I heard a creaking in the massive structure as it struggled to maintain the weight of the bronze lion. Noticing my obvious concern and the ailing statue, Abraxos smiled widely and shot a number of rapid light-force bolts directly at the base.

Rubble exploded all around me.

"Run, Jonathan!" I managed to shout before I extended my wings and wrapped them around my body, as the tumbling masonry engulfed me.

Crouching between my wings, I covered my head with my arms and waited for the falling rocks to subside.

The weight was becoming unbearable and I only hoped that the rubble wasn't superseded by a couple of tons of bronze lion.

Curiosity found this moment to remind me of the tale of Big Ben and his association with the lions: if Big Ben were ever to chime thirteen, the massive lions would come to life.

Doubled over, under rocks, I pleaded with Big Ben to make that thirteenth chime so the lion could walk away from its plinth rather than land on me... Yeah, that didn't happen. I felt the ground shudder around me and I knew the immense structure was falling.

I was stuck: immobilized and weighed down by the rubble that had already fallen. Now I waited for my demise, crushed under seven tons of bronze. A thud of epic proportions resounded beside me and dislodged the concrete on top of me.

A second, louder thud reverberated throughout Trafalgar Square, shaking the earth. It quaked and shuddered uncontrollably.

Dust plummeted up, choking me temporarily. Coughing hard and splitting out clay-like saliva, I forced my eyes to open and surveyed my environment. I was encased in an air pocket surrounded by rock, dust, electric cables, and scattered puddles of water.

Concluding that the lion had, indeed, fallen and that I wasn't dead, I tentatively flexed my wings. They were still heavily laden with building detritus but with every movement of my wings, it started to fall.

Concentrating on excavating myself, I dropped my fangs and released my claws, relieving their constant pent-up pressure. I felt the immediate relief and began clawing at the rubble in front of me through the small gap I could create with my wing movement.

Gradually, my movement was becoming less restrictive as rubble fell. I was frequently adapting to the stagnant dusty air that was impeding my breathing. I took a few moments to gather my thoughts and rest my body. Lacerations and bruises covered my skin: I was healing but at a slower rate as I tried to escape my stone tomb.

Inhaling deeply, I forced my strength into my legs and wings and with a short, sharp burst of energy, I stood up. The remaining rubble cascaded down my wings and my legs shook slightly as I found my balance. Still enveloped within the air pocket, I was able to see shards of moonlight illuminating the space. Straining to see, I went into one of the tiny gaps to my left. I saw only more rubble: the lion had, indeed, fallen from his base.

Turning and retracting my wings tighter to my back, I found a small, dimly lit hole. Putting my eye up to the hole, I could see very little. The hole tunnelled through the rubble, reducing in diameter.

Straining to see, I spotted something. Possibly a claw? The lion's claw! It had missed landing on me by centimetres. I shuddered with relief. I could get myself out and the overturned lion would give me some temporary protection from the demons and angels.

I smiled with renewed confidence and began clawing at the hole, my momentum gathering as the hole expanded, allowing me to see more of the lion. The bronze statue had fallen sideways, its base facing me while its head led toward where Lucifer and Abraxos had been standing.

As soon as the hole was big enough, I squeezed my body through, remaining hidden by the prostrate lion. Poking my head briefly around its enormous form, I reassessed my situation.

Two demons were walking towards me with weapons drawn, sent by Lucifer to ensure my demise. Behind them, a second pair of demons escorted Lucifer and Abraxos towards the fallen statue. Kicking rocks out of their path and creating grey plumes of dusty mortar in their wake, the leaders of heaven and hell discussed my potential crushing and when purgatory should have its portal destroyed.

I smirked at their premature thinking. Were they really that naive to think something so minor as tumbled rock would stop me?

My mouth was still dry from the inhaled rock dust. Pulling as much saliva as I could from the inside of my mouth, I spat out the clay-like substance. Replenishing my lungs with an elongated breath, I prepared for my attack.

Currently, they thought I was either dead or injured. Little did they realise I was going nowhere without a pretty big fight.

I crouched with my sai in hand. Testing my wings, I fluttered them in the minute cavity space. They were sore but healing: I would be able to fly.

Closing the gap between the demons and my hiding place, the group continued forward.

Lucifer had sheathed his dagger, whereas Abraxos held his lightly by its hilt, at his side. Arrogance played across both of their features as they lazily stomped in my direction.

Five feet… Four feet… Three feet… They were getting closer. Two feet… One foot... HERE!

Chapter 40

I leapt as high as I could from the small caves and straight up. Bursting into the moonlight, I immediately released my wings and ignoring the pain that accompanied their release, I readied my sai.

The first two demons were standing on the lion at the edge of the hole I had created as I erupted through the rubble. Flying past them, I stretched out my toxin-laced sai and swiped their heads from their bodies.

Two demon heads with expressions of sheer shock were carried upwards with the momentum of my elevation. A grin played upon my lips as the heads reached their pinnacle height and began to fall down to their wilting bodies.

I stopped flying and held myself in the air. The demons flanking Lucifer and Abraxos had stopped their masters and were preparing to protect them.

Lucifer scanned the area, confused by what was happening. He had been too involved in talking with Abraxos that he hadn't yet seen me or noticed that two of his demons were relieved of their heads.

"Purgatory!" Abraxos exclaimed, beside Lucifer. His eyes locked onto mine.

Following Abraxos's stare, Lucifer found me. His expression barely changed and he showed little emotion when he realized that his demons would not be descending.

Keeping my eyes trained on the four individuals, I allowed myself to return to the earth and came to a standstill directly on top of the lion's mane.

"Kill her!" Lucifer screamed, and the two remaining demons took to the sky.

Standing firm, I waited for them. The two middle-aged demons flew swiftly towards me. I was not intimidated by their snarls or verbal attacks and my sai was as ready as I was.

Landing either side of me at each end of the fallen statue, they began running towards me the moment their feet touched the ground. Maintaining my position, I waited. Lucifer and Abraxos were making their way closer, talking between themselves, deep in conversation.

From my left, I heard the scraping of metal against metal. The demon had his sword at his side but as he walked, he drove the tip of his weapon into the bronze statue, scarring it deeply.

With one sai in my right hand, I pulled back my arm, twisting my torso with it. Twisting sharply gave me the advantage of seeing the second demon slightly closer than I had anticipated. Readying myself, I violently spun back around to face the first demon, releasing my sai as I did so. The weapon flew from my hand and deftly pierced the demon's neck, shattering his spine cord.

The sai drove forward until it appeared out of the back of his neck. Reaching haplessly for the offending blade, the demon fell to his knees and began liquifying.

A roar from behind me reminded me of the second demon: he was so close. Continuing to rotate, I spun my remaining sai backwards in my hand. The toxin-filled tip led me to the demon and keeping the sai down, I pushed it directly into the demon's abdomen.

Immediately using his body as my buffer, I controlled my spin and stopped, leaving the demon bent over where the sai had struck. Withdrawing the weapon from the doubled-up demon, I sunk it deep into the his throat. The dark creature managed a gurgling scream before a torrent of black, viscous blood spewed from his mouth.

Removing my weapon from the dying demon, I callously wiped my blade on the fabric of his cape and bade him farewell as he disintegrated into a demon puddle.

The first demon was already completely liquid. Sitting in the middle of his gooey remnants was my sai, sticking straight up. Walking over, I collected it, cleaned it on my sleeve and placed it in its sheath.

The higher beings of heaven and hell had stopped their advance, opting instead to stand motionless, trying to process what had just happened.

"So it is true, Purgatory," Abraxos began. "You have found a weapon to prevent ascension or descension."

"I have," I answered, smugly.

"How?" Lucifer interjected.

I tilted my head and gave him my 'as if' expression.

"I will not divulge my secrets to you, Lucifer, as I'm sure you would never divulge yours to me." Touché, you bastard.

"Stop talking," Abraxos said, abruptly, to Lucifer. "I did not come here for idle chat! I came to kill this bitch."

Lucifer glared back at Abraxos, pinning him with 'don't you dare reprimand me' eyes.

"Be my guest," he spat at him, stepping sideways, allowing Abraxos a clear path to me. A smirk played upon Lucifer's face as a determined Abraxos drew his dagger and ran at me.

I braced myself for his attack. Closing the gap between us, he gave freedom to the light force imprisoned within the dagger. Blast after blast he aimed at me. I ducked and moved away from each shot, allowing them to pass me. As they did, they hit the statue's remaining base, shattering it further. I found myself avoiding both Abraxos's light force and falling rubble.

Every missed shot Abraxos delivered was accompanied by a deep laugh from Lucifer, behind him.

Deciding that I needed to get out of my corner, I extended my wings and took to the sky, followed by an array of light-force splinters as I went. Abraxos rose, too, consistent with his attacks. My sai had absorbed a large amount of the angel's light weapon as I evaded his attack shots. Feeling its energy pulsing against my palm, I fought back: light against light.

My first shot missed, giving Abraxos the opportunity to mock me further. My second shot, however, caught him directly on his left shoulder, throwing him backwards and tearing a bundle of feathers from his wing.

Pure, dove-white feathers floated around Abraxos's falling body and the language the angel was yelling was more like that of a demon.

Booming laughter sounded, once again, behind the angel as Lucifer enjoyed watching his temporary ally taking an arse-whooping. The cracks in the forced relationship were beginning to show as Abraxos righted himself abruptly, scored the remaining expletive he had and directed them at the angel of hell.

The laughter stopped.

"Abraxos – do not toy with me!" Lucifer warned him, sternly.

"Desist with your laughter," Abraxos countered briefly, before turning back to face me.

I didn't give him the satisfaction of releasing a light force beam, I flew straight at him; my sai extended and aiming for his chest, for his heart: the epicentre that kept him alive.

Meeting me in defence with his dagger, we fought on our wings. Diving – attack, defend, dive, attack, defend – we were matched, unable to inflict wounds on each other in this form of combat.

Deciding that I needed an alternative, I folded my wings and abruptly dived downwards. Abraxos was not expecting my sudden movements. It took him a few moments for the realization of where I had gone to kick in, before he followed.

He was fast. Turning to watch him gather speed to catch up with me I took the opportunity I needed: I slowed and waited for Abraxos to come closer. He encroached fast. Taking a breath, I spun and catapulted myself back up towards him.

I was aiming for his chest. However, as he once again realized I had maneuvered, he countered my actions. Missing his chest, I attacked his right wing, slicing at it mercilessly and enveloping us both in a torrent of feathers, reminiscent of the outcome of an epic pillow fight

He fell: his wings were too damaged to hold him in flight. Hovering and wiping the torn feathers from me, I watched him fall; his rapid speed accompanied by his screams of terror as his fell.

Inhaling and exhaling deeply, I began to establish my equilibrium. I had eliminated Abraxos from the air combat but on the ground he would still be able to fight.

Abraxos fell awkwardly into Nelson's Column, his body implanted neatly in the middle of the structure before momentum from the hit pushed him away from the monument and alongside a large tumble of bricks. Falling down the side of the column and landing with a bone-breaking thud at the bottom, his dilapidated wings fell limply over his body.

"Meh!" I thought. "He will heal."

Pinning him with my eyes, I looked for signs of life, hoping he was hurt enough to ascend. He moved slightly but he wasn't going anywhere.

Nelson's Column leaned precariously to the side as the weight of Nelson, himself, began to compromise the integrity of the structure. It would not fall just yet but another hit from an angel would definitely bring it down.

"Fuck it!" I spat, as Lucifer slammed into me. He had taken the opportunity to take to the sky and attack while I was distracted by Abraxos falling.

I defended my body with my wings and sai as Lucifer bombarded me. Conscious of my need to avoid his venom-filled claws, I skirted around him quickly.

He was relentless, alternating between claw and dagger. I was sustaining superficial scratches and burns from his weapons but nothing my body couldn't cope with.

Every hit he made toward me, I countered. Matched in every sense, physically and mentally, we danced our battle, momentarily admiring each other's ability.

I swung my sai at Lucifer, cutting through his arm and hoping I had released some of the toxin. The smallest amount would not kill him as it would a lower demon: however, it would help to slow him down.

Lucifer clutched at his arm as the toxin invaded his bloodstream. Taking the opportunity to breathe, I pulled back from him and the fight.

A flurry on the ground caught my eye: Abraxos was fighting with someone. I strained my eyes and dropped down towards the earth.

"Jonathan!" I exclaimed. Folding my wings behind me, I sped my way down to the child demon.

I did not stop as I reached the ground, instead opting to plough into Abraxos, grabbing Jonathan as I did so. Using my wings to move us away from the head angel, I took Jonathan out of Trafalgar Square and landed roughly on the outskirts.

"Thank you," Jonathan whispered. "For not giving me to the devil and saving me. Again." His eyes glossed over with a thin, dark liquid which rolled down over his cheek as he blinked.

Embracing him, I hugged him hard. Examining his wounds, I whispered words of reassurance.

"Your wounds... Any of them feel like they are not healing

correctly?" I questioned, releasing him enough to turn him around and examine his back. All external lacerations and scratches seemed to be healing but I probed further for a definitive answer from him.

"They feel fine, honestly, Tory. I can't feel any venom apart from my own," he replied.

Internally, I breathed a sigh of relief. I did not want him descending to Lucifer.

"Good. That's fantastic," I replied, as he adjusted his armour, replacing it in a comfortable position following my inspection.

"Jonathan – I need you to find Ryan and Connor. Both Lucifer and Abraxos are coming for me and although individually I could whoop both their arses, when they're together, I am vulnerable."

"I can help."

"No, Jonathan. Lucifer wants both of us. I need you safe. My PCD is broken. What about yours? Is it working?"

He shrugged, deeply.

"Busted, when the lion collapsed. I crushed it moving out of the way."

"Okay, then. Go and find the twins but try not to engage on the way. Go back through the portal and ask Porter for a new PCD." As I lightly demanded his duties, Jonathan nodded obediently and prepared his wings to fly.

"Be careful," I uttered.

Rushing at me, Jonathan wrapped his arms around me. I held him. No words were necessary. We both understood what was going to happen, yet neither of us wanted to acknowledge it.

"I will see you later," I whispered into the top of his head before planting a kiss in the middle. I felt him smile against the small amount of skin I had not enveloped in armour. "Go, little Demon," I ordered, with a slight push to encourage him to go.

"Bye, Tory," he whispered and took to the sky.

I watched him go: his blackened demon body was immaculately cloaked by the evening sky. Releasing the breath I had been holding, I watched him fly out of sight. Slowly, I turned away and began walking back to Trafalgar Square to finish my war.

Chapter 41
Connor

"I can't hear her, Porter. What the fuck is going on? She isn't responding. No! I don't think so. Anyone hear from Tory in the last ten minutes? NO? Fuck! Porter – can you patch in and locate her? Cheers, mate." Not hearing from Tory was playing with my concentration. Demons and angels were relentlessly attacking and I lost sight of her.

"Connor?" Florence's voice crackled through my headset.

"Florence – are you all right?" I asked.

"We can't find Jonathan either. Stephen and I lost sight of him," she replied.

"Okay. That may be a good thing, Florence. Hopefully, they're together," I told her, knowing that Tory would ensure the young demon was safe.

"I hope so," she answered, before allowing the communication to go silent.

"Connor?"

"Go, Porter – what do you know?"

"It would seem that her communication device is offline. It is either damaged or failed but, interestingly, everyone else's is working fine, apart from Tory's and Jonathan's."

"Did they go offline at the same time?"

"Yes – within seconds of each other," Porter reported.

"Okay. So let's assume they must be together. And Porter – try to pinpoint their last location."

"Will do. I'll let you know when I find something." Porter signed off and silence descended over our group.

The realization that Tory was currently untraceable was disconcerting. The group had reformed into our heptagon leaving the space at the front which should have contained Tory. I needed to know if she was safe; I needed to see her face and hold her in my arms. The waiting was torture. Every second that ticked by reminded me that I had failed her.

"Yo! Bro', wake up!" Ryan yelling at me brought my attention back to the present reality. I looked up just in time to see an angel, moments away from skewering me with a pair of shiny light-force infused daggers.

"Whoah! No, you don't!" Ducking sideways, I moved myself out of his way. Turning sharply, with a fresh arrow in my hand, I drove it deep into the angel's torso. Running the arrow through the back of the angel, I could feel the energy release as the tip of the arrow pierced his heart, allowing light force to escape.

As the angel screamed at the injected venom infiltrating his body, I withdrew my light-force renewed arrow and placed it back in my quiver.

Shattering, the newly glass-made angel fell to the ground amongst the already smashed angel glass and demon puddles.

I chastised myself for my stupidity and lack of concentration. Had I responded any later, it would have been me descending to meet the wrath of Lucifer.

It didn't take long for my mother to realise my near miss as a torrent of verbal abuse cascaded through the privacy setting on my PCD. Reassuring her that it would not happen again, she told me she loved me and to sort myself out.

I chuckled to myself. I am a demon/angel hybrid: I fight hard and fast. I am quick and personally, I would also say quite a badass, yet my mum still threatens to 'tan my hide' if I don't buck my ideas up.

Around the heptagon, angels and demons were dying at an immense rate. The ground was becoming a difficult terrain of glass-infused tar. As a collective, we moved as one to the left and further away from the portal. No sooner had we moved, we were bombarded with new attackers.

"Connor! UP!" Dad yelled in my ear, obviously engaged in battle. "Right... up! Jonathan!"

Looking up, I spotted the small demon irrationally flapping his wings. He was exhausted, bloodstained and trying to stay airborne. Releasing my wings, I flew upright and caught him as his exhaustion overtook him and he lost consciousness.

A quick visual showed me a multitude of slowly healing lacerations, his earpiece was missing and his wings torn. The lacerations he had sustained were evident of battling both angels and demons, the poor boy.

Before my feet had a chance to touch the ground, Florence and Stephen surrounded me. Immediately, Florence took Jonathan from my arms and pushed her way deep into the army to create a safe place to heal the young demon.

Stephen and I followed. Florence had already begun assisting Jonathan's body to heal faster as she hovered over him, sending her light force into him.

Jonathan's eyes began flickering slowly as he forced them to open and focus.

"Tory..." he whispered, before closing his eyes.

Kneeling beside him, I shook him slightly, begging him to tell me where she was. Florence cleared her throat and shaking her head, slowly discouraged any further questioning of the small demon.

I waited, impatiently tapping my fingers on my knee and willing the young demon to regain consciousness. Five long minutes ticked slowly by as I watched Jonathan's chest rise and fall with his rhythmic breathing. His eyes flickered numerous times but never stayed open long enough to wake himself up.

My eyes met Florence's, pleading with her to allow me to shake him awake. Shaking her head slowly, she mouthed 'No'. Anger pulsed through me until Florence leaned close to her charge and gently shook him herself, whispering words of encouragement.

Patting my shoulder from behind, Stephen reassured me. He knew the worry I was feeling for Tory and my need to find her.

Eventually, Jonathan awoke. His eyes widened as he scanned his surroundings and struggled to get up. Kneeling directly behind him, Stephen supported the young demon as he focused on Florence, then turned his eyes to me.

"Tory," he rasped. "She needs you and Ryan. She needs your help."

"Where is she, Jonathan?" I asked impatiently, but softly.

"The lions – one has fallen. She is there. Her earpiece is broken." He paused, swallowing hard to lubricate his throat. "She is fighting Lucifer and Abraxas."

"Together?" I interrupted.

Jonathan nodded, sombrely. "I tried to help but she told me to get

280

you and Ryan. She needs you, Connor."

"Thank you, Jonathan. Stay here with the army."

Standing, I contacted my brother. He was fighting on the right of the dislodged heptagon. I began to head towards him, explaining as I sidestepped my comrades and placed my dagger through oncoming enemies.

"We need to go," I told Ryan, as I reached his position. "Dad!"

My father's voice echoed through my headpiece. "Go! We will protect the Portal," he responded.

"You're in charge, dad," I informed him, nudging Ryan to hurry up and dispatch the demon he was fighting.

Seconds later, he was done and we took to the skies. Looking back, I nodded to my father as he acknowledged me with a brief wave. From my elevated position, I scanned the area for the fallen lion. Only one remained upright: the majority of the others had been destroyed yet this one's legs remained firmly on its base.

"Where is she?"

The fallen lions diagonally faced each other.

"Split!" Ryan shouted at me. "I'll take this one – you go there!" he continued, pointing in the directions he suggested we should try.

"Keep in contact," I told him, before turning away from my twin and propelling myself towards the furthest lion.

Trafalgar Square was a disaster zone. Nelson's Column was teetering on the edge of collapse and below him, carnage was occupying every inch of the ground. I was relieved to see that the majority of victims were undescended demons and grounded angels. Tory's plan was working and we were winning.

Attacks came frequently as I flew. My mood was dictating the ease with which I was dispatching my attackers. Angel glass fell to the earth like collapsing chandeliers, smashing into a million more pieces as they hit the hard ground below them.

Demon remains splattered against the remaining standing buildings surrounding me. Fires had broken out, burning and destroying all angel glass and removing the evidence of their existence.

Out of the corner of my eye, I saw a flash. One after another, the flashes lit up the lion resting heavily on its side. Rubble surrounded it but

I could not see Tory, Lucifer or Abraxos.

Bringing my wings in close to my body, I dropped my altitude. I needed to see better and follow the light bursts.

I scanned, still unable to see Tory. Panic started to envelope me. I could feel my demonic side edging forward and wishing to take control. Pushing him back, I retained myself and persevered, flying close to the ground, searching.

I doubted my position, considering I was searching for three of the most powerful people in the afterlife. I was confused by how elusive they were.

A large flash to my right commanded my attention and I heard a scream. Ice particles speared each blood cell circulating within my veins as my blood ran cold. It was Tory. She was in pain.

I could feel her pain slicing into my heart as she screamed in agony. I needed to get down to her, and quickly. Informing Ryan of my position, I prepared to fly low.

I could not see Tory. Her screams radiated throughout the concrete jungle below, but she was hidden from my view. Rounding a corner through a tiny side street, I found what I had been looking for.

Tory was being held by Lucifer against a battle-damaged church. He was arched over her, whilst Abraxos stood next to him jabbing something at her and infiltrating her body with light force.

"Connor!"

"Not now, bro!" I spat between my teeth, as I prepared to fight.

"Connor, back up. I can feel the change happening. Step back and control it first," Ryan replied. "I am nearly with you. Don't let him take you over."

"Shut the fuck up, Ryan. Tory is being attacked by Lucifer and Abraxos, simultaneously. Do you really think I'm going to back up?"

Anger was feeding my temper and Ryan was right: my demonic side was absorbing my anger to strengthen itself. I paused briefly but as another, more pain-ridden scream assaulted my ears, I forgot my reasoning and dived towards Tory.

Focusing more as I closed the gap between us, I could see that Lucifer had one hand around Tory's neck, lodging her against the church wall and the other, which held his venom-impregnated claw, was pierced into the middle of her chest.

I could feel myself grow pale as I flapped rapidly to reach her. Beside Lucifer, Abraxos held Tory with his hand by her shoulder; in his right hand, a light-force dagger. Light strikes flared as he repeatedly stabbed her in the chest, close to where Lucifer had embedded his claw.

I had no control. The pent-up demon that had rested in the background of my subconscious, dormant and restrained, leapt forward, crushing my angel into the space between my reasoning and self-awareness.

"Connor!" Ryan's panicked voice yelled at me.

"Fuck off, brother!" I replied, and allowed the demon to overtake me as I welcomed him to the surface.

"CONNOR!" Ryan shouted louder.

Ignoring him, I ripped the earpiece from my ear and crushed it in the palm of my hand. My body rippled as my muscle mass strengthened and a light black sheen overtook the pink pigments in my skin.

I had never allowed my demon freedom over my body. I waited in excited anticipation as my body continued to develop.

Pain seared through my mouth. Clasping my hands over my lips, I stifled a scream to avoid detection by either Lucifer or Abraxos. Once the pain had subsided, I removed my hands and used my tongue to explore my mouth.

I had fangs: a metallic taste briefly tainted my tongue. My fangs descended and had split my lip. Licking the remaining droplets of metallic blood from my mouth, I caught sight of my newly acquired claws.

"Shit," I breathed, turning my hands over and observing my integrated weapons. Deep within my subconscious, my inner angel shuddered with fright at my transformation. He persistently tried to voice his concern but was immediately silenced by my demon counterpart.

Tory's screams once again echoed within my auditory canals, sparking my attention away from my whining angel. With my newly enlarged wings, I bolted closer. Approaching fast, I swiped past her, taking Lucifer and Abraxos with me as we tumbled violently through a window and into a hardware shop.

The contents of the shop exploded around us on impact, sending numerous DIY items flying through the air, until they embedded themselves into the nearest stationary objects.

I stood. Superficial lacerations from the shattered glass were healing over my blackened, minutely scaled body.

Searching the store for the head angel and his demonic buddy, I kicked tools away from under my feet and upturned the nearby sales counter.

Abraxos lay unconscious against the wall where he had been concealed by the counter. With Lucifer temporarily absent, I made my way over to the bastard angel. His cuts were healing, blood covered his hands and clothing: it was Tory's blood. Rage pulsed inside my veins, pumping my demon-grade adrenaline throughout my system and allowing every pent-up, restricted, anger-filled feeling to raise itself into the uppermost part of my demon-controlled brain.

My love for Tory fuelled my demon and as I took hold of Abraxos by his neck, I shook the consciousness back into him and slammed him up against a load-bearing wall, laden with nails supporting a multitude of DIY necessities.

"Wake up, you bastard!" I hissed through my gritted teeth and fangs. "Face me, Abraxos, before I kill you!" One last slam against the wall and I hung Abraxos on the penetrating nails like an angelic tapestry. The longer nails spiked through his body emerged, covered in blood and tissue from where they had ripped Abraxos's flesh as they speared through him.

He moaned a dull rasp, deep within his throat: it was pathetic. The sound was reminiscent of the feeble cry of a near-death wounded animal, reaching out for mercy.

"Abraxos!" I slapped him hard. He groaned again. Preparing to hit him again, I realized what he was attempting to do. He was trying to regenerate without the normal routine of ascending back to heaven. Clever!

Placing my hands either side of his head, I brought my face close into his.

"I know what you are doing, Abraxos. Cease now and face me or die as you are: a weak, feeble-minded excuse for an angel."

Abraxos's head nodded slightly: it was the only part of him not

284

embedded on the nails behind him. His eyes flickered rapidly before focusing on mine.

"Fuck you, Connor. Ascend me so I may return and kill you and your purgatory bitch..."

"No, Abraxos," I breathed, maintaining in close proximity to his face. "I shall not give you the pleasure of ascension. I shall give you death," I smirked.

He laughed; a guttural laugh intended to mock me.

"Your weapons cannot work on me, fool. I am the highest angel of heaven. I cannot die," he said, before the weight of his own head drew his attention back to the floor below him.

"Oh, okay" I retorted, my voice laced with sarcasm. "Try this."

Reaching back to my quiver, I pulled one of purgatory's venom-filled weapons and drove it deep into Abraxos's chest.

Abraxos looked up at me, shock crossing his features: for the first time in his angel existence, he felt pain.

He screamed as the toxin tracked throughout his body with every pathetic beat of his failing heart. The mix of demonic venom and light force created a rip in his equilibrium. Abraxos's skin started to become transparent as his body threw itself into mouth-foaming convulsions, desperately trying to relieve itself of the deadly toxin.

I stood, watching him suffer, my arms folded on my chest and my wings hanging relaxed at my back. I kept Abraxos pinned with my stare, encouraging the pain to increase and rip him from the inside out. Abraxos met my eyes with his own. I was unsure if he was pleading with me or cursing me out.

"Does it hurt?" I goaded, remembering Tory's screams as Lucifer and Abraxos dove their weapons into her.

"Fu...ck... yo...u," he stuttered, between screams.

I smiled. Shaking my head at him, I tutted.

"I believe, Abraxos, that it is you – not I – who is fucked."

Abraxos closed his eyes briefly, desperately stifling his screams as the pain from the toxin pulsed through his transparenting body. Temporarily bored with Abraxos's elongated death, I searched for Lucifer. He didn't seem to be present in the store but I maintained vigilance as I turned my attention back to the impaled angel. Abraxos opened his eyes and held my gaze, his body tremoring violently.

"'Bye, Abraxos. Enjoy death," I quipped, waving softly at him.

He kept his eyes focused on me as the angelic body he had inhabited for hundreds of years began to implode. A vortex of swirling light force spun irrationally out from my toxin-laced arrow. The spinning slowly started to pull the body of the angel as if a tornado had touched down on his chest and was dragging him into it.

Abraxos's cold stare began crushing into itself, shards of light force gradually etched out of the spaces where his eyes should have been. His left eye was completely gone, replaced by light force; his right eye sank into the depths of his eye socket before detaching, and was then swept up into the swirl on Abraxos's chest.

Screaming loudly, Abraxos finally disappeared into the vortex and imploded completely around my arrow, leaving just one pure white feather wedged in the plume of the arrow.

Pulling the arrow from the wall, I resettled it back into my quiver.

"Now!" I spoke out loud to myself. "Where's that fucking demon?"

Chapter 42
Tory

Whoever slammed Lucifer and Abraxos away from me caused their weapons to rip within my chest as they moved: not that I wasn't grateful, but fuck – it hurt. A lot. The impact left me with a wound representative of that made by a cardio-thoracic surgeon and the pain was intense.

Slumping forward over myself, I allowed my back to slide down the building supporting me as my legs gave in and failed to keep me upright. Pain radiated within my exhausted, blood-covered body.

"Tory! What the fuck happened? Are you okay? Well – obviously not." Ryan's concerned voice disrupted the ringing in my ears.

"Lucifer and Abraxos attacked me together. My chest is open... Can you help me heal?" I asked, gasping for the breaths that came in insignificant little air pockets.

"Of course." Immediately, Ryan knelt before me and extended his hands, allowing them to hoover millimetres from the open wound. Ryan's light force penetrated my body, soothing the pain created by the demon venom and Abraxos's light force.

"What's changed?" I asked the top of Ryan's head, as he remained kneeling. "Ryan, who was the demon that saved me? And why do you look different? More shiny..."

"How do you know that it was a demon that saved you?" Ryan questioned back.

"I could feel hell surrounding the demon: a deep, dark essence that was strong and powerful," I answered. Suddenly, it dawned on me who it might have been.

"Connor?" I whispered.

Ryan nodded slowly.

"He allowed his demon to overtake him. Jonathan found us and explained what had happened to you. I don't know, Tory, if he will be the same man he was before his demon rose."

"So his change made you more angel?"

"Yes. My angel arose to counterbalance his demon; to maintain the equilibrium throughout the afterlife and human domain." He paused. "Your chest is healed."

Gradually, Ryan stood. Holding his hand out to me, he supported me as stood.

"Thank you," I breathed, gently passing my hand over my chest and feeling for any evidence of the gaping wound. I smiled and leaning into Ryan, hugged him.

"We need to find him," I said, silently begging Ryan to assist with his twin sense and find him quickly. "Do you feel him?"

"I don't sense him yet. However, I do feel an enormous demonic signature. It could be him," Ryan replied turning east, where the demon essence remained. "We need to go now. I'll sense him more the closer we get to him."

I nodded in acknowledgement and released my wings, allowing them the extension they desired. Taking to the skies, I hovered, waiting for Ryan to join me. As soon as he was airborne, we rapidly began to fly east in a bid to find my demon.

We flew for at least five minutes before Ryan could identify Connor's scent.

"He is not hurt, but he is fighting. An angel, I think," Ryan reported. "Abraxos?"

"It must be: the angel signature is one of a hierarchal angel."

"And Lucifer? Can you feel him?"

"No, I don't sense any other being."

"Lead the way," I encouraged, hanging slightly behind Ryan as we took off once more.

"Wait!" Ryan suddenly stopped, mid-flight, concern crossing his features as he paused and closed his eyes. "Abraxos's essence has diminished."

"Connor is defeating him and stopping his ascension. Thank fuck for that," I smirked. "Lucifer?"

"Nothing," Ryan replied.

Having Lucifer temporarily indisposed ensured that Connor had ample time to heal any superficial wounds. Deciding that Ryan and I should get to Connor as soon as we could, we sped up and dived back into the mist-formed clouds that peppered the sky before us.

Within minutes of exhaustingly rapid flying, Ryan and I were brought to a stop on a small road littered with rubble. The carnage surrounding us was evidence enough of Connor's presence but I needed to see him to appease my mind.

Following the trail of mortar and bricks, Ryan and I stepped through the shattered window of a hardware store.

"Yep! Connor's here," Ryan stated, glancing around at the carnage created by the altercation between Connor and Abraxos. I chuckled. Connor was an intelligent, handsome hybrid but he was as messy as a puppy with toilet paper.

Glass crunched underneath my feet as Ryan and I made our way further into the shop.

"'Bye, Abraxos. Enjoy death," Connor's voice echoed lightly from the back of the building.

Ryan and I ran towards Connor's voice, dodging obstacles that were strewn in our path throughout the war-torn DIY shop. Stopping short of where Connor stood, Ryan and I watched as the pinned body of Abraxos began to crumple underneath its own weight and spiral into a vortex of dissipation.

We stood in collective silence as Connor nonchalantly stepped up to his arrow and retrieved it from the crumbling wall. He placed it securely in his quiver.

"Now," he spoke out loud to himself. "Where's that fucking demon?"

Turning swiftly on his heels, Connor turned to face us. His brow was furrowed, his skin littered with healing lacerations and his hair white with dust from the decimated building.

His eyes remained downcast as he roughly beat his blood-stained hands against the trouser fabric on his outer thighs.

"Connor..." I called, softly.

Connor paused and raised his eyes to meet mine. Concerned indentations assaulted his forehead as he straightened, allowing his rigid body to relax.

"Tory!" he breathed, quickening his pace to close the gap between us, refusing to pause until he had me in his arms. Connor immediately swept me into his embrace and held me tightly, peppering the top of my head with kisses.

"Babe, are you okay? Are you healed?" he whispered.

"I am healed," I replied, pulling gently away from him to look at his face. "Ryan helped me heal quicker..."

Mid-sentence, Connor crushed my lips with his own, shutting me up and kissing me with as much passion as he could muster in that moment. I reciprocated, pulling myself further into his body until we moulded into one.

This... Now... This is where I wanted to be and what I wanted to be. I don't think I took a breath as our kiss deepened and my light-headedness cascaded with my feelings and my love for Connor.

His embrace was strong and his hands gradually explored my body, coming to rest on each of my upper arms before he pulled me away from him.

"Breathe, Tory," he softly demanded. Temporary confusion echoed within my head as my oxygen starved-brain processed his words.

Inhaling sharply, I welcomed the new oxygen into my body and my lungs rejoiced in the new saturations of O2.

"That's better," Connor smiled and planted a soft kiss on the end of my nose.

"Where is Lucifer?" I asked.

"I have no idea," he began. "The three of us blasted through the shop so fast, I didn't see where he went. Abraxos is dead," he proudly stated.

"We saw him implode," I replied, shifting my eyes to the white-plumed arrow protruding from Connor's quiver.

"Well done, mate," Ryan interjected, and offered his brother the obligatory high five, which Connor accepted after placing me back on my feet. I rolled my eyes as the hybrids praised each other before they remembered the wayward leader of hell was here somewhere and he was probably in a foul mood.

The sound of movement in the store jolted us from our celebration of Abraxos's death. We now had Lucifer to deal with. Ryan placed his hand up to his ear as his PCD crackled into life.

"It's mum," he reported. "All the angels have left the human realm.

They ascended shortly after you killed Abraxos." Ryan continued to proudly explain to Elena how Abraxos met his end, and Connor and I entered further into the shop.

"They are all on their way here," Ryan continued, following us.

At the very back of the shop, we heard sounds of rubble being cleared, rocks tumbling and wood clattering violently to the floor.

"He's here," I stated, through a barely audible whisper.

The hybrids acknowledged me as Ryan placed one finger over his mouth and Connor pointed to our intended direction. With weapons drawn, our trio edged forward.

Chapter 43

The stench of recently spilled demonic blood assaulted my senses as I reached the rear aspect of the DIY wreckage. Precarious detritus fragments threatened to fall as we passed by the unstable shop walls.

Blood-saturated splatters adorned our surroundings creating a macabre tapestry on the previously off-white plastered walls.

"Lucifer must have been badly injured," I commented as I brought my attention away from the obscure wall murals and settled my focus back on Connor.

"I managed to hit him with the arrow head numerous times as we fell through the window. Our toxin must be preventing him from healing," Connor said, following the trail of blood drops which disappeared behind an enormous, ancient, woodworm-infected oak shelving unit.

Approaching the unit as a trio, we stood ready to fight with our weapons drawn and our focus sharp. A number of coarse growls erupted and reverberated throughout the shops. Lucifer growled once more and burst through the middle of the wooden shelving unit, causing splinters of jagged wood spears to fly in every direction.

Encasing myself with my wings, I felt them deflect the shards away from my body. Taking the opportunity to glance between my feathers, I noted that the hybrids had adopted the same posture, shielding themselves also. Focusing on the commotion unfolding before me, I opened my wings just enough to see a blood-stained, deeply lacerated Lucifer catapult himself from the remnants of the shattered oak structure.

Blood and venom dripped effortlessly from an elongated slash running from a horrendous split lip on the right side of his mouth. Drooling uncontrollably, Lucifer spat a gob of clotted blood from his mouth and wiped his chin with the back of his hand, causing the bleeding waterfall to continue.

Retracting my wings behind me, I retrieved my sai and standing between the battle-eager hybrids, we faced Lucifer, the devil himself.

A rabid force of nature pushed through Lucifer's veins as he attacked us without thought or self-awareness. For every action he initiated, either one of the hybrids or I countered it effortlessly.

Lucifer's frenzied attack was brutal: he was relentless in his advances, yet he remained weak.

"Fucking die, Purgatory," Lucifer spat through his bloodied lips. "Die and take your two half-breed bastards with you."

Pacing in front of us, Lucifer spat more congealed blood before continuing his abusive tantrum.

"My army approaches. I have called the armies of heaven and hell to me."

Temporarily, I sheathed my sai and shook my head softly whilst watching Lucifer's battered body pass from left to right.

"Lucifer! Abraxos is dead, Connor killed him. He was not able to ascend: in fact, he imploded like a suctioning black hole," I informed the demon.

Lucifer snapped his head towards me with such force that I was surprised that he didn't snap his neck in the process. The news was obviously new to him, although I was a little surprised that he hadn't noticed that Abraxos was absent from this domain.

"Heaven has deserted you, Lucifer. The remaining angels ascended to avoid their own deaths."

"My demons will tear you limb from limb!" Lucifer retaliated.

"Yeah… I think not," Ryan calmly retorted, smirking at the leader of hell as his pacing began to slow and his demeanour became more aggressive.

"Hybrid!" Lucifer shouted.

"Ryan," Ryan corrected.

"Hybrid!" Lucifer shouted again.

"Ryan," Ryan repeated. "And this is Connor," he continued, pointing at his twin.

"Hi," Connor waved back, whilst casually winking at his brother.

I felt my eyes roll as I realized the twins were chasing Lucifer into their stupid game; a game to torment the demon king to the point of drawing his sword once more.

Lucifer's red eyes deepened, allowing a crimson waterfall to cascade across his irises.

"Do not goad me, children. My army approaches. Tory will choose which one of you to watch die first." He sniggered, finding my eyes with his own and speaking directly to me. "I am guessing this one," he said, pointing to Ryan. "Since you are fucking the other," he spat, directing his gaze briefly to Connor, then back to me.

I stood firm and slowly shook my head at him.

"Lucifer, from what I can see, you have two options available to you right now. One: you have a quick death. Or two: I can make it extremely slow. Whichever way, today you die. You do not descend and become reborn; you just cease to exist. Your choice," I stated, watching his reaction as I finished talking.

Throwing his head back, Lucifer opened his lacerated, blood-smeared mouth and laughed, each laugh splitting his lip further and increasing the downpour of blood dripping from his chin.

"I do not think so, Purgatory," he replied, continuing to spit the crimson clots from his mouth.

Around us, the atmosphere changed. Ripples within the veil of the human domain began to form, waving and creasing expeditiously.

"Behold, my army has arrived!" Lucifer screeched.

Portholes began to form around the deconstructed shop, one after the other, rippling apart, allowing the demon army to step through. We were surrounded, the three of us backed up against each other to fight as a unit.

"Ryan," I glanced, sideways. "How far away are they?" Ryan began talking into the PCD as I regained my composure and readied myself to fight.

"Minutes," he responded, without taking his eyes from the Demons standing before us.

Demons surrounded us, weapons ready and awaiting the order to attack from Lucifer. The pregnant pause increased with each new demonic presence as they continued to pour from hell through the veil and into the human domain.

"Sweetheart – breathe," Connor whispered next to me, nudging me gently with his wing.

Casting a glimpse in his direction, I saw Connor wink and offer me a small smile of reassurance. I smiled back before returning my focus to Lucifer. He was healing but at an immensely slower pace. His arrogant figure cut a huge shadow over his army, waiting for all to be present before unleashing them on us.

Hundreds of fetid-smelling demons packed their rancid, putrefying bodies together, surrounding us completely. One by one, they continued to step through the veil from hell; pushing and fighting with each other for space within the confines of the small shop. Row upon row they stood, forming a huge, deep blackened circle; hundreds of demons all awaiting their opportunity to attack.

Lucifer stood high upon a stainless steel unit to address his army.

"Demons! Before you stands the trio who intend to bring about my downfall. Purgatory and her twin hybrids wish to see us all die - never to descend. Today, my loyal demon army, we bring about their demise and rule the three domains. KILL THEM."

Chapter 44

The space around me filled swiftly with the foul breath from the demons' battle cries. Hordes of vicious, red-eyed monsters lurched forward toward Ryan, Connor, and me, encasing us in a circle comprising thousands of rancid bodies.

My rage pulsed through my veins, charging my adrenaline and fuelling my anger. With my sai drawn, I awaited the first demon attack. Running towards me, a knife wielding demon began the offense. Neither Ryan, Connor or I were on the defensive: we were on the attack, needing to keep ourselves alive until my army arrived.

Our trio remained in close proximity, ensuring we protected each other as we fought. It became evident that the demons were continuously trying to come between us, to split up our small triangle in order to fight us individually. Unfortunately for them, we were aware of their intentions and avoided their attempts at every failed attack.

Ryan continued a commentary of the progress of my approaching army, distracting me slightly. Facing forward, I stabbed my sai into the neck of an oncoming large and rotund demon, who held onto my weapon as he began to implode into his own body.

Shivers struck my spine as the eyes of the demon met mine: he smiled over his gritted teeth, refusing to acknowledge the pain he was experiencing as his internal body structure ruptured, broke, and liquified within him.

His blackened hand moved with unexpected agility and seized my right hand holding the Sai that was destroying him.

"Release me, Demon!" I screeched, as his grip tightened and his extended, razor-sharp claws began to tentatively pierce my skin.

His eyes remained on mine, searching my soul for explanation or reason, his smile fixed, his teeth forced together and his screaming silent.

Struggling to pull my hand from under his, I withdrew my sai in my left hand and prepared myself to stab his collapsing body once more.

"Release me, Demon!" I commanded again.

His grip tightened this time: each claw spliced effortlessly through my hand. I screamed as his rancid venom began to pulse from him into me. Immediately, I repeatedly stabbed him with my left sai, allowing my own toxin to invade his forlorn body, assisting to bring about his death.

The demon's venom tracked through my hand, reaching out to every one of my pain receptors and pulling on it relentlessly until they screamed back at me.

"Connor..." I breathed through the pain. Ripping my eyes away from the demon, I searched for my hybrid. Connor abruptly turned to my voice and without hesitation, pushed his hand into his armour, pulling from it a black cylinder and putting it up to his mouth, biting off the lid and exposing a thin needle. He took a step closer to me, winked, and drove the needled cylinder into my shoulder. The adrenaline pulsed through my body, immediately taking up the newly injected antidote and delivering it into my bloodstream. Within seconds I could feel my strength returning as the antidote devoured the venom from the demon-claw penetration.

Remaining steadfast on the end of my sai, the demon continued his slow, pathetic death.

"Goodbye..." I grinned, and with the new energy the antidote had given to me, I brought my left sai to his neck. Pulling my left hand to the left and the embedded right sai in the opposite direction, I sourced my strength and decapitated the demon's head from his dissolving body.

The bloodied head rolled over its shoulders before coming to land with a squelch at my feet.

"Awesome!" Connor yelled at me, mid-fight, causing a smile to tug at my mouth. Before me, the remaining demon body disappeared, his head becoming more transparent. However, my impatience whispered softly to me and rather than watch this continued monotonous death, I kicked his head as hard as I could away from me and in the direction of Lucifer.

Catching Lucifer's eye as the demon head swiftly flew past him, I smiled and offered him my middle finger before the dead demon was replaced by a live one.

Engaging this demon, I took an elongated breath and held it as my sai made its first rip into the saturnine and foul-smelling body. He choked, frantically clawing at my weapon as it delivered its crippling toxin. This demon evaporated quickly, leaving nothing more than a viscous mordant gloop of his disappearing remains.

Black, glutinous fluid spread over the floor of the demon-crammed shop. I fought to remain on my feet as the ex-demon body sluggishly disappeared through the gaps in the floorboards.

"They are here," Ryan announced, dispatching his own vengeful demon. Within moments of Ryan's announcement, the angels and demons of my army burst through doors, windows, walls, and the roof. Immediately, the army made their way to Connor, Ryan and me. Eventually we all stood together, back to back, facing outwards and towards Lucifer's demon army.

"STOP!" Lucifer screamed to his army, as they prepared to attack. Each demon stood rigid, awaiting further instruction from their Demon king.

"I want Purgatory alive. And ensure that you descend her hybrid lover. Dispose of the rest," Lucifer commanded. "Continue!" he ordered, flicking his hand towards his army and re-taking his position toward the back of the shop to watch the carnage unfold.

I spun to face Connor with confusion crossing my features. Connor shrugged, smiled, and winked before blocking the attack from an oncoming demon. Connor's 'devil-may-care' irony soothed my soul: he didn't give a shit about Lucifer or the demons before him. He fought for what he believed in and, at present, that was me.

With our numbers greatly enlarged, dispatching the demons became quicker as their numbers gradually decreased. Demons no longer appeared from the tears in the domain walls: they were dying without descending.

Ryan and Connor's new appearance had not gone unnoticed by the army, especially their parents. Ryan held his hand up to his PCD as it crackled into life.

"Dad, its fine – honest. Connor went off on one and brought his demon forward: hence, my angel took over."

I could hear Devon's voice continuing over the headset as Ryan attempted to appease his father. Connor and I both turned towards him:

he was shaking his head while explaining that both Connor and I had lost our headsets and no - Connor hadn't completely lost his mind.

Taking the chance to evaluate the battle, I found myself enveloped into a circle, protected by my army as they continued to fight for me. The demons were relentlessly attacking: one after the other they fought until they died, only to be replaced immediately by another.

My army never fluctuated, never paused, but remained focused and brave. I watched as my army received wounds from demon weapons, the antidote proving itself as the wounds healed immediately, forcing out the venom as the skin knitted itself together.

A number of feelings crashed through my head, drowning my subconsciousness with a cacophony of pride, guilt and regret. Regretting the war, guilt-driven for the people I loved and admired; those same people fighting for me. I glanced towards Lucifer. He retained his power over his army by spitting abuse or threatening their deaths by his own hand if they failed.

"Enough," my conscious whispered to me. I had seen enough. Taking a deep cleansing breath, I silently began to make my way through the protective circle and into the crowd of writhing demon bodies. Unnoticed by my army, I made my way towards the back of the shop, towards my nemesis. Towards Lucifer.

Approaching Lucifer undetected through the sea of demons was easy. They were focused on stepping over their dead and evaporating comrades in an effort to fight my army. I kept Lucifer in my periphery as I silently moved, taking out the demons that did notice me before they had the chance to draw attention to me moving within them.

Lucifer remained high on the pile of rubble which once held the cash register. He was devoid of concern for the falling demon numbers; instead, focusing on his need for Connor's descension.

I continued by circulating around and through Lucifer's army of the evil dead, watching him as I crept. His eyes never left Connor: the red color held within Lucifer's irises illuminated to the demon currently engaging Connor. Moving closer to Lucifer's position, I held my sai firmly within my hands. I rounded the last rubble mountain; the last obstacle between him and me.

"Descend him! You have one objective, you failures: descend the demon hybrid!" Lucifer's attention focused constantly on Connor as he continued to spew orders to his army.

"He will end in hell!" Lucifer continued. "He will kill you all – do not let him gain his powers." His words were senseless: Connor had no more powers, as far as I knew. His demon had been brought forward, which was assisting in his ability to fight so hard, but what powers? I questioned myself.

Stopping and standing firm, I held my toxin-laced sai at Lucifer's back.

"I do not believe in killing a demon without him facing me," I said behind Lucifer, forcing him into silence and allowing him the opportunity to process what was happening. "TURN!" I demanded, keeping my sai trained on his body.

Slowly, Lucifer turned and faced me: he seemed neither fazed nor concerned as he eyed my sai before him.

"Tory," he hissed. "Fuck off!" He smirked, waiting for my reaction, flapping his hand at my outstretched weapons.

I did not react. I grounded myself and entered into my zone, battle ready and waiting.

"I said F..U..C..K O..F..F" he enunciated slowly, spittle dribbling down his chin and the fires of his own anger burning with frustration within his eyes. "You, Tory, are no longer of interest to me."

"Why?" I demanded, keeping my sai aimed at the nonchalant devil.

"Because you will never rule hell; you are insignificant and unworthy to even set foot into my domain. You are of no importance to me," he retorted.

"I will rule hell, just as I will rule heaven and its angels," I hissed back.

Lucifer rolled his eyes before smiling. "I shall humour you Purgatory. Prepare to die at my hand," he said, withdrawing his sword from its sheath at his waist.

"I am prepared but I shall not die," I winked back at him.

He lunged forward at me, swinging his sword violently and forcing me to take a step back. Briefly losing my footing, I began fighting with my surroundings for balance. Eventually, I stabilized and within seconds I heard Lucifer's sword swish a fraction of a millimetre past my ear, taking a lock of wayward hair with it.

Rotating towards him, I tucked the remaining strand of hair behind my ear and leapt forward.

Engaging with his blade, my sai clashed repeatedly against it. Our strength was now matched and I fought with conviction, pushing him harder with my oncoming momentum.

From my position, elevated slightly on the pile of bricks and mortar, I could see my army remaining strong and fighting hard. The demons surrounding them were still reducing in numbers and I could see that their circle maintained a constant level of protection.

"Now!" Lucifer yelled and from behind me I felt the ripple of an opening into the human domain. I felt a presence encroach into the space behind me. Hands clawed at my arms from both sides, lacerating my skin and spilling my viscous, antidote-filled blood. I felt the red sticky liquid trace over my skin and pool at my hands. My sai became slippery in my grip. I now concentrated on Lucifer in front of me, releasing myself from the demons behind me, along with maintaining my grasp on my weapon.

"Hold her!" Lucifer ordered, as claws mercilessly clutched at my arms, shredding my skin.

Reluctantly, I stopped fighting back. I was losing too much blood to protect myself against the demon toxin. Demon fingers encircled my arm roughly and purposely, digging the tips of their claws superficially into my skin and holding me firm.

Lucifer stepped towards me, resheathing his sword while closing the space between us. I inhaled deeply, tracing his steps with my eyes, waiting for my nemesis to stand before me.

Extending a filthy, elongated toxin-filled claw, Lucifer stood millimetres from my face. Using his forefinger, he traced the outline of my face, over my cheek and along my cheekbone; not hard enough to break my skin but enough to mark it.

"Purgatory, I pity you, my darling. Your fight is futile. You will watch your army descend and you will watch as I tear your angel hybrid apart. Then, my dear, you shall descend and I, Purgatory, will rule the three domains. Death for all will become hell."

Throwing his head back, Lucifer laughed, encouraged by the laughter from his fellow demons. I remained standing, allowing his words to wash over me. As he spoke, I calculated my next move. I was ready: I just needed my moment.

Further behind me, I felt a ripple in the atmosphere and felt the presence of more demons to my right.

"Sire," one spoke, bowing his head as he addressed the devil.

"Speak!" Lucifer howled back.

"Sire, the angels have failed in their attempts of war," the demon reported, keeping his eyes downcast.

Lucifer turned from me, diverting his attention to the newly arrived demon.

"I am aware of this: I saw the hybrid kill Abraxos. The angels are weak! They do not contain the power and strength of hell and its demons," he boasted.

"Yes, Sire."

"Continue," Lucifer demanded

"The demons are fighting for you, your highness. Our numbers have reduced but we remain determined," his servant responded.

"How many?" Lucifer growled.

Withdrawing slightly, the demon was reluctant to answer.

"Thousands."

"HOW MANY THOUSANDS?" Lucifer countered, his eyes glowing iridescent red with anger.

"Hundreds of thousands, Sire. Too many to count. No demon descended: they were all killed."

The message delivered by this demon was not what Lucifer wanted to hear.

"Fuck!" Lucifer screamed. His frustration was evident in his demeanour. Without pause, Lucifer backhanded the demon messenger, sending him flying backwards, hitting a wooden pillar behind him that snapped under the force of the demon's body.

The demon stood. Righting himself, he wiped the blood from his newly split lip.

"Dismissed!" Lucifer spat at him. Bowing, the demon took a few steps backwards and disappeared.

I watched Lucifer pace back and forth. The grip on my arms had subsided gradually. The demons were distracted by the information that had just been received. We had killed thousands of un-descending demons, reducing Lucifer's army extensively.

The smile tugging at the side of my lips finally broke. I felt it take over my face as I let out an uncontrollable laugh. This resulted in my captors increasing their grip and causing Lucifer to spin violently towards me.

He said nothing: the leader of hell just stood and looked at me for a moment before punching me hard in the stomach. Pain exploded within my core, reaching to every aspect of my inner body. I was silent, defiant in the face of the pain Lucifer had caused. Unable to move, due to my demon restraints, I inhaled and raised my head to look directly into the evil red eyes of the devil. Antagonizing him further, I shrugged, thus angering him more, resulting in my own smack in the face with Lucifer's backhand.

My head snapped violently to the left reacting to his strike. Immediately, my tastebuds were flooded with the metallic, copper taste of my own blood. Tentatively, I traced my blood-covered lips with my tongue. I felt the jagged split. Toxin from Lucifer's claw was released as he hit me, preventing the split from healing.

The tingling feeling associated with attempted healing fizzed at the sides of the laceration, waiting for my body to metabolize and neutralize the toxin, allowing it to move forward and heal me.

I smirked: we were winning. The pain I was feeling right now was so insignificant compared to the elation of knowing that we had beaten the angels into submission and reduced the demon numbers.

Lifting my head, I looked past the monotonously pacing Lucifer towards my army.

"Connor..." I whispered softly and immediately his head snapped up towards me.

His features filled with horror as he processed my situation. He took a step forward.

"No," I shook my head "Stay where you are. I have got this."

He frowned and took another step.

"Please – no!" I reiterated.

Lowering his eyes and bowing his head slightly, he acknowledged my words and engaged with the demon in front of him. He continued to flick his eyes up towards me and I smiled back at him. This was my moment, my time to execute my possibly foolish plan. I needed to end this conflict now, to end Lucifer.

Chapter 46

My attention was brought back to Lucifer as he administered another lip-wrenching punch to my face. Another toxin-filled split tore its way through my lip and I inhaled sharply as the pain ricocheted throughout my head.

"Bastard," I thought, disappointed by my own distraction. Blood trickled over my chin and dripped rhythmically onto my chest.

Lucifer boomed with laughter.

"Your inability to ignore distraction will be your downfall, Purgatory. I can see that knocking the shit out of you before you die is of no consequence: it is your hybrid that will cause you pain." He lurched forward and took my bloodstained chin in his rough, scaly hand. Leaning forward, he brought his face close into mine.

"You will watch him descend before his powers rear up. You will see his body disintegrate around my claws and I will absorb his power before I descend you and rule this world."

This was the second time Lucifer had mentioned that Connor had powers: I was not aware that he had more than had already developed. Maybe his demon coming forth had brought with it the power Lucifer was so concerned with.

Smack! Lucifer's fist hit me once again, sending my head snapping to the side.

"Distracted, Purgatory?" he goaded.

"Nope, just bored," I retorted.

Smack! I received another punch to the stomach, followed by a fierce upper-cut, sending my head backwards and causing stars to appear in my eyes.

"Better?" Lucifer asked, jeered on by his laughing demons behind me.

"It's a little better." I spoke through blood-stained teeth, spitting a mouthful of blood onto the floor below me. Only then did it dawn on me that maybe I should keep my mouth shut. I realized that the demons' grip on my arms was causing a steady stream of blood to cascade as their claws dug deeper.

I felt dizzy with the rapid exsanguination of blood, alongside the recently acquired concussion. Hanging my head, I gave myself a short reprieve, gathering my thoughts and cleansing my body with a deep inhalation of oxygen.

Deep within my thoughts, I reached out to find Connor. As I called, his essence answered, relaxing my mind and flooding me with confidence.

Opening my eyes and raising my head, I released the breath that I had been holding.

Lucifer had his back towards me, firing orders at the demons below him, his arms gesturing while his animated body acted out the actions required. Taking one more breath, I allowed my wings the freedom they demanded. Both heavy with healing lacerations, yet strong with determination, they extended from my back with such speed the demons holding my arms were not aware of the moment they cut sharply through their bodies. Slicing them like hot metal through ice, the demons fell apart where they stood, creating two perfect halves of the once-whole body on the floor at my sides.

Toxin-filled demon blood dripped from the outer aspects of my wings and filtered back onto the decapitated bodies of the demons.

The lacerations on my arms began healing, pushing the demon venom out of the wounds as they healed from the inside out. Lucifer spun around sharply and took in the sight that was presented to him. He was rigid, gob wide open and his face draining of colour.

"Are you ready to fight me now, Lucifer?" I asked, my sai settled in my hands which, in turn, rested calmly on my hips.

I did not hesitate. Lunging forward and taking Lucifer by surprise, I attacked. My sai slid effortlessly into their intended target. Lucifer roared as the cold metal rested in his chest cavity, between his fourth and fifth ribs.

Looking down, Lucifer stared at the protruding weapons, both impregnated with the lethal cocktail engineered to prevent the descension or ascension of either demon or angel.

Retracting my weapons, I brought each one gently over my armoured, gauntlet-covered forearm and wiped Lucifer's blood from them. Lucifer, now clutching his chest, was semi-bent over, his facial contortions betraying his silence, indicating the enormous amount of pain he was experiencing.

I took the opportunity and lunged for a second time, Lucifer blocked my right sai, meeting my gauntlet with his sword. As the momentum of the block forced me to my left, I concentrated on wounding him with my right sai. I was successful: forcing my body to the left gave me the ability to utilize the movement and dig my weapon with renewed strength into Lucifer's side.

He screamed out, releasing his sword and allowing it to fall to the floor as he swung round to his left to cover the sai-shaped wound with his right hand.

Lucifer's blood-curdling scream attracted the attention of the demons below us.

Ever faithful, a large portion of the demons fled from fighting my army and began to make their way to where the fallen leader stood, crippled by the toxin.

I held my breath and awaited their arrival. One by one, demons appeared and took their place, surrounding Lucifer. This was obviously a pre-organized strategy and slowly Lucifer disappeared behind a sea of blackened, scaly, red-eyed, weapon-wielding, low-ranking demons.

"Shit!" I whispered to myself. I knew he was being hidden in order to heal but I was not prepared for what I witnessed next.

A small gap between demons gave me the perfect opportunity to observe the disgusting act that played out before me. Lucifer was healing slowly due to the venom contained within my sai and administered as they tore through his flesh.

I watched in stunned disbelief and horror as Lucifer grabbed a young demon close to him. It was at that moment I learnt that Lucifer also had fangs. The razor-sharp incisors dropped down from his top gums at either side of his mouth. The corn-tinted teeth developed into jagged points at the end and hung like a pair of broken clothes pegs over his bottom lip.

The young demon acknowledged his master and without complaint or question knelt in front of the frail devil. Leaning back on his heels, the demon raised his chin. Hyperextending his neck backwards, he exposed his soft tissue towards Lucifer and closed his eyes.

Without pause, Lucifer leapt forward and clasped one hand onto the demon's head and the other on his chest. Pushing the kneeling demon's head back a little further, Lucifer dived for his throat and embedded his fangs into him.

The young demon winced but neither fought or moved, completely giving himself to his master.

Greedily, Lucifer ripped at his throat, rapidly ingesting the pure, untainted demon blood. Within seconds, Lucifer had thrown the lifeless demon's body to the side.

"MORE!" he screamed. Without hesitation, another demon knelt before him and adopted the same position. Again, Lucifer tore the throat of the second demon until his lifeless, blood-let body was limp.

"MORE!" Lucifer shrieked. I could see his strength gathering with each self-sacrificing demon.

"MORE!"

"MORE!"

"MORE!" he continued, until a pile of seven, dead, undescended demons lay at his side.

Lucifer remained shielded by his army. Remnants of demon flesh gently came away from his mouth as he teased them from his teeth with his bloodstained tongue and spat them onto the pile of demon corpses.

My stomach tumbled, churning with disbelief at what I had just witnessed. Lucifer demanded respect from his army, yet rewarded them with dishonour and disrespect, throwing away their sacrificed bodies without thought or care.

Nausea waved over me, encouraging bile to bubble up into my throat, threatening to expel itself from my body.

"You barbaric bastard," I hissed, disgusted by his actions and appalled by the realization of what I had witnessed.

Lucifer remained behind his safeguarding demon circle and nonchalantly wiped the blood from his chin with the back of his hand. I forced the bile back down into the pit of my stomach, breathing deeply to dissuade any recurrence.

Pushing two of his demons aside, Lucifer broke his protective circle as he stepped in front of it.

"Let me educate you, Tory. What you have just witnessed is loyalty. My army sacrifices themselves daily to keep me alive. They do it willingly knowing that their blood nourishes their king," he boasted.

"NO!" I screamed "They are people!"

"Demons," Lucifer interjected.

"People who are demons: don't try to justify this, Lucifer," I spat back.

"Demons... Filth of the earth destined to be demons in death; to be commanded by their true king and to sacrifice their worthless bodies when I demand it. Demons, some of whom you judged, Tory. Demons you sent down to hell, down to me to control and do with as I felt fit."

Lucifer's words filtered through my ears: his words fired the synapses in my brain causing realization to force a flurry of emotions over me. Guilt, pain, anger.

"What have I done?" I mumbled deep into my soul, questioning at what point I had become so disconnected by my judgement. "No..." I whispered under my breath. Lucifer was not going to get away with this. Demons or not, these were once living people.

"I beg your pardon?" Lucifer brought his face close to mine, spitting the blood of the fallen demons over me as he spoke.

The demons gathered behind their king: red-glowing eyes fell upon me, their stare burning deep into my skin.

He was close enough, right now. Why was I not moving? Something inside of me reminded me what I needed to do.

Inhaling deeply, I fixed my eyes on Lucifer as he continued to educate me and shower me with a tirade of insults. I could not hear him: I could only hear his heart beating inside his evil chest, pumping stolen blood from the demons who forfeited their lives so he could remain living.

The demons behind him became engrossed in their leader's speeches; encouraging him, laughing with him, praising his wit and goading him to finish me.

Abruptly, Lucifer shut his mouth, choking on the words trapped within it. His eyes found mine and instantaneously he understood what was happening. Dead air filled the atmosphere surrounding the demons behind him as they searched for the reason for his impromptu muteness.

Lucifer inhaled slowly through his nose and opening his mouth, he lost control of his jaw as it unceremoniously fell open, followed by an avalanche of claret, sanguine fluid.

The waterfall of blood spilled continuously, during which time Lucifer frantically gasped for air. Gradually, he began to asphyxiate from the gelatinous blood solidifying in his throat, briskly settling itself into his rapidly hypoxic lungs.

Lucifer began to drown in the life-giving, stolen blood he had embezzled from the seven demons. Coughing, he spat blood out of his mouth, convulsing in pain as the inability to draw in any oxygen sent his body into panic.

Gradually, the surrounding demons became aware of Lucifer's situation. Confusion crossed their faces as they tried to determine what was unfolding before them.

Mumbling broke out throughout the ranks, yet not one demon moved. Each remained rooted to where they stood; numerous red eyes looked at me, yet they still remained immobile.

Glancing over Lucifer's shoulder, I watched as realization hit the demon army: Lucifer was dying.

As Lucifer had stepped closer to me, just moments before, venting his speech on why this whole situation was my fault, I attacked.

Preoccupied by his own words and jeering demons, Lucifer hadn't noticed me grind my feet into the hard rock beneath me. His overarching arrogance ensured that he did not see me bending my knees slightly, in preparation, and he certainly wasn't aware as I gradually released my claws and thrust them deep within his chest, without him having time to react.

Holding Lucifer steady on my claws, I readjusted myself as his body convulsed. Turning my head to the side as the stolen blood fell from his open mouth, I revelled in the knowledge that he was dying and that his demons stood by.

"Lucifer…" I whispered softly, leaning forward towards his ear.

"Goodbye."

Bringing my body back up to stand straight, I withdrew my right claw from his chest, maintaining his upright position with my left claw, thoroughly embedded inside him. Lucifer rolled his eyes up to meet mine, moments before another mouthful of congealed blood slumped out of his mouth.

Raising my right claw, I slashed out towards the demon king. My claw pierced his throat and with deft speed, I separated his head from his body and watched as it rolled backwards off of his shoulders and fell to the unforgiving concrete below.

I retracted my claws, allowing his decapitated, bleeding, lifeless body to slide to the floor. Slumping heavily next to Lucifer's head, I exhaled: the breath I had been holding had become stagnant in my lungs and begged for release.

Immediately, I clutched at the oxygen-rich air around me and renewed my lung capacity with the element it craved.

"Tory?" Connor spoke softly from behind me. "Are you okay?"

Words had temporarily given themselves leave. Unable to find one at that precise moment, I nodded as I wiped the demon king's blood from my hands. I felt Connor close the gap between our bodies and felt his breath warming my neck. His arms encircled me and pulling me close, he whispered.

"Look, babe… Look what you did."

Lifting my head, I watched: one by one, demons re-sheathed their weapons and knelt before me. We had taken back heaven and hell after a millennium of corrupt rule by Lucifer and Abraxos.

"Return to your domain and await my instructions," I ordered the remaining demons. It took moments for them to disappear back into their kingless domain, leaving my army standing together, catching their breath and assessing their wounds.

Turning in Connor's arms, I took his face in my hands and brought his lips to mine. I kissed him as he enveloped my body with his arms, bringing me tighter into his chest.

A short moment passed before I felt a collection of familiar demon and angel essences surround us.

"Get a room!" Ryan mumbled behind us, forcing our embrace to be cut short.

Connor begrudgingly released me and I turned to face my army. Elenor raced towards me and hugged me tightly.

"Well done, Tory! You have taken back the domains of heaven and hell. I knew that you would succeed." Elena released me, smiling, and wiped a clotted blob of Lucifer's blood from my arm as Devon walked to her side.

"Congratulations, Tory," he said, echoing his wife.

"Come - we need to return to Purgatory and decide what to do next," I said and taking Connor's hand, I led my army back home.

Chapter 47

Six weeks have passed since my army and I defeated the rulers of heaven and hell, allowing me to take back the ruling of the human realm, judging newly deceased humans to either ascend or descend.

During those six weeks, I have worked tirelessly to maintain calm and order in the domains of heaven and hell. There are no longer barriers to my entrance and exit into these domains, although the reception I have received has been a little icy. Neither demons residing in hell, nor angels inhabiting heaven are permitted into the human realm since the deaths of Lucifer and Abraxos. Human souls are harvested by my army and me, and are brought to purgatory for judgement. All souls, good or bad, have their decision to either descend or ascend.

A member of my army will escort that soul to their intended domain. The thresholds of heaven and hell are governed to ensure that no angel nor demon can cross the domains unless I summon them.

I got what I wanted: after years of fighting with Abraxos and his angels, alongside Lucifer and his demons, for the human souls, I finally took back what I had created.

On returning to purgatory after the war, neither Ryan nor Connor regained their original hybrid status. They remained hybrids, yet because Connor's demon pushed through during the fighting, it forced Ryan's angel to come to the forefront of his hybrid DNA, also. The change had never subsided: Connor remains guided by his demon as Ryan is by his angel.

The changes are subtle, yet evident to those closest to them. My only hope for them both is that they never lose themselves fully within their demon/angel personas.

I stood with my wings extended outside the bedroom door and encouraged them to beat gently against the cooling breeze that whipped around them. Thoughts paraded through my mind, intentionally stomping on my musings and leaving muddy footprints on my rationalization, cascading the confidence of my decision into an abyss of self-doubt.

"Do you realise that you frown when you think hard?" Connor had slid the door open to the bedroom and made his way over to where I stood.

"You are beautiful," he continued, gently tickling the tips of my feathers as he walked past my wings to stand with me.

I smiled as he placed a soft kiss on my forehead before drawing back to question my frown. In that moment, I felt my heart crack slightly, creating a fragility that threatened to chip, dislodge and fall apart. Changing the subject rapidly, I stroked his cheek with my thumb.

"I have a judgement," I said. "Would you walk with me?"

"Of course," Connor said, reaching for my hands and walking back through the house with me.

"You stand before me for judgement. Your life as a human has ceased; therefore your afterlife begins today."

I performed my opening speech to all judgements. I looked down upon a scrawny, bald, evil-looking man and smiled. It was not a smile for him: it was mine as I awaited the plea he was just about to make. Scrawny, bald man showed no remorse. His posture was arrogant, his stare nonchalant and his plea of 'Who fucking cares?' confirmed the case for descension.

"I have evaluated the life you led as a human: your actions contain a level of evil fitting for your human crimes. I hereby sentence you to descension from purgatory immediately. Guards – remove this man to the holding cell."

Raven and Poet stood up beside the newly judged human and taking an arm each, escorted him out of my court.

I would escort the human to hell, accompanied by Connor and Elena. Once through the gates of hell, higher appointed demons, who chose to follow me after seeing me kill Lucifer during the war, would take their new charge to begin his afterlife.

Ascending souls were escorted to heaven by me but accompanied by Ryan and Devon. To this day, no demon will be permitted into heaven and no angel into hell, helping me to maintain the equilibrium of the afterlife.

Once back home, Connor and I returned to our favourite place; the place that grounded us, that allowed us to be alone and ensured we had the privacy we craved.

"Next steps?" Connor asked, as I settled down beside him and slid myself under his muscular arms.

"I need to prepare hell and heaven for new leaders. Both domains are lacking the authority that a ruler provides."

"Any ideas?"

"Not yet: the decision is hard." I cringed as I turned my face away from my hybrid.

"You will make the right decision," Connor said. "You always do."

"Maybe."

"Tired?" Connor asked, planting a small soft kiss on my head.

"Not really, but I could persuaded to go to bed."

"Perfect."

Seconds later, I was in Connor's arms with his lips crushing mine as he carried me into the bedroom and gently placed me down on the bed.

"I love you," I whispered against his lips.

"I love you, too, and always will," Connor responded.

Allowing his wings freedom, Connor enveloped us both in his fire-red feathers. He growled lightly as he began to kiss my neck and down to my chest. His new demonic status had me fall in love with him over again as his passion and protectiveness increased and our lovemaking became epic.

Throughout the night, Connor never let go of me. My heart was beating just for him and as I fell asleep within his arms, I thanked my own god for my audacity, all those months ago, to challenge heaven and hell and harvest myself a hybrid.

My demon hybrid. My Connor.